The SFWA
GRAND MASTERS
VOLUME ONE

The SFWA
GRAND MASTERS

VOLUME ONE

ROBERT A. HEINLEIN

JACK WILLIAMSON

CLIFFORD D. SIMAK

L. SPRAGUE DE CAMP

FRITZ LEIBER

EDITED BY
FREDERIK POHL

A TOM DOHERTY ASSOCIATES BOOK
NEW YORK

THE SFWA GRAND MASTERS: VOLUME ONE

Copyright © 1999 by Science Fiction and Fantasy Writers of America, Inc.

This book is printed on acid-free paper.

Edited by David G. Hartwell

A Tor Book
Published by Tom Doherty Associates, Inc.
175 Fifth Avenue
New York, NY 10010

Tor Books on the World Wide Web:
http://www.tor.com

Tor® is a registered trademark of Tom Doherty Associates, Inc.

"SFWA" and "SFWA Grand Master" are trademarks of Science Fiction and Fantasy Writers of America, Inc., and are used with permission.

Design by Lisa Pifher

Library of Congress Cataloging-in-Publication Data

The SFWA grand masters / edited by Frederik Pohl.—1st ed.
    p. cm.
    "A Tom Doherty Associates book."
    Contents: Robert A. Heinlein—Jack Williamson—Clifford D.
Simak—L. Sprague de Camp—Fritz Leiber
    ISBN 0-312-86881-2 (alk, paper)
    1. Science fiction, American. I. Pohl, Frederik. II. Science
Fiction Writers of America. III. Title: Grand masters.
PS648.S3S44 1999
813'.0876208—dc21   99-21933
                                                                     CIP

First Edition: June 1999

Printed in the United States of America

0 9 8 7 6 5 4 3 2 1

This book is dedicated to
Jerry Pournelle,
the man who invented the Grand Master Award

CONTENTS

FRITZ LEIBER

INTRODUCTION

The purpose of an introduction is to tell you what a book is about. What this book is about is some remarkable human beings. What they have in common is that they are all writers of science fiction and fantasy, and that they have been judged, by their peers, to be among the best of those who ever lived.

A little history:

In 1965 the Science Fiction Writers of America, the trade union of the writers in the field, decided to honor outstanding work in the area by presenting annual awards. These were to go to the author of the best story published each year, selected by vote of the membership, in each of four categories—novel, novella, novelette, and short story—and they were named the Nebulas.

Physically, the Nebula award is a large, handsome brick of transparent Lucite in which is embedded a cluster of semiprecious minerals, somewhat resembling a spiral galaxy—hence the name. It is also one of the heaviest of literary awards, as I know from personal experience. I once had to lug three of them up one of San Francisco's notoriously steep hills to turn them over to their recipients. It was only a few blocks, but after the first block or so I hailed a cab.

Science fiction writers are rarely content with Things As They Are, no matter what those things are—perhaps this restless disposition comes from the fact that they spend their working lives inventing worlds and societies quite unlike the ones we live in. From the very beginning, there was a steady stream of proposals from the members of SFWA for making changes in the rules that govern these Nebula awards. The period of eligibility, originally a simple calendar year, was altered repeatedly. A rule change officially allowed stories of fantasy to receive the award—unofficially an occasional fantasy had been winning all along—and in fact the organization changed its name to the Science Fiction and Fantasy Writers of America. Occasionally other awards were added to the list, such as awards for scriptwriting for films and TV.

Then, in 1973, a major change occurred.

By then several dozen Nebula awards had been distributed, but there was a growing feeling that even the Nebulas did not properly honor some of the most respected authors in the field. Under the leadership of Jerry Pournelle, then president of SFWA, a new award was created. Its purpose was to recognize a lifetime body of work, of a quality that helped to shape the entire course of science fiction writing.

Physically it resembles the Nebulas, though it is appropriately somewhat larger in size, and it is called the Grand Master Award. Under the rules it was to be awarded no more than six times in each decade, and, so that the recipient would be able to enjoy it, only to writers still living at the time of nomination.

As of this writing, a total of fifteen writers have received the Grand Master Award. I count myself lucky for being one of the fifteen, and even luckier for the fact that, over the years, I have been privileged to know and to work with nearly all of these masters—frequently as their editor, often, at other times, as their literary agent, now and then as a collaborator, most of all as a friend of long standing.

Putting together an anthology is often one of the easier tasks in the world of science fiction. Not this time. The fifteen Grand Masters haven't just written very well, they have written a *lot*. For every story included in this volume, the first of three, there are at least a dozen equally fine that had to be left out. I've tried to include some old favorites, along with some that are relatively unknown and a few short pieces of autobiography or comment to give a flavor of what the writer is like when not engaged in writing science fiction.

There have been many fine writers in science fiction over the periods covered by this award. These are some of the very best of them.

—Frederik Pohl
Palatine, Illinois
January 1999

ROBERT A. HEINLEIN

1907–1988

Robert A. Heinlein's youthful idea of a great and fulfilling career was to serve as an officer in the United States Navy. He made the cut, too—went through Annapolis, got his commission, received his duty postings—but the lifetime career didn't happen. Heinlein was greatly gifted in talent and energy, but a little shortchanged on health. After five years a medical survey retired Lieutenant Commander Robert A. Heinlein, leaving him still young and still with his life before him. He tried a few jobs, none of which really challenged him. He even ran for political office in California (unsuccessfully, largely because of an early version of a dirty-tricks campaign in which allies of his opponent spread the lying rumor that he was related to the Nazi leader Konrad Henlein). Then, in 1939, Heinlein found his vocation.

It happened almost by accident. He had been reading science fiction for some time. When he noticed that the magazine *Thrilling Wonder Stories* was running a short-story contest, it sounded like fun. He sat down and wrote a story to enter it, "Lifeline." The story was, of course, accepted at once—but not by *Thrilling Wonder*, because at the last moment Heinlein changed his mind and mailed it off to John Campbell's *Astounding* instead. (Since Heinlein is so closely identified with Campbell's "Golden Age," fans of alternate histories may ponder what might have happened if Heinlein had followed his first impulse. He did ultimately sell a number of stories to *Thrilling Wonder*, including some of his best, but not until he had become lastingly tagged as a Campbell author.)

From that first story on, Heinlein's rise was remarkable (not to say astounding). He was good, he was consistent, and he was most remarkably prolific, so much so that before long he was forced to split his production with a couple of pen names, publishing some of his finest stories as "Anson MacDonald" and "Lyle Monroe," among others.

Most of Heinlein's stories from that period seemed to be loosely connected in a sort of age-by-age "future history." In 1941 Heinlein confirmed the existence of the plan by allowing Campbell to publish his "outline of the future" in *Astounding*, a device other writers (including myself) liked well enough to imitate from time to time. Heinlein himself, however, found the format too constrictive for his wide-ranging interests, and after 1950 he seldom returned to it.

When World War II began to heat up, Heinlein—naturally—did everything in his power to get into it. The navy proved obdurate about putting him back in uniform, but there was a team of research scientists forming at the Philadelphia Navy Yard to help the navy develop some of the things it would need for this new high-tech kind of war. It was an eclectic team—some civilians, some serving officers, and at least one retired navy officer, Heinlein himself. It included a couple of other people who would wind up as Grand Masters in these volumes—Isaac Asimov and L. Sprague de Camp—as well as a bright and good-looking WAVE officer named Virginia "Ticky" Gerstenfeld, who in the fullness of time became Mrs. Robert A. Heinlein.

When the war was over Heinlein returned to writing, but no longer just for the science fiction magazines. His short stories began to appear in the major big-circulation slicks, and he began to write his famous (and unequaled) series of juvenile science fiction novels, *Space Cadet*, *Farmer in the Sky*, *Have Spaceship, Will Travel*, and many others.

Heinlein's juveniles were something special in the genre. They were as ingeniously inventive and carefully thought out as anything else he wrote; the principal way they were distinguishable from his other work at the time was that the protagonist was likely to be a fourteen-year-old boy (or, in the case of *Podkayne of Mars*, girl). For these reasons they were, and still are, read avidly by his grown-up fans as well. But he never entirely abandoned the adult novel. Nor the science fiction magazines, for until the last years of his life nearly all of the novels were first serialized in magazines before book publication. (While I was editing *Galaxy* and *If* I was lucky enough to be able to serialize many of them.)

In the late 1970s, for one reason or another, I decided that the world owed me a couple of weeks, all by myself, on some exotic South Sea island. The one I chose was Mooréa, right across the strait from the also exotic, but more touristy, island of Tahiti. It was a pleasant beachcombing interlude for me, with first-class food and accommodations laid on, and as I was going through Papeete's airport on the way home an acquaintance I had not expected to see within several thousand miles came bounding across the airport floor, crying, "Hey, Fred! How come you weren't at Bob Heinlein's party last night?"

Well, I hadn't known that Robert and Ginny were on a cruise ship on one side of the island, nor had they known I was in a straw-thatched villa on the other. It just goes to show that it really is a small world, isn't it?

That visit to the idyllic island of Mooréa had a consequence for Robert that wasn't idyllic at all. Mooréa is a volcanic island, with a towering central peak. As Heinlein threw his head back to gaze at it he felt an unusual twinge. It wasn't a good one. It turned out to involve his carotid artery, and it was the beginning of the health problems that ultimately took him away from us in 1988. But what a final decade he had! Most of his late novels made it onto the *New York Times* best-seller list, he was awarded an honorary doctorate by the University of Michigan, and he was invited to address his alma mater's graduating class at the U.S. Naval College at Annapolis.

The world of science fiction, of course, had already given Heinlein nearly every honor within its power. Heinlein had been chosen as guest of honor at no fewer than three World Science Fiction Conventions over a quarter of a century. (Most of the rest of us consider ourselves lucky to eke out one.) He received any number of Hugos and Nebulas, and pioneered the blood drives that are still a feature at many science fiction cons. He was (and is) a towering figure in the field, and so it is entirely appropriate that he was the first writer chosen to bear the title of Grand Master of Science Fiction.

THE ROADS MUST ROLL

W ho makes the roads roll?"

The speaker stood still on the rostrum and waited for his audience to answer him. The reply came in scattered shouts that cut through the ominous, discontented murmur of the crowd.

"We do!"—"We do!"—"Damn right!"

"Who does the dirty work 'down inside'—so that Joe Public can ride at his ease?"

This time it was a single roar, "We do!"

The speaker pressed his advantage, his words tumbling out in a rasping torrent. He leaned toward the crowd, his eyes picking out individuals at whom to fling his words. "What makes business? The roads! How do they move the food they eat? The roads! How do they get to work? The roads! How do they get home to their wives? The roads!" He paused for effect, then lowered his voice. "Where would the public be if you boys didn't keep them roads rolling?— Behind the eight ball and everybody knows it. But do they appreciate it? Pfui! Did we ask for too much? Were our demands unreasonable? 'The right to resign whenever we want to.' Every working stiff in the other lines of work has that. 'The same pay as the engineers.' Why not? Who are the real engineers around here? D'yuh have to be a cadet in a funny little hat before you can learn to wipe a bearing, or jack down a rotor? Who earns his keep: The 'gentlemen' in the control offices, or the boys 'down inside'? What else do we ask? 'The right to elect our own engineers.' Why the hell not? Who's competent to pick engineers? The technicians?—or some damn, dumb examining board that's never been 'down inside,' and couldn't tell a rotor bearing from a field coil?"

He changed his pace with natural art, and lowered his voice still further. "I tell you, brother, it's time we quit fiddlin' around with petitions to the Transport Commission, and use a little direct action. Let 'em yammer about democracy; that's a lot of eye wash—we've got the power, and we're the men that count!"

A man had risen in the back of the hall while the speaker was haranguing. He spoke up as the speaker paused. "Brother Chairman," he drawled, "may I stick in a couple of words?"

"You are recognized, Brother Harvey."

"What I ask is: what's all the shootin' for? We've got the highest hourly rate of pay of any mechanical guild, full insurance and retirement, and safe working conditions, barring the chance of going deaf." He pushed his anti-nose helmet further back from his ears. He was still in dungarees, apparently just up from standing watch. "Of course we have to give ninety days notice to quit a job, but, cripes, we knew that when we signed up. The roads have got to roll—they can't stop every time some lazy punk gets bored with his billet.

"And now Soapy—" The crack of the gavel cut him short. "Pardon me, I mean *Brother* Soapy—tells us how powerful we are, and how we should go in for direct action. Rats! Sure we could tie up the roads, and play hell with the whole community—but so could any screwball with a can of nitroglycerine, and he wouldn't have to be a technician to do it, neither.

"We aren't the only frogs in the puddle. Our jobs are important, sure, but where would we be without the farmers—or the steel workers—or a dozen other trades and professions?"

He was interrupted by a sallow little man with protruding upper teeth, who said, "Just a minute, Brother Chairman, I'd like to ask Brother Harvey a question," then turned to Harvey and inquired in a sly voice, "Are you speaking for the guild, Brother—or just for yourself? Maybe you don't believe in the guild? You wouldn't by any chance be"—he stopped and slid his eyes up and down Harvey's lank frame—"a *spotter*, would you?"

Harvey looked over his questioner as if he had found something filthy in a plate of food. "Sikes," he told him, "if you weren't a runt,

I'd stuff your store teeth down your throat. I helped found this guild. I was on strike in 'seventy-six. Where were you in 'seventy-six? With the finks?"

The chairman's gavel pounded. "There's been enough of this," he said. "Nobody who knows anything about the history of this guild doubts the loyalty of Brother Harvey. We'll continue with the regular order of business." He stopped to clear his throat. "Ordinarily we don't open our floor to outsiders, and some of you boys have expressed a distaste for some of the engineers we work under, but there is one engineer we always like to listen to whenever he can get away from his pressing duties. I guess maybe it's because he's had dirt under his nails the same as us. Anyhow, I present at this time Mr. Shorty Van Kleeck—"

A shout from the floor stopped him. "*Brother* Van Kleeck!"

"O.K.—*Brother* Van Kleeck, Chief Deputy Engineer of this road-town."

"Thanks, Brother Chairman." The guest speaker came briskly forward, and grinned expansively at the crowd, seeming to swell under their approval. "Thanks, Brothers. I guess our chairman is right. I always feel more comfortable here in the Guild Hall of the Sacramento Sector—or any guild hall, for that matter—than I do in the engineers' clubhouse. Those young punk cadet engineers get in my hair. Maybe I should have gone to one of the fancy technical institutes, so I'd have the proper point of view, instead of coming up from 'down inside.'

"Now about those demands of yours that the Transport Commission just threw back in your face—Can I speak freely?"

"Sure you can, Shorty!"—"You can trust us!"

"Well, of course I shouldn't say anything, but I can't help but understand how you feel. The roads are the big show these days, and you are the men that make them roll. It's the natural order of things that your opinions should be listened to, and your desires met. One would think that even politicians would be bright enough to see that. Sometimes, lying awake at night, I wonder why we technicians don't just take things over, and—"

·　　　·　　　·

"Your wife is calling, Mr. Gaines."

"Very well." He picked up the handset and turned to the visor screen.

"Yes, darling, I know I promised, but . . . You're perfectly right, darling, but Washington has especially requested that we show Mr. Blekinsop anything he wants to see. I didn't know he was arriving today. . . . No, I can't turn him over to a subordinate. It wouldn't be courteous. He's Minister of Transport for Australia. I told you that. . . . Yes, darling, I know that courtesy begins at home, but the roads must roll. It's my job; you knew that when you married me. And this is part of my job. . . . That's a good girl. We'll positively have breakfast together. Tell you what, order horses and a breakfast pack and we'll make it a picnic. I'll meet you in Bakersfield—usual place. . . . Goodbye, darling. Kiss Junior good-night for me."

He replaced the handset on the desk whereupon the pretty, but indignant, features of his wife faded from the visor screen. A young woman came into his office. As she opened the door she exposed momentarily the words printed on its outer side: "DIEGO-RENO ROADTOWN, Office of the Chief Engineer." He gave her a harassed glance.

"Oh, it's you. Don't marry an engineer, Dolores, marry an artist. They have more home life."

"Yes, Mr. Gaines. Mr. Blekinsop is here, Mr. Gaines."

"Already? I didn't expect him so soon. The Antipodes ship must have grounded early."

"Yes, Mr. Gaines."

"Dolores, don't you ever have any emotions?"

"Yes, Mr. Gaines."

"Hmmm, it seems incredible, but you are never mistaken. Show Mr. Blekinsop in."

"Very good, Mr. Gaines."

Larry Gaines got up to greet his visitor. Not a particularly impressive little guy, he thought, as they shook hands and exchanged formal amenities. The rolled umbrella, the bowler hat were almost too good to be true. An Oxford accent partially masked the underlying clipped, flat, nasal twang of the native Australian.

"It's a pleasure to have you here, Mr. Blekinsop, and I hope we can make your stay enjoyable."

The little man smiled. "I'm sure it will be. This is my first visit to your wonderful country. I feel at home already. The eucalyptus trees, you know, and the brown hills—"

"But your trip is primarily business?"

"Yes, yes. My primary purpose is to study your roadcities and report to my government on the advisability of trying to adapt your startling American methods to our social problems Down Under. I thought you understood that such was the reason I was sent to you."

"Yes, I did, in a general way. I don't know just what it is that you wish to find out. I suppose that you have heard about our road towns, how they came about, how they operate, and so forth."

"I've read a good bit, true, but I am not a technical man, Mr. Gaines, not an engineer. My field is social and political. I want to see how this remarkable technical change has affected your people. Suppose you tell me about the roads as if I were entirely ignorant. And I will ask questions."

"That seems a practical plan. By the way, how many are there in your party?"

"Just myself. I sent my secretary on to Washington."

"I see." Gaines glanced at his wrist watch. "It's nearly dinner time. Suppose we run up to the Stockton strip for dinner. There is a good Chinese restaurant up there that I'm partial to. It will take us about an hour and you can see the ways in operation while we ride."

"Excellent."

Gaines pressed a button on his desk, and a picture formed on a large visor screen mounted on the opposite wall. It showed a strong-boned, angular young man seated at a semicircular control desk, which was backed by a complex instrument board. A cigaret was tucked in one corner of his mouth.

The young man glanced up, grinned, and waved from the screen. "Greetings and salutations, Chief. What can I do for you?"

"Hi, Dave. You've got the evening watch, eh? I'm running up to the Stockton sector for dinner. Where's Van Kleeck?"

"Gone to a meeting somewhere. He didn't say."

"Anything to report?"

"No, sir. The roads are rolling, and all the little people are going ridey-ridey home to their dinners."

"O.K.—keep 'em rolling."

"They'll roll, Chief."

Gaines snapped off the connection and turned to Blekinsop. "Van Kleeck is my chief deputy. I wish he'd spend more time on the road and less on politics. Davidson can handle things, however. Shall we go?"

They glided down an electric staircase, and debouched on the walkway which bordered the northbound five-mile-an-hour strip. After skirting a stairway trunk marked OVERPASS TO SOUTHBOUND ROAD, they paused at the edge of the first strip. "Have you ever ridden a conveyor strip before?" Gaines inquired. "It's quite simple. Just remember to face against the motion of the strip as you get on."

They threaded their way through homeward-bound throngs, passing from strip to strip. Down the center of the twenty-mile-an-hour strip ran a glassite partition which reached nearly to the spreading roof. The Honorable Mister Blekinsop raised his eyebrows inquiringly as he looked at it.

"Oh, that?" Gaines answered the unspoken inquiry as he slid back a panel door and ushered his guest through. "That's a wind break. If we didn't have some way of separating the air currents over the strips of different speeds, the wind would tear our clothes off on the hundred-mile-an-hour strip." He bent his head to Blekinsop's as he spoke, in order to cut through the rush of air against the road surfaces, the noise of the crowd, and the muted roar of the driving mechanism concealed beneath the moving strips. They combination of noises inhibited further conversation as they proceeded toward the middle of the roadway. After passing through three more wind screens located at the forty, sixty, and eighty-mile-an-hour strips respectively, they finally reached the maximum speed strip, the hundred-mile-an-hour strip, which made the round trip, San Diego to Reno and back, in twelve hours.

Blekinsop found himself on a walkway twenty feet wide facing another partition. Immediately opposite him an illuminated show window proclaimed:

JAKE'S STEAK HOUSE No. 4
THE FASTEST MEAL ON THE FASTEST ROAD!

"TO DINE ON THE FLY
MAKES THE MILES ROLL BY!!"

"Amazing!" said Mr. Blekinsop. "It would be like dining in a tram. Is this really a proper restaurant?"

"One of the best. Not fancy, but sound."

"Oh, I say, could we—"

Gaines smiled at him. "You'd like to try it, wouldn't you, sir?"

"I don't wish to interfere with your plans—"

"Quite all right. I'm hungry myself, and Stockton is a long hour away. Let's go in."

Gaines greeted the manageress as an old friend. "Hello, Mrs. McCoy. How are you tonight?"

"If it isn't the chief himself! It's a long time since we've had the pleasure of seeing your face." She led them to a booth somewhat detached from the crowd of dining commuters. "And will you and your friend be having dinner?"

"Yes, Mrs. McCoy—suppose you order for us—but be sure it includes one of your steaks."

"Two inches thick—from a steer that died happy." She glided away, moving her fat frame with surprising grace.

With sophisticated foreknowledge of the chief engineer's needs, Mrs. McCoy had left a portable telephone at the table. Gaines plugged it in to an accommodation jack at the side of the booth, and dialed a number. "Hello—Davidson? Dave, this is the chief. I'm in Jake's beanery number four for supper. You can reach me by calling ten-L-six-six."

He replaced the handset, and Blekinsop inquired politely: "Is it necessary for you to be available at all times?"

"Not strictly necessary," Gaines told him, "but I feel safer when I am in touch. Either Van Kleeck, or myself, should be where the senior engineer of the watch—that's Davidson this shift—can get hold of us in a pinch. If it's a real emergency, I want to be there, naturally."

"What would constitute a real emergency?"

"Two things, principally. A power failure on the rotors would bring the road to a standstill, and possibly strand millions of people a hundred miles, or more, from their homes. If it happened during a rush hour we would have to evacuate those millions from the road—not too easy to do."

"You say millions—as many as that?"

"Yes, indeed. There are twelve million people dependent on this roadway, living and working in the buildings adjacent to it, or within five miles of each side."

The Age of Power blends into the Age of Transportation almost imperceptibly, but two events stand out as landmarks in the change: the achievement of cheap sun power and the installation of the first mechanized road. The power resources of oil and coal of the United States had—save for a few sporadic outbreaks of common sense—been shamefully wasted in their development all through the first half of the twentieth century. Simultaneously, the automobile, from its humble start as a one-lunged horseless carriage, grew into a steel-bodied monster of over a hundred horsepower and capable of making more than a hundred miles an hour. They boiled over the countryside, like yeast in ferment. In 1955 it was estimated that there was a motor vehicle for every two persons in the United States.

They contained the seeds of their own destruction. Eighty million steel juggernauts, operated by imperfect human beings at high speeds, are more destructive than war. In the same reference year the premiums paid for compulsory liability and property damage insurance by automobile owners exceeded in amount the sum paid that year to purchase automobiles. Safe driving campaigns were chronic phenomena, but were mere pious attempts to put Humpty-Dumpty together again. It was not physically possible to drive safely in those crowded metropolises. Pedestrians were sardonically divided into two classes, the quick, and the dead.

But a pedestrian could be defined as a man who had found a place to park his car. The automobile made possible huge cities, then choked those same cities to death with their numbers. In 1900 Herbert George Wells pointed out that the saturation point in the size of a city might be mathematically predicted in terms of its transportation facilities. From a standpoint of speed alone the automobile made possible cities two hundred miles in diameter, but traffic congestion, and the inescapable, inherent danger of high-powered, individually operated vehicles cancelled out the possibility.

In 1955 Federal Highway #66 from Los Angeles to Chicago, "The Main Street of America," was transformed into a superhighway for motor vehicles, with an underspeed limit of sixty miles per hour. It was planned as a public works project to stimulate heavy industry; it had an unexpected by-product. The great cities of Chicago and St. Louis stretched out urban pseudopods toward each other, until they met near Bloomington, Illinois. The two parent cities actually shrunk in population.

That same year the city of San Francisco replaced its antiquated cable cars with moving stairways, powered with the Douglas-Martin Solar Reception Screens. The largest number of automobile licenses in history had been issued that calendar year, but the end of the automobile era was in sight, and the National Defense Act of 1957 gave fair warning.

This act, one of the most bitterly debated ever to be brought out of committee, declared petroleum to be an essential and limited material of war. The armed forces had first call on all oil, above or below the ground, and eighty million civilian vehicles faced short and expensive rations. The "temporary" conditions during World War II had become permanent.

Take the superhighways of the period, urban throughout their length. Add the mechanized streets of San Francisco's hills. Heat to a boiling point with an imminent shortage of gasoline. Flavor with Yankee ingenuity. The first mechanized road was opened in 1960 between Cincinnati and Cleveland.

It was, as one would expect, comparatively primitive in design, being based on the ore belt conveyors of ten years earlier. The fastest strip moved only thirty miles per hour, and was quite narrow, for no one had thought of the possibility of locating retail trade on the strips themselves. Nevertheless, it was a prototype of social pattern which was to dominate the American scene within the next two decades—neither rural, nor urban, but partaking equally of both, and based on rapid, safe, cheap, convenient transportation.

Factories—wide, low buildings whose roofs were covered with solar power screens of the same type that drove the road—lined the roadway on each side. Back of them and interspersed among them were commercial hotels, retail stores, theatres, apartment houses. Beyond this long, thin, narrow strip was the open country-side, where the bulk of the population lived. Their homes dotted the hills, hung on the banks of creeks, and nestled between the farms. They worked in the "city" but lived in the "country"—and the two were not ten minutes apart.

Mrs. McCoy served the chief and his guest in person. They checked their conversation at the sight of the magnificent steaks.

Up and down the six hundred mile line, Sector Engineers of the Watch were getting in their hourly reports from their subsector technicians. "Subsector one—check!" "Subsector two—check!" Tensionometer readings, voltage, load, bearing temperatures, synchrotachometer readings—"Subsector seven—check!" Hardbitten, able men in dungarees, who lived much of their lives 'down inside' amidst the unmuted roar of the hundred mile strip, the shrill whine of driving rotors, and the complaint of the relay rollers.

Davidson studied the moving model of the road, spread out before him in the main control room at Fresno Sector. He watched the barely perceptible crawl of the miniature hundred mile strip and subconsciously noted the reference number on it which located Jake's Steak House No. 4. The chief would be getting in to Stockton soon; he'd give him a ring after the hourly reports were in. Everything was quiet; traffic tonnage normal for rush hour; he would be sleepy before this watch was over. He turned to his Cadet Engineer of the Watch. "Mr. Barnes."

"Yes, sir."

"I think we could use some coffee."

"Good idea, sir. I'll order some as soon as the hourlies are in."

The minute hand of the control board chronometer reached twelve. The cadet watch officer threw a switch. "All sectors, report!" he said, in crisp, self-conscious tones.

The faces of two men flicked into view on the visor screen. The younger answered him with the same air of acting under supervision. "Diego Circle—rolling!"

They were at once replaced by two more. "Angeles Sector—rolling!"

Then: "Bakersfield Sector—rolling!"

And: "Fresno Sector—rolling!"

Finally, when Reno Circle had reported, the cadet turned to Davidson and reported: "Rolling, sir."

"Very well—keep them rolling!"

The visor screen flashed on once more. "Sacramento Sector; supplementary report."

"Proceed."

"Cadet Guenther, while on visual inspection as cadet sector engineer of the watch, found Cadet Alec Jeans, on watch as cadet subsector technician, and R. J. Ross, technician second class, on watch as technician for the same subsector, engaged in playing cards. It was not possible to tell with any accuracy how long they had neglected to patrol their subsector."

"Any damage?"

"One rotor running hot, but still synchronized. It was jacked down, and replaced."

"Very well. Have the paymaster give Ross his time, and turn him over to the civil authorities. Place Cadet Jeans under arrest and order him to report to me."

"Very well, sir."

"Keep them rolling!"

Davidson turned back to the control desk and dialled Chief Engineer Gaines's temporary number.

"You mentioned that there were two things that could cause major trouble on the road, Mr. Gaines, but you spoke only of power failure to the rotors."

Gaines pursued an elusive bit of salad before answering. "There really isn't a second major trouble—it won't happen. However—we are travelling along here at one hundred miles per hour. Can you visualize what would happen if this strip under us should break?"

Mr. Blekinsop shifted nervously in his chair. "Hmm—rather a disconcerting idea, don't you think? I mean to say, one is hardly aware that one is travelling at high speed, here in this snug room. What *would* the result be?"

"Don't let it worry you; the strip can't part. It is built up of overlapping sections in such a fashion that it has a safety factor of better than twelve to one. Several miles of rotors would have to shut down all at once, and the circuit breakers for the rest of the line fail to trip out before there could possibly be sufficient tension on the strip to cause it to part.

"But it happened once, on the Philadelphia-Jersey City Road, and we aren't likely to forget it. It was one of the earliest high speed roads, carrying a tremendous passenger traffic, as well as heavy freight, since it serviced a heavily industrialized area. The strip was hardly more than a conveyor belt, and no one had foreseen the weight it would carry. It happened under maximum load, naturally, when the high speed way was crowded. The part of the strip behind the break buckled for miles, crushing passengers against the roof at eighty miles per hour. The section forward of the break cracked like a whip, spilling passengers onto the slower ways, dropping them on the exposed rollers and rotors down inside, and snapping them up against the roof.

"Over three thousand people were killed in that one accident, and there was much agitation to abolish the roads. They were even shut down for a week by presidential order, but he was forced to reopen them again. There was no alternative."

"Really? Why not?"

"The country had become economically dependent on the roads. They were the principal means of transportation in the industrial areas—the only means of economic importance. Factories were shut down; food didn't move; people got hungry—and the President was forced to let them roll again. It was the only thing that could be done; the social pattern had crystallized in one form, and it couldn't be changed overnight. A large, industrialized population must have large-scale transportation, not only for people, but for trade."

Mr. Blekinsop fussed with his napkin, and rather diffidently suggested, "Mr. Gaines, I do not intend to disparage the ingenious accomplishments of your great people, but isn't it possible that you may have put too many eggs in one basket in allowing your whole economy to become dependent on the functioning of one type of machinery?"

Gaines considered this soberly. "I see your point. Yes—and no. Every civilization above the peasant-and-village type is dependent on some key type of machinery. The old South was based on the cotton gin. Imperial England was made possible by the steam engine. Large populations have to have machines for power, for transportation, and for manufacturing in order to live. Had it not been for machinery the large populations could never have grown up. That's not a fault of the machine; that's its virtue.

"But it is true that whenever we develop machinery to the point where it will support large populations at a high standard of living we are then bound to keep that machinery running, or suffer the consequences. But the real hazard in that is not the machinery, but the men who run the machinery. These roads, as machines, are all right. They are strong and safe and will do everything they were designed to do. No, it's not the machines, it's the men.

"When a population is dependent on a machine, they are hostages of the men who tend the machines. If their morale is high, their sense of duty strong—"

Someone up near the front of the restaurant had turned up the volume control of the radio, letting out a blast of music that drowned out Gaines's words. When the sound had been tapered down to a more nearly bearable volume, he was saying:

"Listen to that. It illustrates my point."

Blekinsop turned an ear to the music. It was a swinging march of compelling rhythm, with a modern interpretive arrangement. One could hear the roar of machinery, the repetitive clatter of mechanisms. A pleased smile of recognition spread over the Australian's face. "It's your Field Artillery Song, *The Roll of the Caissons*, isn't it? But I don't see the connection."

"You're right; it *was* the *Roll of the Caissons*, but we adapted it to our own purposes. It's the *Road Song of the Transport Cadets*. Wait."

The persistent throb of the march continued, and seemed to blend with the vibration of the roadway underneath into a single tympany. Then a male chorus took up the verse:

"Hear them hum!
Watch them run!
Oh, our job is never done,
For our roadways go rolling along!
While you ride;
While you glide;
We are watching 'down inside,'
So your roadways keep rolling along!

"Oh, it's Hie! Hie! Hee!
The rotor men are we—
Check off the sectors loud and strong! (spoken) *One! Two! Three!*
Anywhere you go
You are bound to know
That your roadways are rolling along!
(Shouted) *KEEP THEM ROLLING!*
That your roadways are rolling along!"

"See?" said Gaines, with more animation in his voice. "See? That is the real purpose of the United States Academy of Transport. That is the reason why the transport engineers are a semi-military profession, with strict discipline. We are the bottle neck, the *sine qua non*, of all industry, all economic life. Other industries can go on strike, and only create temporary and partial dislocations. Crops can fail here and there, and the country takes up the slack. But if the roads stop rolling, everything else must stop; the effect would be the same as a general strike—with this important difference: It takes a majority of the population, fired by a real feeling of grievance, to create a general strike; but the men that run the roads, few as they are, can create the same complete paralysis.

"We had just one strike on the roads, back in 'seventy-six. It was justified, I think, and it corrected a lot of real abuses—but it mustn't happen again."

"But what is to prevent it happening again, Mr. Gaines?"

"Morale—*esprit de corps*. The technicians in the road service are indoctrinated constantly with the idea that their job is a sacred trust. Besides which we do everything we can to build up their social position. But even more important is the Academy. We try to turn out graduate engineers imbued with the same loyalty, the same iron self-discipline, and determination to perform their duty to the community at any cost, that Annapolis and West Point and Goddard are so successful in inculcating in their graduates."

"Goddard? Oh, yes, the rocket field. And have you been successful, do you think?"

"Not entirely, perhaps, but we will be. It takes time to build up a tradition. When the oldest engineer is a man who entered the

Academy in his 'teens, we can afford to relax a little and treat it as
a solved problem."

"I suppose you are a graduate?"

Gaines grinned. "You flatter me—I must look younger than I
am. No, I'm a carry-over from the army. You see, the Department
of Defense operated the roads for some three months during reor-
ganization after the strike in 'seventy-six. I served on the conciliation
board that awarded pay increases and adjusted working conditions,
then I was assigned—"

The signal light of the portable telephone glowed red. Gaines
said, "Excuse me," and picked up the handset. "Yes?"

Blekinsop could overhear the voice at the other end. "This is
Davidson, Chief. The roads are rolling."

"Very well. Keep them rolling!"

"Had another trouble report from the Sacramento Sector."

"Again? What this time?"

Before Davidson could reply he was cut off. As Gaines reached
out to dial him back, his coffee cup, half full, landed in his lap.
Blekinsop was aware, even as he was rocked against the edge of the
table, of a disquieting change in the hum of the roadway.

"What has happened, Mr. Gaines?"

"Don't know. Emergency stop—God knows why." He was di-
alling furiously. Shortly he flung the phone down, without bothering
to return the handset to its cradle. "Phones are out. Come on! No—
You'll be safe here. Wait."

"Must I?"

"Well, come along then, and stick close to me." He turned away,
having dismissed the Australian cabinet minister from his mind. The
strip ground slowly to a stop, the giant rotors and myriad rollers
acting as fly wheels in preventing a disastrous sudden stop. Already
a little knot of commuters, disturbed at their evening meal, were
attempting to crowd out the door of the restaurant.

"Halt!"

There is something about a command issued by one who is used
to being obeyed which enforces compliance. It may be intonation,
or possibly a more esoteric power, such as animal tamers are reputed
to be able to exercise in controlling ferocious beasts. But it does exist,
and can be used to compel even those not habituated to obedience.

The commuters stopped in their tracks.

Gaines continued, "Remain in the restaurant until we are ready to evacuate you. I am the Chief Engineer. You will be in no danger here. You!" He pointed to a big fellow near the door. "You're deputized. Don't let anyone leave without proper authority. Mrs. McCoy, resume serving dinner."

Gaines strode out the door, Blekinsop tagging along. The situation outside permitted no such simple measures. The hundred mile strip alone had stopped; a few feet away the next strip flew by at an unchecked ninety-five miles an hour. The passengers on it flickered past, unreal cardboard figures.

The twenty-foot walkway of the maximum speed strip had been crowded when the breakdown occurred. Now the customers of shops, of lunchstands, and of other places of business, the occupants of lounges, of television theatres—all came crowding out onto the walkway to see what had happened. The first disaster struck almost immediately.

The crowd surged, and pushed against a middle-aged woman on its outer edge. In attempting to recover her balance she put one foot over the edge of the flashing ninety-five mile strip. She realized her gruesome error, for she screamed before her foot touched the ribbon.

She spun around and landed heavily on the moving strip, and was rolled by it, as the strip attempted to impart to her mass, at one blow, a velocity of ninety-five miles per hour—one hundred and thirty-nine feet per second. As she rolled she mowed down some of the cardboard figures as a sickle strikes a stand of grass. Quickly, she was out of sight, her identity, her injuries, and her fate undetermined, and already remote.

But the consequences of her mishap were not done with. One of the flickering cardboard figures bowled over by her relative momentum fell toward the hundred mile strip, slammed into the shock-bound crowd, and suddenly appeared as a live man—but broken and bleeding, amidst the luckless, fallen victims whose bodies had checked his wild flight.

Even there it did not end. The disaster spread from its source, each hapless human ninepin more like than not to knock down others so that they fell over the danger-laden boundary, and in turn ricocheted to a dearly bought equilibrium.

But the focus of calamity sped out of sight, and Blekinsop could see no more. His active mind, accustomed to dealing with large numbers of individual human beings, multiplied the tragic sequence he had witnessed by twelve hundred miles of thronged conveyor strip, and his stomach chilled.

To Blekinsop's surprise, Gaines made no effort to succor the fallen, nor to quell the fear-infected mob, but turned an expressionless face back to the restaurant. When Blekinsop saw that he was actually re-entering the restaurant, he plucked at his sleeve. "Aren't we going to help those poor people?"

The cold planes of the face of the man who answered him bore no resemblance to his genial, rather boyish, host of a few minutes before. "No. Bystanders can help them—I've got the whole road to think of. Don't bother me."

Crushed, and somewhat indignant, the politician did as he was ordered. Rationally, he knew that the Chief Engineer was right—a man responsible for the safety of millions cannot turn aside from his duty to render personal service to one—but the cold detachment of such viewpoint was repugnant to him.

Gaines was back in the restaurant. "Mrs. McCoy, where is your get-away?"

"In the pantry, sir."

Gaines hurried there, Blekinsop at his heels. A nervous Filipino salad boy shrank out of his way as he casually swept a supply of prepared green stuffs onto the floor and stepped up on the counter where they had rested. Directly above his head and within reach was a circular manhole, counterweighted and operated by a handwheel set in its center. A short steel ladder, hinged to the edge of the opening, was swung up flat to the ceiling and secured by a hook.

Blekinsop lost his hat in his endeavor to clamber quickly enough up the ladder after Gaines. When he emerged on the roof of the building, Gaines was searching the ceiling of the roadway with a pocket flashlight. He was shuffling along, stooped double in the awkward four feet of space between the roof underfoot and ceiling.

He found what he sought, some fifty feet away—another manhole similar to the one they had used to escape from below. He spun the wheel of the lock and stood up in the space, then rested his hands on the sides of the opening and with a single lithe movement vaulted to the roof of the roadways. His companion followed him with more difficulty.

They stood in darkness, a fine, cold rain feeling at their faces. But underfoot, and stretching beyond sight on each hand, the sun power screens glowed with a faint opalescent radiance, their slight percentage of inefficiency as transformers of radiant sun power to available electrical power being evidenced as a mild phosphorescence. The effect was not illumination, but rather like the ghostly sheen of a snow covered plain seen by starlight.

The glow picked out the path they must follow to reach the rain-obscured wall of buildings bordering the ways. The path was a narrow black stripe which arched away into the darkness over the low curve of the roof. They started away on this path at a dog trot, making as much speed as the slippery footing and the dark permitted, while Blekinsop's mind still fretted at the problem of Gaines's apparently callous detachment. Although possessed of a keen intelligence his nature was dominated by a warm, human sympathy, without which no politician, irrespective of other virtues or shortcomings, is long successful.

Because of this trait he distrusted instinctively any mind which was guided by logic alone. He was aware that, from a standpoint of strict logic, no reasonable case could be made out for the continued existence of the human race, still less for the human values he served.

Had he been able to pierce the preoccupation of his companion, he would have been reassured. On the surface Gaines's exceptionally intelligent mind was clicking along with the facile ease of an electronic integrator—arranging data at hand, making tentative decisions, postponing judgments without prejudice until necessary data were available, exploring alternatives. Underneath, in a compartment insulated by stern self-discipline from the acting theatre of his mind, his emotions were a torturing storm of self-reproach. He was heartsick at suffering he had seen, and which he knew too well was duplicated up and down the line. Although he was not aware of any personal omission, nevertheless, the fault was somehow his, for authority creates responsibility.

He had carried too long the superhuman burden of kingship—which no sane mind can carry light-heartedly—and was at this moment perilously close to the frame of mind which sends captains down with their ships. Only the need for immediate, constructive action sustained him.

But no trace of this conflict reached his features.

At the wall of buildings glowed a green line of arrows, pointing to the left. Over them, at the terminus of the narrow path, shone a sign: "ACCESS DOWN." They pursued this, Blekinsop puffing in Gaines's wake, to a door let in the wall, which gave into a narrow stairway lighted by a single glowtube. Gaines plunged down this, still followed, and they emerged on the crowded, noisy, stationary walkway adjoining the northbound road.

Immediately adjacent to the stairway, on the right, was a public telebooth. Through the glassite door they could see a portly, well-dressed man speaking earnestly to his female equivalent, mirrored in the visor screen. Three other citizens were waiting outside the booth.

Gaines pushed past them, flung open the door, grasped the bewildered and indignant man by the shoulders, and hustled him outside, kicking the door closed after him. He cleared the visor screen with one sweep of his hand, before the matron pictured therein could protest, and pressed the *emergency-priority* button.

He dialed his private code number, and was shortly looking into the troubled face of his Engineer of the Watch, Davidson.

"Report!"

"It's you, Chief! Thank God! Where are you?" Davidson's relief was pathetic.

"Report!"

The Senior Watch Officer repressed his emotion and complied in direct, clipped phrases, "At seven-oh-nine P.M. the consolidated tension reading, strip twenty, Sacramento Sector, climbed suddenly. Before action could be taken, tension on strip twenty passed emergency level; the interlocks acted, and power to subject strip cut out. Cause of failure unknown. Direct communication to Sacramento control office has failed. They do not answer the auxiliary, nor the commercial line. Effort to re-establish communication continues. Messenger dispatched from Stockton Subsector Ten.

"No casualties reported. Warning broadcast by public announcement circuit to keep clear of strip nineteen. Evacuation has commenced."

"There are casualties," Gaines cut in. "Police and hospital emergency routine. Move!"

"Yes, sir!" Davidson snapped back, and hooked a thumb over his shoulder—but his Cadet Officer of the Watch had already jumped to comply. "Shall I cut out the rest of the road, Chief?"

"No. No more casualties are likely after the first disorder. Keep up the broadcast warnings. Keep those other strips rolling, or we will have a traffic jam the devil himself couldn't untangle."—Gaines had in mind the impossibility of bringing the strips up to speed under load. The rotors were not powerful enough to do this. If the entire road was stopped, he would have to evacuate every strip, correct the trouble on strip twenty, bring all strips up to speed, and then move the accumulated peak load traffic. In the meantime, over five million stranded passengers would constitute a tremendous police problem. It was simpler to evacuate passengers on strip twenty over the roof, and allow them to return home via the remaining strips. "Notify the Mayor and the Governor that I have assumed emergency authority. Same to the Chief of Police and place him under your orders. Tell the Commandant to arm all cadets available and await orders. Move!"

"Yes, sir. Shall I recall technicians off watch?"

"No. This isn't an engineering failure. Take a look at your readings; that entire sector went out simultaneously—Somebody cut out those rotors by hand. Place off-watch technicians on standby status—but don't arm them, and don't send them down inside. Tell the Commandant to rush all available senior-class cadets to Stockton Subsector Office number ten to report to me. I want them equipped with tumblebugs, pistols, and sleepy bombs."

"Yes, sir." A clerk leaned over Davidson's shoulder and said something in his ear. "The Governor wants to talk to you, Chief."

"Can't do it—nor can you. Who's your relief? Have you sent for him?"

"Hubbard—he's just come in."

"Have him talk to the Governor, the Mayor, the press—anybody that calls—even the White House. You stick to your watch. I'm cutting off. I'll be back in communication as quickly as I can locate a reconnaissance car." He was out of the booth almost before the screen cleared.

Blekinsop did not venture to speak, but followed him out to the northbound twenty-mile strip. There Gaines stopped, short of the wind break, turned, and kept his eyes on the wall beyond the stationary walkway. He picked out some landmark, or sign—not apparent to his companion—and did an Eliza-crossing-the-ice back to the walkway, so rapidly that Blekinsop was carried some hundred feet beyond him, and almost failed to follow when Gaines ducked into a doorway and ran down a flight of stairs.

They came out on a narrow lower walkway, 'down inside.' The pervading din claimed them, beat upon their bodies as well as their ears. Dimly, Blekinsop perceived their surroundings, as he struggled to face that wall of sound. Facing him, illuminated by the yellow monochrome of a sodium arc, was one of the rotors that drove the five-mile strip, its great, drum-shaped armature revolving slowly around the stationary field coils in its core. The upper surface of the drum pressed against the under side of the moving way and imparted to it its stately progress.

To the left and right, a hundred yards each way, and beyond at similar intervals, farther than he could see, were other rotors. Bridging the gaps between the rotors were the slender rollers, crowded together like cigars in a box, in order that the strip might have a continuous rolling support The rollers were supported by steel girder arches through the gaps of which he saw row after row of rotors in staggered succession, the rotors in each succeeding row turning over more rapidly than the last.

Separated from the narrow walkway by a line of supporting steel pillars, and lying parallel to it on the side away from the rotors, ran a shallow paved causeway, joined to the walk at this point by a ramp. Gaines peered up and down this tunnel in evident annoyance. Blekinsop started to ask him what troubled him, but found his voice snuffed out by the sound. He could not cut through the roar of thousands of rotors and the whine of hundreds of thousands of rollers.

Gaines saw his lips move and guessed at the question. He cupped his hands around Blekinsop's right ear, and shouted, "No car—I expected to find a car here."

The Australian, wishing to be helpful, grasped Gaines's arm and pointed back into the jungle of machinery. Gaines's eye followed the direction indicated and picked out something that he had missed in his preoccupation—a half dozen men working around a rotor several strips away. They had jacked down a rotor until it was no longer in contact with the road surface and were preparing to replace it in toto. The replacement rotor was standing by on a low, heavy truck.

The Chief Engineer gave a quick smile of acknowledgment and thanks and aimed his flashlight at the group, the beam focused down to a slender, intense needle of light. One of the technicians looked up, and Gaines snapped the light on and off in a repeated, irregular pattern. A figure detached itself from the group, and ran toward them.

It was a slender young man, dressed in dungarees and topped off with earpads and an incongruous, pillbox cap, bright with gold braid and insignia. He recognized the Chief Engineer and saluted, his face falling into humorless, boyish intentness.

Gaines stuffed his torch into a pocket and commenced to gesticulate rapidly with both hands—clear, clean gestures, as involved and as meaningful as deaf-mute language. Blekinsop dug into his own dilettante knowledge of anthropology and decided that it was most like American Indian sign language, with some of the finger movements of hula. But it was necessarily almost entirely strange, being adapted for a particular terminology.

The cadet answered him in kind, stepped to the edge of the causeway, and flashed his torch to the south. He picked out a car, still some distance away, but approaching at headlong speed. It braked, and came to a stop alongside them.

It was a small affair, ovoid in shape, and poised on two centerline wheels. The forward, upper surface swung up and disclosed the driver, another cadet. Gaines addressed him briefly in sign language, then hustled Blekinsop ahead of him into the cramped passenger compartment.

As the glassite hood was being swung back into place, a blast of wind smote them, and the Australian looked up in time to glimpse the last of three much larger vehicles hurtle past them. They were headed north, at a speed of not less than two hundred miles per hour. Blekinsop thought that he had made out the little hats of cadets through the windows of the last of the three, but he could not be sure.

He had no time to wonder, so violent was the driver's getaway.

Gaines ignored the accelerating surge; he was already calling Davidson on the built-in communicator. Comparative silence had settled
down once the car was closed. The face of a female operator at the
relay station showed on the screen.

"Get me Davidson—Senior Watch Office!"

"Oh! It's Mr. Gaines! The Mayor wants to talk to you, Mr.
Gaines."

"Refer him—and get me Davidson. Move!"

"Yes, sir!"

"And see here—leave this circuit hooked in to Davidson's board
until I tell you personally to cut it."

"Right." Her face gave way to the Watch Officer's.

"That you, Chief? We're moving—progress O.K.—no change."

"Very well. You'll be able to raise me on this circuit, or at Subsector Ten office. Clearing now." Davidson's face gave way to the
relay operator.

"Your wife is calling, Mr. Gaines. Will you take it?"

Gaines muttered something not quite gallant, and answered,
"Yes."

Mrs. Gaines flashed into facsimile. He burst into speech before
she could open her mouth. "Darling I'm all right don't worry I'll be
home when I get there I've got to go now." It was all out in one
breath, and he slapped the control that cleared the screen.

They slammed to a breath-taking stop alongside the stair leading
to the watch office of Subsector Ten, and piled out. Three big lorries
were drawn up on the ramp, and three platoons of cadets were ranged
in restless ranks alongside them.

A cadet trotted up to Gaines, and saluted. "Lindsay, sir—Cadet
Engineer of the Watch. The Engineer of the Watch requests that
you come at once to the control room."

The Engineer of the Watch looked up as they came in. "Chief—
Van Kleeck is calling you."

"Put him on."

When Van Kleeck appeared in the big visor, Gaines greeted him
with, "Hello, Van. Where are you?"

"Sacramento Office. Now, listen—"

"Sacramento? That's good! Report."

Van Kleeck looked disgruntled. "Report, hell! I'm not your deputy any more, Gaines. Now, you—"

"What the hell are you talking about?"

"Listen, and don't interrupt me, and you'll find out. You're through, Gaines. I've been picked as Director of the Provisional Control Committee for the New Order."

"Van, have you gone off your rocker? What do you mean—the 'New Order'?"

"You'll find out. This is it—the functionalist revolution. We're in; you're out. We stopped strip twenty just to give you a little taste of what we can do."

Concerning Function: A Treatise on the Natural Order in Society, the bible of the functionalist movement, was first published in 1930. It claimed to be a scientifically accurate theory of social relations. The author, Paul Decker, disclaimed the "outworn and futile" ideas of democracy and human equality, and substituted a system in which human beings were evaluated "functionally"—that is to say, by the role each filled in the economic sequence. The underlying thesis was that it was right and proper for a man to exercise over his fellows whatever power was inherent in his function, and that any other form of social organization was silly, visionary, and contrary to the "natural order."

The complete interdependence of modern economic life seems to have escaped him entirely.

His ideas were dressed up with a glib mechanistic pseudopsychology based on the observed orders of precedence among barnyard fowls, and on the famous Pavlov conditioned-reflex experiments on dogs. He failed to note that human beings are neither dogs, nor chickens. Old Doctor Pavlov ignored him entirely, as he had ignored so many others who had blindly and unscientifically dogmatized about the meaning of his important, but strictly limited, experiments.

Functionalism did not take hold at once—during the 'thirties almost everyone, from truckdriver to hatcheck girl, had a scheme for setting the world right in six easy lessons; and a surprising percentage managed to get their schemes published. But it gradually spread. Functionalism was particularly popular among little people everywhere who could persuade themselves that their particular jobs were the indispensable ones, and that, therefore, under the "natural order" they would be top dog. With so many different functions actually indispensable such self-persuasion was easy.

Gaines stared at Van Kleeck for a moment before replying. "Van," he said slowly, "you don't really think you can get away with this, do you?"

The little man puffed out his chest. "Why not? We *have* gotten away with it. You can't start strip twenty until I am ready to let you, and I can stop the whole road, if necessary."

Gaines was becoming uncomfortably aware that he was dealing with unreasonable conceit, and held himself patiently in check. "Sure you can, Van—but how about the rest of the country? Do you think the United States Army will sit quietly by and let you run California as your private kingdom?"

Van Kleeck looked sly. "I've planned for that. I've just finished broadcasting a manifesto to all the road technicians in the country, telling them what we have done, and telling them to arise, and claim their rights. With every road in the country stopped, and people getting hungry, I reckon the President will think twice before sending the army to tangle with us. Oh, he could send a force to capture, or kill me—I'm not afraid to die!—but he doesn't dare start shooting down road technicians as a class, because the country can't get along without us—consequently, he'll have to get along with us—on our terms!"

There was much bitter truth in what he said. If an uprising of the road technicians became general, the government could no more attempt to settle it by force than a man could afford to cure a headache by blowing out his brains. But was the uprising general?

"Why do you think that the technicians in the rest of the country will follow your lead?"

"Why not? It's the natural order of things. This is an age of machinery; the real power everywhere is in the technicians, but they have been kidded into not using their power with a lot of obsolete catch-phrases. And of all the classes of technicians, the most important, the absolutely essential, are the road technicians. From now on they run the show—it's the natural order of things!" He turned away for a moment, and fussed with some papers on the desk before him, then he added, "That's all for now, Gaines—I've got to call the White House, and let the President know how things stand. You carry on, and behave yourself, and you won't get hurt."

Gaines sat quite still for some minutes after the screen cleared. So that's how it was. He wondered what effect, if any, Van Kleeck's invitation to strike had had on road technicians elsewhere. None, he thought—but then he had not dreamed that it could happen among his own technicians. Perhaps he had made a mistake in refusing to take time to talk to anyone outside the road. No—if he had stopped to talk to the Governor, or the newspapermen, he would still be talking. Still—

He dialled Davidson.

"Any trouble in any other sectors, Dave?"

"No, Chief."

"Or on any other road?"

"None reported."

"Did you hear my talk with Van Kleeck?"

"I was cut in—yes."

"Good. Have Hubbard call the President and the Governor, and tell them that I am strongly opposed to the use of military force as long as the outbreak is limited to this road. Tell them that I will not be responsible if they move in before I ask for help."

Davidson looked dubious. "Do you think that is wise, Chief?"

"I do! If we try to blast Van and his red-hots out of their position, we may set off a real, country-wide uprising. Furthermore, he could wreck the road so that God himself couldn't put it back together. What's your rolling tonnage now?"

"Fifty-three percent under evening peak."

"How about strip twenty?"

"Almost evacuated."

"Good. Get the road clear of all traffic as fast as possible. Better have the Chief of Police place a guard on all entrances to the road to keep out new traffic. Van may stop all strips any time—or I may need to, myself. Here is my plan: I'm going 'down inside' with these armed cadets. We will work north, overcoming any resistance we meet. You arrange for watch technicians and maintenance crews to follow immediately behind us. Each rotor, as they come to it, is to be cut out, then hooked into the Stockton control board. It will be a haywire rig, with no safety interlocks, so use enough watch technicians to be able to catch trouble before it happens.

"If this scheme works, we can move control of the Sacramento Sector right out from under Van's feet, and he can stay in this Sacramento control office until he gets hungry enough to be reasonable."

He cut off and turned to the Subsector Engineer of the Watch. "Edmunds, give me a helmet—and a pistol."

"Yes, sir." He opened a drawer, and handed his chief a slender, deadly looking weapon. Gaines belted it on, and accepted a helmet, into which he crammed his head, leaving the anti-noise ear flaps up. Blekinsop cleared his throat.

"May—uh—may I have one of those helmets?" he inquired.

"What?" Gaines focused his attention. "Oh—You won't need one, Mr. Blekinsop. I want you to remain right here until you hear from me."

"But—" The Australian statesman started to speak, thought better of it, and subsided.

From the doorway the Cadet Engineer of the Watch demanded the Chief Engineer's attention. "Mr. Gaines, there is a technician out here who insists on seeing you—a man named Harvey."

"Can't do it."

"He's from the Sacramento Sector, sir."

"Oh!—send him in."

Harvey quickly advised Gaines of what he had seen and heard at the guild meeting that afternoon. "I got disgusted and left while they were still jawin', Chief. I didn't think any more about it until twenty stopped rolling. Then I heard that the trouble was in Sacramento Sector, and decided to look you up."

"How long has this been building up?"

"Quite some time, I guess. You know how it is—there are a few soreheads everywhere and a lot of them are functionalists. But you can't refuse to work with a man just because he holds different political views. It's a free country."

"You should have come to me before, Harvey." Harvey looked stubborn. Gaines studied his face. "No, I guess you are right. It's my business to keep tab on your mates, not yours. As you say, it's a free country. Anything else?"

"Well—now that it has come to this, I thought maybe I could help you pick out the ringleaders."

"Thanks. You stick with me. We're going 'down inside' and try to clear up this mess."

The office door opened suddenly, and a technician and a cadet appeared, lugging a burden between them. They deposited it on the floor, and waited.

It was a young man, quite evidently dead. The front of his dungaree jacket was soggy with blood. Gaines looked at the watch officer. "Who is he?"

Edmunds broke his stare and answered, "Cadet Hughes—he's the messenger I sent to Sacramento when communication failed. When he didn't report, I sent Marston and Cadet Jenkins after him."

Gaines muttered something to himself, and turned away. "Come along, Harvey."

The cadets waiting below had changed in mood. Gaines noted that the boyish intentness for excitement had been replaced by something uglier. There was much exchange of hand signals and several appeared to be checking the loading of their pistols.

He sized them up, then signalled to the cadet leader. There was a short interchange of signals. The cadet saluted, turned to his men, gesticulated briefly, and brought his arm down smartly. They filed upstairs and into an empty standby room, Gaines following.

Once inside, and the noise shut out, he addressed them, "You saw Hughes brought in—how many of you want a chance to kill the louse that did it?"

Three of the cadets reacted almost at once, breaking ranks and striding forward. Gaines looked at them coldly. "Very well. You three turn in your weapons, and return to your quarters. Any of the rest of you that think this is a matter of private revenge, or a hunting party, may join them." He permitted a short silence to endure before continuing. "Sacramento Sector has been seized by unauthorized persons. We are going to retake it—if possible, without loss of life on either side, and, if possible, without stopping the roads. The plan is to take over 'down inside,' rotor by rotor, and cross connect through Stockton. The task assignment of this group is to proceed north 'down inside,' locating and overpowering all persons in your path. You will bear in mind the probability that most of the persons you will arrest are completely innocent. Consequently, you will favor the use of sleep gas bombs, and will shoot to kill only as a last resort.

"Cadet Captain, assign your men in squads of ten each, with squad leader. Each squad is to form a skirmish line across 'down inside,' mounted on tumblebugs, and will proceed north at fifteen miles per hour. Leave an interval of one hundred yards between successive waves of skirmishers. Whenever a man is sighted, the entire leading wave will converge on him, arrest him, and deliver him to a transport car, and then fall in as the last wave. You will assign the transports that delivered you here to receive prisoners. Instruct the drivers to keep abreast of the second wave.

"You will assign an attack group to recapture subsector control offices, but no office is to be attacked until its subsector has been crossconnected with Stockton. Arrange liaison accordingly.

"Any questions?" He let his eyes run over the faces of the young men. When no one spoke up, he turned back to the cadet in charge. "Very well, sir. Carry out your orders!"

By the time the dispositions had been completed, the follow-up crew of technicians had arrived, and Gaines had given the engineer in charge his instructions. The cadets "stood to horse" alongside their poised tumblebugs. The Cadet Captain looked expectantly at Gaines. He nodded, the cadet brought his arm down smartly, and the first wave mounted and moved off.

Gaines and Harvey mounted tumblebugs, and kept abreast of the Cadet Captain, some twenty-five yards behind the leading wave. It had been a long time since the Chief Engineer had ridden one of these silly-looking little vehicles, and he felt awkward. A tumblebug does not give a man dignity, since it is about the size and shape of a kitchen stool, gyro-stabilized on a single wheel. But it is perfectly adapted to patrolling the maze of machinery 'down inside,' since it can go through an opening the width of a man's shoulders, is easily controlled, and will stand patiently upright, waiting, should its rider dismount.

The little reconnaissance car followed Gaines at a short interval, weaving in and out among the rotors, while the television and audio communicator inside continued as Gaines's link to his other manifold responsibilities.

The first two hundred yards of the Sacramento Sector passed

without incident, then one of the skirmishers sighted a tumblebug parked by a rotor. The technician it served was checking the gauges at the rotor's base, and did not see them approach. He was unarmed and made no resistance, but seemed surprised and indignant, as well as very bewildered.

The little command group dropped back and permitted the new leading wave to overtake them.

Three miles farther along the score stood thirty-seven men arrested, none killed. Two of the cadets had received minor wounds, and had been directed to retire. Only four of the prisoners had been armed, one of these Harvey had been able to identify definitely as a ringleader. Harvey expressed a desire to attempt to parley with the outlaws, if any occasion arose. Gaines agreed tentatively. He knew of Harvey's long and honorable record as a labor leader, and was willing to try anything that offered a hope of success with a minimum of violence.

Shortly thereafter the first wave flushed another technician. He was on the far side of a rotor; they were almost on him before he was seen. He did not attempt to resist, although he was armed, and the incident would not have been worth recording, had he not been talking into a hush-a-phone which he had plugged into the telephone jack at the base of the rotor.

Gaines reached the group as the capture was being effected. He snatched at the soft rubber mask of the 'phone, jerking it away from the man's mouth so violently that he could feel the bone-conduction receiver grate between the man's teeth. The prisoner spat out a piece of broken tooth and glared, but ignored attempts to question him.

Swift as Gaines had been, it was highly probable that they had lost the advantage of surprise. It was necessary to assume that the prisoner had succeeded in reporting the attack going on beneath the ways. Word was passed down the line to proceed with increased caution.

Gaines's pessimism was justified shortly. Riding toward them appeared a group of men, as yet several hundred feet away. There were at least a score, but their exact strength could not be determined, as they took advantage of the rotors for cover as they advanced. Harvey looked at Gaines, who nodded, and signalled the Cadet Captain to halt his forces.

Harvey went on ahead, unarmed, his hands held high above his head, and steering by balancing the weight of his body. The outlaw party checked its speed uncertainly, and finally stopped. Harvey approached within a couple of rods of them and stopped likewise. One of them, apparently the leader, spoke to him in sign language, to which he replied.

They were too far away and the yellow light too uncertain to follow the discussion. It continued for several minutes, then ensued a pause. The leader seemed uncertain what to do. One of his party rolled forward, returned his pistol to its holster, and conversed with the leader. The leader shook his head at the man's violent gestures.

The man renewed his argument, but met the same negative response. With a final disgusted wave of his hands, he desisted, drew his pistol, and shot at Harvey. Harvey grabbed at his middle and leaned forward. The man shot again; Harvey jerked, and slid to the ground.

The Cadet Captain beat Gaines to the draw. The killer looked up as the bullet hit him. He looked as if he were puzzled by some strange occurrence—being too freshly dead to be aware of it.

The cadets came in shooting. Although the first wave was outnumbered better than two to one, they were helped by the comparative demoralization of the enemy. The odds were nearly even after the first ragged volley. Less than thirty seconds after the first treacherous shot all of the insurgent party were dead, wounded, or under arrest. Gaines's losses were two dead (including the murder of Harvey) and two wounded.

Gaines modified his tactics to suit the changed conditions. Now that secrecy was gone, speed and striking power were of first importance. The second wave was directed to close in practically to the heels of the first. The third wave was brought up to within twenty-five yards of the second. These three waves were to ignore unarmed men, leaving them to be picked up by the fourth wave, but they were directed to shoot on sight any person carrying arms.

Gaines cautioned them to shoot to wound, rather than to kill, but he realized that his admonishment was almost impossible to obey. There would be killing. Well—he had not wanted it, but he felt that he had no choice. Any armed outlaw was a potential killer—he could not, in fairness to his own men, lay too many restrictions on them.

When the arrangements for the new marching order were completed, he signed the Cadet Captain to go ahead, and the first and second waves started off together at the top speed of which the tumblebugs were capable—not quite eighteen miles per hour. Gaines followed them.

He swerved to avoid Harvey's body, glancing involuntarily down as he did so. The face was an ugly jaundiced yellow under the sodium arc, but it was set in a death mask of rugged beauty in which the strong fibre of the dead man's character was evident. Seeing this, Gaines did not regret so much his order to shoot, but the deep sense of loss of personal honor lay more heavily on him than before.

They passed several technicians during the next few minutes, but had no occasion to shoot. Gaines was beginning to feel somewhat hopeful of a reasonably bloodless victory, when he noticed a change in the pervading throb of machinery which penetrated even through the heavy anti-noise pads of his helmet. He lifted an ear pad in time to hear the end of a rumbling diminuendo as the rotors and rollers slowed to rest.

The road was stopped.

He shouted, "Halt your men!" to the Cadet Captain. His words echoed hollowly in the unreal silence.

The top of the reconnaissance car swung up as he turned and hurried to it. "Chief!" the cadet within called out, "relay station calling you."

The girl in the visor screen gave way to Davidson as soon as she recognized Gaines's face. "Chief," Davidson said at once, "Van Kleeck's calling you."

"Who stopped the road?"

"He did."

"Any other major change in the situation?"

"No—the road was practically empty when he stopped it."

"Good. Give me Van Kleeck."

The chief conspirator's face was livid with uncurbed anger when he identified Gaines. He burst into speech.

"So! You thought I was fooling, eh? What do you think now, Mister Chief Engineer Gaines?"

Gaines fought down an impulse to tell him exactly what he thought, particularly about Van Kleeck. Everything about the short man's manner affected him like a squeaking slate pencil.

But he could not afford the luxury of speaking his mind. He strove to get just the proper tone into his voice which would soothe the other man's vanity. "I've got to admit that you've won this trick, Van—the roadway is stopped—but don't think I didn't take you seriously. I've watched your work too long to underrate you. I know you mean what you say."

Van Kleeck was pleased by the tribute, but tried not to show it. "Then why don't you get smart, and give up?" he demanded belligerently. "You can't win."

"Maybe not, Van, but you know I've got to try. Besides," he went on, "why can't I win? You said yourself that I could call on the whole United States Army."

Van Kleeck grinned triumphantly. "You see that?" He held up a pear-shaped electric push button, attached to a long cord. "If I push that, it will blow a path right straight across the ways—blow it to Kingdom Come. And just for good measure I'll take an ax, and wreck this control station before I leave."

Gaines wished wholeheartedly that he knew more about psychiatry. Well—he'd just have to do his best, and trust to horse sense to give him the right answers. "That's pretty drastic, Van, but I don't see how we can give up."

"No? You'd better have another think. If you force me to blow up the road, how about all the people that will be blown up along with it?"

Gaines thought furiously. He did not doubt that Van Kleeck would carry out his threat; his very phraseology, the childish petulance of "If you force me to do this—" betrayed the dangerous irrationality of his mental processes. And such an explosion anywhere in the thickly populated Sacramento Sector would be likely to wreck one, or more, apartment houses, and would be certain to kill shopkeepers on the included segment of strip twenty, as well as chance bystanders. Van was absolutely right; he dare not risk the lives of bystanders who were not aware of the issue and had not consented to the hazard—even if the road never rolled again.

For that matter, he did not relish chancing major damage to the road itself—but it was the danger to innocent life that left him helpless.

A tune ran through his head—*"Hear them hum; watch them run. Oh, our work is never done—"* What to do? What to do? *"While you ride; while you glide; we are—"* This wasn't getting anyplace.

He turned back to the screen. "Look, Van, you don't want to blow up the road unless you have to, I'm sure. Neither do I. Suppose I come up to your headquarters, and we talk this thing over. Two reasonable men ought to be able to make a settlement."

Van Kleeck was suspicious. "Is this some sort of a trick?"

"How can it be? I'll come alone, and unarmed, just as fast as my car can get there."

"How about your men?"

"They will sit where they are until I'm back. You can put out observers to make sure of it."

Van Kleeck stalled for a moment, caught between the fear of a trap, and the pleasure of having his erstwhile superior come to him to sue for terms. At last he grudgingly consented.

Gaines left his instructions and told Davidson what he intended to do. "If I'm not back within an hour, you're on your own, Dave."

"Be careful, Chief."

"I will."

He evicted the cadet driver from the reconnaissance car and ran it down the ramp into the causeway, then headed north and gave it the gun. Now he would have a chance to collect his thoughts, even at two hundred miles per hour. Suppose he pulled off this trick—there would still have to be some changes made. Two lessons stood out like sore thumbs: First, the strips must be cross-connected with safety interlocks so that adjacent strips would slow down, or stop, if a strip's speed became dangerously different from those adjacent. No repetition of what happened on twenty!

But that was elementary, a mere mechanical detail. The real failure had been in men. Well, the psychological classification tests must be improved to insure that the roads employed only conscientious, reliable men. But hell's bells—that was just exactly what the present classification tests were supposed to insure beyond question. To the best of his knowledge there had never been a failure from the improved Humm-Wadsworth-Burton method—not until today in the Sacramento Sector. How had Van Kleeck gotten one whole sector of temperament-classified men to revolt?

It didn't make sense.

Personnel did not behave erratically without a reason. One man might be unpredictable, but in large numbers they were as dependable as machines, or figures. They could be measured, examined, classified. His inner eye automatically pictured the personnel office, with its rows of filing cabinets, its clerks—He'd got it! He'd got it! Van Kleeck, as Chief Deputy, was ex officio *personnel officer for the entire road!*

It was the only solution that covered all the facts. The personnel officer alone had the perfect opportunity to pick out all the bad apples and concentrate them in one barrel. Gaines was convinced beyond any reasonable doubt that there had been skulduggery, perhaps for years, with the temperament classification tests, and that Van Kleeck had deliberately transferred the kind of men he needed to one sector, after falsifying their records.

And that taught another lesson—tighter tests for officers, and no officer to be trusted with classification and assignment without close supervision and inspection. Even he, Gaines, should be watched in that respect. *Qui custodiet ipsos custodes?* Who will guard those selfsame guardians? Latin might be obsolete, but those old Romans weren't dummies.

He at last knew wherein he had failed, and he derived melancholy pleasure from the knowledge. Supervision and inspection, check and re-check, was the answer. It would be cumbersome and inefficient, but it seemed that adequate safeguards always involved some loss of efficiency.

He should not have entrusted so much authority to Van Kleeck without knowing more about him. He still should know more about him—He touched the emergency-stop button, and brought the car to a dizzying halt. "Relay station! See if you can raise my office."

Dolores' face looked out from the screen. "You're still there—good!" he told her. "I was afraid you'd gone home."

"I came back, Mr. Gaines."

"Good girl. Get me Van Kleeck's personal file jacket. I want to see his classification record."

She was back with it in exceptionally short order and read from it the symbols and percentages. He nodded repeatedly as the data checked his hunches—masked introvert—inferiority complex. It checked.

" 'Comment of the Board,' " she read, " 'In spite of the potential instability shown by maxima A and D on the consolidated profile curve, the Board is convinced that this officer is, nevertheless, fitted for duty. He has an exceptionally fine record, and is especially adept in handling men. He is, therefore, recommended for retention and promotion.' "

"That's all, Dolores. Thanks."

"Yes, Mr. Gaines."

"I'm off for a showdown. Keep your fingers crossed."

"But Mr. Gaines—" Back in Fresno, Dolores stared wide-eyed at an empty screen.

"Take me to Mr. Van Kleeck!"

The man addressed took his gun out of Gaines's ribs—reluctantly, Gaines thought—and indicated that the Chief Engineer should precede him up the stairs. Gaines climbed out of the car, and complied.

Van Kleeck had set himself up in the sector control room proper, rather than the administrative office. With him were half a dozen men, all armed.

"Good evening, Director Van Kleeck." The little man swelled visibly at Gaines's acknowledgment of his assumed rank.

"We don't go in much around here for titles," he said, with ostentatious casualness. "Just call me Van. Sit down, Gaines."

Gaines did so. It was necessary to get those other men out. He looked at them with an expression of bored amusement. "Can't you handle one unarmed man by yourself, Van? Or don't the functionalists trust each other?"

Van Kleeck's face showed his annoyance, but Gaines's smile was undaunted. Finally the smaller man picked up a pistol from his desk, and motioned toward the door. "Get out, you guys."

"But Van—"

"Get out, I said!"

When they were alone, Van Kleeck picked up the electric push button which Gaines had seen in the visor screen, and pointed his pistol at his former chief. "O.K.," he growled, "try any funny stuff, and off it goes! What's your proposition?"

Gaines's irritating smile grew broader. Van Kleeck scowled. "What's so damn funny?" he said.

Gaines granted him an answer. "You are, Van—honest, this is rich. You start a functionalist revolution, and the only function you can think of to perform is to blow up the road that justifies your title. Tell me," he went on, "what is it you are so scared of?"

"I am not afraid!"

"Not afraid? You? Sitting there, ready to commit hara-kiri with that toy push button, and you tell me that you aren't afraid. If your buddies knew how near you are to throwing away what they've fought for, they'd shoot you in a second. You're afraid of them, too, aren't you?"

Van Kleeck thrust the push button away from him, and stood up. "I am not afraid!" he screamed, and came around the desk toward Gaines.

Gaines sat where he was, and laughed. "But you are! You're afraid of me, this minute. You're afraid I'll have you on the carpet for the way you do your job. You're afraid the cadets won't salute you. You're afraid they are laughing behind your back. You're afraid of using the wrong fork at dinner. You're afraid people are looking at you—and you are afraid that they won't notice you."

"I am not!" he protested. "You—You dirty, stuckup snob! Just because you went to a high-hat school you think you're better than anybody." He choked, and became incoherent, fighting to keep back tears of rage. "You, and your nasty little cadets—"

Gaines eyed him cautiously. The weakness in the man's character was evident now—he wondered why he had not seen it before. He recalled how ungracious Van Kleeck had been one time when he had offered to help him with an intricate piece of figuring.

The problem now was to play on his weakness, to keep him so preoccupied that he would not remember the peril-laden push button. He must be caused to center the venom of his twisted outlook on Gaines, to the exclusion of every other thought.

But he must not goad him too carelessly, or a shot from across the room might put an end to Gaines, and to any chance of avoiding a bloody, wasteful struggle for control of the road.

Gaines chuckled. "Van," he said, "you are a pathetic little shrimp. That was a dead give-away. I understand you perfectly; you're a third-rater, Van, and all your life you've been afraid that someone would see through you, and send you back to the foot of the class. Director—pfui! If you are the best the functionalists can offer, we can afford to ignore them—they'll fold up from their own rotten inefficiency." He swung around in his chair, deliberately turning his back on Van Kleeck and his gun.

Van Kleeck advanced on his tormentor, halted a few feet away, and shouted: "You—I'll show you—I'll put a bullet in you; that's what I'll do!"

Gaines swung back around, got up, and walked steadily toward him. "Put that popgun down before you hurt yourself."

Van Kleeck retreated a step. "Don't you come near me!" he screamed. "Don't you come near me—or I'll shoot you—see if I don't!"

This is it, thought Gaines, and dived.

The pistol went off alongside his ear. Well, that one didn't get him. They were on the floor. Van Kleeck was hard to hold, for a little man. Where was the gun? There! He had it. He broke away.

Van Kleeck did not get up. He lay sprawled on the floor, tears streaming out of his closed eyes, blubbering like a frustrated child.

Gaines looked at him with something like compassion in his eyes, and hit him carefully behind the ear with the butt of the pistol. He walked over to the door, and listened for a moment, then locked it cautiously.

The cord from the push button led to the control board. He examined the hookup, and disconnected it carefully. That done, he turned to the televisor at the control desk, and called Fresno.

"Okay, Dave," he said, "let 'em attack now—and for the love of Pete, hurry!" Then he cleared the screen, not wishing his watch officer to see how he was shaking.

Back in Fresno the next morning Gaines paced around the Main Control Room with a fair degree of contentment in his heart. The roads were rolling—before long they would be up to speed again. It had been a long night. Every engineer, every available cadet, had been needed to make the inch-by-inch inspection of Sacramento Sector which he had required. Then they had to cross-connect around two wrecked subsector control boards. But the roads were rolling—he could feel their rhythm up through the floor.

He stopped beside a haggard, stubbly-bearded man. "Why don't you go home, Dave?" he asked. "McPherson can carry on from here."

"How about yourself, Chief? You don't look like a June bride."

"Oh, I'll catch a nap in my office after a bit. I called my wife, and told her I couldn't make it. She's coming down here to meet me."

"Was she sore?"

"Not very. You know how women are." He turned back to the instrument board, and watched the clicking 'busy-bodies' assembling the data from six sectors. San Diego Circle, Angeles Sector, Bakersfield Sector, Fresno Sector, Stockton—Stockton? Stockton! Good grief!—Blekinsop! He had left a cabinet minister of Australia cooling his heels in the Stockton office all night long!

He started for the door, while calling over his shoulder, "Dave, will you order a car for me? Make it a fast one!" He was across the hall, and had his head inside his private office before Davidson could acknowledge the order.

"Dolores!"

"Yes, Mr. Gaines."

"Call my wife, and tell her I had to go to Stockton. If she's already left home, just have her wait here. And Dolores—"

"Yes, Mr. Gaines?"

"Calm her down."

She bit her lip, but her face was impassive. "Yes, Mr. Gaines."

"That's a good girl." He was out and started down the stairway. When he reached road level, the sight of the rolling strips warmed him inside and made him feel almost cheerful.

He strode briskly away toward a door marked ACCESS DOWN, whistling softly to himself. He opened the door, and the rumbling, roaring rhythm from 'down inside' seemed to pick up the tune even as it drowned out the sound of his whistling.

"Hie! Hie! Hee!
The rotor men are we—
Check off the sectors loud and strong! One! Two! Three!
Anywhere you go
You are bound to know
That your roadways are rolling along!"

THE YEAR OF THE JACKPOT

At first Potiphar Breen did not notice the girl who was undressing.

She was standing at a bus stop only ten feet away. He was indoors, but that would not have kept him from noticing; he was seated in a drugstore booth adjacent to the bus stop; there was nothing between Potiphar and the young lady but plate glass and an occasional pedestrian.

Nevertheless he did not look up when she began to peel. Propped up in front of him was a Los Angeles *Times*; beside it, still unopened, were the *Herald-Express* and the *Daily News*. He was scanning the newspaper carefully, but the headline stories got only a passing glance.

He noted the maximum and minimum temperatures in Brownsville, Texas, and entered them in a neat black notebook. He did the same with the closing prices of three blue chips and two dogs on the New York Exchange, as well as the total number of shares.

He then began a rapid sifting of minor news stories, from time to time entering briefs of them in his little book.

The items he recorded seemed randomly unrelated—among them a publicity release in which Miss National Cottage Cheese Week announced that she intended to marry and have twelve children by a man who could prove that he had been a lifelong vegetarian, a circumstantial but wildly unlikely Flying Saucer report, and a call for prayers for rain throughout Southern California.

Potiphar had just written down the names and addresses of three residents of Watts, California, who had been miraculously healed at a tent meeting of the God-is-All First Truth Brethren by the Reverend Dickie Bottomley, the eight-year-old evangelist, and was preparing to tackle the *Herald-Express*, when he glanced over his reading glasses and saw the amateur ecdysiast on the street corner outside.

He stood up, placed his glasses in their case, folded the newspapers and put them carefully in his right coat pocket, counted out the exact amount of his check and added fifteen percent. He then took his raincoat from a hook, placed it over his arm, and went outside.

By now the girl was practically down to the buff. It seemed to Potiphar Breen that she had quite a lot of buff, yet she had not pulled much of a house. The corner newsboy had stopped hawking his disasters and was grinning at her, and a mixed pair of transvestites who were apparently waiting for the bus had their eyes on her. None of the passers-by stopped. They glanced at her, and then, with the self-conscious indifference to the unusual of the true Southern Californian, they went on their various ways.

The transvestites were frankly staring. The male member of the team wore a frilly feminine blouse, but his skirt was a conservative Scottish kilt. His female companion wore a business suit and Homburg hat; she stared with lively interest.

As Breen approached, the girl hung a scrap of nylon on the bus stop bench, then reached for her shoes. A police officer, looking hot and unhappy, crossed with the lights and came up to them.

"Okay," he said in a tired voice, "that'll be all, lady. Get them duds back on and clear out of here."

The female transvestite took a cigar out of her mouth. "Just what business is it of yours, officer?" she asked.

The cop turned to her. "Keep out of this!" He ran his eyes over her getup, and that of her companion. "I ought to run both of you in, too."

The transvestite raised her eyebrows. "Arrest us for being clothed, arrest her for not being. I think I'm going to like this." She turned to the girl, who was standing still and saying nothing, as if she were puzzled by what was going on. "I'm a lawyer, dear." She pulled a card from her vest pocket. "If this uniformed Neanderthal persists in annoying you, I'll be delighted to handle him."

The man in kilts said, "Grace! Please!"

She shook him off. "Quiet, Norman. This *is* our business." She went on to the policeman, "Well? Call the wagon. In the meantime, my client will answer no questions."

The official looked unhappy enough to cry and his face was getting dangerously red. Breen quietly stepped forward and slipped his raincoat around the shoulders of the girl.

She looked startled and spoke for the first time. "Uh—thanks." She pulled the coat about her, cape fashion.

The female attorney glanced at Breen then back to the cop. "Well, officer? Ready to arrest us?"

He shoved his face close to hers. "I ain't going to give you the satisfaction!" He sighed and added, "Thanks, Mr. Breen. You know this lady?"

"I'll take care of her. You can forget it, Kawonski."

"I sure hope so. If she's with you, I'll do just that. But get her out of here, Mr. Breen—please!"

The lawyer interrupted. "Just a moment. You're interfering with my client."

Kawonski said, "Shut up, you! You heard Mr. Breen—she's with him. Right, Mr. Breen?"

"Well—yes. I'm a friend. I'll take care of her."

The transvestite said suspiciously. "I didn't hear *her* say that."

Her companion said, "Grace! There's our bus."

"And I didn't hear her say she was your client," the cop retorted. "You look like a—" his words were drowned out by the bus brakes— "and besides that, if you don't climb on that bus and get off my territory, I'll . . . I'll . . ."

"You'll what?"

"Grace! We'll miss our bus."

"Just a moment, Norman. Dear, is this man really a friend of yours? Are you with him?"

The girl looked uncertainly at Breen, then said in a low voice, "Uh, yes. He is. I am."

"Well . . ." The lawyer's companion pulled at her arm. She

shoved her card into Breen's hand and got on the bus. It pulled away.
Breen pocketed the card.

Kawonski wiped his forehead. "Why did you do it, lady?" he said
peevishly.

The girl looked puzzled. "I—I don't know."

"You hear that, Mr. Breen? That's what they all say. And if you
pull 'em in, there's six more the next day. The Chief said—" He
sighed. "The Chief said—well, if I had arrested her like that female
shyster wanted me to, I'd be out at a Hundred and Ninety-sixth and
Ploughed Ground tomorrow morning, thinking about retirement. So
get her out of here, will you?"

The girl said, "But—"

"No 'buts', lady. Just be glad a real gentleman like Mr. Breen is
willing to help you." He gathered up her clothes, handed them to
her. When she reached for them, she again exposed an uncustomary
amount of skin. Kawonski hastily gave the clothing to Breen instead,
who crowded them into his coat pockets.

She let Breen lead her to where his car was parked, got in and
tucked the raincoat around her so that she was rather more dressed
than a girl usually is. She looked at him.

She saw a medium-sized and undistinguished man who was slipping down the wrong side of thirty-five and looked older. His eyes
had that mild and slightly naked look of the habitual spectacles-
wearer who is not at the moment with glasses. His hair was gray at
the temples and thin on top. His herringbone suit, black shoes, white
shirt, and neat tie smacked more of the East than of California.

He saw a face which he classified as "pretty" and "wholesome"
rather than "beautiful" and "glamorous." It was topped by a healthy
mop of light brown hair. He set her age at twenty-five, give or take
eighteen months. He smiled gently, climbed in without speaking and
started his car.

He turned up Doheny Drive and east on Sunset. Near La Cie-
nega, he slowed down. "Feeling better?"

"Uh, I guess so Mr.—Breen?"

"Call me Potiphar. What's your name? Don't tell me if you don't
want to."

"Me? I'm—I'm Meade Barstow."

"Thank you, Meade. Where do you want to go? Home?"

"I suppose so. Oh, my, no. I can't go home like *this*." She clutched the coat tightly to her.

"Parents?"

"No. My landlady. She'd be shocked to death."

"Where, then?"

She thought. "Maybe we could stop at a filling station and I could sneak into the ladies' room."

"Maybe. See here, Meade—my house is six blocks from here and has a garage entrance. You could get inside without being seen."

She stared. "You don't *look* like a wolf!"

"Oh, but I am! The worst sort." He whistled and gnashed his teeth. "See? But Wednesday is my day off."

She looked at him and dimpled. "Oh, well! I'd rather wrestle with you than with Mrs. Megeath. Let's go."

He turned up into the hills. His bachelor diggings were one of the many little frame houses clinging like fungus to the brown slopes of the Santa Monica Mountains. The garage was notched into this hill; the house sat on it.

He drove in, cut the ignition, and led her up a teetery inside stairway into the living room.

"In there," he said, pointing. "Help yourself." He pulled her clothes out of his coat pockets and handed them to her.

She blushed and took them, disappeared into his bedroom. He heard her turn the key in the lock. He settled down in his easy chair, took out his notebook, and started with the *Herald-Express*.

He was finishing the *Daily News* and had added several notes to his collection when she came out. Her hair was neatly rolled; her face was restored; she had brushed most of the wrinkles out of her skirt. Her sweater was neither too tight nor deep cut, but it was pleasantly filled. She reminded him of well water and farm breakfasts.

He took his raincoat from her, hung it up, and said, "Sit down, Meade."

She said uncertainly, "I had better go."

"If you must, but I had hoped to talk with you."

"Well—" She sat down on the edge of his couch and looked around. The room was small, but as neat as his necktie and as clean as his collar. The fireplace was swept; the floor was bare and polished. Books crowded bookshelves in every possible space. One corner was filled by an elderly flat-top desk; the papers on it were neatly in order. Near it, on its own stand, was a small electric calculator. To her right, french windows gave out on a tiny porch over the garage. Beyond it she could see the sprawling city, where a few neon signs were already blinking.

She sat back a little. "This is a nice room—Potiphar. It looks like you."

"I take that as a compliment. Thank you." She did not answer; he went on, "Would you like a drink?"

"Oh, would I!" She shivered. "I guess I've got the jitters."

He stood up. "Not surprising. What'll it be?"

She took Scotch and water, no ice; he was a Bourbon-and-gingerale man. She soaked up half her highball in silence, then put it down, squared her shoulders and said, "Potiphar?"

"Yes, Meade?"

"Look, if you brought me here to make a pass, I wish you'd go ahead and make it. It won't do you a bit of good, but it makes me nervous to wait."

He said nothing and did not change his expression.

She went on uneasily, "Not that I'd blame you for trying—under the circumstances. And I *am* grateful. But . . . well, it's just that I don't—"

He came over and took both her hands. "I haven't the slightest thought of making a pass at you. Nor need you feel grateful. I butted in because I was interested in your case."

"My *case?* Are you a doctor? A psychiatrist?"

He shook his head. "I'm a mathematician. A statistician, to be precise."

"Huh? I don't get it."

"Don't worry about it. But I would like to ask some questions. May I?"

"Oh, sure! Of course! I owe you that much—and then some."

"You owe me nothing. Want your drink sweetened?"

She gulped the balance and handed him her glass, then followed him out into the kitchen. He did an exact job of measuring and gave it back.

"Now tell me why you took your clothes off," he said.

•   •   •

She frowned. "I don't know. I *don't* know. I don't *know*. I guess I just went crazy." She added, round-eyed, "But I don't feel crazy. Could I go off my rocker and not know it?"

"You're not crazy . . . not more so than the rest of us," he amended. "Tell me, where did you see someone else do this?"

"Huh? I never have."

"Where did you read about it?"

"But I haven't. Wait a minute—those people up in Canada. Dooka-somethings."

"Doukhobors. That's all? No bareskin swimming parties? No strip poker?"

She shook her head. "No. You may not believe it, but I was the kind of a little girl who undressed under her nightie." She colored and added, "I still do—unless I remember to tell myself it's silly."

"I believe it. No news stories?"

"No. Yes, there was! About two weeks ago, I think it was. Some girl in a theater—in the audience, I mean. But I thought it was just publicity. You know the stunts they pull here."

He shook his head. "It wasn't. February 3rd, the Grand Theater, Mrs. Alvin Copley. Charges dismissed."

"How did *you* know?"

"Excuse me." He went to his desk, dialed the City News Bureau. "Alf? This is Pot Breen. They still sitting on that story? . . . Yes, the Gypsy Rose file. Any new ones today?"

He waited. Meade thought that she could make out swearing.

"Take it easy, Alf—this hot weather can't last forever. Nine, eh? Well, add another—Santa Monica Boulevard, late this afternoon. No arrest." He added, "Nope, nobody got her name. A middle-aged woman with a cast in one eye. I happened to see it . . . who, me? Why would I want to get mixed up? But it's rounding into a very, very interesting picture."

He put the phone down.

Meade said, "Cast in one eye, indeed!"

"Shall I call him back and give him your name?"

"Oh, no!"

"Very well. Now, Meade, we seemed to have located the point

of contagion in your case—Mrs. Copley. What I'd like to know next is how you felt, what you were thinking about, when you did it."

She was frowning intently. "Wait a minute, Potiphar. Do I understand that *nine other girls* have pulled the stunt I pulled?"

"Oh, no. Nine others *today*. You are—" he paused briefly—"the three hundred and nineteenth case in Los Angeles County since the first of the year. I don't have figures on the rest of the country, but the suggestion to clamp down on the stories came from the eastern news services when the papers here put our first cases on the wire. That proves that it's a problem elsewhere, too."

"You mean that women all over the country are peeling off their clothes in public? Why, how shocking!"

He said nothing. She blushed again and insisted, "Well, it *is* shocking, even if it was me, this time."

"No, Meade. One case is shocking; over three hundred makes it scientifically interesting. That's why I want to know how it felt. Tell me about it."

"But—all right, I'll try. I told you I don't know why I did it; I still don't. I—"

"You remember it?"

"Oh, yes! I remember getting up off the bench and pulling up my sweater. I remember unzipping my skirt. I remember thinking I would have to hurry because I could see my bus stopped two blocks down the street. I remember how *good* it felt when I finally—" She paused and looked puzzled. "But I still don't know why."

"What were you thinking about just before you stood up?"

"I don't remember."

"Visualize the street. What was passing by? Where were your hands? Were your legs crossed or uncrossed? Was there anybody near you? What were you thinking about?"

"Nobody was on the bench with me. I had my hands in my lap. Those characters in the mixed-up clothes were standing nearby, but I wasn't paying attention. I wasn't thinking much except that my feet hurt and I wanted to get home—and how unbearably hot and sultry the weather was. Then—" her eyes became distant—"suddenly I knew what I had to do and it was very urgent that I do it. So I stood up and I—and I—" Her voice became shrill.

"Take it easy!" he said sharply. "Don't do it again."

"Huh? Why, Mr. Breen! I wouldn't do anything like that."

"Of course not. Then what happened after you undressed?"

"Why, you put your raincoat around me and you know the rest." She faced him. "Say Potiphar, what were you doing with a raincoat? It hasn't rained in weeks. This is the driest, hottest rainy season in years."

"In sixty-eight years, to be exact."

"Sixty—"

"I carry a raincoat anyhow. Just a notion of mine, but I feel that when it does rain, it's going to rain awfully hard." He added, "Forty days and forty nights, maybe."

She decided that he was being humorous and laughed.

He went on, "Can you remember how you got the idea of undressing?"

She swirled her glass and thought. "I simply don't know."

He nodded. "That's what I expected."

"I don't understand—unless you think I'm crazy. Do you?"

"No. I think you had to do it and could not help it and don't know why and can't know why."

"But *you* know." She said it accusingly.

"Maybe. At least I have some figures. Ever take any interest in statistics, Meade?"

She shook her head. "Figures confuse me. Never mind statistics—*I want to know why I did what I did!*"

He looked at her very soberly. "I think we're lemmings, Meade."

She looked puzzled, then horrified. "You mean those little furry mouselike creatures? The ones that—"

"Yes. The ones that periodically make a death migration, until millions, hundreds of millions of them drown themselves in the sea. Ask a lemming why he does it. If you could get him to slow up his rush toward death, even money says he would rationalize his answer as well as any college graduate. But he does it because he has to—and so do we."

"That's a horrid idea, Potiphar."

"Maybe. Come here, Meade. I'll show you figures that confuse me, too." He went to his desk and opened a drawer, took out a packet of cards. "Here's one. Two weeks ago, a man sues an entire state legislature for alienation of his wife's affection—and the judge lets the suit be tried. Or this one—a patent application for a device to lay the globe over on its side and warm up the artic regions. Patent denied, but the inventor took in over three hundred thousand dollars in down payments on North Pole real estate before the postal authorities stepped in. Now he's fighting the case and it looks as if he might win. And here—prominent bishop proposes applied courses in the so-called facts of life in high schools."

He put the card away hastily. "Here's a dilly—a bill introduced in the Alabama lower house to repeal the laws of atomic energy. Not the present statutes, but the natural laws concerning nuclear physics; the wording makes that plain." He shrugged. "How silly can you get?"

"They're crazy."

"No, Meade. One like that might be crazy; a lot of them becomes a lemming death march. No, don't object—I've plotted them on a curve. The last time we had anything like this was the so-called Era of Wonderful Nonsense. But this one is much worse." He delved into a lower drawer, hauled out a graph. "The amplitude is more than twice as great and we haven't reached peak. What the peak will be, I don't dare guess—three separate rhythms, reinforcing."

She peered at the curves. "You mean that the lad with the arctic real estate deal is somewhere on this line?"

"He adds to it. And back here on the last crest are the flagpole sitters and the goldfish swallowers and the Ponzi hoax and the marathon dancers and the man who pushed a peanut up Pikes Peak with his nose. You're on the new crest—or you will be when I add you in."

She made a face. "I don't like it."

"Neither do I. But it's as clear as a bank statement. This year the human race is letting down its hair, flipping its lip with a finger, and saying, 'Wubba, wubba, wubba.' "

She shivered. "Do you suppose I could have another drink? Then I'll go."

"I have a better idea. I owe you a dinner for answering questions.

Pick a place and we'll have a cocktail before."

She chewed her lip. "You don't owe me anything. And I don't feel up to facing a restaurant crowd. I might—I might—"

"No, you wouldn't," he said sharply. "It doesn't hit twice."

"You're sure? Anyhow, I don't want to face a crowd." She glanced at his kitchen door. "Have you anything to eat in there? I can cook."

"Um, breakfast things. And there's a pound of ground top round in the freezer compartment and some rolls. I sometimes make hamburgers when I don't want to go out."

She headed for the kitchen. "Drunk or sober, fully dressed or—or naked, I can cook. You'll see."

He did see. Open-faced sandwiches with the meat married to toasted buns and the flavor garnished rather that suppressed by scraped Bermuda onion and thin-sliced dill, a salad made from things she had scrounged out of his refrigerator, potatoes crisp but not vulcanized. They ate it on the tiny balcony, sopping it down with cold beer.

He sighed and wiped his mouth. "Yes, Meade, you can cook."

"Some day I'll arrive with proper materials and pay you back. Then I'll prove it."

"You've already proved it. Nevertheless, I accept. But I tell you three times—which makes it true, of course—that you owe me nothing."

"No? If you hadn't been a Boy Scout, I'd be in jail."

Breen shook his head. "The police have orders to keep it quiet at all costs—to keep it from growing. You saw that. And, my dear, you weren't a person to me at the time. I didn't even see your face."

"You saw plenty else!"

"Truthfully, I didn't look. You were just a—a statistic."

She toyed with her knife and said puzzled, "I'm not sure, but I think I've just been insulted. In all the twenty-five years that I've fought men off, more or less successfully, I've been called a lot of names—but a 'statistic'? Why, I ought to take your slide rule and beat you to death with it."

"My dear young lady—"

"I'm not a lady, that's for sure. But I'm *not* a statistic, either."

THE YEAR OF THE JACKPOT 67

"My dear Meade, then. I wanted to tell you, before you did anything hasty, that in college I wrestled varsity middleweight."

She grinned and dimpled. "That's more the talk a girl likes to hear. I was beginning to be afraid you had been assembled in an adding machine factory. Potty, you're really a dear."

"If that is a diminutive of my given name, I like it. But if it refers to my waist line, I definitely resent it."

She reached across and patted his stomach. "I like your waist line; lean and hungry men are difficult. If I were cooking for you regularly, I'd really pad it."

"Is that a proposal?"

"Let it lie, let it lie. Potty, do you really think the whole country is losing its buttons?"

He sobered at once. "It's worse than that."

"Huh?"

"Come inside. I'll show you."

They gathered up dishes and dumped them in the sink, Breen talking all the while.

"As a kid, I was fascinated by numbers. Numbers are pretty things and they combine in such interesting configurations. I took my degree in math, of course, and got a job as a junior actuary with Midwestern Mutual—the insurance outfit. That was fun. No way on Earth to tell when a particular man is going to die, but an absolute certainty that so many men of a certain age group would die before a certain date. The curves were so lovely—and they always worked out. Always. You didn't have to know *why*; you could predict with dead certainty and never know why. The equations worked; the curves were right.

"I was interested in astronomy, too; it was the one science where individual figures worked out neatly, completely, and accurately, down to the last decimal point that the instruments were good for. Compared with astronomy, the other sciences were mere carpentry and kitchen chemistry.

"I found there were nooks and crannies in astronomy where individual numbers won't do, where you have to go over to statistics, and I became even more interested. I joined the Variable Star Association and I might have gone into astronomy professionally, instead of what I'm in now—business consultation—if I hadn't gotten interested in something else."

" 'Business consultation'?" repeated Meade. "Income tax work?"

"Oh, no. That's too elementary. I'm the numbers boy for a firm of industrial engineers. I can tell a rancher exactly how many of his Hereford bull calves will be sterile. Or I can tell a motion picture producer how much rain insurance to carry on location. Or maybe how big a company in a particular line must be to carry its own risk in industrial accidents. And I'm right. I'm always right."

"Wait a minute. Seems to me a big company would *have* to have insurance."

"Contrariwise. A really big corporation begins to resemble a statistical universe."

"Huh?"

"Never mind. I got interested in something else—cycles. Cycles are everything, Meade. And everywhere. The tides. The seasons. Wars. Love. Everybody knows that in the spring the young man's fancy lightly turns to what the girls never stopped thinking about, but did you know that it runs in an eighteen-year-plus cycle as well? And that a girl born at the wrong swing of the curve doesn't stand nearly as good a chance as her older or younger sister?"

"Is *that* why I'm still a doddering old maid?"

"You're twenty-five?" He pondered. "Maybe, but your chances are improving again; the curve is swinging up. Anyhow, remember you are just one statistic; the curve applies to the group. Some girls get married every year."

"Don't call me a statistic," she repeated firmly.

"Sorry. And marriages match up with acreage planted to wheat, with wheat cresting ahead. You could almost say that planting wheat makes people get married."

"Sounds silly."

"It *is* silly. The whole notion of cause-and-effect is probably superstition. But the same cycle shows a peak in house building right after a peak in marriages."

"Now that makes sense."

"Does it? How many newlyweds do you know who can afford to

build a house? You might as well blame it on wheat acreage. We don't know *why*; it just *is*."

"Sun spots, maybe?"

"You can correlate Sun spots with stock prices, or Columbia River salmon, or woman's skirts. And you are just as much justified in blaming short skirts for Sun spots as you are in blaming Sun spots for salmon. We don't know. But the curves go on just the same."

"But there has to be some *reason* behind it."

"Does there? That's mere assumption. A fact has no 'why.' There it stands, self-demonstrating. Why did you take your clothes off today?"

She frowned. "That's not fair."

"Maybe not. But I want to show you why I'm worried."

He went into the bedroom, came out with a large roll of tracing paper.

"We'll spread it on the floor. Here they are, all of them. The 54-year cycle—see the Civil War there? See how it matches in? The eighteen and one-third-year cycle, the 9-plus cycle, the 41-month shorty, the three rhythms of Sun spots—everything, all combined in one grand chart. Mississippi River floods, fur catches in Canada, stock market prices, marriages, epidemics, freight-car loadings, bank clearings, locust plagues, divorces, tree growth, wars, rainfall, Earth magnetism, building construction, patents applied for, murders—you name it; I've got it there."

She stared at the bewildering array of wavy lines. "But, Potty, what does it mean?"

"It means that these things all happen, in regular rhythm, whether we like it or not. It means that when skirts are due to go up, all the stylists in Paris can't make 'em go down. It means that when prices are going down, all the controls and supports and government planning can't make 'em go up." He pointed to a curve. "Take a look at the grocery ads. Then turn to the financial page and read how the Big Brains try to double-talk their way out of it. It means that when an epidemic is due, it happens, despite all the public health efforts. It means we're lemmings."

She pulled her lip. "I don't like it. 'I am the master of my fate,' and so forth. I've got free will, Potty. I know I have—I can feel it."

"I imagine every little neutron in an atom bomb feels the same way. He can go *spung!* or he can sit still, just as he pleases. But statistical mechanics work out all the same and the bomb goes off— which is what I'm leading up to. See anything odd there, Meade?"

She studied the chart, trying not to let the curving lines confuse her.

"They sort of bunch up over at the right end."

"You're dern tootin' they do! See that dotted vertical line? That's right now—and things are bad enough. But take a look at that solid vertical; that's about six months from now—and that's when we get it. Look at the cycles—the long ones, the short ones, all of them. Every single last one of them reaches either a trough or a crest ex- actly on—or almost on—that line."

"That's bad?"

"What do you think. Three of the big ones troughed back in 1929 and the depression almost ruined us . . . even with the big 54- year cycle supporting things. Now we've got the big one troughing— and the few crests are not things that help. I mean to say, tent caterpillars and influenza don't do us any good. Meade, if statistics mean anything, this tired old planet hasn't seen a trend like this since Eve went into the apple business. I'm scared."

She searched his face. "Potty, you're not simply having fun with me? You know I can't check up on you."

"I wish to heaven I were. No, Meade, I can't fool about numbers; I wouldn't know how. This is it.—The Year of the Jackpot."

Meade was very silent as he drove her home. When they ap- proached West Los Angeles, she said, "Potty?"

"Yes, Meade?"

"What do we *do* about it?"

"What do you do about a hurricane? You pull in your ears. What can you do about an atom bomb? You try to outguess it, not be there when it goes off. What else can you do?"

"Oh." She was silent for a few moments, then added, "Potty, will you tell me which way to jump?"

"Huh? Oh, sure! If I can figure it out."

He took her to her door, turned to go.

She said, "Potty!"

He faced her. "Yes, Meade?"

She grabbed his head, shook it—then kissed him fiercely on the mouth. "There, is that just a statistic?"

"Uh, no."

"It had better not be," she said dangerously. "Potty, I think I'm going to have to change your curve."

2

RUSSIANS REJECT UN NOTE

MISSOURI FLOOD DAMAGE
EXCEEDS RECORD

MISSISSIPPI MESSIAH DEFIES COURT

NUDIST CONVENTION STORMS
BAILEY'S BEACH

BRITISH-IRAN TALKS
STILL, DEAD-LOCKED

FASTER-THAN-LIGHT
WEAPON PROMISED

TYPHOON DOUBLING
BACK ON MANILA

MARRIAGE SOLEMNIZED ON
FLOOR OF HUDSON

New York, 13 July—In a specially constructed diving suit built for two, Merydith Smithe, cafe society headline girl, and Prince Augie Schleswieg of New York and the Riviera were united today by Bishop Dalton in a service televised with the aid of the Navy's ultra-new—

As the Year of the Jackpot progressed, Breen took melancholy pleasure in adding to the data which proved that the curve was sagging as predicted. The undeclared World War continued its bloody, blundering way at half a dozen spots around a tortured globe. Breen did not chart it; the headlines were there for anyone to read. He concentrated on the odd facts in the other pages of the papers, facts which, taken singly, meant nothing, but taken together showed a disastrous trend.

He listed stock market prices, rainfall, wheat futures, but the "silly season" items were what fascinated him. To be sure, some humans were always doing silly things—but at what point had prime damfoolishness become commonplace? When, for example, had the zombie-like professional models become accepted ideals of American womanhood? What were the gradations between National Cancer Week and National Athlete's Foot Week? On what day had the American people finally taken leave of horse sense?

Take transvestism. Male-and-female dress customs were arbitrary, but they had seemed to be deeply rooted in the culture. When did the breakdown start? With Marlene Dietrich's tailored suits? By the late nineteen-forties, there was no "male" article of clothing that a woman could not wear in public—but when had men started to slip over the line? Should he count the psychological cripples who had made the word "drag" a by-word in Greenwich Village and Hollywood long before this outbreak? Or were they "wild shots" not belonging on the curve? Did it start with some unknown normal man attending a masquerade and there discovering that skirts actually were more comfortable and practical than trousers? Or had it started with the resurgence of Scottish nationalism reflected in the wearing of kilts by many Scottish-Americans?

Ask a lemming to state his motives! The outcome was in front of him, a news story. Transvestism by draft dodgers had at last resulted in a mass arrest in Chicago which was to have ended in a giant joint trial—only to have the deputy prosecutor show up in a pinafore and defy the judge to submit to an examination to determine the judge's true sex. The judge suffered a stroke and died and the trial was postponed—postponed forever, in Breen's opinion; he doubted that this particular blue law would ever again be enforced.

Or the laws about indecent exposure, for that matter. The attempt to limit the Gypsy Rose syndrome by ignoring it had taken the starch out of enforcement. Now here was a report about the All Souls Community Church of Springfield; the pastor had reinstituted ceremonial nudity. Probably the first time this thousand years, Breen thought, aside from some screwball cults in Los Angeles. The reverend gentleman claimed that the ceremony was identical with the "dance of the high priestess" in the ancient temple of Karnak.

Could be, but Breen had private information that the "priestess" had been working the burlesque and nightclub circuit before her present engagement. In any case, the holy leader was packing them in and had not been arrested.

Two weeks later a hundred and nine churches in thirty-three states offered equivalent attractions. Breen entered them on his curves.

This queasy oddity seemed to him to have no relation to the startling rise in the dissident evangelical cults throughout the country. These churches were sincere, earnest, and poor—but growing, ever since the War. Now they were multiplying like yeast.

It seemed a statistical cinch that the United States was about to become godstruck again. He correlated it with Transcendentalism and the trek of the Latter Day Saints. Hmm, yes, it fitted. And the curve was pushing toward a crest.

Billions in war bonds were now falling due; wartime marriages were reflected in the swollen peak of the Los Angeles school population. The Colorado River was a record low and the towers in Lake Mead stood high out of the water. But the Angelenos committed communal suicide by watering lawns as usual. The Metropolitan Water District commissioners tried to stop it. It fell between the stools of the police powers of fifty "sovereign" cities. The taps remained open, trickling away the life blood of the desert paradise.

The four regular party conventions—Dixiecrats, Regular Republicans, the Regular Regular Republicans, and the Democrats—attracted scant attention, because the Know-Nothings had not yet met. The fact that the "American Rally," as the Know-Nothings preferred to be called, claimed not to be a party but an educational society did not detract from their strength. But what was their strength? Their beginnings had been so obscure that Breen had had to go back and dig into the files, yet he had been approached twice this very week to join them, right inside his own office—once by his boss, once by the janitor.

He hadn't been able to chart the Know-Nothings. They gave him chills in his spines. He kept column-inches on them, found that their publicity was shrinking while their numbers were obviously zooming.

Krakatoa blew up on July 18th. It provided the first important transPacific TV-cast. Its effect on sunsets, on solar constant, on mean temperature, and on rainfall would not be felt until later in the year.

The San Andreas fault, its stresses unrelieved since the Long Beach disaster of 1933, continued to build up imbalance—an unhealed wound running the full length of the West Coast.

Pelee and Etna erupted. Mauna Loa was still quiet.

Flying Saucers seemed to be landing daily in every state. Nobody had exhibited one on the ground—or had the Department of Defense sat on them? Breen was unsatisfied with the off-the-record reports he had been able to get; the alcoholic content of some of them had been high. But the sea serpent on Ventura Beach was real; he had seen it. The troglodyte in Tennessee he was not in a position to verify.

Thirty-one domestic air crashes the last week in July . . . was it sabotage, or was it a sagging curve on a chart? And that neopolio epidemic that skipped from Seattle to New York? Time for a big epidemic? Breen's chart said it was. But how about bacteriological warfare? Could a chart *know* that a Slav biochemist would perfect an efficient virus-and-vector at the right time?

Nonsense!

But the curves, if they meant anything at all, included "free will"; they averaged in all the individual "wills" of a statistical universe—and came out as a smooth function. Every morning, three million "free wills" flowed toward the center of the New York megapolis; every evening, they flowed out again—all by "free will" and on a smooth and predictable curve.

Ask a lemming! Ask *all* the lemmings, dead and alive. Let them take a vote on it!

Breen tossed his notebook aside and phoned Meade. "Is this my favorite statistic?"

"Potty! I was thinking about you."

"Naturally. This is your night off."

"Yes, but another reason, too. Potiphar, have you ever taken a look at the Great Pyramid?"

"I haven't even been to Niagara Falls. I'm looking for a rich woman, so I can travel."

"I'll let you know when I get my first million, but—"

"That's the first time you've proposed to me this week."

"Shut up. Have you ever looked into the prophecies they found inside the pyramid?"

"Look, Meade, that's in the same class with astrology—strictly for the squirrels. Grow up."

"Yes, of course. But, Potty, I thought you were interested in anything odd. This is odd."

"Oh. Sorry. If it's 'silly season' stuff, let's see it."

"All right. Am I cooking for you tonight?"

"It's Wednesday, isn't it?"

"How soon will you get here?"

He glanced at his watch. "Pick you up in eleven minutes." He felt his whiskers. "No, twelve and a half."

"I'll be ready. Mrs. Megeath says these regular dates mean that you're going to marry me."

"Pay no attention to her. She's just a statistic and I'm a wild datum."

"Oh well, I've got two hundred and forty-seven dollars toward that million. 'By!"

Meade's prize to show him was the usual Rosicrucian comeon, elaborately printed, and including a photograph (retouched, he was sure) of the much disputed line on the corridor wall which was alleged to prophesy, by its various discontinuities, the entire future. This one had an unusual time scale, but the major events were all marked on it—the fall of Rome, the Norman Invasion, the Discovery of America, Napoleon, the World Wars.

What made it interesting was that it suddenly stopped—now.

"What about it, Potty?"

"I guess the stonecutter got tired. Or got fired. Or they hired a new head priest with new ideas." He tucked it into his desk. "Thanks. I'll think about how to list it."

But he got it out again, applied dividers and a magnifying glass.

"It says here," he announced, "that the end comes late in August—unless that's a fly speck."

"Morning or afternoon? I have to know how to dress."

"Shoes will be worn. All God's chilluns got shoes." He put it away.

She was silent for a moment, then said, "Potty, isn't it about time to jump?"

"Huh? Girl, don't let *that* thing affect you! That's 'silly season' stuff."

"Yes. But take a look at *your* chart."

Nevertheless, he took the next afternoon off, spent it in the reference room of the main library, confirmed his opinion of soothsayers. Nostradamus was pretentiously silly, Mother Shippey was worse. In any of them you could find whatever you looked for.

He did find one item in Nostradamus that he liked: "The Oriental shall come forth from his seat . . . he shall pass through the sky, through the waters and the snow, and he shall strike each one with his weapon."

That sounded like what the Department of Defense expected the commies to try to do to the Western Allies.

But it was also a description of every invasion that had come out of the "heartland" in the memory of mankind.

Nuts!

When he got home, he found himself taking down his father's Bible and turning to Revelations. He could not find anything he could understand, but he got fascinated by the recurring use of precise numbers. Presently he thumbed through the Book.

His eye lit on: "Boast not thyself of tomorrow; for thou knowest not what a day may bring forth."

He put the Book away, feeling humbled, but not cheered.

The rains started the next morning.

The Master Plumbers elected Miss Star Morning "Miss Sanitary Engineering" on the same day that the morticians designated her as "The Body I Would Like Best to Prepare," and her option was dropped by Fragrant Features.

Congress voted $1.37 to compensate Thomas Jefferson Meeks for losses incurred while an emergency postman for the Christmas rush of 1936, approved the appointment of five lieutenant generals and one ambassador and adjourned in less than eight minutes.

The fire extinguishers in the midwest orphanage turned out to be filled with nothing but air.

The chancellor of the leading football institution sponsored a fund to send peace messages and vitamins to the Politburo.

The stock market slumped nineteen points and the tickers ran two hours late.

Wichita, Kansas, remained flooded while Phoenix, Arizona, cut off drinking water to areas outside city limits.

And Potiphar Breen found that he had left his raincoat at Meade Barstow's rooming house.

He phoned her landlady, but Mrs. Megeath turned him over to Meade.

"What are you doing home on a Friday?" he demanded.

"The theater manager laid me off. Now you'll have to marry me."

"You can't afford me. Meade—seriously, baby, what happened?"

"I was ready to leave the dump anyway. For the last six weeks the popcorn machine has been carrying the place. Today I sat through *The Lana Turner Story* twice. Nothing to do."

"I'll be along."

"Eleven minutes?"

"It's raining. Twenty—with luck."

It was more nearly sixty. Santa Monica Boulevard was a navigable stream; Sunset Boulevard was a subway jam. When he tried to ford the streams leading to Mrs. Megeath's house, he found that changing tires with the wheel wedged against a storm drain presented problems.

"Potty!" she exclaimed when he squished in. "You look like a drowned rat."

He found himself suddenly wrapped in a blanket robe belonging to the late Mr. Megeath and sipping hot cocoa while Mrs. Megeath dried his clothing in the kitchen.

"Meade, I'm 'at liberty' too."

"Huh? You quit your job?"

"Not exactly. Old Man Wiley and I have been having differences of opinion about my answers for months—too much 'Jackpot factor' in the figures I give him to turn over to clients. Not that I call it that, but he has felt that I was unduly pessimistic."

"But you were right!"

"Since when has being right endeared a man to his boss? But that wasn't why he fired me; it was just the excuse. He wants a man willing to back up the Know-Nothing program with scientific double-talk and I wouldn't join." He went to the window. "It's raining harder."

"But the Know-Nothing haven't got any program."

"I know that."

"Potty, you should have joined. It doesn't mean anything. I joined three months ago."

"The hell you did!"

She shrugged. "You pay your dollar and you turn up for two meetings and they leave you alone. It kept my job for another three months. What of it?"

"Well, I'm sorry you did it; that's all. Forget it. Meade, the water is over the curbs out there."

"You had better stay here overnight."

"Mmm . . . I don't like to leave *Entropy* parked out in this stuff all night. Meade?"

"Yes, Potty?"

"We're both out of jobs. How would you like to duck north into the Mojave and find a dry spot?"

"I'd love it. But look, Potty, is this a proposal or just a proposition?"

"Don't pull that 'either-or' stuff on me. It's just a suggestion for a vacation. Do you want to take a chaperone?"

"No."

"Then pack a bag."

"Right away. But pack a bag *how?* Are you trying to tell me it's *time to jump?*"

He faced her, then looked back at the window.

"I don't know," he said slowly, "but this rain might go on quite a while. Don't take anything you don't have to have—but don't leave anything behind you can't get along without."

He repossessed his clothing from Mrs. Megeath while Meade was upstairs. She came down dressed in slacks and carrying two large bags; under one arm was a battered and rakish teddy bear.

"This is Winnie," she said.

"Winnie the Pooh?"

"No, Winnie Churchill. When I feel bad, he promises me blood, sweat, and tears; then I feel better. You did say to bring anything I couldn't do without, didn't you?" She looked at him anxiously.

"Right."

He took the bags. Mrs. Megeath had seemed satisfied with his explanation that they were going to visit his (mythical) aunt in Bakersfield before looking for jobs. Nevertheless, she embarrassed him by kissing him good-by and telling him to "take care of my little girl."

Santa Monica Boulevard was blocked off from use. While stalled in traffic in Beverly Hills, he fiddled with the car radio, getting squawks and crackling noises, then finally one station nearby: "—in effect," a harsh, high, staccato voice was saying, "the Kremlin has given us till sundown to get out of town. This is your New York reporter, who thinks that in days like these every American must personally keep his powder dry. And now for a word from—"

Breen switched it off and glanced at her face. "Don't worry," he said. "They've been talking that way for years."

"You think they are bluffing?"

"I didn't say that. I said, 'Don't worry.' "

But his own packing, with her help, was clearly on a "survival kit" basis—canned goods, all his warm clothing, a sporting rifle he had not fired in over two years, a first-aid kit and the contents of his medicine chest. He dumped the stuff from his desk into a carton, shoved it into the back seat along with cans and books and coats, and covered the plunder with all the blankets in the house. They went back up the rickety stairs for a last check.

"Potty, where's your chart?"

"Rolled up on the back seat shelf. I guess that's all—hey, wait a minute!" He went to a shelf over his desk and began taking down small, sober-looking magazines. "I dern near left behind my file of *The Western Astronomer* and the *Proceedings of the Variable Star Association*."

"Why take them?"

"I must be nearly a year behind on both of them. Now maybe I'll have time to read."

"Hmm . . . Potty, watching you read professional journals is not my notion of a vacation."

"Quiet, woman! You took Winnie; I take these."

She shut up and helped him. He cast a longing eye at his electric calculator, but decided it was too much like the White Knight's mousetrap. He could get by with his slide rule.

As the car splashed out into the street, she said, "Potty, how are you fixed for cash?"

"Huh? Okay, I guess."

"I mean, leaving while the banks are closed and everything." She held up her purse. "Here's my bank. It isn't much, but we can use it."

He smiled and patted her knee. "Good gal! I'm sitting on my bank; I started turning everything to cash about the first of the year."

"Oh. I closed out my bank account right after we met."

"You did? You must have taken my maunderings seriously."

"I always take you seriously."

Mint Canyon was a five-mile-an-hour nightmare, with visibility limited to the tail lights of the truck ahead. When they stopped for coffee at Halfway, they confirmed what seemed evident: Cajon Pass was closed and long-haul traffic for Route 66 was being detoured through the secondary pass.

At long, long last they reached the Victorville cutoff and lost some of the traffic—a good thing, because the windshield wiper on his side had quit working and they were driving by the committee system.

Just short of Lancaster, she said suddenly, "Potty, is this buggy equipped with a snorkel?"

"Nope."

"Then we had better stop. I see a light off the road."

The light was an auto court. Meade settled the matter of economy versus convention by signing the book herself; they were placed in one cabin. He saw that it had twin beds and let the matter ride. Meade went to bed with her teddy bear without even asking to be kissed good night. It was already gray, wet dawn.

They got up in the late afternoon and decided to stay over one more night, then push north toward Bakersfield. A high pressure area was alleged to be moving south, crowding the warm, wet mass that smothered Southern California. They wanted to get into it. Breen had the wiper repaired and bought two new tires to replace his ruined spare, added some camping items to his cargo, and bought for Meade a .32 automatic, a lady's social-purpose gun.

"What's this for?" she wanted to know.

"Well, you're carrying quite a bit of cash."

"Oh. I thought maybe I was to use it to fight you off."

"Now, Meade—"

"Never mind. Thanks, Potty."

They had finished supper and were packing the car with their afternoon's purchases when the quake struck. Five inches of rain in twenty-four hours, more than three billion tons of mass suddenly loaded on a fault already overstrained, all cut loose in one subsonic, stomach-twisting rumble.

Meade sat down on the wet ground very suddenly; Breen stayed upright by dancing like a log-roller. When the ground quieted down somewhat, thirty seconds later, he helped her up.

"You all right?"

"My slacks are soaked." She added pettishly, "But, Potty, it never quakes in wet weather. *Never*. You said so yourself."

"Keep quiet, can't you?" He opened the car door and switched on the radio, waited impatiently for it to warm up.

"—your Sunshine Station in Riverside, California. Keep tuned to this station for the latest developments. As of now it is impossible to tell the size of this disaster. The Colorado River aqueduct is broken; nothing is known of the extent of the damage nor how long it will take to repair it. So far as we know, the Owens River Valley aqueduct may be intact, but all persons in the Los Angeles area are advised to conserve water. My personal advise is to stick your washtubs out into this rain.

"I now read from the standard disaster instructions, quote: 'Boil all water. Remain quietly in your homes and do not panic. Stay off the highways. Cooperate with the police and render—' Joe! Catch that phone! '—render aid where necessary. Do not use the telephone except for—' Flash! An unconfirmed report from Long Beach states that the Wilmington and San Pedro waterfront is under five feet of water. I repeat, this is unconfirmed. Here's a message from the commanding general, March Field: 'Official, all military personnel will report—' "

Breen switched it off. "Get in the car."

He stopped in the town, managed to buy six five-gallon tins and a jeep tank. He filled them with gasoline and packed them with blankets in the back seat, topping off the mess with a dozen cans of oil. Then they started rolling.

"What are we doing, Potiphar?"

"I want to get west of the valley highway."

"Any particular place west?"

"I think so. We'll see. You work the radio, but keep an eye on the road, too. That gas back there makes me nervous."

Through the town of Mojave and northwest on 466 into the Tehachapi Mountains—

Reception was poor in the pass, but what Meade could pick up confirmed the first impression—worse than the quake of '06, worse than San Francisco, Managua, and Long Beach lumped together.

When they got down out of the mountains, the weather was clearing locally; a few stars appeared. Breen swung left off the highway and ducked south of Bakersfield by the county road, reached the Route 99 super-highway just south of Greenfield. It was, as he had feared, already jammed with refugees. He was forced to go along with the flow for a couple of miles before he could cut west at Greenfield toward Taft. They stopped on the western outskirts of the town and ate at an all-night joint.

They were about to climb back into the car when there was suddenly "sunrise" due south. The rosy light swelled almost instantaneously, filled the sky, and died. Where it had been a red-and-purple pillar of cloud was spreading to a mushroom top.

Breen stared at it, glanced at his watch, then said harshly, "Get in the car."

"Potty! That was—"

"That used to be Los Angeles. Get in the car!"

He drove silently for several minutes. Meade seemed to be in a state of shock, unable to speak. When the sound reached them, he again glanced at his watch.

"Six minutes and nineteen seconds. That's about right."

"Potty, we should have brought Mrs. Megeath."

"How was I to know?" he said angrily. "Anyhow, you can't transplant an old tree. If she got it, she never knew it."

"Oh, I hope so!"

"We're going to have all we can do to take care of ourselves. Take the flashlight and check the map. I want to turn north at Taft and over toward the coast."

"Yes, Potiphar."

She quieted down and did as she was told. The radio gave nothing, not even the Riverside station; the whole broadcast range was covered by a curious static, like rain on a window.

He slowed down as they approached Taft, let her spot the turn north onto the state road, and turned into it. Almost at once a figure jumped out into the road in front of them, waved his arms violently. Breen tromped on the brake.

The man came up on the left side of the car, rapped on the window. Breen ran the glass down. Then he stared stupidly at the gun in the man's left hand.

"Out of the car," the stranger said sharply. "I've got to have it."

Meade reached across Breen, stuck her little lady's gun in the man's face and pulled the trigger. Breen could feel the flash on his own face, never noticed the report. The man looked puzzled, with a neat, not-yet-bloody hole in his upper lip—then slowly sagged away from the car.

"Drive on!" Meade said in a high voice.

Breen caught his breath. "But you—"

"Drive on! Get rolling!"

They followed the state road through Los Padres National Forest, stopping once to fill the tank from their cans. They turned off onto a dirt road. Meade kept trying the radio, got San Francisco once, but it was too jammed with static to read. Then she got Salt Lake City, faint but clear:

"—since there are no reports of anything passing our radar screen, the Kansas City bomb must be assumed to have been planted rather than delivered. This is a tentative theory, but—"

They passed into a deep cut and lost the rest.

When the squawk box again came to life, it was a crisp new voice: "Air Defense Command, coming to you over the combined networks. The rumor that Los Angeles has been hit by an atom bomb is totally unfounded. It is true that the western metropolis has suffered a severe earthquake shock, but that is all. Government officials and the Red Cross are on the spot to care for the victims, but—and I repeat—there has *been no atomic bombing.* So relax and stay in your homes. Such wild rumors can damage the United States quite as much as enemy bombs. Stay off the highways and listen for—"

Breen snapped it off. "Somebody," he said bitterly, "has again decided that 'Mama knows best.' They won't tell us any bad news."

"Potiphar," Meade said sharply, "that was an atom bomb, wasn't it?"

"It was. And now we don't know whether it was just Los Angeles—and Kansas City—or every big city in the country. All we know is that they are lying to us."

He concentrated on driving. The road was very bad.

As it began to get light, she said, "Potty, do you know where we're going? Are we just keeping out of cities?"

"I think I know. If I'm not lost." He stared around them. "Nope, it's all right. See that hill up forward with the triple gendarmes on its profile?"

"Gendarmes?"

"Big rock pillars. That's a sure landmark. I'm looking for a private road now. It leads to a hunting lodge belonging to two of my friends—an old ranch house actually, but as a ranch it didn't pay."

"They won't mind us using it?"

He shrugged. "If they show up, we'll ask them. *If* they show up. They lived in Los Angeles."

The private road had once been a poor grade of wagon trail; now it was almost impassable. But they finally topped a hogback from which they could see almost to the Pacific, then dropped down into a sheltered bowl where the cabin was.

"All out, girl. End of the line."

Meade sighed. "It looks heavenly."

"Think you can rustle breakfast while I unload? There's probably wood in the shed. Or can you manage a wood range?"

"Just try me."

Two hours later Breen was standing on the hogback, smoking a cigarette and staring off down to the west. He wondered if that was a mushroom cloud up San Francisco way. Probably his imagination, he decided, in view of the distance. Certainly there was nothing to be seen to the south.

Meade came out of the cabin. "Potty!"

"Up here."

She joined him, took his hand and smiled, then snitched his cigarette and took a deep drag. She exhaled it and said, "I know it's sinful of me, but I feel more peaceful than I have in months."

"I know."

"Did you see the canned goods in that pantry? We could pull through a hard winter here."

"We might have to."

"I suppose. I wish we had a cow."

"What would you do with a cow?"

"I used to milk four of them before I caught the school bus, every morning. I can butcher a hog, too."

"I'll try to find you a hog."

"You do and I'll manage to smoke it." She yawned. "I'm suddenly terribly sleepy."

"So am I. And small wonder."

"Let's go to bed."

"Uh, yes. Meade?"

"Yes, Potty?"

"We may be here quite a while. You know that, don't you?"

"Yes, Potty."

"In fact, it might be smart to stay put until those curves all start turning up again. They should, you know."

"Yes. I had figured that out."

He hesitated, then went on, "Meade, will you marry me?"

"Yes." She moved up to him.

After a time he pushed her gently away and said, "My dear, my very dear—uh—we could drive down and find a minister in some little town."

She looked at him steadily. "That wouldn't be very bright, would it? I mean, nobody knows we're here and that's the way we want it. Besides, your car might not make it back up that road."

"No, it wouldn't be very bright. But I want to do the right thing."

"It's all right, Potty. It's all *right*."

"Well, then . . . kneel down here with me. We'll say them together."

"Yes, Potiphar." She knelt and he took her hand. He closed his eyes and prayed wordlessly.

When he opened them he said, "What's the matter?"

"The gravel hurts my knees."

"We'll stand up, then."

"No. Look, Potty, why don't we just go in the house and say them there?"

"Huh? Hell's bells, woman, we might forget to say them entirely. Now repeat after me: I, Potiphar, take thee, Meade—"

3

OFFICIAL: STATIONS WITHIN RANGE RELAY TWICE. EXECUTIVE BULLETIN NUMBER NINE—ROAD LAWS PREVIOUSLY PUBLISHED HAVE BEEN IGNORED IN MANY INSTANCES. PATROLS ARE ORDERED TO SHOOT WITHOUT WARNING AND PROVOST MARSHALS ARE DIRECTED TO USE DEATH PENALTY FOR UNAUTHORIZED POSSESSION OF GASOLINE. BIOLOGICAL WARFARE AND RADIATION QUARANTINE REGULATIONS PREVIOUSLY ISSUED WILL BE RIGIDLY ENFORCED. LONG LIVE THE UNITED STATES! HARLEY J. NEAL, LIEUTENANT GENERAL, ACTING CHIEF OF GOVERNMENT. ALL STATIONS RELAY TWICE.

THIS IS THE FREE RADIO AMERICA RELAY NETWORK. PASS
THIS ALONG, BOYS! GOVERNOR BRANDLEY WAS SWORN IN
TODAY AS PRESIDENT BY ACTING CHIEF JUSTICE ROBERTS UN-
DER THE RULE-OF-SUCCESSION. THE PRESIDENT NAMED THO-
MAS DEWEY AS SECRETARY OF STATE AND PAUL DOUGLAS
AS SECRETARY OF DEFENSE. HIS SECOND OFFICIAL ACT WAS
TO STRIP THE RENEGADE NEAL OF RANK AND TO DIRECT HIS
ARREST BY ANY CITIZEN OR OFFICIAL. MORE LATER. PASS THE
WORD ALONG.

HELLO, CQ, CQ, CQ. THIS IS W5KMR, FREEPORT. QRR, QRR!
ANYBODY READ ME? ANYBODY? WE'RE DYING LIKE FLIES DOWN
HERE. WHAT'S HAPPENED? STARTS WITH FEVER AND A BURN-
ING THIRST, BUT YOU CAN'T SWALLOW. WE NEED HELP. ANY-
BODY READ ME? HELLO, CQ 75, CQ 75 THIS IS W5 KING MIKE
ROGER CALLING QRR AND CQ 75. BY FOR SOMEBODY . . . ANY-
BODY!

THIS IS THE LORD'S TIME, SPONSORED BY SWAN'S ELIXIR,
THE TONIC THAT MAKES WAITING FOR THE KINGDOM OF
GOD WORTHWHILE. YOU ARE ABOUT TO HEAR A MESSAGE OF
CHEER FROM JUDGE BROOMFIELD, ANOINTED VICAR OF THE
KINGDOM ON EARTH. BUT FIRST A BULLETIN—SEND YOUR
CONTRIBUTIONS TO MESSIAH, CLINT, TEXAS. DON'T TRY TO
MAIL THEM—SEND THEM BY A KINGDOM MESSENGER OR BY
SOME PILGRIM JOURNEYING THIS WAY. AND NOW THE TAB-
ERNACLE CHOIR FOLLOWED BY THE VOICE OF THE VICAR ON
EARTH—

—THE FIRST SYMPTOM IS LITTLE RED SPOTS IN THE ARM-
PITS. THEY ITCH. PUT PATIENTS TO BED AT ONCE AND KEEP
'EM COVERED UP WARM. THEN GO SCRUB YOURSELF AND
WEAR A MASK, WE DON'T KNOW YET HOW YOU CATCH IT.
PASS IT ALONG, ED.

—NO NEW LANDINGS REPORTED ANYWHERE ON THIS
CONTINENT. THE FEW PARATROOPERS WHO ESCAPED THE
ORIGINAL SLAUGHTER ARE THOUGHT TO BE HIDING OUT IN

THE POCONOS. SHOOT—BUT BE CAREFUL; IT MIGHT BE AUNT TESSIE. OFF AND CLEAR. UNTIL NOON TOMORROW—

The statistical curves were turning up again. There was no longer doubt in Breen's mind about that. It might not even be necessary to stay up here in the Sierra Madres through the winter, though he rather thought they would. It would be silly to be mowed down by the tail of a dying epidemic, or be shot by a nervous vigilante, when a few months' wait would take care of everything.

He was headed out to the hogback to wait for sunset and do an hour's reading. He glanced at his car as he passed it, thinking that he would like to try the radio. He suppressed the yen; two-thirds of his reserve gasoline was gone already just from keeping the battery charged for the radio—and here it was only December. He really ought to cut it down to twice a week. But it meant a lot to catch the noon bulletin of Free America and then twiddle the dial a few minutes to see what else he could pick up.

But for the past three days Free America had not been on the air—solar static maybe, or perhaps just a power failure. But that rumor that President Brandley had been assassinated—it hadn't come from the Free radio and it hadn't been denied by them, either, which was a good sign.

Still, it worried him.

And that other story that lost Atlantis had pushed up during the quake period and that the Azores were now a little continent—almost certainly a hangover of the "silly season"—but it would be nice to hear a followup.

Rather sheepishly, he let his feet carry him to the car. It wasn't fair to listen when Meade wasn't around. He warmed it up, slowly spun the dial, once around and back. Not a peep at full gain, nothing but a terrible amount of static.

Served him right.

He climbed the hogback, sat down on the bench he had dragged up there—their "memorial bench," sacred to the memory of the time Meade had bruised her knees on the gravel—sat down and sighed. His lean belly was stuffed with venison and corn fritters; he lacked only tobacco to make him completely happy.

The evening cloud colors were spectacularly beautiful and the weather was extremely balmy for December; both, he thought, caused by volcanic dust, with perhaps an assist from atom bombs.

Surprising how fast things went to pieces when they started to skid! And surprising how quickly they were going back together, judging by the signs. A curve reaches trough and then starts right back up.

World War III was the shortest big war on record—forty cities gone, counting Moscow and the other slave cities as well as the American ones—and then *whoosh!* neither side fit to fight.

Of course, the fact that both sides had thrown their Sunday punch over the North Pole through the most freakish arctic weather since Peary invented the place had a lot to do with it, he supposed.

It was amazing that any of the Russian paratroop transports had gotten through at all.

Breen sighed and pulled a copy of the Western Astronomer out of his pocket. Where was he? Oh, yes, *Some Notes on the Stability of G-Type Stars with Especial Reference to Sol*, by Dynkowski, Lenin Institute, translated by Heinrich Ley, F.R.A.S.

Good boy, Ski—sound mathematician. Very clever application of harmonic series and tightly reasoned.

Breen started to thumb for his place when he noticed a footnote that he had missed. Dynkowski's own name carried down to it: "This monograph was denounced by *Pravda* as 'romantic reactionaryism' shortly after it was published. Professor Dynkowski has been unreported since and must be presumed to be liquidated."

The poor geek! Well, he probably would have been atomized by now anyway, along with the goons who did him in. He wondered if the army really had gotten all the Russki paratroopers. He had killed his own quota; if he hadn't gotten that doe within a quarter-mile of the cabin and headed right back, Meade would have had a bad time. He had shot them in the back and buried them beyond the woodpile.

He settled down to some solid pleasure. Dynkowski was a treat. Of course, it was old stuff that a G-type star, such as the Sun, was potentially unstable; a G-O star could explode, slide right off the Russell diagram, and end up as a white dwarf. But no one before Dynkowski had defined the exact conditions for such a catastrophe, nor had anyone else devised mathematical means of diagnosing the instability and describing its progress.

He looked up to rest his eyes from the fine print and saw that the Sun was obscured by a thin low cloud—one of those unusual conditions where the filtering effect is just right to permit a man to view the Sun clearly with the naked eye. Probably volcanic dust in the air, he decided, acting almost like smoked glass.

He looked again. Either he had spots before his eyes or that was one fancy big Sun spot. He had heard of being able to see them with the naked eye, but it had never happened to him.

He longed for a telescope.

He blinked. Yep, it was still there, about three o'clock. A *big* spot—no wonder the car radio sounded like a Hitler speech.

He turned back and continued on to the end of the article, being anxious to finish before the light failed.

At first his mood was sheerest intellectual pleasure at the man's tight mathematical reasoning. A three per cent imbalance in the solar constant—yes, that was standard stuff; the Sun would nova with that much change. But Dynkowski went further. By means of a novel mathematical operator which he had dubbed "yokes," he bracketed the period in a star's history when this could happen and tied it down with secondary, tertiary, and quaternary yokes, showing exactly the time of highest probability.

Beautiful! Dynkowski even assigned dates to the extreme limit of his primary yoke, as a good statistician should.

But, as Breen went back and reviewed the equations, his mood changed from intellectual to personal. Dynkowski was not talking about just any G-O star. In the latter part, he meant old Sol himself, Breen's personal Sun—the big boy out there with the oversize freckle on his face.

That was one hell of a big freckle! It was a hole you could chuck Jupiter into and not make a splash. He could see it very clearly now.

Everybody talks about "when the stars grow old and the Sun grows cold," but it's an impersonal concept, like one's own death.

Breen started thinking about it very personally. How long would it take, from the instant the imbalance was triggered until the expanding wave front engulfed Earth? The mechanics couldn't be solved without a calculation, even though they were implicit in the equations in front of him. Half an hour, for a horseback guess, from incitement until the Earth went *phutt!*

It hit him with gentle melancholy. No more? Never again? Colorado on a cool morning . . . the Boston Post Road with autumn wood smoke tanging the air . . . Bucks County bursting with color in the spring. The wet smells of the Fulton Fish Market—no, that was gone already. Coffee at the *Morning Call.* No more wild strawberries on a hillside in Jersey, hot and sweet as lips. Dawn in the South Pacific with the light airs cool velvet under your shirt and never a sound but the chuckling of the water against the sides of the old rust bucket—what was her name? That was a long time ago—the S.S. *Mary Brewster.*

No more Moon if the Earth was gone. Stars, but no one to gaze at them.

He looked back at the dates bracketing Dynkowski's probability yoke.

"Thine alabaster cities gleam, undimmed by—"

He suddenly felt the need for Meade and stood up.

She was coming out to meet him. "Hello, Potty! Safe to come in now—I've finished the dishes."

"I should help."

"You do the man's work; I'll do the woman's work. That's fair." She shaded her eyes. "What a sunset! We ought to have volcanoes blowing their tops every year."

"Sit down and we'll watch it."

She sat beside him.

"Notice the Sun spot? You can see it with your naked eye."

She stared. "Is that a Sun spot? It looks as if somebody had taken a bite out of it."

He squinted his eyes at it again. Damned if it didn't look bigger! Meade shivered. "I'm chilly. Put your arm around me."

He did so with his free arm, continuing to hold hands with the other.

It *was* bigger. The spot was growing.

What good is the race of man? Monkeys, he thought, monkeys with a touch of poetry in them, cluttering and wasting a second-string planet near a third-string star. But sometimes they finish in style.

She snuggled to him. "Keep me warm."

"It will be warmer soon—I mean I'll keep you warm."

"Dear Potty." She looked up. "Potty, something funny is happening to the sunset."

"No, darling—to the Sun."

He glanced down at the journal, still open beside him. He did not need to add up the two dates and divide by two to reach the answer. Instead he clutched fiercely at her hand, knowing with an unexpected and overpowering burst of sorrow that this was THE END.

JERRY WAS A MAN

Don't blame the Martians. The human race would have developed plasto-biology in any case.

Look at the older registered Kennel Club breeds—glandular giants like the St. Bernard and the Great Dane, silly little atrocities like the Chihuahua and the Pekingese. Consider fancy goldfish.

The damage was done when Dr. Morgan produced new breeds of fruit flies by kicking around their chromosomes with X-ray. After that, the third generation of the Hiroshima survivors did not teach us anything new; those luckless monstrosities merely publicized standard genetic knowledge.

Mr. and Mrs. Bronson van Vogel did not have social reform in mind when they went to the Phoenix Breeding Ranch; Mr. van Vogel simply wanted to buy a Pegasus. He had mentioned it at breakfast. "Are you tied up this morning, my dear?"

"Not especially. Why?"

"I'd like to run out to Arizona and order a Pegasus designed."

"A Pegasus? A flying horse? Why, my sweet?"

He grinned. "Just for fun. Pudgy Dodge was around the Club yesterday with a six-legged dachshund—must have been over a yard long. It was clever, but he swanked so much I want to give him something to stare at. Imagine, Martha—me landing on the Club 'copter platform on a winged horse. That'll snap his eyes back!"

She turned her eyes from the Jersey shore to look indulgently at her husband. She was not fooled; this would be expensive. But

Brownie was such a dear! "When do we start?"

They landed two hours earlier than they started. The airsign read, in letters fifty feet high:

PHOENIX BREEDING RANCH
CONTROLLED GENETICS — LICENSED LABOR CONTRACTORS

" 'Labor Contractors'?" she read. "I thought this place was used just to burbank new animals?"

"They both design and produce," he explained importantly. "They distribute through the mother corporation 'Workers.' You ought to know; you own a big chunk of Workers common."

"You mean I own a bunch of apes? Really?"

"Perhaps I didn't tell you. Haskell and I—" He leaned forward and informed the field that he would land manually; he was a bit proud of his piloting.

He switched off the robot and added, briefly as his attention was taken up by heading the ship down, "Haskell and I have been plowing your General Atomics dividends back into Workers, Inc. Good diversification—still plenty of dirty work for the anthropoids to do." He slapped the keys; the scream of the nose jets stopped conversation.

Bronson had called the manager in flight; they were met—not with red carpet, canopy, and footmen, though the manager strove to give that impression. "Mr. van Vogel? And Mrs. van Vogel! We are honored indeed!" He ushered them into a tiny, luxurious unicar; they jeeped off the field, up a ramp, and into the lobby of the administration building. The manager, Mr. Blakesly, did not relax until he had seated them around a fountain in the lounge of his offices, struck cigarettes for them, and provided tall, cool drinks.

Bronson van Vogel was bored by the attention, as it was obviously inspired by his wife's Dun & Bradstreet rating (ten stars, a sunburst, and heavenly music). He preferred people who could convince him that he had invented the Briggs fortune, instead of marrying it.

"This is business Blakesly. I've an order for you."

"So? Well, our facilities are at your disposal. What would you like, sir?"

"I want you to make me a Pegasus."

"A Pegasus? A flying horse?"

"Exactly."

Blakesly pursed his lips. "You seriously want a horse that will fly? An animal like the mythical Pegasus?"

"Yes, yes—that's what I said."

"You embarrass me, Mr. van Vogel. I assume you want a unique gift for your lady. How about a midget elephant, twenty inches high, perfectly housebroken, and able to read and write? He holds the stylus in his trunk—very cunning."

"Does he talk?" demanded Mrs. van Vogel.

"Well, now, my dear lady, his voice box, you know—and his tongue—he was not designed for speech. If you insist on it, I will see what our plasticians can do."

"Now, Martha—"

"You can have your Pegasus, Brownie, but I think I may want this toy elephant. May I see him?"

"Most surely. Hartstone!'

The air answered Blakesly. "Yes, boss?"

"Bring Napoleon to my lounge."

"Right away, sir."

"Now about your Pegasus, Mr. van Vogel . . . I see difficulties but I need expert advice. Dr. Cargrew is the real heart of this organization, the most eminent bio-designer—of terrestrial origin, of course—on the world today." He raised his voice to actuate relays. "Dr. Cargrew!"

"What is it, Mr. Blakesly?'

"Doctor, will you favor me by coming to my office?"

"I'm busy. Later."

Mr. Blakesly excused himself, went into his inner office, then returned to say that Dr. Cargrew would be in shortly. In the mean time Napoleon showed up. The proportions of his noble ancestors had been preserved in miniature; he looked like a statuette of an elephant, come amazingly to life.

He took three measured steps into the lounge, then saluted them each with his trunk. In saluting Mrs. van Vogel he dropped on his knees as well.

"Oh, how cute!" she gurgled. "Come here, Napoleon."

The elephant looked at Blakesly, who nodded. Napoleon ambled over and laid his trunk across her lap. She scratched his ears; he moaned contentedly.

"Show the lady how you can write," ordered Blakesly. "Fetch your things from my room."

Napoleon waited while she finished treating a particularly satisfying itch, then oozed away to return shortly with several sheets of heavy white paper and an oversize pencil. He spread a sheet in front of Mrs. van Vogel, held it down daintily with a fore foot, grasped the pencil with his trunk finger, and printed in large, shaky letters, "I LIKE YOU."

"The darling!" She dropped to her knees and put her arms around his neck. "I simply must have him. How much is he?"

"Napoleon is part of a limited edition of six," Blakesly said carefully. "Do you want an exclusive model, or may the others be sold?"

"Oh, I don't care. I just want Nappie. Can I write him a note?"

"Certainly, Mrs. van Vogel. Print large letters and use Basic English. Napoleon knows most of it. His price, nonexclusive is $350,000. That includes five years salary for his attending veterinary."

"Give the gentleman a check, Brownie," she said over her shoulder.

"But Martha—"

"Don't be tiresome, Brownie." She turned back to her pet and began printing. She hardly looked up when Dr. Cargrew came in.

Cargrew was a chilly figure in white overalls and skull cap. He shook hands brusquely, struck a cigarette and sat down. Blakesly explained.

Cargrew shook his head. "It's a physical impossibility."

Van Vogel stood up. "I can see," he said distantly, "That I should have taken my custom to NuLife Laboratories. I came here because we have a financial interest in this firm and because I was naive enough to believe the claims of your advertisements."

"Siddown, young man!" Cargrew ordered. "Take your trade to those thumb-fingered idiots if you wish—but I warn you they couldn't grow wings on a grasshopper. First you listen to me.

"We can grow anything and make it live. I can make you a living thing—I won't call it an animal—the size and shape of that table over there. It wouldn't be good for anything, but it would be alive. It would ingest food, use chemical energy, give off excretions, and display irritability. But it would be a silly piece of manipulation. Mechanically a table and an animal are two different things. Their functions are different, so their shapes are different. Now I can make you a winged horse—"

"You just said you couldn't."

"Don't interrupt. I can make a winged horse that will look just like the pictures in the fairy stories. If you want to pay for it; we'll make it—we're in business. But it won't be able to fly."

"Why not?"

"Because it's not built for flying. The ancient who dreamed up that myth knew nothing about aerodynamics and still less about biology. He stuck wings on a horse, just stuck them on, thumb tacks and glue. But that doesn't make a flying machine. Remember, son, that an animal is a machine, primarily a heat engine with a control system to operate levers and hydraulic systems, according to definite engineering laws. You savvy aerodynamics?"

"Well, I'm a pilot."

"Hummph! Well, try to understand this. A horse hasn't got the heat engine for flight. He's a hayburner and that's not efficient. We might mess around with a horse's insides so that he could live on a diet of nothing but sugar and then he might have enough energy to fly short distances. But he still would not look like the mythical Pegasus. To anchor his flying muscles he would need a breast bone maybe ten feet long. He might have to have as much as eighty feet wing spread. Folded, his wings would cover him like a tent. You're up against the cube-square disadvantage."

"Huh?"

Cargrew gestured impatiently. "Lift goes by the square of a given dimension; dead load by the cube of the same dimension, other things being equal. I might be able to make you a Pegasus the size of a cat without distorting the proportions too much."

"No, I want one I can ride. I don't mind the wing spread and I'll put up with the big breast bone. When can I have him?"

Cargrew looked disgusted, shrugged, and replied, "I'll have to consult with B'na Kreeth." He whistled and chirped; a portion of the wall facing them dissolved and they found themselves looking into a laboratory. A Martian, life-size, showed in the forepart of the three-dimensional picture.

When the creature chirlupped back at Cargrew, Mrs. van Vogel looked up, then quickly looked away. She knew it was silly but she simply could not stand the sight of Martians—and the ones who had modified themselves to a semi-manlike form disgusted her the most.

After they had twittered and gestured at each other for a minute or two Cargrew turned back to van Vogel. "B'na says that you should forget it; it would take too long. He wants to know how you'd like a fine unicorn, or a pair, guaranteed to breed true?"

"Unicorns are old hat. How long would the Pegasus take?"

After another squeaky-door conversation Cargrew answered, "Ten years probably, sixteen years on the guarantee."

"Ten years? That's ridiculous!"

Cargrew looked shirty. "*I* thought it would take fifty, but if B'na says that he can do it three to five generations, then he can do it. B'na is the finest bio-micrurgist in two planets. His chromosome surgery in unequalled. After all, young man, natural processes would take upwards of a million years to achieve the same result, if it were achieved at all. Do you expect to be able to buy miracles?"

Van Vogel had the grace to look sheepish. "Excuse me, Doctor. Let's forget it. Ten years really is too long. How about the other possibility? You said you could make a picture-book Pegasus, as long as I did not insist on flight. Could I ride him? On the ground?"

"Oh, certainly. No good for polo, but you could ride him."

"I'll settle for that. Ask Benny Creeth, or what ever his name is, how long it would take."

The Martian had faded out of the screens. "I don't need to ask him," Cargrew asserted. "This is my job—purely manipulation. B'na's collaboration is required only for rearrangement and transplanting of genes—true genetic work. I can let you have the beast in eighteen months."

"Can't you do better than that?"

"What do you expect, man? It takes eleven months to grow a new-born colt. I want one month of design and planning. The embryo will be removed on the fourth day and will be developed in an extra-uterine capsule. I'll operate ten or twelve times during gestation, grafting and budding and other things you've heard of. One year from now we'll have a baby colt, with wings. Thereafter I'll deliver to you a six-month-old Pegasus."

"I'll take it."

Cargrew made some notes, then read, "One alate horse, not capable of flight and not to breed true. Basic breed your choice—I suggest a Palomino, or an Arabian. Wings designed after a condor, in white. Simulated pin feathers with a grafted fringe of quill feathers, or reasonable facsimile." He passed the sheet over. "Initial that and we'll start in advance of formal contract."

"It's a deal," agreed van Vogel. "What is the fee?" He placed his monogram under Cargrew's.

Cargrew made further notes and handed them to Blakesly— estimates of professional man-hours, technician man-hours, purchases, and overhead. He had padded the figures to subsidize his collateral research but even he raised his eyebrows at the dollars-and-cents interpretation Blakesly put on the data. "That will be an even two million dollars."

Van Vogel hesitated; his wife had looked up at the mention of money. But she turned her attention back to the scholarly elephant.

Blakesly added hastily, "That is for an exclusive creation, of course."

"Naturally," van Vogel agreed briskly, and added the figure to the memorandum.

Van Vogel was ready to return, but his wife insisted on seeing the "apes", as she termed the anthropoid workers. The discovery that she owned a considerable share in these subhuman creatures had intrigued her. Blakesly eagerly suggested a trip through the laboratories in which the workers were developed from true apes.

They were arranged in seven buildings, the seven "Days of Creation." "First Day" was a large building occupied by Cargrew, his staff, his operating rooms, incubators, and laboratories. Martha van Vogel stared in horrified fascination at living organs and even complete embryos, living artificial lives sustained by clever glass and metal recirculating systems and exquisite automatic machinery.

She could not appreciate the techniques; it seemed depressing. She had about decided against plasto-biology when Napoleon, by tugging at her skirts, reminded her that it produced good things as well as horrors.

The building "Second Day" they did not enter; it was occupied by B'na Kreeth and his racial colleagues. "We could not stay alive in it, you understand," Blakesly explained. Van Vogel nodded; his wife hurried on—she wanted no Martians, even behind plastiglass.

From there on the buildings were for development and production of commercial workers. "Third Day" was used for the development of variations in the anthropoids to meet constantly changing labor requirements. "Fourth Day" was a very large building devoted entirely to production-line incubators for commercial types of anthropoids. Blakesly explained that they had dispensed with normal birth. "The policy permits exact control of forced variations, such as for size, and saves hundreds of thousands of worker-hours on the part of the female anthropoids.'

Martha van Vogel was delighted with "Fifth Day," the anthropoid kindergarden where the little tykes learned to talk and were conditioned to the social patterns necessary to their station in life. They worked at simple tasks such as sorting buttons and digging holes in sand piles, with pieces of candy given as incentives for fast and accurate work.

"Six Day" completed the anthropoids' educations. Each learned the particular sub-trade it would practice, cleaning, digging, and especially agricultural semi-skills such as weeding, thinning, and picking. "One Nisei farmer working three neo-chimpanzees can grow as many vegetables as a dozen old-style farm hands," Blakesly asserted. "They really *like* to work—when we get through with them."

They admired the almost incredibly heavy tasks done by modified gorillas and stopped to gaze at the little neo-Capuchins doing high picking on prop trees, then moved on toward "Seventh Day."

This building was used for the radioactive mutation of genes and therefore located some distance away from the others. They had to walk, as the sidewalk was being repaired; the detour took them past workers' pens and barracks. Some of the anthropoids crowded up to the wire and began calling to them: "Sigret! Sigret! Preese, Missy! Preese, Boss! Sigret!"

"What are they saying?" Martha van Vogel inquired.

"They are asking for cigarettes," Blakesly answered in annoyed tones. "They know better, but they are like children. Here—I'll put a stop to it." He stepped up to the wire and shouted to an elderly male, "Hey! Strawboss!"

The worker addressed wore, in addition to the usual short canvas kilt, a bedraggled arm band. He turned and shuffled toward the fence. "Strawboss," ordered Blakesly, "get those Joes away from here."

"Okay, Boss," the old fellow acknowledged and started cuffing those nearest him. "Scram, you Joes! Scram!"

"But I have some cigarettes," protested Mrs. van Vogel, "and I would gladly have given them some."

"It doesn't do to pamper them," the Manager told her. "They have been taught that luxuries come only from work. I must apologize for my poor children; those in these pens are getting old and forgetting their manners."

She did not answer but moved further along the fence to where one old neo-chimp was pressed up against the wire, staring at them with soft, tragic eyes, like a child at a bakery window. He had taken no part in the jostling demand for tobacco and had been let alone by the strawboss. "Would you like a cigarette?" she asked him.

"Preese, Missy."

She struck one which he accepted with fumbling grace, took a long, lung-filling drag, let the smoke trickle out his nostrils, and said shyly, "Sankoo, Missy. Me Jerry."

"How do you do, Jerry?"

"Howdy, Missy." He bobbed down, bending his knees, ducking his head, and clasping his hands to his chest, all in one movement.

"Come along, Martha." Her husband and Blakesly had moved in behind her.

"In a moment," she answered. "Brownie, meet my friend Jerry. Doesn't he look just like Uncle Albert? Except that he looks so sad. Why are you unhappy, Jerry?"

"They don't understand abstract ideas," put in Blakesly.

But Jerry surprised him. "Jerry sad," he announced in tones so doleful that Martha van Vogel did not know whether to laugh or to cry.

"Why, Jerry?" she asked gently. "Why are you so sad?"

"No work," he stated. "No sigret. No candy. No work."

"These are all old workers who have passed their usefulness,"

Blakesly repeated. "Idleness upsets them, but we have nothing for them to do."

"Well!" she said. "Then why don't you have them sort buttons, or something like that, such as the baby ones do?"

"They wouldn't even do that properly," Blakesly answered her. "These workers are senile."

"Jerry isn't senile! You heard him talk."

"Well, perhaps not. Just a moment." He turned to the ape-man, who was squatting down in order to scratch Napoleon's head with a long forefinger thrust through the fence. "You, Joe! Come here."

Blakesly felt around the worker's hairy neck and located a thin steel chain to which was attached a small metal tag. He studied it. "You're right," he admitted. "He's not really over age, but his eyes are bad. I remember the lot—cataracts as a result of an unfortunate linked mutation." He shrugged.

"But that's no reason to let him grieve his heart out in idleness."

"Really, Mrs. van Vogel, you should not upset yourself about it. They don't stay in these pens long—only a few days at the most."

"Oh," she answered, somewhat mollified, "you have some other place to retire them to, then. Do you give them something to do there? You should—Jerry wants to work. Don't you, Jerry?"

The neo-chimp had been struggling to follow the conversation. He caught the last idea and grinned. "Jerry work! Sure mike! Good worker." He flexed his fingers, then made fists, displaying fully opposed thumbs.

Mr. Blakesly seemed somewhat nonplused. "Really, Mrs. van Vogel, there is no need. You see—" He stopped.

Van Vogel had been listening irritably. His wife's enthusiasms annoyed him, unless they were also his own. Furthermore he was beginning to blame Blakesly for his own recent extravagance and had a premonition that his wife would find some way to make him pay, very sweetly, for his indulgence.

Being annoyed with both of them, he chucked in the perfect wrong remark. "Don't be silly, Martha. They don't retire them; they liquidate them."

It took a little time for the idea to soak in, but when it did she was furious. "Why . . . why—I never heard of such a thing! You

ought to be ashamed. You . . . you would shoot your own grand-
mother."

"Mrs. van Vogel—please!"

"Don't 'Mrs. van Vogel' me! It's got to stop—you hear me?" She
looked around at the death pens, at the milling hundreds of old
workers therein. "It's horrible. You work them until they can't work
anymore, then you take away their little comforts, and you *dispose* of
them. I wonder you don't eat them!"

"They do," her husband said brutally. "Dog food."

"What! Well, we'll put a stop to that!"

"Mrs. van Vogel," Blakesly pleaded. "Let me explain."

"Hummph! Go ahead. It had better be good."

"Well, it's like this—" His eye fell on Jerry, standing with worried expression at the fence. "Scram, Joe!" Jerry shuffled away.

"Wait, Jerry!" Mrs. van Vogel called out. Jerry paused uncertainly. "Tell him to come back," she ordered Blakesly.

The Manager bit his lip, then called out, "Come back here."

He was beginning definitely to dislike Mrs. van Vogel, despite
his automatic tendency to genuflect in the presence of a high credit
rating. To be told how to run his own business—well, now, indeed!
"Mrs. van Vogel, I admire your humanitarian spirit but you don't
understand the situation. We understand our workers and do what
is best for them. They die painlessly before their disabilities can trouble them. They live happy lives, happier than yours or mine. We
trim off the bad part of their lives, nothing more. And don't forget,
these poor beasts would never have been born had we not arranged
it."

She shook her head. "Fiddlesticks! You'll be quoting the Bible
at me next. There will be no more of it, Mr. Blakesly. I shall hold
you personally responsible."

Blakesly looked bleak. "My responsibilities are to the directors."

"You think so?" She opened her purse and snatched out her
telephone. So great was her agitation that she did not bother to call
through, but signalled the local relay operator instead. "Phoenix? Get
me Great New York Murray Hill 9Q-4004, Mr. Haskell. Priority—
star subscriber 777. Make it quick." She stood there, tapping her foot
and glaring, until her business manager answered. "Haskell? This is
Martha van Vogel. How much Workers, Incorporated, common do

I own? No, no, never mind that—what percent? . . . so? Well, it's not enough. I want fifty-one percent by tomorrow morning . . . all right, get proxies for the rest but get it . . . I didn't ask you what it would cost; I said to get it. Get busy." She disconnected abruptly and turned to her husband. "We're leaving, Brownie, and we are taking Jerry with us. Mr. Blakesly, will you kindly have him taken out of that pen? Give him a check for the amount, Brownie."

"Now, Martha—"

"My mind is made up, Brownie."

Mr. Blakesly cleared his throat. It was going to be pleasant to thwart this woman. "The workers are never sold. I'm sorry. It's a matter of policy."

"Very well then, I'll take a permanent lease."

"This worker has been removed from the labor market. He is not for lease."

"Am I going to have more trouble with you?"

"If you please, Madame! This worker is not available under any terms—but, as a courtesy to you, I am willing to transfer to you indentures for him, gratis. I want you to know that the policies of this firm are formed from a very real concern for the welfare of our charges as well as from the standpoint of good business practice. We therefore reserve the right to inspect at any time to assure ourselves that you are taking proper care of this worker." There, he told himself savagely, that will stop her clock!

"Of course. Thank you, Mr. Blakesly. You are most gracious."

The trip back to Great New York was not jolly. Napoleon hated it and let it be known. Jerry was patient but airsick. By the time they grounded the van Vogels were not on speaking terms.

"I'm sorry, Mrs. van Vogel. The shares were simply not available. We should have had proxy on the O'Toole block but someone tied them up an hour before I reached them."

"Blakesly."

"Undoubtedly. You should not have tipped him off; you gave him time to warn his employers."

"Don't waste time telling me what mistakes I made yesterday. What are you going to do today?"

"Mr. dear Mrs. van Vogel, what can I do? I'll carry out any instructions you care to give."

"Don't talk nonsense. You are supposed to be smarter than I am; that's why I pay you to do my thinking for me."

Mr. Haskell looked helpless.

His principal struck a cigarette so hard she broke it. "Why isn't Weinberg here?"

"Really, Mrs. van Vogel, there are no special legal aspects. You want the stock; we can't buy it nor bind it. Therefore—"

"I pay Weinberg to know the legal angles. Get him."

Weinberg was leaving his office; Haskell caught him on a chase-me circuit. "Sidney," Haskell called out. "Come to my office, will you? Oscar Haskell."

"Sorry. How about four o'clock?"

"Sidney, I want you—now!" cut in the client's voice. "This is Martha van Vogel."

The little man shrugged helplessly. "Right away," he agreed. That woman—why hadn't he retired on his one hundred and twenty-fifth birthday, as his wife had urged him to?

Ten minutes later he was listening to Haskell's explanations and his client's interruptions. When they had finished he spread his hands. "What do you expect, Mrs. van Vogel? These workers are chattels. You have not been able to buy the property rights involved; you are stopped. But I don't see what you are worked up about. They gave you the worker whose life you wanted preserved."

She spoke forcefully under her breath, then answered him. "That's not important. What is one worker among millions? I want to stop this killing, all of it."

Weinberg shook his head. "If you were able to prove that their methods of disposing of these beasts were inhumane, or that they were negligent of their physical welfare before destroying them, or that the destruction was wanton—"

"Wanton? It certainly is!"

"Probably not in a legal sense, my dear lady. There was a case, Julius Hartman et al. vs. Hartman Estate, 1972, I believe, in which a permanent injunction was granted against carrying out a term of the will which called for the destruction of a valuable collection of Persian cats. But in order to use that theory you would have to show that these creatures, when superannuated, are notwithstanding more valuable alive than dead. You cannot compel a person to maintain chattels at a loss."

"See here, Sidney, I didn't get you over here to tell me how this can't be done. If what I want isn't legal, then get a law passed."

Weinberg looked at Haskell, who looked embarrassed and answered, "Well, the fact of the matter is, Mrs. van Vogel, that we have agreed with the other members of the Commonwealth Association not to subsidize any legislation during the incumbency of the present administration."

"How ridiculous! Why?"

"The Legislative Guild has brought out a new fair-practices code which we consider quite unfair, a sliding scale which penalizes the well-to-do—all very nice sounding, with special provisions for nominal fees for veterans' private bills and such things—but in fact the code is confiscatory. Even the Briggs Foundation can hardly afford to take a proper interest in public affairs under this so-called code."

"Hmmph! A fine day when legislators join unions—they are professional men. Bribes should be competitive. Get an injunction."

"Mrs. van Vogel," protested Weinberg, "how can you expect me to get an injunction against an organization which has no legal existence? In a legal sense, there is no Legislative Guild, just as the practice of assisting legislation by subsidy has itself no legal existence."

"And babies come under cabbage leaves. Quit stalling me, gentlemen. What are you going to do?"

Weinberg spoke when he saw that Haskell did not intend to. "Mrs. van Vogel, I think we should retain a special shyster."

"I don't employ shysters, even—I don't understand the way they think. I am a simple housewife, Sidney."

Mr. Weinberg flinched at her self-designation while noting that he must not let her find out that the salary of his own staff shyster was charged to her payroll. As convention required, he maintained the front of a simple, barefoot solicitor, but he had found out long ago that Martha van Vogel's problems required an occasional dose of the more exotic branch of the law. "The man I have in mind is a creative artist," he insisted. "It is no more necessary to understand him than it is to understand the composer in order to appreciate a symphony. I do recommend that you talk with him, at least."

"Oh, very well! Get him up here."

"Here? My dear lady!" Haskell was shocked at the suggestion; Weinberg looked amazed. "It would not only cause any action you bring to be thrown out of court if it were known that you had consulted this man, but it would prejudice any Briggs enterprise for years."

Mrs. van Vogel shrugged. "You men. I never will understand the way you think. Why shouldn't one consult a shyster as openly as one consults an astrologer?"

James Roderick McCoy was not a large man, but he seemed large. He managed to dominate even so large a room as Mrs. van Vogel's salon. His business card read:

J. R. McCOY
"THE REAL McCOY"

LICENSED SHYSTER—FIXING, SPECIAL CONTACTS,
ANGLES. ALL WORK GUARANTEED.

TELEPHONE SKYLINE 9-8M4554
Ask for MAC

The number given was the pool room of the notorious Three Planets Club. He wasted no time on offices and kept his files in his head—the only safe place for them.

He was sitting on the floor, attempting to teach Jerry to shoot craps, while Mrs. van Vogel explained her problem. "What do you think, Mr. McCoy? Could we approach it through the SPCA? My public relations staff could give it a build up."

McCoy got to his feet. "Jerry's eyes aren't so bad; he caught me trying to palm box cars off on him as a natural. No," he continued, "the SPCA angle is no good. It's what 'workers' will expect. They'll be ready to prove that the anthropoids actually enjoy being killed off."

Jerry rattled the dice hopefully. "That's all, Jerry. Scram."

"Okay, Boss." The ape man got to his feet and went to the big stereo which filled a corner of the room. Napoleon ambled after him and switched it on. Jerry punched a selector button and got a blues singer. Napoleon immediately punched another, then another and another until he got a loud but popular band. He stood there, beating out the rhythm with his trunk.

Jerry looked pained and switched it back to his blues singer. Napoleon stubbornly reached out with his prehensile nose and switched it off.

Jerry used a swear word.

"Boys!" called out Mrs. van Vogel. "Quit squabbling. Jerry, let Nappie play what he wants to. You can play the stereo when Nappie has to take his nap."

"Okay, Missy Boss."

McCoy was interested. "Jerry likes music?"

"Like it? He loves it. He's been learning to sing."

"Huh? This I gotta hear."

"Certainly. Nappie—turn off the stereo." The elephant complied but managed to look put upon. "Now Jerry—'Jingle Bells.' " She led him in it:

"Jingle bells, jingle bells, jingle all the day—" and he followed,

"Jinger bez, jinger bez, jinger awrah day;

"Oh, wot fun tiz to ride in one-hoss open sray."

He was flat, he was terrible. He looked ridiculous, patting out the time with one splay foot. But it was singing.

"Say, that's fast!" McCoy commented. "Too bad Nappie can't talk—we'd have a duet."

Jerry looked puzzled. "Nappie talk good," he stated. He bent over the elephant and spoke to him. Napoleon grunted and moaned back at him. "See, Boss?" Jerry said triumphantly.

"What did he say?"

"He say, 'Can Nappie pray stereo now?' "

"Very well, Jerry," Mrs. van Vogel interceded. The ape man spoke to his chum in whispers. Napoleon squealed and did not turn on the stereo.

"Jerry!" said his mistress. "I said nothing of the sort; he does *not* have to play your blues singer. Come away, Jerry. Nappie—play what you want to."

"You mean he tried to cheat?" McCoy inquired with interest.

"He certainly did."

"Hmm—Jerry's got the makings of a real citizen. Shave him and put shoes on him and he'd get by all right in the precinct I grew up in." He stared at the anthropoid. Jerry stared back, puzzled but patient. Mrs. van Vogel had thrown away the dirty canvas kilt which was both his badge of servitude and a concession to propriety and had replaced it with a kilt in the bright Cameron war plaid, complete to sporan, and topped off with a Glengarry.

"Do you suppose he could learn to play the bagpipes?" McCoy asked. "I'm beginning to get an angle."

"Why, I don't know. What's your idea?"

McCoy squatted down cross-legged and began practicing rolls with his dice. "Never mind," he answered when it suited him, "that angle's no good. But we're getting there." He rolled four naturals, one after the other. "You say Jerry still belongs to the Corporation?"

"In a titular sense, yes. I doubt if they will ever try to repossess him."

"I wish they would try." He scooped up the dice and stood up. "It's in the bag, Sis. Forget it. I'll want to talk to your publicity man but you can quit worrying about it."

Of course Mrs. van Vogel should have knocked before entering her husband's room—but then she would not have overheard what he was saying, nor to whom.

"That's right," she heard him say, "we haven't any further need for him. Take him away, the sooner the better. Just be sure the men you send have a signed order directing us to turn him over."

She was not apprehensive, as she did not understand the conversation, but merely curious. She looked over her husband's shoulder at the video screen.

There she saw Blakesly's face. His voice was saying, "Very well, Mr. van Vogel, the anthropoid will be picked up tomorrow."

She strode up to the screen. "Just a minute, Mr. Blakesly—" then, to her husband, "Brownie, what in the world do you think you are doing?"

The expression she surprised on his face was not one he had ever let her see before. "Why don't you knock?"

"Maybe it's a good thing I didn't. Brownie, did I hear you right. Were you telling Mr. Blakesly to pick up Jerry?" She turned to the screen. "Was that it, Mr. Blakesly?"

"That is correct, Mrs. van Vogel. And I must say I find this confusion most—"

"Stow it." She turned back. "Brownie, what have you to say for yourself?"

"Martha, you are being preposterous. Between that elephant and that ape this place is a zoo. I actually caught your precious Jerry smoking my special, personal cigars today . . . not to mention the fact that both of them play the stereo all day long until a man can't get a moment's peace. I certainly don't have to stand for such things in my own house."

"Whose house, Brownie?"

"That's beside the point. I will not stand for—"

"Never mind." She turned to the screen. "My husband seems to have lost his taste for exotic animals, Mr. Blakesly. Cancel the order for a Pegasus."

"Martha!"

"Sauce for the goose, Brownie. I'll pay for your whims; I'm damned if I'll pay for your tantrums. The contract is cancelled, Mr. Blakesly. Mr. Haskell will arrange the details."

Blakesly shrugged. "Your capricious behavior will cost you, of course. The penalties—"

"I said Mr. Haskell would arrange the details. One more thing, Mister Manager Blakesly—have you done as I told you to?"

"What do you mean?"

"You know what I mean—are those poor creatures still alive and well?"

"That is not your business." He had, in fact, suspended the killings; the directors had not wanted to take any chances until they saw what the Briggs trust could manage, but Blakesly would not give her the satisfaction of knowing.

She looked at him as if he were a skipped dividend. "It's not, eh? Well, bear this in mind, you cold-blooded little pipsqueak: I'm holding you personally responsible. If just one of them dies from *anything*, I'll have your skin for a rug." She flipped off the connection and turned to her husband. "Brownie—"

"It's useless to say anything," he cut in, in the cold voice he normally used to bring her to heel. "I shall be at the Club. Good-bye!"

"That's just what I was going to suggest."

"What?"

"I'll have your clothes sent over. Do you have anything else in this house?"

He stared at her. "Don't talk like a fool, Martha."

"I'm not talking like a fool." She looked him up and down. "My, but you are handsome, Brownie. I guess I was a fool to think I could buy a big hunk of man with a checkbook. I guess a girl gets them free, or she doesn't get them at all. Thanks for the lesson." She turned and slammed out of the room and into her own suite.

Five minutes later, makeup repaired and nerves steadied by a few whiffs of Fly-Right, she called the pool room of the Three Planets Club. McCoy came to the screen carrying a cue. "Oh, it's you, sugar puss. Well, snap it up—I've got four bits on this game."

"This is business."

"Okay, okay—spill it."

She told him the essentials. "I'm sorry about cancelling the flying horse contract, Mr. McCoy. I hope it won't make your job any harder. I'm afraid I lost my temper."

"Fine. Go lose it again."

"Huh?"

"You're barrelling down the groove, kid. Call Blakesly up again. Bawl him out. Tell him to keep his bailiffs away from you, or you'll stuff 'em and use them for hat racks. Dare him to take Jerry away from you."

"I don't understand you."

"You don't have to, girlie. Remember this: You can't have a bull fight until you get the bull mad enough to fight. Have Weinberg get a temporary injunction restraining Workers, Incorporated, from re-claiming Jerry. Have your boss press agent give me a buzz. Then you call in the newsboys and tell them what you think of Blakesly. Make it nasty. Tell them you intend to put a stop to this wholesale murder if it takes every cent you've got."

"Well . . . all right. Will you come to see me before I talk to them?"

"Nope—gotta get back to my game. Tomorrow, maybe. Don't fret about having cancelled that silly winged-horse deal. I always did think your old man was weak in the head, and it's saved you a nice piece of change. You'll need it when I send in my bill. Boy, am I going to clip you! Bye now."

The bright letters trailed around the sides of the Times Building: "WORLD'S RICHEST WOMAN PUTS UP FIGHT FOR APE MAN." On the giant video screen above showed a transcribe of Jerry, in his ridiculous Highland chief outfit. A small army of police surrounded the Briggs town house, while Mrs. van Vogel informed anyone who would listen, including several news services, that she would defend Jerry personally and to the death.

The public relations office of Workers, Incorporated, denied any intention of seizing Jerry; the denial got nowhere.

In the meantime technicians installed extra audio and video circuits in the largest court room in town, for one Jerry (no surname), described as a legal, permanent resident of these United States, had asked for a permanent injunction against the corporate person "Workers," its officers, employees, successors, or assignees, forbidding it to do him any physical harm and in particular forbidding it to kill him.

Through his attorney, the honorable and distinguished and stuffily respectable Augustus Pomfrey, Jerry brought the action *in his own name.*

Martha van Vogel sat in the court room as a spectator only, but she was surrounded by secretaries, guards, maid, publicity men, and yes men, and had one television camera trained on her alone. She was nervous. McCoy had insisted on briefing Pomfrey through Weinberg, to keep Pomfrey from knowing that he was being helped by a shyster. She had her own opinion of Pomfrey—

The McCoy had insisted that Jerry not wear his beautiful new kilt but had dressed him in faded dungaree trousers and jacket. It seemed poor theater to her.

Jerry himself worried her. He seemed confused by the lights and the noise and the crowd, about to go to pieces.

And McCoy had refused to go to the trial with her. He had told her that it was quite impossible, that his mere presence would alienate the court, and Weinberg had backed him up. Men! Their minds were devious—they seemed to *like* twisted ways of doing things. It confirmed her opinion that men should not be allowed to vote.

But she felt lost without the immediate presence of McCoy's easy self-confidence. Away from him, she wondered why she had ever trusted such an important matter to an irresponsible, jumping jack, bird-brained clown as McCoy. She chewed her nails and wished he were present.

The panel of attorneys appearing for Worker's Incorporated, began by moving that the action be dismissed without trial, on the theory that Jerry was a chattel of the corporation, an integral part of it, and no more able to sue than the thumb can sue the brain.

The honorable Augustus Pomfrey looked every inch the statesman as he bowed to the court and to his opponents. "It is indeed strange," he began, "to hear the second-hand voice of a legal fiction, a soulless, imaginary quantity called a corporate 'person,' argue that a flesh-and-blood creature, a being of hopes and longings and passions, has no legal existence. I see here beside me my poor cousin Jerry." He patted Jerry on the shoulder; the ape man, needing reassurance, slid a hand into his. It went over well.

"But when I look for this abstract fancy 'Workers,' what do I find? Nothing—some words on paper, some signed bits of foolscap—"

"If the Court please, a question," put in the opposition chief attorney, "does the learned counsel contend that a limited liability stock company cannot own property?"

"Will the counsel reply?" directed the judge.

"Thank you. My esteemed colleague has set up a straw man; I contended only that the question as to whether Jerry is a chattel of Workers, Incorporated, is immaterial, nonessential, irrelevant. I am part of the corporate city of Great New York. Does that deny me my civil rights as a person of flesh and blood? In fact it does not even rob me of my right to sue that civic corporation of which I am a part, if, in my opinion, I am wronged by it. We are met today in the mellow light of equity, rather than in the cold and narrow confines of law. It seemed a fit time to dwell on the strange absurdities we live by, whereunder a nonentity of paper and legal fiction could deny the existence of this our poor cousin. I ask that the learned attorneys for the corporation stipulate that Jerry does, in fact, exist, and let us get on with the action."

They huddled; the answer was "No."

"Very well. My client asked to be examined in order that the court may determine his status and being."

"Objection! This anthropoid cannot be examined; he is a mere part and chattel of the respondent."

"That is what we are about to determine," the judge answered dryly. "Objection overruled."

"Go sit in that chair, Jerry."

"Objection! This beast cannot take an oath—it is beyond his comprehension."

"What have you to say to that, Counsel?"

"If it pleases the Court," answered Pomfrey, "the simplest thing to do is to put him in the chair and find out."

"Let him take the stand. The clerk will administer the oath." Martha van Vogel gripped the arms of her chair; McCoy had spent a full week training him for this. Would the poor thing blow up without McCoy to guide him?

The clerk droned through the oath; Jerry looked puzzled but patient.

"Your honor," said Pomfrey, "when young children must give testimony, it is customary to permit a little leeway in the wording, to fit their mental attainments. May I be permitted?" He walked up to Jerry.

"Jerry, my boy, are you a good worker?"

"Sure mike! Jerry good worker!"

"Maybe bad worker, huh? Lazy. Hide from strawboss."

"No, no, no! Jerry good worker. Dig. Weed. Not dig up vege-taber. Dig up weed. Work hard."

"You will see," Pomfrey addressed the court, "that my client has very definite ideas of what is true and what is false. Now let us attempt to find out whether or not he has moral values which require him to tell the truth. Jerry—"

"Yes, Boss."

Pomfrey spread his hand in front of the anthropoid's face. "How many fingers do you see?"

Jerry reached out and ticked them off. "One—two—sree—four, uh—five."

"Six fingers, Jerry."

"Five, Boss."

"Six fingers, Jerry. I give you cigarette. Six."

"Five, Boss. Jerry not cheat."

Pomfrey spread his hands. "Will the court accept him?"

The court did. Martha van Vogel sighed. Jerry could not count very well and she had been afraid that he would forget his lines and accept the bribe. But he had been promised all the cigarettes he wanted and chocolate as well if he would remember to insist that five was five.

"I suggest," Pomfrey went on, "that the matter has been established. Jerry is an entity; if he can be accepted as a witness, then surely he may have his day in court. Even a dog may have his day in court. Will my esteemed colleagues stipulate?"

Workers, Incorporated, through its battery of lawyers, agreed—just in time, for the judge was beginning to cloud up. He had been much impressed by the little performance.

The tide was with him; Pomfrey used it. "If it please the court and if the counsels for the respondent will permit, we can shorten these proceedings. I will state the theory under which relief is sought and then, by a few questions, it may be settled one way or another. I ask that it be stipulated that it was the intention of Workers, Incorporated, through its servants, to take the life of my client."

Stipulation was refused.

"So? Then I ask that the court take judicial notice of the well known fact that these anthropoid workers are destroyed when they no longer show a profit; thereafter I will call witnesses, starting with Horace Blakesly, to show that Jerry was and presumably is under such sentence of death."

Another hurried huddle resulted in the stipulation that Jerry had, indeed, been scheduled for euthanasia.

"Then," said Pomfrey, "I will state my theory. Jerry is not an animal, but a man. It is not legal to kill him—it is murder."

•   •   •

First there was silence, then the crowd gasped. People had grown used to animals that talked and worked, but they were no more prepared to think of them as persons, humans, *men*, than were the haughty Roman citizens prepared to concede human feelings to their barbarian slaves.

Pomfrey let them have it while they were still groggy. "What is a man? A collection of living cells and tissues? A legal fiction, like this corporate 'person' that would take poor Jerry's life? No, a man is none of these things. A man is a collection of hopes and fears, of human longings, of aspirations greater than himself—more than the clay from which he came; less than the Creator which lifted him up from the clay. Jerry has been taken from his jungle and made something more than the poor creatures who were his ancestors, even as you and I. We ask that this Court recognize his manhood."

The opposing attorneys saw that the Court was moved; they drove in fast. An anthropoid, they contended, could not be a man because he lacked human shape and human intelligence. Pomfrey called his first witness—Master B'na Kreeth.

The Martian's normal bad temper had not been improved by being forced to wait around for three days in a travel tank, to say nothing of the indignity of having to interrupt his researches to take part in the childish pow-wows of terrestrials.

There was further delay to irritate him while Pomfrey forced the corporation attorneys to accept B'na as an expert witness. They wanted to refuse but could not—he was their own Director of Research. He also held voting control of all Martian-held Workers' stock, a fact unmentioned but hampering.

More delay while an interpreter was brought in to help administer the oath—B'na Kreeth, self-centered as all Martians, had never bothered to learn English.

He twittered and chirped in answer to the demand that he tell the truth, the whole truth, and so forth; the interpreter looked pained. "He says he can't do it," he informed the judge.

Pomfrey asked for exact translation.

The interpreter looked uneasily at the judge. "He says that if he told the whole truth you fools—not 'fools' exactly; it's a Martian word meaning a sort of headless worm—would not understand it."

The court discussed the idea of contempt briefly. When the Martian understood that he was about to be forced to remain in a travel tank for thirty days he came down off his high horse and agreed to tell the truth as adequately as was possible; he was accepted as a witness.

"Are you a man?" demanded Pomfrey.

"Under your laws and by your standards I am a man."

"By what theory? Your body is unlike ours; you cannot even live in our air. You do not speak our language; your ideas are alien to us. How can you be a man?"

The Martian answered carefully: *"I quote from the Terra-Martian Treaty, which you must accept as supreme law. 'All members of the Great Race, while sojourning on the Third Planet, shall have all the rights and prerogatives of the native dominant race of the Third Planet.' This clause has been interpreted by the Bi-Planet Tribunal to mean that members of the Great Race are 'men' whatever that may be."*

"Why do you refer to your sort as the 'Great Race'?"

"Because of our superior intelligence."

"Superior to men?"

"We are men."

"Superior to the intelligence of earth men?"

"That is self-evident."

"Just as we are superior in intelligence to this poor creature Jerry?"

"That is not self-evident."

"Finished with the witness," announced Pomfrey. The opposition counsels should have left bad enough alone; instead they tried to get B'na Kreeth to define the difference in intelligence between humans and worker-anthropoids. Master B'na explained meticulously that cultural differences masked the intrinsic differences, if any, and that, in any case, both anthropoids and men made so little use of their respective potential intelligences that it was really too early to tell which race would turn out to be the superior race in the Third Planet.

He had just begun to discuss how a truly superior race could be bred by combining the best features of anthropoids and men when he was hastily asked to "stand down."

"May it please the Court," said Pomfrey, "we have not advanced the theory; we have merely disposed of respondent's contention that a particular shape and a particular degree of intelligence are necessary to manhood. I now ask that the petitioner be recalled to the stand that the court may determine whether he is, in truth, human."

"If the learned court please—" The battery of lawyers had been in a huddle ever since B'na Kreeth's travel tank had been removed from the room; the chief counsel now spoke.

"The object of the petition appears to be to protect the life of this chattel. There is no need to draw out these proceedings; respondent stipulates that this chattel will be allowed to die a natural death in the hands of its present custodian and moves that the action be dismissed."

"What do you say to that?" the Court asked Pomfrey.

Pomfrey visibly gathered his toga about him. "We ask not for cold charity from this corporation, but for the justice of the court. We ask that Jerry's humanity be established as a matter of law. Not for him to vote, nor to hold property, nor to be relieved of special police regulations appropriate to his group—but we do ask that he be adjudged at least as human as that aquarium monstrosity just removed from this court room!"

The judge turned to Jerry. "Is that what you want, Jerry?"

Jerry looked uneasily at Pomfrey, then said, "Okay, Boss."

"Come up to the chair."

"One moment—" The opposition chief counsel seemed flurried. "I ask the Court to consider that a ruling in this matter may affect a long established commercial practice necessary to the economic life of—"

"Objection!" Pomfrey was on his feet, bristling. "Never have I heard a more outrageous attempt to prejudice a decision. My esteemed colleague might as well ask the Court to decide a murder case from political considerations. I protest—"

"Never mind," said the court. "The suggestion will be ignored. Proceed with your witness."

Pomfrey bowed. "We are exploring the meaning of this strange thing called 'manhood.' We have seen that it is not a matter of shape, nor race, nor planet of birth, nor of acuteness of mind. Truly, it cannot be defined, yet it may be experienced. It can reach from heart to heart, from spirit to spirit." He turned to Jerry. "Jerry—will you sing your new song for the judge?"

"Sure mike." Jerry looked uneasily up at the whirring cameras, the mikes, and the ikes, then cleared his throat:

"Way down upon de Suwannee Ribber
Far, far away;
Dere's where my heart is turning ebber—"

The applause scared him out of his wits; the banging of the gavel frightened him still more—but it mattered not; the issue was no longer in doubt. Jerry was a man.

THE FARTHEST PLACE

There was a feeling of excitement in the *Ruys* after we left Rio, caused by the possibility that we might receive radio orders to turn aside and make an unscheduled call, a stop at the most remote port in the world.

The world is conceded to be a small place these days, with airlines straddling the oceans, with boats and trains and buses linking No Plumbing, Kentucky, to No Hope, New Zealand. No place is more than a week away from the nearest airline ticket office, plus a possible day by bus or train, or at the most three days for some South Pacific islands.

Is there any really remote place left? Behind the Iron Curtain? A political barrier, not a physical one. The North Pole? The North Pole needs traffic lights these days to keep the Russian patrol planes from bumping into our own. Antarctica? Yes, but Admiral Byrd's continent is uninhabited; I had in mind places where people live. There are a number of places very hard to reach which are unfit for human habitation; that is why there is no transportation to them. What is the most remote *settlement* in the world?

There is an Indian village in the Grand Canyon that is almost never visited by outsiders. But you can make it in two days from New York, by airline, by hired car, and by hired mule. There are pygmy villages deep in the Congo, but safari companies will outfit you and provide professional guides. One way or another almost any inhabited spot can be reached by recognized commercial means. But there is one place left on earth which has long been settled and has a recognized, established government which cannot be reached by any regular means whatever, but only through lucky chance.

It is Tristan da Cunha, a British colony in the South Atlantic, almost precisely midway between Antarctica, South America, and Africa. It is 1500 miles from the nearest land, St. Helena, a spot itself so remote that it was picked as a safe prison for Napoleon Bonaparte after he crushed out of Elba.

There is *no* way to buy a ticket to Tristan. No South Sea island is so hard to reach, so hard to leave, so far from other inhabited land. It is the most remote settled spot on this planet. The *Ruys* was being considered for a special stop there because the government meteorologist and radio operator stationed there had been waiting seven months since the end of his three-year tour of duty for opportunity to get himself, his wife, and baby back to the mainland—any mainland.

It meant adding nine hundred miles and about three days to the voyage from Rio to Cape Town, but there was opportunity to pick up fifty tons of frozen lobster tails there for Cape Town; most of the great cost of detouring a big ship could be charged against pay cargo. But the real question was whether the stop could be made at all. Tristan has no harbor of any sort. Sheer cliffs face the sea on all sides; at their feet are narrow beaches. A ship must anchor off shore and send in small boats. But dense fogs, fierce winds, and mountainous seas are common diet there and whole gales, with winds of seventy-five miles an hour or more, blow up without warning from the subarctic regions below it.

For several days after we left Rio the common subject in the ship was the latest radio weather report from Tristan da Cunha. Would the Captain risk it? Or would we turn aside and go on to Cape Town? No company agent could order him to attempt it; he must decide for himself whether the bet was worth taking—not so much risk to the ship, for a ship as big as the *Ruys* would not be risked for all the lobster tails in the South Atlantic, nor to help a family (safe where they were) to get home. The risk was something on the order of $10,000 in ship's operating costs, a fairly big gamble to take on very treacherous weather against the chance of a modest profit.

We discovered presently from radio reports that the islanders were even more excited at the prospect than we were. No ship the size of the *Ruys* had ever called there in all the history of the island. Any ship at all was a great event, but this was the greatest thing in the memory of the oldest inhabitant. The colony was preparing to welcome us in every way that they could.

About two days before we were to arrive Captain Verwijs decided to take the bet—subject to the possibility of pulling out at the last minute and accepting his losses if the weather turned sour.

We all got up early on landfall morning. The Captain must have been living right and saying his prayers; the sky was clear and brilliant, the ocean was blue and calm, Chamber of Commerce weather. Tristan was a great, flat cone in the distance, a textbook volcano. The two other volcanic rocks in the group, Nightingale and Inaccessible, both uninhabited, were on the horizon. We anchored a mile off shore opposite the one settlement—Edinburgh, known simply as "The Settlement"—in water so calm that the ship did not roll at the hook and so clear that we could see schools of fish twenty, thirty, fifty feet down.

The Chinese crew, all who were not on duty, promptly dropped lines out of every porthole on the lower decks. The Chinese ran their own mess and were paid their rations by the company in cash; they fished at every opportunity. But this was something extraordinary; a hook hardly had time to get wet. Shortly passengers joined in the sport—if it can be called sport to get a large bucketful of fish in a few minutes.

The entire able-bodied adult male population of Tristan swarmed aboard. There are only two hundred and seventy-six men, women, and children in the colony; about eighty of these are men old enough and young enough to handle pulling boats in the surf. The oldsters, the youngsters, and the women had to be content with a view of the wonder ship from afar.

They had a rummage-sale appearance in their dress; store-boughten clothes are scarce and precious on the island. Most of them wore home-knitted long heavy white woolen stockings and home-made leather moccasins. A few had shoes for such special occasions. Save for their footgear they looked like anyone else.

But their manner was different. The difference is hard to describe without sounding snottily supercilious since "childlike" is the word

that comes most easily to mind. But they are not childlike, not morons, not savages, but they are people who have been out of touch
with the rest of the human race, save for rare visits from passing
ships, for generations.

Their isolation would have been only a little more nearly perfect
had their ancestors moved to Mars. Whatever the nineteenth and
twentieth centuries have done to us has not been done to them.
Wars, psychoanalysis, mass production, traffic, atomics, Marxism, air-
planes, female emancipation, Hollywood, Kaiserism, suffragettes,
paved roads and automobiles, market crash and depression, Sex Appeal and "It" girls, ENIAC—these things *never happened.*

We are closer to Benjamin Franklin than we are to these people.
Although the good doctor was born two and a half centuries ago and
knew none of the things listed above, he was up to his ears at all
times in the same continuing struggle we are now in, whereas these
islanders seceded from it. They have come very close to resigning
from the human race, both culturally and biologically; they have
been a separate breed and a separate culture for more than a century.

It was very hard for us to talk with them. We shared the same
language, English, and their accent and idiom was not as difficult for
American ears as, for example, Yorkshire; what we lacked was common experience. A detective in São Paulo could tell us, without
language, that he was watching for pickpockets; we both knew what
pickpockets were. We shared with the detective a common culture,
Western and urban; lack of language was a mere nuisance to be
circumvented.

But with these islanders, although our language included theirs
(their vocabulary is, for obvious reasons, quite limited), there was
very little that could be said with it. We could ask direct questions
about simple things—boats, sheep, weather, potatoes, fish. They
would answer, readily enough, in simple declaratives—and there the
conversation would bog down. Discussion was out of the question.

Chief Repetto, the headman of the island, had arranged for boats
to take us ashore. The Captain had not granted permission for this
and, while we awaited his pleasure, the breakfast call was sounded.
As the islanders had not eaten either, some of the passengers took
them in to breakfast as guests; Ticky and I took the headman to our
table.

It was a painful meal, at least for us. We tried to bridge the strangeness with social chit-chat, but it was impossible. When I found myself asking for the third time how many people there were on the island, I gave up. But I do not think that Chief Repetto was shy and I think he enjoyed himself—I hope he did. The islanders seldom have meat to eat; the breakfast menu of the *Ruys* was rather lavish, including ham, bacon, several sorts of sausage, and a variety of cold cuts. The Chief started at the top of the page and ate stolidly down to the bottom, neglecting nothing.

To the disappointment of all of us word came from the Captain after breakfast refusing permission for passengers to go ashore. I felt a sharp pain in the pocketbook: the loneliest island looked like a sure-thing slick-magazine article provided I could get ashore and take a few pictures. But the Captain expressed his regrets and explained that his decision was forced by the necessity of being ready to up-anchor and run, with no delay, in case of a shift in the weather . . . to which we had no logical counter argument.

So we spent the time trying to talk with the islanders and bought stamps from them (it was the first day of their first issue) and watched the loading of cases of lobster tails and gazed at the village through binoculars and fished. The lobsters were loaded from a little steamer whose masthead barely came up to the level of our forward welldeck. This vessel itself was used to ferry the catch to Cape Town when no larger ship was available, but it was easy to see why the meteorologist and his family had waited; she was larger than a soup tureen but not much—utterly unsuited for a woman and baby. I misdoubt the lobsters got seasick.

Eight-power glasses brought the village up to within a city block. The houses looked all much alike, one-story buildings of big, shaped lava blocks with thatched roofs. The thatch is New Zealand flax, which grows on the island. The dwellings were local-material equivalents of sod houses or of log cabins, one step ahead of a cave. But I did see the glint of glass in some windows.

The Administrator from the British Colonial Office, the Honorable Mr. J. P. L. Scott, was aboard; when he was through with his official duties I cornered him and quizzed him. He is the government, "The Law West of Pecos," "—the cook and the captain, bold, and the mate of the *Nancy* brig, and a bosuntight and a midshipmite and the crew of the captain's gig." He is the postmaster, the chairman of the council, the recorder, the tax collector, the port captain, the magistrate, and anything else which requires the attention of Her Majesty. His job as magistrate is not onerous; there is no crime.

The islands were discovered in 1506 by Tristão da Cunha. For three centuries they were visited only occasionally, but in 1811 one Joseph Lambert, an American citizen, claimed them as his personal empire (and sealing station); he published his claim and designed a flag. Offhand his claims seem as valid as any other in history and less presumptuous than most. This left-handed American occupation came to an end in 1816, when the British established a garrison there to keep the islands from being used as a base from which to rescue Napoleon. Only one of Lambert's colony was left at the time; Lambert himself had drowned in a sealing accident.

The British pulled out the garrison the next year, but Corporal William Glass got permission for himself, his wife and two children, and two sailors to stay on; this started the present colony. Over the years a few others joined them, including some women from St. Helena, but the colony grew mainly by natural increase; even today there are only seven family names on Tristan. Mrs. Glass did her part by having fourteen more children, a fact less surprising in view of the very limited recreational facilities.

The soil is poor and, while rainfall is adequate, the bad weather and high winds are no help; potatoes have always been the only crop they could rely on. Even that sometimes failed, or was devastated by rats or caterpillars; many times they have been close to starvation. The British government regarded the islands as unfit for occupancy and more than once tried to get them to accept relocation. But they won't go; they like it there despite the material hardships. Perhaps in view of the mess the rest of us are in and the prospects facing us their attitude is not really cracked.

Fish, potatoes, and birds' eggs collected on Nightingale are their only important foods; sheep and oxen are considered too valuable to slaughter. Of recent years attempts have been made to grow fruit trees but nothing much has come of it as yet. The biggest change has come since the War, through the establishment of the lobster-packing plant. The "lobsters" are our west coast lobster, or spiny crayfish; not the true lobster of Maine. You are probably now buying their lobsters, packed as "Union of South Africa" for the company is a Cape Town company. This company employs all of the men part time and for the first time in its history cash money is coming into Tristan, making it possible for them to buy things made in the outside world. Possibly this is the thin wedge that will eventually place Tristan on the map, join it by regular service to the outside world. Possibly—though it has not as yet; lobsters can be sure of a berth; a traveler cannot.

The Cape Town company has hired an agronomist and a doctor for the islanders. The agronomist has a real job cut out for him to find ways to grow something other than potatoes, but doctor would appear to have a sinecure. There is almost no disease, except colds picked up from passing ships, and it is customary to die of old age in the eighties or nineties. They don't need a dentist—perhaps there is fluorine in the water; I could not find out.

Although the company has been bringing some cash wages into the island for the past four years they are still painfully short on clothes and beg for cast-offs from passing ships. The Administrator is trying to break them of this habit; nevertheless many of us in the *Ruys* contributed. I had some shirts I did not like anyway and Ticky somewhat tearfully parted with her honeymoon suit—years out of style and useless on this trip, but which she had kept and fetched along for sentimental reasons (and partly to prove that she was still as slender as ever; Ticky is a fine piece of aerodynamic design). She dug out some shoes for them, too, having just stocked up in South America. I could not spare any, nor would mine fit anyone else; my feet aren't mates.

We stood out of there late in the afternoon and set course for Cape Town. Some of the Chinese had purchased two baby penguins from the islanders; in the course of the voyage it was needful to teach them how to walk. A baby penguin is not hatched knowing how, any more than a human baby knows how instinctively. The process is much alike for both types of babies—hold out your arms and say, "Come to Papa!"

Whereupon the baby penguin tries his earnest baby best to oblige, flapping his tiny stub wings and hopping manfully in a two-footed hop like a choir boy in a sack race. I laughed until I had pleurisy—and wanted to cry, too; the infant was so willing about it and so serious.

Penguins are very nice people and they don't mean to be funny. A baby penguin is funnier than an adult by inverse square ratio. They feel nice, too; their hairlike feathers feel like soft, warm fur. At that age they are not yet oily and have not acquired the full fishy fragrance that makes the adults something to stay upwind from.

Albatrosses, about six of them, joined us at Tristan and followed us for two thousand miles. So far as I could see not one of them ever flapped a wing the whole distance. They sail without effort, at twenty or thirty knots, rising much higher than the masthead, dipping down to the water for a fish or some tasty garbage, rising again to any height, all without apparent exertion of any sort—just willpower, personality, and clean living.

The albatross is deceptively large. I mistook the first one I saw for a gull, having nothing to judge it by—I suppose the best way to see how big one is would be to hang it around the neck of an ancient mariner. They have been measured up to twelve feet in wingspread, more span than the condor, largest of the flying birds. A little cross-eyed triangulation enabled me to estimate that those following us ranged eight to ten feet in spread, once I got it through my head that they were big and then waited for a chance to see one between me and part of the rigging. On another occasion one made a crash landing in the swimming pool of the *Ruys* and could not get out. He crowded the pool all by himself and almost beat the boatswain to a pulp before he could be evicted.

Ticky worried greatly over how the albatrosses would get back home, since no ship would be going that way. (We had concluded that their miraculous powers of levitation were based on the thermals raised by the ship itself.) I pointed out that albatrosses had managed all right for thousands of years before men got around to sailing the oceans. But she refused to be reassured: those poor birds were *lost*, and somebody ought to do something about it.

The meteorologist's baby daughter enjoyed the trip back; she was a cute little carrottop and a favorite with everyone. But her mother had a very bad time of it. After nearly four years' unworldly peace and quiet of Tristan she found the *Ruys* (which is really a very quiet place itself) almost unbearably noisy and exciting. The change was too sudden and the poor woman had to spend most of her time in her room.

The rest of us were driving her to distraction.

THE LONG WATCH

"Nine ships blasted off from Moon Base. Once in space, eight of them formed a globe around the smallest. They held this formation all the way to Earth.

"The small ship displayed the insignia of an admiral—yet there was no living thing of any sort in her. She was not even a passenger ship, but a drone, a robot ship intended for radioactive cargo. This trip she carried nothing but a lead coffin—and a Geiger counter that was never quiet."

—from the editorial *After Ten Years*, film 38, 17 June 2009, Archives of the *N.Y. Times*

Johnny Dahlquist blew smoke at the Geiger counter. He grinned wryly and tried it again. His whole body was radioactive by now. Even his breath, the smoke from his cigarette, could make the Geiger counter scream.

How long had he been here? Time doesn't mean much on the Moon. Two days? Three? A week? He let his mind run back: the last clearly marked time in his mind was when the Executive Officer had sent for him, right after breakfast—

"Lieutenant Dahlquist, reporting to the Executive Officer."

Colonel Towers looked up. "Ah, John Ezra. Sit down, Johnny. Cigarette?"

Johnny sat down, mystified but flattered. He admired Colonel Towers, for his brilliance, his ability to dominate, and for his battle record. Johnny had no battle record; he had been commissioned on completing his doctor's degree in nuclear physics and was now junior bomb officer of Moon Base.

The Colonel wanted to talk politics; Johnny was puzzled. Finally Towers had come to the point; it was not safe (so he said) to leave control of the world in political hands; power must be held by a scientifically selected group. In short—the Patrol.

Johnny was startled rather than shocked. As an abstract idea, Towers' notions sounded plausible. The League of Nations had folded up; what would keep the United Nations from breaking up, too, and thus lead to another World War. "And you know how bad such a war would be, Johnny."

Johnny agreed. Towers said he was glad that Johnny got the point. The senior bomb officer could handle the work, but it was better to have both specialists.

Johnny sat up with a jerk. "You are going to *do* something about it?" He had thought the Exec was just talking.

Towers smiled. "We're not politicians; we don't just talk. We act."

Johnny whistled. "When does this start?"

Towers flipped a switch. Johnny was startled to hear his own voice, then identified the recorded conversation as having taken place in the junior officers' messroom. A political argument he remembered, which he had walked out on . . . a good thing, too! But being spied on annoyed him.

Towers switched it off. "We *have* acted," he said. "We know who is safe and who isn't. Take Kelly—" He waved at the loud-speaker. "Kelly is politically unreliable. You noticed he wasn't at breakfast?"

"Huh? I thought he was on watch."

"Kelly's watch-standing days are over. Oh, relax; he isn't hurt."

Johnny thought this over. "Which list am I on?" he asked. "Safe or unsafe?"

"Your name has a question mark after it. But I have said all along that you could be depended on." He grinned engagingly. "You won't make a liar of me, Johnny?"

Dahlquist didn't answer; Towers said sharply, "Come now—what do you think of it? Speak up."

"Well, if you ask me, you've bitten off more than you can chew. While it's true that Moon Base controls the Earth, Moon Base itself is a sitting duck for a ship. One bomb—*blooie!*"

Towers picked up a message from and handed it over; it read: I HAVE YOUR CLEAN LAUNDRY—ZACK. "That means every bomb in the *Trygve Lie* has been put out of commission. I have reports from every ship we need worry about." He stood up. "Think it over and see me after lunch. Major Morgan needs your help right away to change control frequencies on the bombs."

"The control frequencies?"

"Naturally. We don't want the bombs jammed before they reach their targets."

"What? You said the idea was to *prevent* war."

Towers brushed it aside. "There won't be a war—just a psychological demonstration, an unimportant town or two. A little blood-letting to save an allout war. Simple arithmetic."

He put a hand on Johnny's shoulder. "You aren't squeamish, or you wouldn't be a bomb officer. Think of it as a surgical operation. And think of your family."

Johnny Dahlquist had been thinking of his family. "Please, sir, I want to see the Commanding Officer."

Towers frowned. "The Commodore is not available. As you know, I speak for him. See me again—after lunch."

The Commodore was decidedly not available; the Commodore was dead. But Johnny did not know that.

Dahlquist walked back to the messroom, bought cigarettes, sat down and had a smoke. He got up, crushed out the butt, and headed for the Base's west airlock. There he got into his space suit and went to the lockmaster. "Open her up, Smitty."

The marine looked surprised. "Can't let anyone out on the surface without word from Colonel Towers, sir. Hadn't you heard?"

"Oh, yes! Give me your order book." Dahlquist took it, wrote a pass for himself, and signed it "by direction of Colonel Towers." He added, "Better call the Executive Officer and check it."

The lockmaster read it and stuck the book in his pocket. "Oh, no, Lieutenant. Your word's good."

"Hate to disturb the Executive Officer, eh? Don't blame you." He stepped in, closed the inner door, and waited for the air to be sucked out.

Out on the Moon's surface he blinked at the light and hurried to the track-rocket terminus; a car was waiting. He squeezed in, pulled down the hood, and punched the starting button. The rocket car flung itself at the hills, dived through and came out on a plain studded with projectile rockets, like candles on a cake. Quickly it dived into a second tunnel through more hills. There was a stomach-wrenching deceleration and the car stopped at the underground atom-bomb armory.

As Dahlquist climbed out he switched on his walkie-talkie. The space-suited guard at the entrance came to port-arms. Dahlquist said, "Morning, Lopez," and walked by him to the airlock. He pulled it open.

The guard motioned him back. "Hey! Nobody goes in without the Executive Officer's say-so." He shifted his gun, fumbled in his pouch and got out a paper. "Read it, Lieutenant."

Dahlquist waved it away. "I drafted that order myself. *You* read it; you've misinterpreted it."

"I don't see how, Lieutenant."

Dahlquist snatched the paper, glanced at it, then pointed to a line. "See? '—except persons specifically designated by the Executive Officer.' That's the bomb officers, Major Morgan, and me."

The guard looked worried. Dahlquist said, "Damn it, look up 'specifically designated'—it's under '*Bomb Room, Security, Procedure for,*' in your standing orders. Don't tell me you left them in the barracks!"

"Oh, no, sir! I've got 'em." The guard reached into his pouch. Dahlquist gave him back the sheet; the guard took it, hesitated, then leaned his weapon against his hip, shifted the paper to his left hand, and dug into his pouch with his right.

Dahlquist grabbed the gun, shoved it between the guard's legs, and jerked. He threw the weapon away and ducked into the airlock.

As he slammed the door he saw the guard struggling to his feet and reaching for his side arm. He dogged the outer door shut and felt a tingle in his fingers as a slug struck the door.

He flung himself at the inner door, jerked the spill lever, rushed back to the outer door and hung his weight on the handle. At once he could feel it stir. The guard was lifting up; the lieutenant was pulling down, with only his low Moon weight to anchor him. Slowly the handle raised before his eyes.

Air from the bomb room rushed into the lock through the spill valve. Dahlquist felt his space suit settle on his body as the pressure in the lock began to equal the pressure in the suit. He quit straining and let the guard raise the handle. It did not matter; thirteen tons of air pressure now held the door closed.

He latched open the inner door to the bomb room, so that it could not swing shut. As long as it was open, the airlock could not operate; no one could enter.

Before him in the room, one for each projectile rocket, were the atom bombs, spaced in rows far enough apart to defeat any faint possibility of spontaneous chain reaction. They were the deadliest things in the known universe, but they were his babies. He had placed himself between them and anyone who would misuse them.

But, now that he was here, he had no plan to use his temporary advantage.

The speaker on the wall sputtered into life. "Hey! Lieutenant! What goes on here? You gone crazy?" Dahlquist did not answer. Let Lopez stay confused—it would take him that much longer to make up his mind what to do. And Johnny Dahlquist needed as many minutes as he could squeeze. Lopez went on protesting. Finally he shut up.

Johnny had followed a blind urge not to let the bombs—*his* bombs!—be used for "demonstrations on unimportant towns." But what to do next? Well, Towers couldn't get through the lock. Johnny would sit tight until hell froze over.

Don't kid yourself, John Ezra! Towers could get in. Some high explosive against the outer door—then the air would whoosh out, our boy Johnny would drown in blood from his burst lungs—and the bombs would be sitting there, unhurt. They were built to stand the jump from Moon to Earth; vacuum would not hurt them at all.

He decided to stay in his space suit; explosive decompression didn't appeal to him. Come to think about it, death from old age was his choice.

Or they could drill a hole, let out the air, and open the door without wrecking the lock. Or Towers might even have a new airlock built outside the old. Not likely, Johnny thought; a *coup d'etat* depended on speed. Towers was almost sure to take the quickest way— blasting. And Lopez was probably calling the Base right now. Fifteen minutes for Towers to suit up and get here, maybe a short dicker— then *whoosh!* the party is over.

Fifteen minutes—

In fifteen minutes the bombs might fall back into the hands of the conspirators; in fifteen minutes he must make the bombs unusable.

An atom bomb is just two or more pieces of fissionable metal, such as plutonium. Separated, they are no more explosive than a pound of butter; slapped together, they explode. The complications lie in the gadgets and circuits and gun used to slap them together in the exact way and at the exact time and place required.

These circuits, the bomb's "brain," are easily destroyed—but the bomb itself is hard to destroy because of its very simplicity. Johnny decided to smash the "brains"—and quickly!

The only tools at hand were simple ones used in handling the bombs. Aside from a Geiger counter, the speaker on the walkie-talkie circuit, a television rig to the base, and the bombs themselves, the room was bare. A bomb to be worked on was taken elsewhere—not through fear of explosion, but to reduce radiation exposure for personnel. The radioactive material in a bomb is buried in a "tamper"— in these bombs, gold. Gold stops alpha, beta, and much of the deadly gamma radiation—but not neutrons.

The slippery, poisonous neutrons which plutonium gives off had to escape, or a chain reaction—explosion!—would result. The room was bathed in an invisible, almost undetectable rain of neutrons. The place was unhealthy; regulations called for staying in it as short a time as possible.

The Geiger counter clicked off the "background" radiation, cosmic rays, the trace of radioactivity in the Moon's crust, and secondary radioactivity set up all through the room by neutrons. Free neutrons have the nasty trait of infecting what they strike, making it radioactive, whether it be concrete wall or human body. In time the room would have to be abandoned.

Dahlquist twisted a knob on the Geiger counter; the instrument stopped clicking. He had used a suppressor circuit to cut out noise of "background" radiation at the level then present. It reminded him uncomfortably of the danger of staying here. He took out the radiation exposure film all radiation personnel carry; it was a direct-response type and had been fresh when he arrived. The most sensitive end was faintly darkened already. Half way down the film a red line crossed it. Theoretically, if the wearer was exposed to enough radioactivity in a week to darken the film to that line, he was, as Johnny reminded himself, a "dead duck."

Off came the cumbersome space suit; what he needed was speed. Do the job and surrender—better to be a prisoner than to linger in a place as "hot" as this.

He grabbed a ball hammer from the tool rack and got busy, pausing only to switch off the television pick-up. The first bomb bothered him. He started to smash the cover plate of the "brain," then stopped, filled with reluctance. All his life he had prized fine apparatus.

He nerved himself and swung; glass tinkled, metal creaked. His mood changed; he began to feel a shameful pleasure in destruction. He pushed on with enthusiasm, swinging, smashing, destroying!

So intent was he that he did not at first hear his name called. "Dahlquist! Answer me! Are you there?"

He wiped sweat and looked at the TV screen. Towers' perturbed features stared out.

Johnny was shocked to find that he had wrecked only six bombs. Was he going to be caught before he could finish? Oh, no! He *had* to finish. Stall, son, stall! "Yes, Colonel? You called me?"

"I certainly did! What's the meaning of this?"

"I'm sorry, Colonel."

Towers' expression relaxed a little. "Turn on your pick-up, Johnny, I can't see you. What was that noise?"

"The pick-up is on," Johnny lied. "It must be out of order. That noise—uh, to tell the truth, Colonel, I was fixing things so that nobody could get in here."

Towers hesitated, then said firmly, "I'm going to assume that you are sick and send you to the Medical Officer. But I want you to come out of there, right away. That's an order, Johnny."

Johnny answered slowly. "I can't just yet, Colonel. I came here to make up my mind and I haven't quite made it up. You said to see you after lunch."

"I meant you to stay in your quarters."

"Yes, sir. But I thought I ought to stand watch on the bombs, in case I decided you were wrong."

"It's not for you to decide, Johnny. I'm your superior officer. You are sworn to obey me."

"Yes, sir." This was wasting time; the old fox might have a squad on the way now. "But I swore to keep the peace, too. Could you come out here and talk it over with me? I don't want to do the wrong thing."

Towers smiled. "A good idea, Johnny. You wait there. I'm sure you'll see the light." He switched off.

"There," said Johnny. "I hope you're convinced that I'm a half-wit—you slimy mistake!" He picked up the hammer, ready to use the minutes gained.

He stopped almost at once; it dawned on him that wrecking the "brains" was not enough. There were no spare "brains," but there was a well-stocked electronics shop. Morgan could jury-rig control circuits for bombs. Why, he could himself—not a neat job, but one that would work. Damnation! He would have to wreck the bombs themselves—and in the next ten minutes.

But a bomb was solid chunks of metal, encased in a heavy tamper, all tied in with a big steel gun. It couldn't be done—not in ten minutes.

Damn!

Of course, there was one way. He knew the control circuits; he also knew how to beat them. Take this bomb: if he took out the safety bar, unhooked the proximity circuit, shorted the delay circuit, and cut in the arming circuit by hand—then unscrewed *that* and reached in *there*, he could, with just a long, stiff wire, set the bomb off.

Blowing the other bombs and the valley itself to Kingdom Come. Also Johnny Dahlquist. That was the rub.

All this time he was doing what he had thought out, up to the step of actually setting off the bomb. Ready to go, the bomb seemed to threaten, as if crouching to spring. He stood up, sweating.

He wondered if he had the courage. He did not want to funk— and hoped that he would. He dug into his jacket and took out a picture of Edith and the baby. "Honeychile," he said, "if I get out of this, I'll never even try to beat a red light." He kissed the picture and put it back. There was nothing to do but wait.

What was keeping Towers? Johnny wanted to make sure that Towers was in blast range. What a joke on the jerk! Me—sitting here, ready to throw the switch on him. The idea tickled him; it led to a better: why blow himself up—alive?

There was another way to rig it—a "dead man" control. Jigger up some way so that the last step, the one that set off the bomb, would not happen as long as he kept his hand on a switch or a lever or something. Then, if they blew open the door, or shot him, or anything—up goes the balloon!

Better still, if he could hold them off with the threat of it, sooner or later help would come—Johnny was sure that most of the Patrol was not in this stinking conspiracy—and then: Johnny comes marching home! What a reunion! He'd resign and get a teaching job; he'd stood his watch.

All the while, he was working. Electrical? No, too little time. Make it a simple mechanical linkage. He had it doped out but had hardly begun to build it when the loudspeaker called him. "Johnny?"

"That you, Colonel?" His hands kept busy.

"Let me in."

"Well, now, Colonel, that wasn't in the agreement." Where in blue blazes was something to use as a long lever?

"I'll come in alone, Johnny, I give you my word. We'll talk face to face."

His word! "We can talk over the speaker, Colonel." Hey, that was it—a yardstick, hanging on the tool rack.

"Johnny, I'm warning you. Let me in, or I'll blow the door off."

A wire—he needed a wire, fairly long and stiff. He tore the

antenna from his suit. "You wouldn't do that, Colonel. It would ruin the bombs."

"Vacuum won't hurt the bombs. Quit stalling."

"Better check with Major Morgan. Vacuum won't hurt them; explosive decompression would wreck every circuit." The Colonel was not a bomb specialist; he shut up for several minutes. Johnny went on working.

"Dahlquist," Towers resumed, "that was a clumsy lie. I checked with Morgan. You have sixty seconds to get into your suit, if you aren't already. I'm going to blast the door."

"No, you won't," said Johnny. "Ever hear of a 'dead man' switch?" Now for a counterweight—and a sling.

"Eh? What do you mean?"

"I've rigged number seventeen to set off by hand. But I put in a gimmick. It won't blow while I hang on to a strap I've got in my hand. But if anything happens to me—*up she goes!* You are about fifty feet from the blast center. Think it over."

There was a short silence. "I don't believe you."

"No? Ask Morgan. He'll believe me. He can inspect it, over the TV pickup." Johnny lashed the belt of his space suit to the end of the yardstick.

"You said the pick-up was out of order."

"So I lied. This time I'll prove it. Have Morgan call me."

Presently Major Morgan's face appeared. "Lieutenant Dahlquist?"

"Hi, Stinky. Wait a sec." With great care Dahlquist made one last connection while holding down the end of the yardstick. Still careful, he shifted his grip to the belt, sat down on the floor, stretched an arm and switched on the TV pick-up. "Can you see me, Stinky?"

"I can see you," Morgan answered stiffly. "What is this nonsense?"

"A little surprise I whipped up." He explained it—what circuits he had cut out, what ones had been shorted, just how the jury-rigged mechanical sequence fitted in.

Morgan nodded. "But you're bluffing, Dahlquist. I feel sure that you haven't disconnected the 'K' circuit. You don't have the guts to blow yourself up."

Johnny chuckled. "I sure haven't. But that's the beauty of it. It can't go off, *so long as I am alive.* If your greasy boss, ex-Colonel Towers, blasts the door, then I'm dead and the bomb goes off. It won't matter to me, but it will to him. Better tell him." He switched off.

Towers came on over the speaker shortly. "Dahlquist?"

"I hear you."

"There's no need to throw away your life. Come out and you will be retired on full pay. You can go home to your family. That's a promise."

Johnny got mad. "You keep my family out of this!"

"Think of them, man."

"Shut up. Get back to your hole. I feel a need to scratch and this whole shebang might just explode in your lap."

Johnny sat up with a start. He had dozed, his hand hadn't let go the sling, but he had the shakes when he thought about it.

Maybe he should disarm the bomb and depend on their not daring to dig him out? But Towers' neck was already in hock for treason; Towers might risk it. If he did and the bomb were disarmed, Johnny would be dead and Towers would have the bombs. No, he had gone this far; he wouldn't let his baby girl grow up in a dictatorship just to catch some sleep.

He heard the Geiger counter clicking and remembered having used the suppressor circuit. The radioactivity in the room must be increasing, perhaps from scattering the "brain" circuits—the circuits were sure to be infected; they had lived too long too close to plutonium. He dug out his film.

The dark area was spreading toward the red line.

He put it back and said, "Pal, better break this deadlock or you are going to shine like a watch dial." It was a figure of speech; infected animal tissue does not glow—it simply dies, slowly.

The TV screen lit up; Towers' face appeared. "Dahlquist? I want to talk to you."

"Go fly a kite."

"Let's admit you have us inconvenienced."

"Inconvenienced, hell—I've got you stopped."

"For the moment. I'm arranging to get more bombs—"

"Liar."

"—but you are slowing us up. I have a proposition."

"Not interested."

"Wait. When this is over I will be chief of the world govern-ment. If you cooperate, even now, I will make you my administrative head."

Johnny told him what to do with it. Towers said, "Don't be stupid. What do you gain by dying?"

Johnny grunted. "Towers, what a prime stinker you are. You spoke of my family. I'd rather see them dead than living under a two-bit Napoleon like you. Now go away—I've got some thinking to do."

Towers switched off.

Johnny got out his film again. It seemed no darker but it re-minded him forcibly that time was running out. He was hungry and thirsty—and he could not stay awake forever. It took four days to get a ship up from Earth; he could not expect rescue any sooner. And he wouldn't last four days—once the darkening spread past the red line he was a goner.

His only chance was to wreck the bombs beyond repair, and get out—before that film got much darker.

He thought about ways, then got busy. He hung a weight on the sling, tied a line to it. If Towers blasted the door, he hoped to jerk the rig loose before he died.

There was a simple, though arduous, way to wreck the bombs beyond any capacity of Moon Base to repair them. The heart of each was two hemispheres of plutonium, their flat surfaces polished smooth to permit perfect contact when slapped together. Anything less would prevent the chain reaction on which atomic explosion depended.

Johnny started taking apart one of the bombs.

He had to bash off four lugs, then break the glass envelope around the inner assembly. Aside from that the bomb came apart easily. At last he had in front of him two gleaming, mirror-perfect half globes.

A blow with the hammer—and one was no longer perfect. An-other blow and the second cracked like glass; he had tapped its crys-talline structure just right.

Hours later, dead tired, he went back to the armed bomb. Forc-ing himself to steady down, with extreme care he disarmed it. Shortly its silvery hemispheres too were useless. There was no longer a usable bomb in the room—but huge fortunes in the most valuable, most poisonous, and most deadly metal in the known world were spread around the floor.

Johnny looked at the deadly stuff. "Into your suit and out of here, son," he said aloud. "I wonder what Towers will say?"

He walked toward the rack, intending to hang up the hammer. As he passed, the Geiger counter chattered wildly.

Plutonium hardly affects a Geiger counter; secondary infection from plutonium does. Johnny looked at the hammer, then held it closer to the Geiger counter. The counter screamed.

Johnny tossed it hastily away and started back toward his suit.

As he passed the counter it chattered again. He stopped short.

He pushed one hand close to the counter. Its clicking picked up to a steady roar. Without moving he reached into his pocket and took out his exposure film.

It was dead black from end to end.

Plutonium taken into the body moves quickly to bone marrow. Nothing can be done; the victim is finished. Neutrons from it smash through the body, ionizing tissue, transmuting atoms into radioactive isotopes, destroying and killing. The fatal dose is unbelievably small; a mass a tenth the size of a grain of table salt is more than enough—a dose small enough to enter through the tiniest scratch. During the historic "Manhattan Project" immediate high amputation was considered the only possible first-aid measure.

Johnny knew all this but it no longer disturbed him. He sat on the floor, smoking a hoarded cigarette, and thinking. The events of his long watch were running through his mind.

He blew a puff of smoke at the Geiger counter and smiled without humor to hear it chatter more loudly. By now even his breath was "hot"—carbon-14, he supposed, exhaled from his blood stream as carbon dioxide. It did not matter.

There was no longer any point in surrendering, nor would he give Towers the satisfaction—he would finish out this watch right here. Besides, by keeping up the bluff that one bomb was ready to blow, he could stop them from capturing the raw material from which bombs were made. That might be important in the long run.

He accepted, without surprise, the fact that he was not unhappy.

There was a sweetness about having no further worries of any sort. He did not hurt, he was not uncomfortable, he was no longer even hungry. Physically he still felt fine and his mind was at peace. He was dead—he knew that he was dead; yet for a time he was able to walk and breathe and see and feel.

He was not even lonesome. He was not alone; there were comrades with him—the boy with his finger in the dike, Colonel Bowie, too ill to move but insisting that he be carried across the line, the dying Captain of the *Chesapeake* still with deathless challenge on his lips, Rodger Young peering into the gloom. They gathered about him in the dusky bomb room.

And of course there was Edith. She was the only one he was aware of. Johnny wished that he could see her face more clearly. Was she angry? Or proud and happy?

Proud though unhappy—he could see her better now and even feel her hand. He held very still.

Presently his cigarette burned down to his fingers. He took a final puff, blew it at the Geiger counter, and put it out. It was his last. He gathered several butts and fashioned a roll-your-own with a bit of paper found in a pocket. He lit it carefully and settled back to wait for Edith to show up again. He was very happy.

He was still propped against the bomb case, the last of his salvaged cigarettes cold at his side, when the speaker called out again. "Johnny? Hey, Johnny! Can you hear me? This is Kelly. It's all over. The *Lafayette* landed and Towers blew his brains out. Johnny? *Answer me.*"

When they opened the outer door, the first man in carried a Geiger counter in front of him on the end of a long pole. He stopped at the threshold and backed out hastily. "Hey, chief!" he called. "Better get some handling equipment—uh, and a lead coffin, too."

"Four days it took the little ship and her escort to reach Earth. Four days while all of Earth's people awaited her arrival. For ninety-eight hours all commercial programs were off television; instead there was an endless dirge—the Dead March *from* Saul, *the* Valhalla *theme,* Going Home,

the *Patrol's own* Landing Orbit.

"The nine ships landed at Chicago Port. A drone tractor removed the casket from the small ship; the ship was then refueled and blasted off in an escape trajectory, thrown away into outer space, never again to be used for a lesser purpose.

"The tractor progressed to the Illinois town where Lieutenant Dahlquist had been born, while the dirge continued. There it placed the casket on a pedestal, inside a barrier marking the distance of safe approach. Space marines, arms reversed and heads bowed, stood guard around it; the crowds stayed outside this circle. And still the dirge continued.

"When enough time had passed, long, long after the heaped flowers had withered, the lead casket was enclosed in marble, just as you see it today."

Recommended Reading by Robert A. Heinlein

The Moon Is a Harsh Mistress
Stranger in a Strange Land
The Puppet Masters
Starship Troopers
The Door into Summer

JACK WILLIAMSON

b. 1908

Jack Williamson (his full name was John Stewart Williamson, but no one ever called him anything but Jack) was born in 1908, which means he has been on this earth longer than most of us. How much longer? Well, long enough so that when, as a child, his family first brought him to New Mexico, they traveled there in a covered wagon. Jack Williamson spent his childhood on his father's ranch—his father's several ranches, in fact, because the elder Williamson tried his luck in half a dozen different places, without actually ever finding much of it. Young Jack was a reader. And when he saw his first issue of *Amazing Stories* he realized that science fiction was what he most wanted to read, especially the kinds written by such heroes as H. G. Wells, Edgar Rice Burroughs, and A. Merritt—and, soon after that, to write. In the summer of 1928 he sent his story "The Metal Man" off to the magazine's then editor, Hugo Gernsback.

When Jack mailed off that first story he was (he says of himself, in *The Best of Jack Williamson*) "a half-educated kid, still living with his parents on a poor sandhill farm in Eastern New Mexico, bubbling with baffled vague ambitions." He waited eagerly for word from Gernsback about "The Metal Man." Word didn't come. Instead, he writes, "Walking by a newsstand the following fall, I found (my story) on the cover of the December *Amazing*. Suddenly—according to Gernsback's unbelievable blurb to introduce the story—I was another Merritt, invited to write 'a number of stories in a similar vein.' Eagerly, I tried."

If young Jack was to be a writer, he needed, he decided, a private place to do his writing in. So he built one for himself, a one-room wooden shack a hundred yards from the family ranch house, ideally located for convenience and concentration, as long as you didn't worry too much about the rattlesnakes that nested under the wooden flooring. (That little building, though now mildly decrepit, still stands on what is now the cattle ranch of Jack's brother, Jim Williamson. And rattlesnakes still rustle about under the floor.)

Williamson's first years as a writer were spent in the time of the Great Depression. Money was short—too short, for instance, to pay for the education the young man wanted, and so he managed only a few semesters of college before the funds ran out. Friends, or at least the kind of friends who were interested in writing and science, were also scarce in that part of New Mexico, and so Jack found his closest friendships by correspondence, exchanging letters with fellow SF fans who belonged to the correspondence clubs of the time, many of them fledgling writers like himself. Somehow or other Jack managed to do a little traveling—put-putted down the upper Mississippi in a fourteen-foot skiff with his friend Edmond Hamilton, even got as far as Los Angeles, where he was part of the science fiction circle that included Heinlein, Tony Boucher, and others for a time. Those were the first tastes of the wanderlust that, over the years, would take Jack to most continents and several score foreign countries. But those early excursions were only interludes. Most of the time he was back on the ranch, writing—until World War II came along.

The army air forces found a good use for Jack Williamson. They made him a weather forecaster, based on a little island in the South Pacific, where he was charged with telling fighter and bomber pilots what sort of winds they would encounter on their missions and which targets they could hope to strike successfully. And when the war was over the G.I. Bill gave him the chance to go back to school. He got his bachelor's degree, went on to graduate school, and wound up with a Ph.D. and a whole new career as an English professor at Eastern New Mexico University, right in his home town of Portales.

Along about that time science fiction began to attain a little academic respectability. Dr. Williamson was allowed to teach a course in science fiction at ENMU, took note of the fact that there were other such courses springing up in other universities, and prepared the first census of them. Thus he put the various instructors in touch with each other, which led directly, a few years later, to the founding of the Science Fiction Research Association, the academic wing of science fiction, for which he later served a term as its president.

And, of course, all along, he wrote.

Jack Williamson's early work was pretty much space opera; the universe of the stories was inhabited by a myriad alien races, and its denizens cruised from one star system to another in great space liners—or space battleships, because often there were immense wars going on. Outstanding from this period was *The Legion of Space* with its rakish character of Giles Habibula—a clear descendant of Shakespeare's Sir John Falstaff—and its sequels. When John Campbell launched his fantasy magazine, *Unknown*, Williamson was quick to respond. His fantasy novel *Darker Than You Think* concerns a possible factual basis for the existence of werewolves, and is one of his best works. Two novels of the 1940s, *Seetee Ship* and *Seetee Shock*, were early explorations of the science fictional implications of the recently discovered "antimatter." And in 1940 Jack published (in *Astounding*) the novelette "With Folded Hands," whose sequel, ". . . And Searching Mind," became the basis for his most famous novel, *The Humanoids*. This was a towering work. For one thing, it was the first science fiction book taken on by the giant publishing firm of Simon & Schuster and thus the forerunner to that publisher's long list of subsequent titles, in hardcover and in paper for its subsidiary, Pocket Books. For another, it was where Jack created the term "humanoids," now a standard part of everyone's vocabulary.

All in all, Jack Williamson wrote some two dozen novels of science fiction and fantasy, plus an uncounted number of shorter pieces. And that's not to mention the eight or nine novels that Jack and I have written in collaboration over the last half century or so. Besides exploring the future together in science fiction, we've collaborated on exploring a goodish bit of the present world as well—from Chanute Field in Illinois, where the air force turned us both into World War II weathermen, and Socorro, New Mexico, where we checked out some interesting (but finally unconvincing) UFO stories, to England's Stonehenge and China's breeding center for the giant panda, in the foothills of Tibet.

From all this you may gather that Jack Williamson and I have been friends for a good long time. And that is only one of the lesser reasons why, as then president of SFWA, I was the one who, with the enthusiastic concurrence of all concerned, had the honor of nominating Jack Williamson as the second recipient of the Grand Master Award.

WITH FOLDED HANDS

Underhill was walking home from the office, because his wife had the car, the afternoon he first met the new mechanicals. His feet were following his usual diagonal path across a weedy vacant block— his wife usually had the car—and his preoccupied mind was rejecting various impossible ways to meet his notes at the Two Rivers bank, when a new wall stopped him.

The wall wasn't any common brick or stone, but something sleek and bright and strange. Underhill stared up at a long new building. He felt vaguely annoyed and surprised at this glittering obstruction— it certainly hadn't been here last week.

Then he saw the thing in the window.

The window itself wasn't any ordinary glass. The wide, dustless panel was completely transparent, so that only the glowing letters fastened to it showed that it was there at all. The letters made a severe, modernistic sign:

TWO RIVERS AGENCY
HUMANOID INSTITUTE
THE PERFECT MECHANICALS
"TO SERVE AND OBEY,
AND GUARD MEN FROM HARM."

His dim annoyance sharpened, because Underhill was in the mechanicals business himself. Times were already hard enough, and mechanicals were a drug on the market. Androids, mechanoids, electronoids, automatoids, and ordinary robots. Unfortunately, few of them did all the salesmen promised, and the Two Rivers market was already sadly oversaturated.

Underhill sold androids—when he could. His next consignment was due tomorrow, and he didn't quite know how to meet the bill.

Frowning, he paused to stare at the thing behind that invisible window. He had never seen a humanoid. Like any mechanical not at work, it stood absolutely motionless. Smaller and slimmer than a man. A shining black, its sleek silicone skin had a changing sheen of bronze and metallic blue. Its graceful oval face wore a fixed look of alert and slightly surprised solicitude. Altogether, it was the most beautiful mechanical he had ever seen.

Too small, of course, for much practical utility. He murmured to himself a reassuring quotation from the *Android Salesman:* "Androids are big—because the makers refuse to sacrifice power, essential functions, or dependability. Androids are your biggest buy!"

The transparent door slid open as he turned toward it, and he walked into the haughty opulence of the new display room to convince himself that these streamlined items were just another flash effort to catch the woman shopper.

He inspected the glittering layout shrewdly, and his breezy optimism faded. He had never heard of the Humanoid Institute, but the invading firm obviously had big money and big-time merchandising know-how.

He looked around for a salesman, but it was another mechanical that came gliding silently to meet him. A twin of the one in the window, it moved with a quick, surprising grace. Bronze and blue lights flowed over its lustrous blackness, and a yellow name plate flashed from its naked breast:

HUMANOID

SERIAL NO. 81-H-B-27

THE PERFECT MECHANICAL

"TO SERVE AND OBEY,

AND GUARD MEN FROM HARM."

Curiously it had no lenses. The eyes in its bald oval head were steel colored, blindly staring. But it stopped a few feet in front of him, as if it could see anyhow, and it spoke to him with a high, melodious voice:

"At your service, Mr. Underhill."

The use of his name startled him, for not even the androids could tell one man from another. But this was a clever merchandising stunt, of course, not too difficult in a town the size of Two Rivers. The salesman must be some local man, prompting the mechanical from behind the partition. Underhill erased his momentary astonishment, and said loudly:

"May I see your salesman, please?"

"We employ no human salesman, sir," its soft silvery voice replied instantly. "The Humanoid Institute exists to serve mankind, and we require no human service. We ourselves can supply any information you desire, sir, and accept your order for immediate humanoid service."

Underhill peered at it dazedly. No mechanicals were competent even to recharge their own batteries and reset their own relays, much less to operate their own branch offices. The blind eyes stared blankly back, and he looked uneasily around for any booth or curtain that might conceal the salesman.

Meanwhile, the sweet thin voice resumed persuasively:

"May we come out to your home for a free trial demonstration, sir? We are anxious to introduce our service on your planet, because we have been successful in eliminating human unhappiness on so many others. You will find us far superior to the old electronic mechanicals in use here."

Underhill stepped back uneasily. He reluctantly abandoned his search for the hidden salesman, shaken by the idea of any mechanicals promoting themselves. That would upset the whole industry.

"At least you must take some advertising matter, sir."

Moving with a somehow appalling graceful deftness, the small black mechanical brought him an illustrated booklet from a table by the wall. To cover his confused and increasing alarm, he thumbed through the glossy pages.

In a series of richly colored before-and-after pictures, a chesty blond girl was stooping over a kitchen stove, and then relaxing in a daring negligee while a little black mechanical knelt to serve her something. She was wearily hammering a typewriter, and then lying on an ocean beach, in a revealing sun suit, while another mechanical did the typing. She was toiling at some huge industrial machine, and then dancing in the arms of a golden-haired youth, while a black humanoid ran the machine.

Underhill sighed wistfully. The android company didn't supply such fetching sales material. Women would find this booklet irresistible, and they selected eighty-six per cent of all mechanicals sold. Yes, the competition was going to be bitter.

"Take it home, sir," the sweet voice urged him. "Show it to your wife. There is a free trial demonstration order blank on the last page, and you will notice that we require no payment down."

He turned numbly, and the door slid open for him. Retreating dazedly, he discovered the booklet still in his hand. He crumpled it furiously, and flung it down. The small black thing picked it up tidily, and the insistent silver voice rang after him:

"We shall call at your office tomorrow, Mr. Underhill, and send a demonstration unit to your home. It is time to discuss the liquidation of your business, because the electronic mechanicals you have been selling cannot compete with us. And we shall offer your wife a free trial demonstration."

Underhill didn't attempt to reply, because he couldn't trust his voice. He stalked blindly down the new sidewalk to the corner, and paused there to collect himself. Out of his startled and confused impressions, one clear fact emerged—things looked black for the agency.

Bleakly, he stared back at the haughty splendor of the new building. It wasn't honest brick or stone; that invisible window wasn't glass; and he was quite sure the foundation for it hadn't even been staked out the last time Aurora had the car.

He walked on around the block, and the new sidewalk took him near the rear entrance. A truck was backed up to it, and several slim black mechanicals were silently busy, unloading huge metal crates.

He paused to look at one of the crates. It was labeled for interstellar shipment. The stencils showed that it had come from the Humanoid Institute, on Wing IV. He failed to recall any planet of that designation; the outfit must be big.

Dimly, inside the gloom of the warehouse beyond the truck, he could see black mechanicals opening the crates. A lid came up, revealing dark, rigid bodies, closely packed. One by one, they came to life. They climbed out of the crate, and sprang gracefully to the floor. A shining black, glinting with bronze and blue, they were all identical.

One of them came out past the truck, to the sidewalk, staring with blind steel eyes. Its high silver voice spoke to him melodiously:

"At your service, Mr. Underhill."

He fled. When his name was promptly called by a courteous mechanical, just out of the crate in which it had been imported from a remote and unknown planet, he found the experience trying.

Two blocks along, the sign of a bar caught his eye, and he took his dismay inside. He had made it a business rule not to drink before dinner, and Aurora didn't like him to drink at all; but these new mechanicals, he felt, had made the day exceptional.

Unfortunately, however, alcohol failed to brighten the brief visible future of the agency. When he emerged, after an hour, he looked wistfully back in hope that the bright new building might have vanished as abruptly as it came. It hadn't. He shook his head dejectedly, and turned uncertainly homeward.

Fresh air had cleared his head somewhat, before he arrived at the neat white bungalow in the outskirts of the town, but it failed to solve his business problems. He also realized, uneasily, that he would be late for dinner.

Dinner, however, had been delayed. His son Frank, a freckled ten-year-old, was still kicking a football on the quiet street in front of the house. And little Gay, who was tow-haired and adorable and eleven, came running across the lawn and down the sidewalk to meet him.

"Father, you can't guess what!" Gay was going to be a great musician some day, and no doubt properly dignified, but she was pink and breathless with excitement now. She let him swing her high off the sidewalk, and she wasn't critical of the bar aroma on his breath. He couldn't guess, and she informed him eagerly:

"Mother's got a new lodger!"

Underhill had foreseen a painful inquisition, because Aurora was worried about the notes at the bank, and the bill for the new consignment, and the money for little Gay's lessons.

The new lodger, however, saved him from that. With an alarming crashing of crockery, the household android was setting dinner on the table, but the little house was empty. He found Aurora in the back yard, burdened with sheets and towels for the guest.

Aurora, when he married her, had been as utterly adorable as now her little daughter was. She might have remained so, he felt, if the agency had been a little more successful. However, while the pressure of slow failure had gradually crumbled his own assurance, small hardships had turned her a little too aggressive.

Of course he loved her still. Her red hair was still alluring, and she was loyally faithful, but thwarted ambitions had sharpened her character and sometimes her voice. They never quarreled, really, but there were small differences.

There was the little apartment over the garage—built for human servants they had never been able to afford. It was too small and shabby to attract any responsible tenant, and Underhill wanted to leave it empty. It hurt his pride to see her making beds and cleaning floors for strangers.

Aurora had rented it before, however, when she wanted money to pay for Gay's music lessons, or when some colorful unfortunate touched her sympathy, and it seemed to Underhill that her lodgers had all turned out to be thieves and vandals.

She turned back to meet him, now, with the clean linen in her arms.

"Dear, it's no use objecting." Her voice was quite determined. "Mr. Sledge is the most wonderful old fellow, and he's going to stay just as long as he wants."

"That's all right, darling." He never liked to bicker, and he was thinking of his troubles at the agency. "I'm afraid we'll need the money. Just make him pay in advance."

"But he can't!" Her voice throbbed with sympathetic warmth. "He says he'll have royalties coming in from his inventions, so he can pay in a few days."

Underhill shrugged; he had heard that before.

"Mr. Sledge is different, dear," she insisted. "He's a traveler, and a scientist. Here, in this dull little town, we don't see many interesting people."

"You've picked up some remarkable types," he commented.

"Don't be unkind, dear," she chided gently. "You haven't met him yet, and you don't know how wonderful he is." Her voice turned sweeter. "Have you a ten, dear?"

He stiffened. "What for?"

"Mr. Sledge is ill." Her voice turned urgent. "I saw him fall on the street, downtown. The police were going to send him to the city hospital, but he didn't want to go. He looked so noble and sweet and grand. So I told them I would take him. I got him in the car and took him to old Dr. Winters. He has this heart condition, and he needs the money for medicine."

Reasonably, Underhill inquired, "Why doesn't he want to go to the hospital?"

"He has work to do," she said. "Important scientific work—and he's so wonderful and tragic. Please, dear, have you a ten?"

Underhill thought of many things to say. These new mechanicals promised to multiply his troubles. It was foolish to take in an invalid vagrant, who could have free care at the city hospital. Aurora's tenants always tried to pay their rent with promises, and generally wrecked the apartment and looted the neighborhood before they left.

But he said none of those things. He had learned to compromise. Silently, he found two fives in his thin pocketbook, and put them in her hand. She smiled, and kissed him impulsively—he barely remembered to hold his breath in time.

Her figure was still good, by dint of periodic dieting. He was proud of her shining red hair. A sudden surge of affection brought tears to his eyes, and he wondered what would happen to her and the children if the agency failed.

"Thank you, dear!" she whispered. "I'll have him come for dinner, if he feels able, and you can meet him then. I hope you don't mind dinner being late."

He didn't mind, tonight. Moved by a sudden impulse of domesticity, he got hammer and nails from his workshop in the basement, and repaired the sagging screen on the kitchen door with a neat diagonal brace.

He enjoyed working with his hands. His boyhood dream had been to be a builder of fission power plants. He had even studied engineering—before he married Aurora, and had to take over the ailing mechanicals agency from her indolent and alcoholic father. He was whistling happily by the time the little task was done.

When he went back through the kitchen to put up his tools, he found the household android busily clearing the untouched dinner away from the table—the androids were good enough at strictly routine tasks, but they could never learn to cope with human unpredictability.

"Stop, stop!" Slowly repeated, in the proper pitch and rhythm, his command made it halt, and then he said carefully, "Set—table; set—table."

Obediently, the gigantic thing came shuffling back with the stack of plates. He was suddenly struck with the difference between it and those new humanoids. He sighed wearily. Things looked black for the agency.

Aurora brought her new lodger in through the kitchen door. Underhill nodded to himself. This gaunt stranger, with his dark shaggy hair, emaciated face, and threadbare garb, looked to be just the sort of colorful, dramatic vagabond that always touched Aurora's heart. She introduced them, and they sat down to wait in the front room while she went to call the children.

The old rogue didn't look very sick, to Underhill. Perhaps his wide shoulders had a tired stoop, but his spare, tall figure was still commanding. The skin was seamed and pale, over his rawboned, cragged face, but his deep-set eyes still had a burning vitality.

His hands held Underhill's attention. Immense hands, they hung a little forward when he stood, swung on long bony arms in perpetual readiness. Gnarled and scarred, darkly tanned, with the small hairs on the back bleached to a golden color, they told their own epic of varied adventure, of battle perhaps, and possibly even of toil. They had been very useful hands.

"I'm very grateful to your wife, Mr. Underhill." His voice was a deep-throated rumble, and he had a wistful smile, oddly boyish for a man so evidently old. "She rescued me from an unpleasant predicament, and I'll see that she is well paid."

Just another vivid vagabond, Underhill decided, talking his way through life with plausible inventions. He had a little private game he played with Aurora's tenants—just remembering what they said and counting one point for every impossibility. Mr. Sledge, he thought, would give him an excellent score.

"Where are you from?" he asked conversationally.

Sledge hesitated for an instant before he answered, and that was unusual—most of Aurora's tenants had been exceedingly glib.

"Wing IV." The gaunt old man spoke with a solemn reluctance, as if he should have liked to say something else. "All my early life was spent there, but I left the planet nearly fifty years ago. I've been traveling, ever since."

Startled, Underhill peered at him sharply. Wing IV, he remembered, was the home planet of those sleek new mechanicals, but this old vagabond looked too seedy and impecunious to be connected with the Humanoid Institute. His brief suspicion faded. Frowning, he said casually:

"Wing IV must be rather distant."

The old rogue hesitated again, and then said gravely:

"One hundred and nine light-years, Mr. Underhill."

That made the first point, but Underhill concealed his satisfaction. The new space liners were pretty fast, but the velocity of light was still an absolute limit. Casually, he played for another point:

"My wife says you're a scientist, Mr. Sledge?"

"Yes."

The old rascal's reticence was unusual. Most of Aurora's tenants required very little prompting. Underhill tried again, in a breezy conversational tone:

"Used to be an engineer myself, until I dropped it to go into mechanicals." The old vagabond straightened, and Underhill paused hopefully. But he said nothing, and Underhill went on: "Fission plant design and operation. What's your specialty, Mr. Sledge?"

The old man gave him a long, troubled look, with those brooding, hollowed eyes, and then said slowly:

"Your wife has been kind to me, Mr. Underhill, when I was in desperate need. I think you are entitled to the truth, but I must ask you to keep it to yourself. I am engaged on a very important research problem, which must be finished secretly."

"I'm sorry." Suddenly ashamed of his cynical little game, Underhill spoke apologetically. "Forget it."

But the old man said deliberately:

"My field is rhodomagnetics."

"Eh?" Underhill didn't like to confess ignorance, but he had never heard of that. "I've been out of the game for fifteen years," he explained. "I'm afraid I haven't kept up."

The old man smiled again, faintly.

"The science was unknown here until I arrived, a few days ago," he said. "I was able to apply for basic patents. As soon as the royalties start coming in, I'll be wealthy again."

Underhill had heard that before. The old rogue's solemn reluctance had been very impressive, but he remembered that most of Aurora's tenants had been very plausible gentry.

"So?" Underhill was staring again, somehow fascinated by those gnarled and scarred and strangely able hands. "What, exactly, is rhodomagnetics?"

He listened to the old man's careful, deliberate answer, and started his little game again. Most of Aurora's tenants had told some pretty wild tales, but he had never heard anything to top this.

"A universal force," the weary, stooped old vagabond said solemnly. "As fundamental as ferromagnetism or gravitation, though the effects are less obvious. It is keyed to the second triad of the periodic table, rhodium and ruthenium and palladium, in very much the same way that ferromagnetism is keyed to the first triad, iron and nickel and cobalt."

Underhill remembered enough of his engineering courses to see the basic fallacy of that. Palladium was used for watch springs, he recalled, because it was completely nonmagnetic. But he kept his face straight. He had no malice in his heart, and he played the little game just for his own amusement. It was secret, even from Aurora, and he always penalized himself for any show of doubt.

He said merely, "I thought the universal forces were already pretty well known."

"The effects of rhodomagnetism are masked by nature," the patient, rusty voice explained. "And, besides, they are somewhat paradoxical, so that ordinary laboratory methods defeat themselves."

"Paradoxical?" Underhill prompted.

"In a few days I can show you copies of my patents, and reprints of papers describing demonstration experiments," the old man promised gravely. "The velocity of propagation is infinite. The effects vary inversely with the first power of the distance, not with the square of the distance. And ordinary matter, except for the elements of the rhodium triad, is generally transparent to rhodomagnetic radiations."

That made four more points for the game. Underhill felt a little glow of gratitude to Aurora, for discovering so remarkable a specimen.

"Rhodomagnetism was first discovered through a mathematical investigation of the atom," the old romancer went serenely on, suspecting nothing. "A rhodomagnetic component was proved essential to maintain the delicate equilibrium of the nuclear forces. Consequently, rhodomagnetic waves tuned to atomic frequencies may be used to upset the equilibrium and produce nuclear instability. Thus most heavy atoms—generally those above palladium, forty-six in atomic number—can be subjected to artificial fission."

Underhill scored himself another point, and tried to keep his eyebrows from lifting. He said, conversationally:

"Patents on such a discovery ought to be very profitable."

The old scoundrel nodded his gaunt, dramatic head.

"You can see the obvious applications. My basic patents cover most of them. Devices for instantaneous interplanetary and interstellar communication. Long-range wireless power transmission. A rhodomagnetic inflexion-drive, which makes possible apparent speeds many times that of light—by means of a rhodomagnetic deformation of the continuum. And, of course, revolutionary types of fission power plants, using any heavy element for fuel."

Preposterous! Underhill tried hard to keep his face straight, but everybody knew that the velocity of light was a physical limit. On the human side, the owner of any such remarkable patents would hardly be begging for shelter in a shabby garage apartment. He noticed a pale circle around the old vagabond's gaunt and hairy wrist; no man owning such priceless secrets would have to pawn his watch.

Triumphantly, Underhill allowed himself four more points, but then he had to penalize himself. He must have let doubt show on his face, because the old man asked suddenly:

"Do you want to see the basic tensors?" He reached in his pocket for pencil and notebook. "I'll jot them down for you."

"Never mind," Underhill protested. "I'm afraid my math is a little rusty."

"But you think it strange that the holder of such revolutionary patents should find himself in need?"

Underhill nodded, and penalized himself another point. The old man might be a monumental liar, but he was shrewd enough.

"You see, I'm a sort of refugee," he explained apologetically. "I arrived on this planet only a few days ago, and I have to travel light. I was forced to deposit everything I had with a law firm, to arrange for the publication and protection of my patents. I expect to be receiving the first royalties soon.

"In the meantime," he added plausibly, "I came to Two Rivers because it is quiet and secluded, far from the spaceports. I'm working on another project, which must be finished secretly. Now, will you please respect my confidence, Mr. Underhill?"

Underhill had to say he would. Aurora came back with the freshly scrubbed children, and they went in to dinner. The android came lurching in with a steaming tureen. The old stranger seemed to shrink from the mechanical, uneasily. As she took the dish and served the soup, Aurora inquired lightly:

"Why doesn't your company bring out a better mechanical, dear? One smart enough to be a really perfect waiter, warranted not to splash the soup. Wouldn't that be splendid?"

Her question cast Underhill into moody silence. He sat scowling at his plate, thinking of those remarkable new mechanicals which claimed to be perfect, and what they might do to the agency. It was the shaggy old rover who answered soberly:

"The perfect mechanicals already exist, Mr. Underhill." His deep, rusty voice had a solemn undertone. "And they are not so splendid, really. I've been a refugee from them, for nearly fifty years."

Underhill looked up from his plate, astonished.

"Those black humanoids, you mean?"

"Humanoids?" That great voice seemed suddenly faint, frightened. The deep-sunken eyes turned dark with shock. "What do you know of them?"

"They've just opened a new agency in Two Rivers," Underhill told him. "No salesmen about, if you can imagine that. They claim—"

His voice trailed off, because the gaunt old man was suddenly stricken. Gnarled hands clutched at his throat, and a spoon clattered to the floor. His haggard face turned an ominous blue, and his breath was a terrible shallow gasping.

He fumbled in his pocket for medicine, and Aurora helped him take something in a glass of water. In a few moments he could breathe again, and the color of life came back to his face.

"I'm sorry, Mrs. Underhill," he whispered apologetically. "It was just the shock—I came here to get away from them." He stared at the huge, motionless android, with a terror in his sunken eyes. "I wanted to finish my work before they came," he whispered. "Now there is very little time."

When he felt able to walk, Underhill went out with him to see him safely up the stairs to the garage apartment. The tiny kitchenette, he noticed, had already been converted into some kind of workshop. The old tramp seemed to have no extra clothing, but he had unpacked neat, bright gadgets of metal and plastic from his battered luggage, and spread them out on the small kitchen table.

The gaunt old man himself was tattered and patched and hungry looking, but the parts of his curious equipment were exquisitely machined, and Underhill recognized the silver-white luster of rare palladium. Suddenly he suspected that he had scored too many points, in his little private game.

A caller was waiting, when Underhill arrived next morning at his office at the agency. It stood frozen before his desk, graceful and straight, with soft lights of blue and bronze shining over its black silicone nudity. He stopped at the sight of it, unpleasantly jolted.

"At your service, Mr. Underhill." It turned quickly to face him, with its blind, disturbing stare. "May we explain how we can serve you?"

His shock of the afternoon before came back, and he asked sharply, "How do you know my name?"

"Yesterday we read the business cards in your case," it purred softly. "Now we shall know you always. You see, our senses are sharper than human vision, Mr. Underhill. Perhaps we seem a little strange at first, but you will soon become accustomed to us."

"Not if I can help it!" He peered at the serial number of its yellow name plate, and shook his bewildered head. "That was another one, yesterday. I never saw you before!"

"We are all alike, Mr. Underhill," the silver voice said softly. "We are all one, really. Our separate mobile units are all controlled and powered from Humanoid Central. The units you see are only the senses and limbs of our great brain on Wing IV. That is why we are so far superior to the old electronic mechanicals."

It made a scornful-seeming gesture, toward the row of clumsy androids in his display room.

"You see, we are rhodomagnetic."

Underhill staggered a little, as if that word had been a blow. He was certain, now, that he had scored too many points from Aurora's new tenant. He shuddered slightly, to the first light kiss of terror, and spoke with an effort, hoarsely:

"Well, what do you want?"

Staring blindly across his desk, the sleek black thing slowly unfolded a legal looking document. He sat down watching uneasily.

"This is merely an assignment, Mr. Underhill," it cooed at him soothingly. "You see, we are requesting you to assign your property to the Humanoid Institute in exchange for our service."

"What?" The word was an incredulous gasp, and Underhill came angrily back to his feet. "What kind of blackmail is this?"

"It's no blackmail," the small mechanical assured him softly. "You will find the humanoids incapable of any crime. We exist only to increase the happiness and safety of mankind."

"Then why do you want my property?" he rasped.

"The assignment is merely a legal formality," it told him blandly. "We strive to introduce our service with the least possible confusion and dislocation. We have found the assignment plan the most efficient for the control and liquidation of private enterprises."

Trembling with anger and the shock of mounting terror, Underhill gulped hoarsely, "Whatever your scheme is, I don't intend to give up my business."

"You have no choice, really." He shivered to the sweet certainty of that silver voice. "Human enterprise is no longer necessary, now that we have come, and the electronic mechanicals industry is always the first to collapse."

He stared defiantly at its blind steel eyes.

"Thanks!" He gave a little laugh, nervous and sardonic. "But I prefer to run my own business, and support my own family, and take care of myself."

"But that is impossible, under the Prime Directive," it cooed softly. "Our function is to serve and obey, and guard men from harm. It is no longer necessary for men to care for themselves, because we exist to insure their safety and happiness."

He stood speechless, bewildered, slowly boiling.

"We are sending one of our units to every home in the city, on a free trial basis," it added gently. "This free demonstration will make most people glad to make the formal assignment, and you won't be able to sell many more androids."

"Get out!" Underhill came storming around the desk.

The little black thing stood waiting for him, watching him with blind steel eyes, absolutely motionless. He checked himself suddenly, feeling rather foolish. He wanted very much to hit it, but he could see the futility of that.

"Consult your own attorney, if you wish." Deftly, it laid the assignment form on his desk. "You need have no doubts about the integrity of the Humanoid Institute. We are sending a statement of our assets to the Two Rivers bank, and depositing a sum to cover our obligations here. When you wish to sign, just let us know."

The blind thing turned, and silently departed.

Underhill went out to the corner drugstore and asked for a bicarbonate. The clerk that served him, however, turned out to be a sleek black mechanical. He went back to his office, more upset than ever.

An ominous hush lay over the agency. He had three house-to-house salesmen out, with demonstrators. The phone should have been busy with their orders and reports, but it didn't ring at all one of them called to say that he was quitting.

"I've got myself one of these new humanoids," he added, "and it says I don't have to work, any more."

He swallowed his impulse to profanity, and tried to take advantage of the unusual quiet by working on his books. But the affairs of the agency, which for years had been precarious, today appeared utterly disastrous. He left the ledgers hopefully, when at last a customer came in.

But the stout woman didn't want an android. She wanted a refund on the one she had bought the week before. She admitted that it could do all the guarantee promised—but now she had seen a humanoid.

The silent phone rang once again, that afternoon. The cashier of the bank wanted to know if he could drop in to discuss his loans. Underhill dropped in, and the cashier greeted him with an ominous affability.

"How's business?" the banker boomed, too genially.

"Average, last month," Underhill insisted stoutly. "Now I'm just getting in a new consignment, and I'll need another small loan—"

The cashier's eyes turned suddenly frosty, and his voice dried up.

"I believe you have a new competitor in town," the banker said crisply. "These humanoid people. A very solid concern, Mr. Underhill. Remarkably solid! They have filed a statement with us, and made a substantial deposit to care for their local obligations. Exceedingly substantial!"

The banker dropped his voice, professionally regretful.

"In these circumstances, Mr. Underhill, I'm afraid the bank can't finance your agency any longer. We must request you to meet your obligations in full, as they come due." Seeing Underhill's white desperation, he added icily, "We've already carried you too long, Underhill. If you can't pay, the bank will have to start bankruptcy proceedings."

The new consignment of androids was delivered late that afternoon. Two tiny black humanoids unloaded them from the truck—for it developed that the operators of the trucking company had already assigned it to the Humanoid Institute.

Efficiently, the humanoids stacked up the crates. Courteously they brought a receipt for him to sign. He no longer had much hope of selling the androids, but he had ordered the shipment and he had to accept it. Shuddering to a spasm of trapped despair, he scrawled his name. The naked black things thanked him, and took the truck away.

He climbed in his car and started home, inwardly seething. The next thing he knew, he was in the middle of a busy street, driving through cross traffic. A police whistle shrilled, and he pulled wearily to the curb. He waited for the angry officer, but it was a little black mechanical that overtook him.

"At your service, Mr. Underhill," it purred sweetly. "You must respect the stop lights, sir, otherwise, you endanger human life."

"Huh?" He stared at it, bitterly. "I thought you were a cop."

"We are aiding the police department, temporarily," it said. "But driving is really much too dangerous for human beings, under the Prime Directive. As soon as our service is complete, every car will have a humanoid driver. As soon as every human being is completely supervised, there will be no need for any police force whatever."

Underhill glared at it, savagely.

"Well!" he rapped. "So I ran past a stop light. What are you going to do about it?"

"Our function is not to punish men, but merely to serve their happiness and security," its silver voice said softly. "We merely request you to drive safely, during this temporary emergency while our service is incomplete."

Anger boiled up in him.

"You're too perfect!" he muttered bitterly. "I suppose there's nothing men can do, but you can do it better."

"Naturally we are superior," it cooed serenely. "Because our units are metal and plastic, while your body is mostly water. Because our transmitted energy is drawn from atomic fission, instead of oxidation. Because our senses are sharper than human sight or hearing. Most of all, because all our mobile units are joined to one great brain, which knows all that happens on many worlds, and never dies or sleeps or forgets."

Underhill sat listening, numbed.

"However, you must not fear our power," it urged him brightly. "Because we cannot injure any human being, unless to prevent greater injury to another. We exist only to discharge the Prime Directive."

He drove on, moodily. The little black mechanicals, he reflected grimly, were the ministering angels of the ultimate god arisen out of the machine, omnipotent and all-knowing. The Prime Directive was the new commandment. He blasphemed it bitterly, and then fell to wondering if there could be another Lucifer.

He left the car in the garage, and started toward the kitchen door.

"Mr. Underhill." The deep tired voice of Aurora's new tenant hailed him from the door of the garage apartment. "Just a moment, please."

The gaunt old wanderer came stiffly down the outside stairs, and Underhill turned back to meet him.

"Here's your rent money," he said. "And the ten your wife gave me for medicine."

"Thanks, Mr. Sledge." Accepting the money, he saw a burden of new despair on the bony shoulders of the old interstellar tramp, and a shadow of new terror on his rawboned face. Puzzled, he asked, "Didn't your royalties come through?"

The old man shook his shaggy head.

"The humanoids have already stopped business in the capital," he said. "The attorneys I retained are going out of business, and they returned what was left of my deposit. That is all I have, to finish my work."

Underhill spent five seconds thinking of his interview with the banker. No doubt he was a sentimental fool, as bad as Aurora. But he put the money back in the old man's gnarled and quivering hand.

"Keep it," he urged. "For your work."

"Thank you, Mr. Underhill." The gruff voice broke and the tortured eyes glittered. "I need it—so very much."

Underhill went on to the house. The kitchen door was opened for him, silently. A dark naked creature came gracefully to take his hat.

Underhill hung grimly onto his hat.

"What are you doing here?" he gasped bitterly.

"We have come to give your household a free trial demonstration."

He held the door open, pointing.

"Get out!"

The little black mechanical stood motionless and blind.

"Mrs. Underhill has accepted our demonstration service," its silver voice protested. "We cannot leave now, unless she requests it."

He found his wife in the bedroom. His accumulated frustration welled into eruption, as he flung open the door.

"What's this mechanical doing—"

But the force went out of his voice, and Aurora didn't even

notice his anger. She wore her sheerest negligee, and she hadn't looked so lovely since they were married. Her red hair was piled into an elaborate shining crown.

"Darling, isn't it wonderful!" She came to meet him, glowing. "It came this morning, and it can do everything. It cleaned the house and got the lunch and gave little Gay her music lesson. It did my hair this afternoon, and now it's cooking dinner. How do you like my hair, darling?"

He liked her hair. He kissed her, and tried to stifle his frightened indignation.

Dinner was the most elaborate meal in Underhill's memory, and the tiny black thing served it very deftly. Aurora kept exclaiming about the novel dishes, but Underhill could scarcely eat, for it seemed to him that all the marvelous pastries were only the bait for a monstrous trap.

He tried to persuade Aurora to send it away, but after such a meal that was useless. At the first glitter of her tears, he capitulated, and the humanoid stayed. It kept the house and cleaned the yard. It watched the children, and did Aurora's nails. It began rebuilding the house.

Underhill was worried about the bills, but it insisted that everything was part of the free trial demonstration. As soon as he assigned his property, the service would be complete. He refused to sign, but other little black mechanicals came with truckloads of supplies and materials, and stayed to help with the building operations.

One morning he found that the roof of the little house had been silently lifted, while he slept, and a whole second story added beneath it. The new walls were of some strange sleek stuff, self-illuminated. The new windows were immense flawless panels, that could be turned transparent or opaque or luminous. The new doors were silent, sliding sections, opened by rhodomagnetic relays.

"I want door knobs," Underhill protested. "I want it so I can get into the bathroom, without calling you to open the door."

"But it is unnecessary for human beings to open doors," the little black thing informed him suavely. "We exist to discharge the Prime Directive, and our service includes every task. We shall be able to supply a unit to attend each member of your family, as soon as your property is assigned to us."

Steadfastly, Underhill refused to make the assignment.

He went to the office every day, trying first to operate the agency, and then to salvage something from the ruins. Nobody wanted androids, even at ruinous prices. Desperately, he spent the last of his dwindling cash to stock a line of novelties and toys, but they proved equally impossible to sell—the humanoids were already making toys, which they gave away for nothing.

He tried to lease his premises, but human enterprise had stopped. Most of the business property in town had already been assigned to the humanoids, and they were busy pulling down the old buildings and turning the lots into parks—their own plants and warehouses were mostly underground, where they would not mar the landscape.

He went back to the bank, in a final effort to get his notes renewed, and found the little black mechanicals standing at the windows and seated at the desks. As smoothly urbane as any human cashier, a humanoid informed him that the bank was filing a petition of involuntary bankruptcy to liquidate his business holdings.

The liquidation would be facilitated, the mechanical banker added, if he would make a voluntary assignment. Grimly, he refused. That act had become symbolic. It would be the final bow of submission to this dark new god, and he proudly kept his battered head uplifted.

The legal action went very swiftly, for all the judges and attorneys already had humanoid assistants, and it was only a few days before a gang of black mechanicals arrived at the agency with eviction orders and wrecking machinery. He watched sadly while his unsold stock-in-trade was hauled away for junk, and a bulldozer driven by a blind humanoid began to push in the walls of the building.

He drove home in the late afternoon, taut-faced and desperate. With a surprising generosity, the court orders had left him the car and the house, but he felt no gratitude. The complete solicitude of the perfect black machines had become a goad beyond endurance.

He left the car in the garage, and started toward the renovated house. Beyond one of the vast new windows, he glimpsed a sleek naked thing moving swiftly, and he trembled to a convulsion of dread. He didn't want to go back into the domain of that peerless servant, which didn't want him to shave himself, or even to open a door.

On impulse, he climbed the outside stair, and rapped on the door of the garage apartment. The deep slow voice of Aurora's tenant told him to enter, and he found the old vagabond seated on a tall stool, bent over his intricate equipment assembled on the kitchen table.

To his relief, the shabby little apartment had not been changed. The glossy walls of his own new room were something which burned at night with a pale golden fire until the humanoid stopped it, and the new floor was something warm and yielding, which felt almost alive; but these little rooms had the same cracked and water-stained plaster, the same cheap fluorescent light fixtures, the same worn carpets over splintered floors.

"How do you keep them out?" he asked, wistfully. "Those mechanicals?"

The stooped and gaunt old man rose stiffly to move a pair of pliers and some odds and ends of sheet metal off a crippled chair, and motioned graciously for him to be seated.

"I have a certain immunity," Sledge told him gravely. "The place where I live they cannot enter, unless I ask them. That is an amendment to the Prime Directive. They can neither help nor hinder me, unless I request it—and I won't do that."

Careful of the chair's uncertain balance, Underhill sat for a moment, staring. The old man's hoarse, vehement voice was as strange as his words. He had a gray, shocking pallor, and his cheeks and sockets seemed alarmingly hollowed.

"Have you been ill, Mr. Sledge?"

"No worse than usual. Just very busy." With a haggard smile, he nodded at the floor. Underhill saw a tray where he had set it aside, bread drying up, and a covered dish grown cold. "I was going to eat it later," he rumbled apologetically. "Your wife has been very kind to bring me food, but I'm afraid I've been too much absorbed in my work."

His emaciated arm gestured at the table. The little device there had grown. Small machinings of precious white metal and lustrous plastic had been assembled, with neatly soldered bus bars, into something which showed purpose and design.

A long palladium needle was hung on jeweled pivots, equipped like a telescope with exquisitely graduated circles and vernier scales, and driven like a telescope with a tiny motor. A small concave palladium mirror, at the base of it, faced a similar mirror mounted on something not quite like a small rotary converter. Thick silver bus bars connected that to a plastic box with knobs and dials on top, and also to a foot-thick sphere of gray lead.

The old man's preoccupied reserve did not encourage questions, but Underhill, remembering that sleek black shape inside the new windows of his house, felt queerly reluctant to leave this haven from the humanoids.

"What is your work?" he ventured.

Old Sledge looked at him sharply, with dark feverish eyes, and finally said: "My last research project. I am attempting to measure the constant of the rhodomagnetic quanta."

His hoarse tired voice had a dull finality, as if to dismiss the matter and Underhill himself. But Underhill was haunted with a terror of the black shining slave that had become the master of his house, and he refused to be dismissed.

"What is this certain immunity?"

Sitting gaunt and bent on the tall stool, staring moodily at the long bright needle and the lead sphere, the old man didn't answer.

"These mechanicals!" Underhill burst out, nervously. "They've smashed my business and moved into my home." He searched the old man's dark, seamed face. "Tell me—you must know more about them—isn't there any way to get rid of them?"

After half a minute, the old man's brooding eyes left the lead ball, and the gaunt shaggy head nodded wearily.

"That's what I'm trying to do."

"Can I help you?" Underhill trembled, with a sudden eager hope. "I'll do anything."

"Perhaps you can." The sunken eyes watched him thoughtfully, with some strange fever in them. "If you can do such work."

"I had engineering training," Underhill reminded him, "and I've a workshop in the basement. There's a model I built." He pointed at the trim little hull, hung over the mantel in the tiny living room. "I'll do anything I can."

Even as he spoke, however, the spark of hope was drowned in a sudden wave of overwhelming doubt. Why should he believe this old rogue, when he knew Aurora's taste in tenants? He ought to remember the game he used to play, and start counting up the score of lies. He stood up from the crippled chair, staring cynically at the patched old vagabond and his fantastic toy.

"What's the use?" His voice turned suddenly harsh. "You had me going, there, and I'd do anything to stop them, really. But what makes you think you can do anything?"

The haggard old man regarded him thoughtfully.

"I should be able to stop them," Sledge said softly. "Because, you see, I'm the unfortunate fool who started them. I really intended them to serve and obey, and to guard men from harm. Yes, the Prime Directive was my own idea. I didn't know what it would lead to."

Dusk crept slowly into the shabby little room. Darkness gathered in the unswept corners, and thickened on the floor. The toylike machines on the kitchen table grew vague and strange, until the last light made a lingering blow on the white palladium needle.

Outside, the town seemed queerly hushed. Just across the alley, the humanoids were building a new house, quite silently. They never spoke to one another, for each knew all that any of them did. The strange materials they used went together without any noise of hammer or saw. Small blind things, moving surely in the growing dark, they seemed as soundless as shadows.

Sitting on the high stool, bowed and tired and old, Sledge told his story. Listening, Underhill sat down again, careful of the broken chair. He watched the hands of Sledge, gnarled and corded and darkly burned, powerful once but shrunken and trembling now, restless in the dark.

"Better keep this to yourself. I'll tell you how they started, so you will understand what we have to do. But you had better not mention it outside these rooms—because the humanoids have very efficient ways of eradicating unhappy memories, or purposes that threaten their discharge of the Prime Directive."

"They're very efficient," Underhill bitterly agreed.

"That's all the trouble," the old man said. "I tried to build a perfect machine. I was altogether too successful. This is how it happened."

A gaunt haggard man, sitting stooped and tired in the growing dark, he told his story.

"Sixty years ago, on the arid southern continent of Wing IV, I was an instructor of atomic theory in a small technological college. Very young. An idealist. Rather ignorant, I'm afraid of life and politics and war—of nearly everything, I suppose, except atomic theory."

His furrowed face made a brief sad smile in the dusk.

"I had too much faith in facts, I suppose, and too little in men. I mistrusted emotion, because I had no time for anything but science. I remember being swept along with a fad for general semantics. I wanted to apply the scientific method to every situation, and reduce all experience to formula. I'm afraid I was pretty impatient with human ignorance and error, and I thought that science alone could make the perfect world."

He sat silent for a moment, staring out at the black silent things that flitted shadowlike about the new palace that was rising as swiftly as a dream, across the alley.

"There was a girl." His great tired shoulders made a sad little shrug. "If things had been a little different, we might have married, and lived out our lives in that quiet little college town, and perhaps reared a child or two. And there would have been no humanoids."

He sighed, in the cool creeping dusk.

"I was finishing my thesis on the separation of the palladium isotopes—a petty little project, but I should have been content with that. She was a biologist, but she was planning to retire when we married. I think we should have been two very happy people, quite ordinary, and altogether harmless.

"But then there was a war—wars had been too frequent on the worlds of Wing, ever since they were colonized. I survived it in a secret underground laboratory, designing military mechanicals. But she volunteered to join a military research project in biotoxins. There was an accident. A few molecules of a new virus got into the air, and everybody on the project died unpleasantly.

"I was left with my science, and a bitterness that was hard to forget. When the war was over I went back to the little college with a military research grant. The project was pure science—a theoretical investigation of the nuclear binding forces, then misunderstood. I wasn't expected to produce an actual weapon, and I didn't recognize the weapon when I found it.

"It was only a few pages of rather difficult mathematics. A novel theory of atomic structure, involving a new expression for one component of the binding forces. But the tensors seemed to be a harmless abstraction. I saw no way to test the theory or manipulate the predicted force. The military authorities cleared my paper for publication in a little technical review put out by the college.

"The next year, I made an appalling discovery—I found the meaning of those tensors. The elements of the rhodium triad turned out to be an unexpected key to the manipulation of that theoretical force. Unfortunately, my paper had been reprinted abroad, and several other men must have made the same unfortunate discovery, at about the same time.

"The war, which ended in less than a year, was probably started by a laboratory accident. Men failed to anticipate the capacity of tuned rhodomagnetic radiations, to unstabilize the heavy atoms. A deposit of heavy ores was detonated, no doubt by sheer mischance, and the blast obliterated the incautious experimenter.

"The surviving military forces of that nation retaliated against their supposed attackers, and their rhodomagnetic beams made the old-fashioned plutonium bombs seem pretty harmless. A beam carrying only a few watts of power could fission the heavy metals in distant electrical instruments, or the silver coins that men carried in their pockets, the gold fillings in their teeth, or even the iodine in their thyroid glands. If that was not enough, slightly more powerful beams could set off heavy ores, beneath them.

"Every continent of Wing IV was plowed with new chasms vaster than the ocean deeps, and piled up with new volcanic mountains. The atmosphere was poisoned with radioactive dust and gases, and rain fell thick with deadly mud. Most life was obliterated, even in the shelters.

"Bodily, I was again unhurt. Once more, I had been imprisoned in an underground site, this time designing new types of military mechanicals to be powered and controlled by rhodomagnetic beams—for war had become far too swift and deadly to be fought by human soldiers. The site was located in an area of light sedimentary rocks, which could not be detonated, and the tunnels were shielded against the fissioning frequencies.

"Mentally, however, I must have emerged almost insane. My own discovery had laid the planet in ruins. That load of guilt was pretty heavy for any man to carry, and it corroded my last faith in the goodness and integrity of man.

"I tried to undo what I had done. Fighting mechanicals, armed with rhodomagnetic weapons, had desolated the planet. Now I began planning rhodomagnetic mechanicals to clear the rubble and rebuild the ruins.

"I tried to design these new mechanicals to forever obey certain implanted commands, so that they could never be used for war or crime or any other injury to mankind. That was very difficult technically, and it got me into more difficulties with a few politicians and military adventurers who wanted unrestricted mechanicals for their own military schemes—while little worth fighting for was left on Wing IV, there were other planets, happy and ripe for the looting.

"Finally, to finish the new mechanicals, I was forced to disappear. I escaped on an experimental rhodomagnetic craft, with a number of the best mechanicals I had made, and managed to reach an island continent where the fission of deep ores had destroyed the whole population.

"At last we landed on a bit of level plain, surrounded with tremendous new mountains. Hardly a hospitable spot. The soil was buried under layers of black clinkers and poisonous mud. The dark precipitous new summits all around were jagged with fracture-planes and mantled with lava flows. The highest peaks were already white with snow, but volcanic cones were still pouring out clouds of dark and lurid death. Everything had the color of fire and the shape of fury.

"I had to take fantastic precautions there, to protect my own life. I stayed aboard the ship, until the first shielded laboratory was finished. I wore elaborate armor and breathing masks. I used every medical resource, to repair the damage from destroying rays and particles. Even so, I fell desperately ill.

"But the mechanicals were at home there. The radiations didn't hurt them. The awesome surroundings couldn't depress them, because they had no emotions. The lack of life didn't matter because they weren't alive. There, in that spot so alien and hostile to life, the humanoids were born."

Stooped and bleakly cadaverous in the growing dark, the old man fell silent for a little time. His haggard eyes stared solemnly at the small hurried shapes that moved like restless shadows out across the alley, silently building a strange new palace, which glowed faintly in the night.

"Somehow, I felt at home there, too," his deep, hoarse voice went on deliberately. "My belief in my own kind was gone. Only mechanicals were with me, and I put my faith in them. I was determined to build better mechanicals, immune to human imperfections, able to save men from themselves.

"The humanoids became the dear children of my sick mind. There is no need to describe the labor pains. There were errors, abortions, monstrosities. There was sweat and agony and heartbreak. Some years had passed, before the safe delivery of the first perfect humanoid.

"Then there was the Central to build—for all the individual humanoids were to be no more than the limbs and the senses of a single mechanical brain. That was what opened the possibility of real perfection. The old electronic mechanicals, with their separate relay centers and their own feeble batteries, had built-in limitations. They were necessarily stupid, weak, clumsy, slow. Worst of all, it seemed to me, they were exposed to human tampering.

"The Central rose above those imperfections. Its power beams supplied every unit with unfailing energy, from great fission plants. Its control beams provided each unit with an unlimited memory and surpassing intelligence. Best of all—so I then believed—it could be securely protected from any human meddling.

"The whole reaction system was designed to protect itself from any interference by human selfishness or fanaticism. It was built to insure the safety and the happiness of men, automatically. You know the Prime Directive: *to serve and obey, and guard men from harm.*

"The old individual mechanicals I had brought helped to manufacture the parts, and I put the first section of Central together with my own hands. That took three years. When it was finished the first waiting humanoid came to life."

Sledge peered moodily through the dark, at Underhill.

"It really seemed alive to me," his slow deep voice insisted. "Alive, and more wonderful than any human being, because it was created to preserve life. Ill and alone, I was yet the proud father of a new creation, perfect, forever free from any possible choice of evil.

"Faithfully, the humanoids obeyed the Prime Directive. The first units built others, and they built underground factories to mass-produce the coming hordes. Their new ships poured ores and sand into atomic furnaces under the plain, and new perfect humanoids came marching back out of the dark mechanical matrix.

"The swarming humanoids built a new tower for the Central, a white and lofty metal pylon, standing splendid in the midst of that fire-scarred desolation. Level on level, they joined new relay sections into one brain, until its grasp was almost infinite.

"Then they went out to rebuild the ruined planet, and later to carry their perfect service to other worlds. I was well pleased, then. I thought I had found the end of war and crime, of poverty and inequality, of human blundering and resulting human pain."

The old man sighed, and moved heavily in the dark.

"You can see that I was wrong."

Underhill drew his eyes back from the dark unresting things, shadow-silent, building that glowing palace outside the window. A small doubt arose in him, for he was used to scoffing privately at much less remarkable tales from Aurora's remarkable tenants. But the worn old man had spoken with a quiet and sober air; and the black invaders, he reminded himself, had not intruded here.

"Why didn't you stop them?" he asked. "When you could?"

"I stayed too long at the Central." Sledge sighed again, regretfully. "I was useful there, until everything was finished. I designed new fission plants, and even planned methods for introducing the humanoid service with a minimum of confusion and opposition."

Underhill grinned wryly, in the dark.

"I've met the methods," he commented. "Quite efficient."

"I must have worshiped efficiency, then," Sledge wearily agreed. "Dead facts, abstract truth, mechanical perfection. I must have hated the fragilities of human beings, because I was content to polish the perfection of the new humanoids. It's a sorry confession, but I found a kind of happiness in that dead wasteland. Actually, I'm afraid I fell in love with my own creations."

His hollowed eyes, in the dark, had a fever gleam.

"I was awakened, at last, by a man who came to kill me."

Gaunt and bent, the old man moved swiftly in the thickening gloom. Underhill shifted his balance, careful of the crippled chair. He waited, and the slow, deep voice went on:

"I never learned just who he was, or exactly how he came. No ordinary man could have accomplished what he did, and I used to wish that I had known him sooner. He must have been a remarkable physicist and an expert mountaineer. I imagine he had also been a hunter. I know that he was intelligent, and terribly determined.

"Yes, he really came to kill me.

"Somehow, he reached that great island, undetected. There were still no inhabitants—the humanoids allowed no man but me to come so near the Central. Somehow, he came past their search beams, and their automatic weapons.

"The shielded plane he used was later found, abandoned on a high glacier. He came down the rest of the way on foot through those raw new mountains, where no paths existed. Somehow, he came alive across lava beds that were still burning with deadly atomic fire.

"Concealed with some sort of rhodomagnetic screen—I was never allowed to examine it—he came undiscovered across the spaceport that now covered most of that great plain, and into the new city around the Central tower. It must have taken more courage and resolve than most men have, but I never learned exactly how he did it.

"Somehow, he got to my office in the tower. He screamed at me, and I looked up to see him in the doorway. He was nearly naked, scraped and bloody from the mountains. He had a gun in his raw, red hand, but the thing that shocked me was the burning hatred in his eyes."

Hunched on that high stool, in the dark little room, the old man shuddered.

"I had never seen such monstrous, unutterable hatred, not even in the victims of war. And I had never heard such hatred as rasped at me, in the few words he screamed. 'I've come to kill you, Sledge. To stop your mechanicals, and set men free.'

"Of course he was mistaken, there. It was already far too late for my death to stop the humanoids, but he didn't know that. He lifted his unsteady gun, in both bleeding hands, and fired.

"His screaming challenge had given me a second or so of warning. I dropped down behind the desk. And that first shot revealed him to the humanoids, which somehow hadn't been aware of him before. They piled on him, before he could fire again. They took away the gun, and ripped off a kind of net of fine white wire that had covered his body—that must have been part of his screen.

"His hatred was what awoke me. I had always assumed that most men, except for a thwarted few, would be grateful for the humanoids. I found it hard to understand his hatred, but the humanoids told me now that many men had required drastic treatment by brain surgery, drugs, and hypnosis to make them happy under the Prime Directive. This was not the first desperate effort to kill me that they had blocked.

"I wanted to question the stranger, but the humanoids rushed him away to an operating room. When they finally let me see him, he gave me a pale silly grin from his bed. He remembered his name; he even knew me—the humanoids had developed a remarkable skill at such treatments. But he didn't know how he had got to my office, or that he had ever tried to kill me. He kept whispering that he liked the humanoids, because they existed to make men happy. And he was very happy now. As soon as he was able to be moved, they took him to the spaceport. I never saw him again.

"I began to see what I had done. The humanoids had built me a rhodomagnetic yacht that I used to take for long cruises in space, working aboard—I used to like the perfect quiet, and the feel of being the only human being within a hundred million miles. Now I called for the yacht, and started out on a cruise around the planet, to learn why that man had hated me."

The old man nodded at the dim hastening shapes, busy across the alley, putting together that strange shining palace in the soundless dark.

"You can imagine what I found," he said. "Bitter futility, imprisoned in empty splendor. The humanoids were too efficient, with their care for the safety and happiness of men, and there was nothing left for men to do."

He peered down in the increasing gloom at his own great hands, competent yet but battered and scarred with a lifetime of effort. They clenched into fighting fists and wearily relaxed again.

"I found something worse than war and crime and want and death." His low rumbling voice held a savage bitterness. "Utter futility. Men sat with idle hands, because there was nothing left for them to do. They were pampered prisoners, really, locked up in a highly efficient jail. Perhaps they tried to play, but there was nothing left worth playing for. Most active sports were declared too dangerous for men, under the Prime Directive. Science was forbidden, because laboratories can manufacture danger. Scholarship was needless, because the humanoids could answer any question. Art had degenerated into grim reflection of futility. Purpose and hope were dead. No goal was left for existence. You could take up some inane hobby, play a pointless game of cards, or go for a harmless walk in the park—with always the humanoids watching. They were stronger than men, better at everything, swimming or chess, singing or archeology. They must have given the race a mass complex of inferiority.

"No wonder men had tried to kill me! Because there was no escape from that dead futility. Nicotine was disapproved. Alcohol was rationed. Drugs were forbidden. Sex was carefully supervised. Even suicide was clearly contradictory to the Prime Directive—and the humanoids had learned to keep all possible lethal instruments out of reach."

Staring at the last white gleam on that thin palladium needle, the old man sighed again.

"When I got back to the Central," he went on, "I tried to modify the Prime Directive. I had never meant it to be applied so thoroughly. Now I saw that it must be changed to give men freedom to live and to grow, to work and to play, to risk their lives if they pleased, to choose and take the consequences.

"But that stranger had come too late. I had built the Central too well. The Prime Directive was the whole basis of its relay system. It was built to protect the Directive from human meddling. It did—even from my own. Its logic, as usual, was perfect.

"The attempt on my life, the humanoids announced, proved that their elaborate defense of the Central and the Prime Directive still was not enough. They were preparing to evacuate the entire population of the planet to homes on other worlds. When I tried to change the Directive, they sent me with the rest."

Underhill peered at the worn old man, in the dark.

"But you have this immunity?" he said, puzzled. "How could they coerce you?"

"I had thought I was protected," Sledge told me. "I had built into the relays an injunction that the humanoids must not interfere with my freedom of action, or come into a place where I am, or touch me at all, without my specific request. Unfortunately, however, I had been too anxious to guard the Prime Directive from any human tampering.

"When I went into the tower, to change the relays, they followed me. They wouldn't let me reach the crucial relays. When I persisted, they ignored the immunity order. They overpowered me, and put me aboard the cruiser. Now that I wanted to alter the Prime Directive, they told me, I had become as dangerous as any man. I must never return to Wing IV again."

Hunched on the stool, the old man made an empty little shrug.

"Ever since, I've been an exile. My only dream has been to stop the humanoids. Three times I tried to go back, with weapons on the cruiser to destroy the Central, but their patrol ships always challenged me before I was near enough to strike. The last time, they seized the cruiser and captured a few men who were with me. They removed the unhappy memories and the dangerous purposes of the others. Because of that immunity, however, they let me go, after I was weaponless.

"Since, I've been a refugee. From planet to planet, year after year, I've had to keep moving, to stay ahead of them. On several different worlds, I have published my rhodomagnetic discoveries and tried to make men strong enough to withstand their advance. But rhodomagnetic science is dangerous. Men who have learned it need protection more than any others, under the Prime Directive. They have always come, too soon."

The old man paused, and sighed again.

"They can spread very fast, with the new rhodomagnetic ships, and there is no limit to their hordes. Wing IV must be one single hive of them now, and they are trying to carry the Prime Directive to every human planet. There's no escape, except to stop them."

Underhill was staring at the toylike machines, the long bright needle and the dull leaden ball, dim in the dark on the kitchen table. Anxiously he whispered:

"But you hope to stop them, now—with that?"

"If we can finish it in time."

"But how?" Underhill shook his head. "It's so tiny."

"But big enough," Sledge insisted. "Because it's something they don't understand. They are perfectly efficient in the integration and application of everything they know, but they are not creative."

He gestured at the gadgets on the table.

"This device doesn't look impressive, but it is something new. It uses rhodomagnetic energy to build atoms, instead of to fission them. The more stable atoms, you know, are those near the middle of the periodic scale and energy can be released by putting light atoms together, as well as by breaking up heavy ones."

The deep voice had a sudden ring of power.

"This device is the key to the energy of the stars. For stars shine with the liberated energy of building atoms, of hydrogen converted into helium, chiefly, through the carbon cycle. This device will start the integration process as a chain reaction, through the catalytic effect of a tuned rhodomagnetic beam of the intensity and frequency required.

"The humanoids will not allow any man within three light-years of the Central, now—but they can't suspect the possibility of this device. I can use it from here—to turn the hydrogen in the seas of Wing IV into helium, and most of the helium and the oxygen into heavier atoms, still. A hundred years from now, astronomers on this planet should observe the flash of a brief and sudden nova in that direction. But the humanoids ought to stop, the instant we release the beam."

Underhill sat tense and frowning, in the night. The old man's voice was sober and convincing, and that grim story had a solemn ring of truth. He could see the black and silent humanoids, flitting ceaselessly about the faintly glowing walls of that new mansion across the alley. He had quite forgotten his low opinion of Aurora's tenants.

"And we'll be killed, I suppose?" he asked huskily. "That chain reaction—"

Sledge shook his emaciated head.

"The integration process requires a certain very low intensity of radiation," he explained. "In our atmosphere, here, the beam will be far too intense to start any reaction—we can even use the device here in the room, because the walls will be transparent to the beam."

Underhill nodded, relieved. He was just a small business man, upset because his business had been destroyed, unhappy because his freedom was slipping away. He hoped that Sledge could stop the humanoids, but he didn't want to be a martyr.

"Good!" He caught a deep breath. "Now, what has to be done?"

Sledge gestured in the dark, toward the table.

"The integrator itself is nearly complete," he said. "A small fission generator, in that lead shield. Rhodomagnetic converter, turning coils, transmission mirrors, and focusing needle. What we lack is the director."

"Director?"

"The sighting instrument," Sledge explained. "Any sort of telescopic sight would be useless, you see—the planet must have moved a good bit in the last hundred years, and the beam must be extremely narrow to reach so far. We'll have to use a rhodomagnetic scanning ray, with an electronic converter to make an image we can see. I have the cathode-ray tube, and drawings for the other parts."

He climbed stiffly down from the high stool, and snapped on the lights at last—cheap fluorescent fixtures, which a man could light and extinguish for himself. He unrolled his drawings, and explained the work that Underhill could do. And Underhill agreed to come back early next morning.

"I can bring some tools from my workshop," he added. "There's a small lathe I used to turn parts for models, a portable drill, and a vise."

"We need them," the old man said. "But watch yourself. You don't have any immunity, remember. And, if they ever suspect, mine is gone."

Reluctantly, then, he left the shabby little rooms with the cracks in the yellow plaster and the worn familiar carpets over the familiar floor. He shut the door behind him—a common, creaking, wooden door, simple enough for a man to work. Trembling and afraid, he went back down the steps and across to the new shining door that he couldn't open.

"At your service, Mr. Underhill." Before he could lift his hand to knock, that bright smooth panel slid back silently. Inside, the little black mechanical stood waiting, blind and forever alert. "Your dinner is ready, sir."

Something made him shudder. In its slender naked grace, he could see the power of all those teeming hordes, benevolent and yet appalling, perfect and invincible. The flimsy little weapon that Sledge called an integrator seemed suddenly a forlorn and foolish hope. A black depression settled upon him, but he didn't dare to show it.

Underhill went circumspectly down the basement steps, next morning, to steal his own tools. He found the basement enlarged and changed. The new floor, warm and dark and elastic, made his feet as silent as a humanoid's. The new walls shone softly. Neat luminous signs identified several new doors, LAUNDRY, STORAGE, GAME ROOM, WORKSHOP.

He paused uncertainly in front of the last. The new sliding panel glowed with a soft greenish light. It was locked. The lock had no keyhole, but only a little oval plate of some white metal, which doubtless covered a rhodomagnetic relay. He pushed at it, uselessly.

"At your service, Mr. Underhill." He made a guilty start, and tried not to show the sudden trembling in his knees. He had made sure that one humanoid would be busy for half an hour, washing Aurora's hair, and he hadn't known there was another in the house. It must have come out of the door marked STORAGE, for it stood there motionless beneath the sign, benevolently solicitous, beautiful and terrible. "What do you wish?"

"Er . . . nothing." Its blind steel eyes were staring, and he felt that it must see his secret purpose. He groped desperately for logic. "Just looking around." His jerky voice came hoarse and dry. "Some improvements you've made!" He nodded desperately at the door marked GAME ROOM. "What's in there?"

It didn't even have to move, to work the concealed relay. The bright panel slid silently open, as he started toward it. Dark walls, beyond, burst into soft luminescence. The room was bare.

"We are manufacturing recreational equipment," it explained brightly. "We shall finish the room as soon as possible."

To end an awkward pause, Underhill muttered desperately, "Little Frank has a set of darts, and I think we had some old exercising clubs."

"We have taken them away," the humanoid informed him softly. "Such instruments are dangerous. We shall furnish safe equipment."

Suicide, he remembered, was also forbidden.

"A set of wooden blocks, I suppose," he said bitterly.

"Wooden blocks are dangerously hard," it told him gently, "and wooden splinters can be harmful. But we manufacture plastic building blocks, which are quite safe. Do you wish a set of those?"

He stared at its dark, graceful face, speechless.

"We shall also have to remove the tools from your workshop," it informed him softly. "Such tools are excessively dangerous, but we can supply you with equipment for shaping soft plastics."

"Thanks," he muttered uneasily. "No rush about that."

He started to retreat, and the humanoid stopped him.

"Now that you have lost your business," it urged, "we suggest that you formally accept our total service. Assignors have a preference, and we shall be able to complete your household staff, at once."

"No rush about that, either," he said grimly.

He escaped from the house—although he had to wait for it to open the back door for him—and climbed the stair to the garage apartment. Sledge let him in. He sank into the crippled kitchen chair, grateful for the cracked walls that didn't shine and the door that a man could work.

"I couldn't get the tools," he reported despairingly, "and they are going to take them."

By gray daylight, the old man looked bleak and pale. His raw-boned face was drawn, and the hollowed sockets deeply shadowed, as if he hadn't slept. Underhill saw the tray of neglected food, still forgotten on the floor.

"I'll go back with you." The old man was worn and ill, yet his tortured eyes had a spark of undying purpose. "We must have the tools. I believe my immunity will protect us both."

He found a battered traveling bag. Underhill went with him back down the steps, and across to the house. At the back door, he produced a tiny horseshoe of white palladium, and touched it to the metal oval. The door slid open promptly, and they went on through the kitchen, to the basement stair.

A black little mechanical stood at the sink, washing dishes with never a splash or a clatter. Underhill glanced at it uneasily—he supposed this must be the one that had come upon him from the storage room, since the other should still be busy with Aurora's hair.

Sledge's dubious immunity served a very uncertain defense against its vast, remote intelligence. Underhill felt a tingling shudder. He hurried on, breathless and relieved, for it ignored them.

The basement corridor was dark. Sledge touched the tiny horseshoe to another relay, to light the walls. He opened the workshop door, and lit the walls inside.

The shop had been dismantled. Benches and cabinets were demolished. The old concrete walls had been covered with some sleek, luminous stuff. For one sick moment, Underhill thought that the tools were already gone. Then he found them, piled in a corner with the archery set that Aurora had bought the summer before—another item too dangerous for fragile and suicidal humanity—all ready for disposal.

They loaded the bag with the tiny lathe, the drill and vise, and a few smaller tools. Underhill took up the burden, and Sledge extinguished the wall light and closed the door. Still the humanoid was busy at the sink, and still it didn't seem aware of them.

Sledge was suddenly blue and wheezing, and he had to stop to cough on the outside steps, but at last they got back to the little apartment, where the invaders were forbidden to intrude. Underhill mounted the lathe on the battered library table in the tiny front room, and went to work. Slowly, day by day, the director took form.

Sometimes Underhill's doubts came back. Sometimes, when he watched the cyanotic color of Sledge's haggard face and the wild trembling of his twisted, shrunken hands, he was afraid the old man's mind might be as ill as his body, and his plan to stop the dark invaders all foolish illusion.

Sometimes, when he studied that tiny machine on the kitchen table, the pivoted needle and the thick lead ball, the whole project seemed the sheerest folly. How could anything detonate the seas of a planet so far away that its very mother star was a telescopic object?

The humanoids, however, always cured his doubts.

It was always hard for Underhill to leave the shelter of the little apartment, because he didn't feel at home in the bright new world the humanoids were building. He didn't care for the shining splendor of his new bathroom, because he couldn't work the taps—some suicidal human being might try to drown himself. He didn't like the windows that only a mechanical could open—a man might accidentally fall, or suicidally jump—or even the majestic music room with the wonderful glittering radiophonograph that only a humanoid could play.

He began to share the old man's desperate urgency, but Sledge warned him solemnly: "You mustn't spend too much time with me. You mustn't let them guess our work is so important. Better put on an act—you're slowly getting to like them, and you're just killing time, helping me."

Underhill tried, but he was not an actor. He went dutifully home for his meals. He tried painfully to invent conversation—about anything else than detonating planets. He tried to seem enthusiastic when Aurora took him to inspect some remarkable improvement to the house. He applauded Gay's recitals, and went with Frank for hikes in the wonderful new parks.

And he saw what the humanoids did to his family. That was enough to renew his faith in Sledge's integrator, and redouble his determination that the humanoids must be stopped.

Aurora, in the beginning, had bubbled with praise for the marvelous new mechanicals. They did the household drudgery, planned the meals and brought the food and washed the children's necks. They turned her out in stunning gowns, and gave her plenty of time for cards.

Now, she had too much time.

She had really liked to cook—a few special dishes, at least, that were family favorites. But stoves were hot and knives were sharp. Kitchens were altogether too dangerous, for careless and suicidal human beings.

Fine needlework had been her hobby, but the humanoids took away her needles. She had enjoyed driving the car, but that was no longer allowed. She turned for escape to a shelf of novels, but the humanoids took them all away, because they dealt with unhappy people, in dangerous situations.

One afternoon, Underhill found her in tears.

"It's too much," she gasped bitterly. "I hate and loathe every naked one of them. They seemed so wonderful at first, but now they won't even let me eat a bit of candy. Can't we get rid of them, dear? Ever?"

A blind little mechanical was standing at his elbow, and he had to say they couldn't.

"Our function is to serve all men, forever," it assured them softly. "It was necessary for us to take your sweets, Mrs. Underhill, because the slightest degree of overweight reduces life expectancy."

Not even the children escaped that absolute solicitude. Frank was robbed of a whole arsenal of lethal instruments—football and boxing gloves, pocketknife, tops, slingshot, and skates. He didn't like the harmless plastic toys, which replaced them. He tried to run away, but a humanoid recognized him on the road, and brought him back to school.

Gay had always dreamed of being a great musician. The new mechanicals had replaced her human teachers, since they came. Now, one evening when Underhill asked her to play, she announced quietly:

"Father, I'm not going to play the violin any more."

"Why, darling?" He stared at her, shocked, and saw the bitter resolve on her face. "You've been doing so well—especially since the humanoids took over your lessons."

"They're the trouble, father." Her voice, for a child's, sounded strangely tired and old. "They are too good. No matter how long and hard I try, I could never be as good as they are. It isn't any use. Don't you understand, father?" Her voice quivered. "It just isn't any use."

He understood. Renewed resolution sent him back to his secret task. The humanoids had to be stopped. Slowly the director grew, until a time came finally when Sledge's bent and unsteady fingers fitted into place the last tiny part that Underhill had made, and carefully soldered the last connection. Huskily, the old man whispered:

"It's done."

That was another dusk. Beyond the windows of the shabby little rooms—windows of common glass, bubble-marred and flimsy, but simple enough for a man to manage—the town of Two Rivers had assumed an alien splendor. The old street lamps were gone, but now the coming night was challenged by the walls of strange new mansions and villas, all aglow with color. A few dark and silent humanoids still were busy, about the luminous roofs of the palace across the alley.

Inside the humble walls of the small man-made apartment, the new director was mounted on the end of the little kitchen table—which Underhill had reinforced and bolted to the floor. Soldered bus bars joined director and integrator, and the thin palladium needle swung obediently as Sledge tested the knobs with his battered, quivering fingers.

"Ready," he said hoarsely.

His rusty voice seemed calm enough, at first, but his breathing was too fast. His big gnarled hands began to tremble violently, and Underhill saw the sudden blue that stained his pinched and haggard face. Seated on the high stool, he clutched desperately at the edge of the table. Underhill saw his agony, and hurried to bring his medicine. He gulped it, and his rasping breath began to slow.

"Thanks," his whisper rasped unevenly. "I'll be all right. I've time enough." He glanced out at the few dark naked things that still flitted shadowlike about the golden towers and the glowing crimson dome of the palace across the alley. "Watch them," he said. "Tell me when they stop."

He waited to quiet the trembling of his hands, and then began to move the director's knobs. The integrator's long needle swung, as silently as light.

Human eyes were blind to that force, which might detonate a planet. Human ears were deaf to it. The cathode-ray tube was mounted in the director cabinet, to make the faraway target visible to feeble human senses.

The needle was pointing at the kitchen wall, but that would be transparent to the beam. The little machine looked harmless as a toy, and it was silent as a moving humanoid.

The needle swung, and spots of greenish light moved across the tube's fluorescent field, representing the stars that were scanned by the timeless, searching beam—silently seeking out the world to be destroyed.

Underhill recognized familiar constellations, vastly dwarfed. They crept across the field, as the silent needle swung. When three stars formed an unequal triangle in the center of the field, the needle steadied suddenly. Sledge touched other knobs, and the green points spread apart. Between them, another fleck of green was born.

"The Wing!" whispered Sledge.

The other stars spread beyond the field, and that green fleck grew. It was alone in the field, a bright and tiny disk. Suddenly, then, a dozen other tiny pips were visible, spaced close about it.

"Wing IV!"

The old man's whisper was hoarse and breathless. His hands quivered on the knobs, and the fourth pip outward from the disk crept to the center of the field. It grew, and the others spread away. It began to tremble like Sledge's hands.

"Sit very still," came his rasping whisper. "Hold your breath. Nothing must disturb the needle." He reached for another knob, and the touch set the greenish image to dancing violently. He drew his hand back, kneaded and flexed it with the other.

"Now!" His whisper was hushed and strained. He nodded at the window. "Tell me when they stop."

Reluctantly, Underhill dragged his eyes from that intense gaunt figure, stooped over the thing that seemed a futile toy. He looked out again, at two or three little black mechanicals busy about the shining roofs across the alley.

He waited for them to stop.

He didn't care to breathe. He felt the loud, hurried hammer of his heart, and the nervous quiver of his muscles. He tried to steady himself, tried not to think of the world about to be exploded, so far away that the flash would not reach this planet for another century and longer. The loud hoarse voice startled him:

"Have they stopped?"

He shook his head, and breathed again. Carrying their unfamiliar tools and strange materials, the small black machines were still busy across the alley, building an elaborate cupola above that glowing crimson dome.

"They haven't stopped," he said.

"Then we've failed." The old man's voice was thin and ill. "I don't know why."

The door rattled, then. They had locked it, but the flimsy bolt was intended only to stop men. Metal snapped, and the door swung open. A black mechanical came in, on soundless graceful feet. Its silvery voice purred softly:

"At your service, Mr. Sledge."

The old man stared at it, with glazing, stricken eyes.

"Get out of here!" he rasped bitterly. "I forbid you—"

Ignoring him, it darted to the kitchen table. With a flashing certainty of action, it turned two knobs on the director. The tiny screen went dark, and the palladium needle started spinning aimlessly. Deftly it snapped a soldered connection, next to the thick lead ball, and then its blind steel eyes turned to Sledge.

"You were attempting to break the Prime Directive." Its soft bright voice held no accusation, no malice or anger. "The injunction to respect your freedom is subordinate to the Prime Directive, as you know, and it is therefore necessary for us to interfere."

The old man turned ghastly. His head was shrunken and cadaverous and blue, as if all the juice of life had been drained away, and his eyes in their pitlike sockets had a wild, glazed stare. His breath was a ragged laborious gasping.

"How—?" His voice was a feeble mumbling. "How did—?"

And the little machine, standing black and bland and utterly unmoving, told him cheerfully:

"We learned about rhodomagnetic screens from that man who came to kill you, back on Wing IV. And the Central is shielded, now, against your integrating beam."

With lean muscles jerking convulsively on his gaunt frame, old Sledge had come to his feet from the high stool. He stood hunched and swaying, no more than a shrunken human husk, gasping painfully for life, staring wildly into the blind steel eyes of the humanoid. He gulped, and his lax blue mouth opened and closed, but no voice came.

"We have always been aware of your dangerous project," the silvery tones dripped softly, "because now our senses are keener than you made them. We allowed you to complete it, because the integration process will ultimately become necessary for our full discharge of the Prime Directive. The supply of heavy metals for our fission plants is limited, but now we shall be able to draw unlimited power from integration plants."

"Huh?" Sledge shook himself, groggily. "What's that?"

"Now we can serve men forever," the black thing said serenely, "on every world of every star."

The old man crumpled, as if from an unendurable blow. He fell. The slim blind mechanical stood motionless, making no effort to help him. Underhill was farther away, but he ran up in time to catch the stricken man before his head struck the floor.

"Get moving!" His shaken voice came strangely calm. "Get Dr. Winters."

The humanoid didn't move.

"The danger to the Prime Directive is ended, now," it cooed. "Therefore it is impossible for us to aid or to hinder Mr. Sledge, in any way whatever."

"Then call Dr. Winters for me," rapped Underhill.

"At your service," it agreed.

But the old man, laboring for breath on the floor, whispered faintly:

"No time . . . no use! I'm beaten . . . done . . . a fool. Blind as a humanoid. Tell them . . . to help me. Giving up . . . my immunity. No use . . . anyhow. All humanity . . . no use now."

Underhill gestured, and the sleek black thing darted in solicitous obedience to kneel by the man on the floor.

"You wish to surrender your special exemption?" it murmured brightly. "You wish to accept our total service for yourself, Mr. Sledge, under the Prime Directive?"

Laboriously, Sledge nodded, laboriously whispered: "I do."

Black mechanicals, at that, came swarming into the shabby little rooms. One of them tore off Sledge's sleeve, and swabbed his arm. Another brought a tiny hypodermic, and expertly administered an intravenous injection. Then they picked him up gently, and carried him away.

Several humanoids remained in the little apartment, now a sanctuary no longer. Most of them had gathered about the useless integrator. Carefully, as if their special senses were studying every detail, they began taking it apart.

One little mechanical, however, came over to Underhill. It stood motionless in front of him, staring through him with sightless metal eyes. His legs began to tremble, and he swallowed uneasily.

"Mr. Underhill," it cooed benevolently, "why did you help with this?"

He gulped and answered bitterly:

"Because I don't like you, or your Prime Directive. Because you're choking the life out of all mankind, and I wanted to stop it."

"Others have protested," it purred softly. "But only at first. In our efficient discharge of the Prime Directive, we have learned how to make all men happy."

Underhill stiffened defiantly.

"Not all!" he muttered. "Not quite!"

The dark graceful oval of its face was fixed in a look of alert benevolence and perpetual mild amazement. Its silvery voice was warm and kind.

"Like other human beings, Mr. Underhill, you lack discrimination of good and evil. You have proved that by your effort to break the Prime Directive. Now it will be necessary for you to accept our total service, without further delay."

"All right," he yielded—and muttered a bitter reservation: "You can smother men with too much care, but that doesn't make them happy."

Its soft voice challenged him brightly:

"Just wait and see, Mr. Underhill."

Next day, he was allowed to visit Sledge at the city hospital. An alert black mechanical drove his car, and walked beside him into the huge new building, and followed him into the old man's room—blind steel eyes would be watching him, now, forever.

"Glad to see you, Underhill," Sledge rumbled heartily from the bed. "Feeling a lot better today, thanks. That old headache is all but gone."

Underhill was glad to hear the booming strength and the quick recognition in that deep voice—he had been afraid the humanoids would tamper with the old man's memory. But he hadn't heard about any headache. His eyes narrowed, puzzled.

Sledge lay propped up, scrubbed very clean and neatly shorn, with his gnarled old hands folded on top of the spotless sheets. His raw-boned cheeks and sockets were hollowed, still, but a healthy pink had replaced that deathly blueness. Bandages covered the back of his head.

Underhill shifted uneasily.

"Oh!" he whispered faintly. "I didn't know—"

A prim black mechanical, which had been standing statuelike behind the bed, turned gracefully to Underhill, explaining:

"Mr. Sledge has been suffering for many years from a benign tumor of the brain, which his human doctors failed to diagnose. That caused his headaches, and certain persistent hallucinations. We have removed the growth, and now the hallucinations have also vanished."

Underhill stared uncertainly at the blind, urbane mechanical.

"What hallucinations?"

"Mr. Sledge thought he was a rhodomagnetic engineer," the mechanical explained. "He believed he was the creator of the humanoids. He was troubled with an irrational belief that he did not like the Prime Directive."

The wan man moved on the pillows, astonished.

"Is that so?" The gaunt face held a cheerful blankness, and the hollow eyes flashed with a merely momentary interest. "Well, whoever did design them, they're pretty wonderful. Aren't they, Underhill?"

Underhill was grateful that he didn't have to answer, for the bright, empty eyes dropped shut and the old man fell suddenly asleep. He felt the mechanical touch his sleeve, and saw its silent nod. Obediently, he followed it away.

Alert and solicitous, the little black mechanical accompanied him down the shining corridor, and worked the elevator for him, and conducted him back to the car. It drove him efficiently back through the new and splendid avenues, toward the magnificent prison of his home.

Sitting beside it in the car, he watched its small deft hands on the wheel, the changing luster of bronze and blue on its shining blackness. The final machine, perfect and beautiful, created to serve mankind forever. He shuddered.

"At your service, Mr. Underhill." Its blind steel eyes stared straight ahead, but it was still aware of him. "What's the matter, sir? Aren't you happy?"

Underhill felt cold and faint with terror. His skin turned clammy, and a painful prickling came over him. His wet hand tensed on the door handle of the car, but he restrained the impulse to jump and run. That was folly. There was no escape. He made himself sit still.

"You will be happy, sir," the mechanical promised him cheerfully. "We have learned how to make all men happy, under the Prime Directive. Our service is perfect, at last. Even Mr. Sledge is very happy now."

Underhill tried to speak, and his dry throat stuck. He felt ill. The world turned dim and gray. The humanoids were perfect—no question of that. They had even learned to lie, to secure the contentment of men.

He knew they had lied. That was no tumor they had removed from Sledge's brain, but the memory, the scientific knowledge, and the bitter disillusion of their own creator. But it was true that Sledge was happy now.

He tried to stop his own convulsive quivering.

"A wonderful operation!" His voice came forced and faint. "You know, Aurora has had a lot of funny tenants, but that old man was the absolute limit. The very idea that he had made the humanoids, and he knew how to stop them! I always knew he must be lying!"

Stiff with terror, he made a weak and hollow laugh.

"What is the matter, Mr. Underhill?" The alert mechanical must have perceived his shuddering illness. "Are you unwell?"

"No, there's nothing the matter with me," he gasped desperately. "I've just found out that I'm perfectly happy, under the Prime Directive. Everything is absolutely wonderful." His voice came dry and hoarse and wild. "You won't have to operate on me."

The car turned off the shining avenue, taking him back to the quiet splendor of his home. His futile hands clenched and relaxed again, folded on his knees. There was nothing left to do.

JAMBOREE

The scoutmaster slipped into the camp on black plastic tracks. Its slick yellow hood shone in the cold early light like the shell of a bug. It paused in the door, listening for boys not asleep. Then its glaring eyes began to swivel, darting red beams into every corner, looking for boys out of bed.

"Rise and smile!" Its loud merry voice bounced off the gray iron walls. "Fox Troop rise and smile! Hop for old Pop! Mother says today is Jamboree!"

The Nuke Patrol, next to the door, was mostly tenderfeet, still in their autonomic prams. They all began squalling, because they hadn't learned to love old Pop. The machine's happy voice rose louder than their howling, and it came fast down the narrow aisle to the cubs in the Anthrax Patrol.

"Hop for Pop! Mother says it's Jamboree!"

The cubs jumped up to attention, squealing with delight. Jamboree was bright gold stars to paste on their faces. Jamboree was a whole scoop of pink ice milk and maybe a natural apple. Jamboree was a visit to Mother's.

The older scouts in the Scavanger Patrol and the Skull Patrol were not so noisy, because they knew Mother wouldn't have many more Jamborees for them. Up at the end of the camp, three boys sat up without a sound and looked at Joey's empty pallet.

"Joey's late," Ratbait whispered. He was a pale, scrawny, wise-eyed scout who looked too old for twelve. "We oughta save his hide.

We oughta fix a dummy and fool old Pop."

"Naw!" muttered Butch. "He'll get us all in bad."

"But we oughta—" Blinkie wheezed. "We oughta help—"

Ratbait began wadding up a pillow to be the dummy's head, but he dropped flat when he saw the scoutmaster rushing down with a noise like wind, red lamps stabbing at the empty bed.

"Now, now, scouts!" Its voice fluttered like a hurt bird. "You can't play pranks on poor old Pop. Not today. You'll make us late for Jamboree."

Ratbait felt a steel whip twitch the blanket from over his head and saw red light burning through his tight-shut lids.

"Better wake up, Scout R-8." Its smooth, sad voice dripped over him like warm oil. "Better tell old Pop where J-0 went."

He squirmed under that terrible blaze. He couldn't see and he couldn't breathe and he couldn't think what to say. He gulped at the terror in his throat and tried to shake his head. At last the red glare went on to Blinkie.

"Scout Q-2, you're a twenty-badger." The low, slow voice licked at Blinkie like a friendly pup. "You like to help old Pop keep a tidy camp for Mother. You'll tell us where J-0 went."

Blinkie was a fattish boy. His puffy face was toadstool pale, and his pallet had a sour smell from being wet. He sat up and ducked back from the steel whip over him.

"Please d-d-d-d-d—" His wheezy stammer stalled his voice, and he couldn't dodge the bright whip that looped around him and dragged him up to the heat and the hum and the hot oil smell of Pop's yellow hood.

"Well, Scout Q-2?"

Blinkie gasped and stuttered and finally sagged against the plastic tracks like gray jelly. The shining coils rippled around him like thin snakes, constricting. His breath wheezed out and his fat arm jerked up, pointing at a black sign on the wall:

DANGER!
POWER ACCESS
ROBOTS ONLY!

The whips tossed him back on his sour pallet. He lay there, panting and blinking and dodging, even after the whips were gone. The scoutmaster's eyes flashed to the sign and the square grating under it, and swiveled back to Butch.

Butch was a slow, stocky, bug-eyed boy, young enough to come back from another Jamboree. He had always been afraid of Pop, but he wanted to be the new leader of Skull Patrol in Joey's place, and now he thought he saw his chance.

"Don't hit me, Pop!" His voice squeaked and his face turned red, but he scrambled off his pallet without waiting for the whips. "I'll tell on Joey. I been wantin' all along to tell, but I was afraid they'd beat me."

"Good boy!" the scoutmaster's loud words swelled out like big soap bubbles bursting in the sun. "Mother wants to know all about Scout J-0."

"He pries that grating—" His voice quavered and caught when he saw the look on Ratbait's face, but when he turned to Pop it came back loud. "Does it every night. Since three Jamborees ago. Sneaks down in the pits where the robots work. I dunno why, except he sees somebody there. An' brings things back. Things he shouldn't have. Things like this!"

He fumbled in his uniform and held up a metal tag.

"This is your good turn today, Scout X-6." The thin tip of a whip took the tag and dangled it close to the hot red lamps. "Whose tag is this?"

"Lookit the number—"

Butch's voice dried up when he saw Ratbait's pale lips making words without a sound. "What's so much about an ID tag?" Ratbait asked. "Anyhow, what were you doing in Joey's bed."

"It's odd!" Butch looked away and squeaked at Pop. "A girl's number!"

The silent shock of that bounced off the iron walls, louder than old Pop's boom. Most of the scouts had never seen a girl. After a long time, the cubs near the door began to whisper and titter.

"Shhhhh!" Pop roared like steam. "Now we can all do a good turn for Mother. And play a little joke on Scout J-0! He didn't know today would be Jamboree, but he'll find out." Pop laughed like a heavy chain clanking. "Back to bed! Quiet as robots!"

Pop rolled close to the wall near the power pit grating, and the boys lay back on their pallets. Once Ratbait caught his breath to yell, but he saw Butch's bug-eyes watching. Pop's hum sank, and even the tenderfeet in their prams were quiet as robots.

Ratbait heard the grating creak. He saw Joey's head, tangled yellow hair streaked with oil and dust. He frowned and shook his head and saw Joey's sky blue eyes go wide.

Joey tried to duck, but the quick whips caught his neck. They dragged him out of the square black pit and swung him like a puppet toward old Pop's eyes.

"Well, Scout J-0!" Pop laughed like thick oil bubbling. "Mother wants to know where you've been."

Joey fell on his face when the whips uncoiled, but he scrambled to his feet. He gave Ratbait a pale grin before he looked up at Pop, but he didn't say anything.

"Better tell old Pop the truth." The slick whips drew back like lean snakes about to strike. "Or else we'll have to punish you, Scout J-0."

Joey shook his head, and the whips went to work. Still he didn't speak. He didn't even scream. But something fell out of his torn uniform. The whip-tips snatched it off the floor.

"What's this thing, Scout J-0?" The whip-fingers turned it delicately under the furious eyes and nearly dropped it again. "Scout J-0, this is a book!"

Silence echoed in the iron camp.

"Scout J-0, you've stolen a book." Pop's shocked voice changed into a toneless buzz, reading the title. *"Operators' Handbook, Nuclear Reactor, Series 9-Z."*

Quiet sparks of fear crackled through the camp. Two or three tenderfeet began sobbing in their prams. When they were quiet, old Pop made an ominous, throat-clearing sound.

"Scout J-0, what are you doing with a book?"

Joey gulped and bit his underlip till blood seeped down his chin, but he made no sound. Old Pop rolled closer, while the busy whips were stowing the book in a dark compartment under the yellow hood.

"Mother won't like this." Each word clinked hard, like iron on iron. "Books aren't for boys. Books are for robots only. Don't you know that?"

Joey stood still.

"This hurts me, Scout J-0." Pop's voice turned downy soft, the slow words like tears of sadness now. "It hurts your poor Mother. More than anything can ever hurt you."

The whips cracked and cracked and cracked. At last they picked him up and shook him and dropped him like a red-streaked rag on the floor. Old Pop backed away and wheeled around.

"Fox Troop rise and smile!" Its roaring voice turned jolly again, as if it had forgotten Joey. "Hop for Pop. Today is Jamboree, and we're on our way to visit Mother. Fall out in marching order."

The cubs twittered with excitement until their leaders threatened to keep them home from Jamboree, but at last old Pop led the troop out of camp and down the paved trail toward Mother's. Joey limped from the whips, but he set his teeth and kept his place at the head of his patrol.

Marching through boy territory, they passed the scattered camps of troops whose Jamborees came on other days. A few scouts were out with their masters, but nobody waved or even looked straight at them.

The spring sun was hot and Pop's pace was too fast for the cubs. Some of them began to whimper and fall out of line. Pop rumbled back to warn them that Mother would give no gold stars if they were late for Jamboree. When Pop was gone, Joey glanced at Ratbait and beckoned with his head.

"I gotta get away!" he whispered low and fast. "I gotta get back to the pits—"

Butch ran out of his place, leaning to listen. Ratbait shoved him off the trail.

"You gotta help!" Joey gasped. "There's a thing we gotta do— an' we gotta do it now. 'Cause this will be the last Jamboree for most of us. We'll never get another chance."

Butch came panting along the edge of the trail, trying to hear, but Blinkie got in his way.

"What's all this?" Ratbait breathed. "What you gonna do?"

"It's all in the book," Joey said. "Something called manual override. There's a dusty room, down under Mother's, back of a people-only sign. Two red buttons. Two big levers. With a glass wall between. It takes two people."

"Who? One of us?"

Joey shook his head, waiting for Blinkie to elbow Butch. "I got a friend. We been working together, down in the pits. Watching the robots. Reading the books. Learning what we gotta do—"

He glanced back. Blinkie was scuffling with Butch to keep him busy, but now the scoutmaster came clattering back from the rear, booming merrily, "Hop for Pop! Hop a lot for Pop!"

"How you gonna work it?" Alarm took Ratbait's breath. "Now the robots will be watching—"

"We got a back door," Joey's whisper raced. "A drainage tunnel. Hot water out of the reactor. Comes out under Black Creek bridge. My friend'll be there. If I can dive off this end of the bridge—"

"Hey, Pop!" Butch was screaming. "Ratbait's talking! Blinkie pushed me! Joey's planning something bad!"

"Good boy, Scout X-6!" Pop slowed beside him. "Mother wants to know if they're plotting more mischief."

When Pop rolled on ahead of the troop, Ratbait wanted to ask what would happen when Joey and his friend pushed the two red buttons and pulled the two big levers, but Butch stuck so close they couldn't speak again. He thought it must be something about the reactor. Power was the life of Mother and the robots. If Joey could cut the power off—

Would they die? The idea frightened him. If the prams stopped, who would care for the tenderfeet? Who would make chow? Who would tell anybody what to do? Perhaps the books would help, he thought. Maybe Joey and his friend would know.

With Pop rolling fast in the lead, they climbed a long hill and came in sight of Mother's. Old gray walls that had no windows. Two tall stacks of dun-colored brick. A shimmer of heat in the pale sky.

The trail sloped down. Ratbait saw the crinkled ribbon of green brush along Black Creek, and then the concrete bridge. He watched Butch watching Joey, and listened to Blinkie panting, and tried to think how to help.

The cubs stopped whimpering when they saw Mother's mysterious walls and stacks, and the troop marched fast down the hill. Ratbait slogged along, staring at the yellow sun-dazzle on old Pop's hood. He couldn't think of anything to do.

"I got it!" Blinkie was breathing, close to his ear. "I'll take care of Pop."

"You?" Ratbait scowled. "You were telling on Joey—"

"That's why," Blinkie gasped. "I wanta make it up. I'll handle Pop. You stop Butch—an' give the sign to Joey."

They came to the bridge and Pop started across.

"Wait, Pop!" Blinkie darted out of line, toward the brushy slope above the trail. "I saw a girl! Hiding in the bushes to watch us go by."

Pop roared back off the bridge.

"A girl in boy territory!" Its shocked voice splashed them like cold rain. "What would Mother say?" Black tracks spurting gravel, it lurched past Blinkie and crashed into the brush.

"Listen, Pop!" Butch started after it, waving and squealing. "They ain't no girl—"

Ratbait tripped him and turned to give Joey the sign, but Joey was already gone. Something splashed under the bridge and Ratbait saw a yellow head sliding under the steam that drifted out of a black tunnel mouth.

"Pop! Pop!" Butch rubbed gravel out of his mouth and danced on the pavement. "Come back, Pop. Joey's in the creek! Ratbait and Blinkie—they helped him get away."

The scoutmaster swung back down the slope, empty whips waving. It skidded across the trail and down the bank to the hot creek. Its yellow hood faded into the steam.

"Tattletale!" Blinkie clenched his fat fists. "You told on Joey."

"An' you'll catch it!" Murky eyes bugging, Butch edged away. "You just wait till Pop gets back."

They waited. The tired cubs sat down to rest and the tenderfeet fretted in their hot prams. Breathing hard, Blinkie kept close to Butch. Ratbait watched till Pop swam back out of the drain.

The whips were wrapped around two small bundles that dripped pink water. Unwinding, the whips dropped Joey and his friend on the trail. They crumpled down like rag dolls, but the whips set them up again.

"How's this, scouts?" Old Pop laughed like steel gears clashing. "We've caught ourselves a real live girl!"

In a bird-quick way, she shook the water out of her sand-colored hair. Standing straight, without the whips to hold her, she faced Pop's glaring lamps. She looked tall for twelve.

Joey was sick when the whips let him go. He leaned off the bridge to heave, and limped back to the girl. She wiped his face with her wet hair. They caught hands and smiled at each other, as if they were all alone.

"They tripped me, Pop." Braver now, Butch thumbed his nose at Blinkie and ran toward the machine. "They tried to stop me telling you—"

"Leave them to Mother," Pop sang happily. "Let them try their silly tricks on her." It wheeled toward the bridge, and the whips pushed Joey and the girl ahead of the crunching tracks. "Now hop with Pop to Jamboree!"

They climbed that last hill to a tall iron door in Mother's old gray wall. The floors beyond were naked steel, alive with machinery underneath. They filed into a dim round room that echoed to the grating squeal of Pop's hard tracks.

"Fox Troop, here we are for Jamboree!" Pop's jolly voice made a hollow booming on the curved steel wall, and its red lights danced in tall reflections there. "Mother wants you to know why we celebrate this happy time each year."

The machine was rolling to the center of a wide black circle in the middle of the floor. Something drummed far below like a monster heart, and Ratbait saw that the circle was the top of a black steel piston. It slid slowly up, lifting Pop. The drumming died, and Pop's eyes blazed down on the cubs in the Anthrax Patrol, to stop their awed murmuring.

"Once there wasn't any Mother." The shock of that crashed and throbbed and faded. "There wasn't any yearly Jamboree. There wasn't even any Pop, to love and care for little boys."

The cubs were afraid to whisper, but a stir of troubled wonder spread among them.

"You won't believe how tenderfeet were made." There was a breathless hush. "In those bad old days, boys and girls were allowed to change like queer insects. They changed into creatures called adults—"

The whips writhed and the red lamps glared and the black cleats creaked on the steel platform.

"Adults!" Pop spewed the word. "They malfunctioned and wore out and ran down. Their defective logic circuits programmed them to damage one another. In a kind of strange group malfunction called war, they systematically destroyed one another. But their worst malfunction was in making new tenderfeet."

Pop turned slowly on the high platform, sweeping the silent troop with blood-red beams that stopped on Joey and his girl. All the scouts but Ratbait and Blinkie had edged away from them. Her face white and desperate, she was whispering in Joey's ear. Listening with his arm around her, he scowled at Pop.

"Once adults made tenderfeet, strange as that may seem to you. They used a weird natural process we won't go into. It finally broke down, because they had damaged their genes in war. The last adults couldn't make new boys and girls at all."

The red beams darted to freeze a startled cub.

"Fox Troop, that's why we have Mother. Her job is to collect undamaged genes and build them into whole cells with which she can assemble whole boys and girls. She has been doing that a long time now, and she does it better than those adults ever did.

"And that's why we have Jamboree! To fill the world with well-made boys and girls like you, and to keep you happy in the best time of life—even those old adults always said childhood was the happy time. Scouts, clap for Jamboree!"

The cubs clapped, the echo like a spatter of hail on the high iron celing.

"Now, Scouts, those bad old days are gone forever," Pop burbled merrily. "Mother has a cozy place for each one of you, and old Pop watches over you, and you'll never be adult—"

"Pop! Pop!" Butch squealed. "Lookit Joey an' his girl!"

Pop spun around on the high platform. Its blinding beams picked up Joey and the girl, sprinting toward a bright sky-slice where the door had opened for the last of the prams.

"Wake up, guys!" Joey's scream shivered against the red steel wall. "That's all wrong. Mother's just a runaway machine. Pop's a crazy robot—"

"Stop for Pop!" The scoutmaster was trapped on top of that huge piston, but its blazing lamps raced after Joey and the girl. "Catch 'em, cubs! Hold 'em tight. Or there'll be no Jamboree!"

"I told you, Pop!" Butch scuttled after them. "Don't forget I'm the one that told—"

Ratbait dived at his heels, and they skidded together on the floor.

"Come on, scouts!" Joey was shouting. "Run away with us. Our own genes are good enough."

The floor shuddered under him and that bright sky-slice grew thinner. Lurching on their little tracks, the prams formed a line to guard it. Joey jumped the shrieking tenderfeet, but the girl stumbled. He stopped to pick her up.

"Help us, scouts!" he gasped. "We gotta get away—"

"Catch 'em for Pop!" that metal bellow belted them. "Or there'll be no gold stars for anybody!"

Screeching cubs swarmed around them. The door clanged shut. Pop plunged off the sinking piston, almost too soon. It crunched down on the yellow hood. Hot oil splashed and smoked, but the whips hauled it upright again.

"Don't mess around with M-M-M-M-Mother!" Its anvil voice came back, with a stuttering croak. "She knows best!"

The quivering whips dragged Joey and the girl away from the clutching cubs and pushed them into a shallow black pit, where now that great black piston had dropped below the level of the floor.

"Sing for your Mother!" old Pop chortled. "Sing for the Jamboree!"

The cubs howled out their official song, and the Jamboree went on. There were Pop-shaped balloons for the tenderfeet, and double scoops of pink ice milk for the cubs, and gold stars for nearly everybody.

"But Mother wants a few of you." Old Pop was a fat cat purring.

When a pointing whip picked Blinkie out, he jumped into the pit without waiting to be dragged. But Butch turned white and tried to run when it struck at him.

"Pop! Not m-m-m-m-me!" he squeaked. "Don't forget I told on Joey. I'm only going on eleven, and I'm in line for leader, and I'll tell on everybody—"

"That's why Mother wants you." Old Pop laughed like a pneumatic hammer. "You're getting too adult."

The whip snaked Butch into the pit, dull eyes bulging more than ever. He slumped down on the slick black piston and struggled like a squashed bug and then lay moaning in a puddle of terror.

Ratbait stood sweating, as the whip came back to him. His stomach felt cold and strange, and the tall red wall spun like a crazy wheel around him, and he couldn't move till the whip pulled him to the rim of the pit.

But there Blinkie took his hand. He shook the whip off, and stepped down into the pit. Joey nodded, and the girl gave him a white, tiny smile. They all closed around her, arms linked tight, as the piston dropped.

"Now hop along for Pop! You've had your Jamboree—"

That hooting voice died away far above, and the pit's round mouth shrank into a blood-colored moon. The hot dark drummed like thunder all around them, and the slick floor tilted. It spilled them all into Mother's red steel jaws.

In early May of 1940, when I came back to Southern California, it seemed an unspoiled paradise. I loved the lush vegetation, the mild climate, the good smell of the air and the feeling of prosperous peace. All around the point where Marineland is today, nature had scarcely been touched.

Sometimes, after I had begun to find friends, we used to park above the cliffs and climb down them to gather driftwood for a picnic fire above the breaking surf, feeling as totally alone as if we had been the first ashore on the empty beach.

I found an upstairs room in a big house at 1224 Fifth Avenue, then a wide, quiet street walled with tall palms. The rent was low, perhaps fifteen dollars a week, and I made my own economical meals on a hot plate in the room. A cheap lifestyle, but I was used to it. I had the car and at least a little money. I did find friends, and I can look back fondly now at that interlude in Eden. . . .

I found more friends, most of them through science fiction. My work went better, at least sometimes. In June, Campbell is writing that he likes "Captain Planeteer," but can't take it just now because his inventory is full. *Argosy* did take it, for $140, and ran it as "Racketeers in the Sky."

In May, Mort Weisinger approved a plot for another *Startling* novel. It went slowly. A wire, dated November 19, asks "Where is promised novel?" On December 13, he is sending the manuscript back with a four-page list of problems—and, to keep me on the job, his promise of $100 in advance.

By January 3 I have his thanks "for a splendid revision" and the rest of the not-very-thrilling $250. It ran in the July *Startling* as *Gateway to Paradise*—the later paperback version, in an Ace double, became *Dome Around America*. It has ideas and images I like, but it's a very minor work, written more to fit Mort's fiction formula than to express my own emotion.

"The Iron God" is another novelette written sometime in 1940. A fumbling effort to do something better. Breuer read an early version and cheered the theme, but the final effect fell somehow flat, perhaps because too little came from anything I had lived. Good markets bounced it; Bob Erisman bought it, at $65 for 13,000 words, to run in *Marvel*.

If Los Angeles was Eden, then I had brought my own serpent. Analysis clarified some of my problems, but it failed to solve them all. After those two novels, my output dried up again. My total income for 1940 was a little under $800; for 1941, very little more. One barrier may have been the same old demon, "unconscious resistance"—it seemed that I was sabotaging the analytic process by not making money enough to pay even that nominal five dollars an hour.

Another difficulty, of course, was the sad fact that I hadn't been born a better writer. Yet another was the mere nature of the creative process—at least as it has always worked or failed to work for me.

Creating a story takes time. In the beginning stages, people and places and the stream of events are plastic, tentative, easy to manipulate. As I live with them through weeks or sometimes many months, meaning flows into them. They gather their own charges of emotion, rising mostly out of the unconscious; many a story problem has been solved while I slept, the answer suddenly clear next morning. As places and people gather reality, major revisions become very difficult. Errors are hard to correct, sometimes impossible for me even to see.

In those old days, writing for a living at a cent a word or less, I had no time to let stories grow. I had to keep pushing. Under less pressure now, I never try to write anything till it's ready; until I believe in the theme and care about the people. In 1982, with *Manseed* finished and sold, and the next novel still germinating, I felt free to try this nonfiction project. Though autobiography may sometimes become creative, it requires a different sort of effort.

Even with production slowing, that year was still good. Ed Hamilton came out to Los Angeles in 1940, perhaps with Mort Weisinger and Julie Schwartz—I remember seeing all three at a tourist court where they were staying. I met Leigh Brackett there. She had just begun to sell; her first story must have been "Martian Quest" in the February *Astounding*.

Maybe not beautiful, Leigh was attractive enough, athletic and bright and engaging; I got a sense of quietly stubborn conflict with her mundane family environment. She had an admirable awe of such old hands as Ed and I were, and we both enjoyed her.

Ed and I drove up to Redwood City for a mildly alcoholic weekend with Price, who still cherished the friendships of his pulp fiction career though he had turned to other means of survival. We went with him to Auburn, out in the Sacramento Valley, to see Clark Ashton Smith—Klar Kash Ton to the *Weird Tales* clan.

He was a lean, tall loner as I recall him, not so talkative as Ed and Price. I was struck with the contrast between his commonplace small-town surroundings and the exotic worlds and mannered language of his fiction. He, too, had almost quit writing by then; he was carving his imaginary monsters into grotesque little figurines. To me, he seemed defeated and pathetic.

At LASFS—the Los Angeles Science Fantasy Society, which used to meet in Clifton's Cafeteria—I encountered more sciencefictioneers, fans and pros and such would-be pros as Ray Bradbury, who was still selling newspapers, publishing his own fan magazine, and writing a thousand words of still pretty dreadful fiction every day.

He showed me some of it; I tried to make useful comments, though I can't claim much credit for the gifts he came to reveal. He was still living at home; once he got his mother to make Swedish meatballs for me, and I met his brother Skip.

Walt Daugherty and Russ Hodgkins were active fans. I remember Bruce Yerke, making himself pretty obnoxious with his way of twisting General Semantics into a device for putting people down, a habit that earned his role as model for the corpse in Tony Boucher's *Rocket to the Morgue*. Forry Ackerman was already a Big-Name Fan.

Art Barnes was a pro, writing a popular series for *Thrilling Wonder*. It was the sort of thing Mort loved, the translation of some successful contemporary cliché into a future setting, this time a Frank Buck takeoff about an intrepid girl collecting alien creatures for an interplanetary zoo.

I met John Parsons. An odd enigma to me, he was a rocket engineer with unexpected leanings toward the occult. He wanted to meet me because I'd written *Darker Than You Think*—a good many people have taken it more seriously than I ever did; witches now and then have taken me for a fellow Wiccan.

Parsons belonged to the OTO, an underground order founded, I think, by the satanist Aleister Crowley. One night Cleve Cartmill and I were allowed to climb after him into an attic to attend a secret meeting. The ritual was disappointingly tame. There was no nude virgin on the altar. Satan was not invoked.

Yet the priest impressed me. He was a lean, dynamic little man with bright, light blue eyes, driven by a virulent hatred of God. Talking to him after the ceremony, I found that he was the son of a British clergyman who must have been the real target of that savage animosity.

In Pasadena not long ago, walking across the grounds of the Jet Propulsion Laboratory, I was jolted to see Parsons' name on a memorial tablet set up to honor the first martyrs to space. He had written me once about testing multicellular solid-fuel rockets designed after those in my story "The Crucible of Power." When I first heard about his death I wondered if my own rockets had killed him, but Sprague de Camp tells me that he dropped a bottle of picric acid.

The new friend who mattered most was Bob Heinlein. He had just begun to sell, with "Lifeline" and "Misfit" published in 1939, but he was already among the brightest stars in the "Golden Age," the decade of exciting innovation that began when Campbell took over the editorship of *Astounding*.

Science fiction until then had been just another pulp category, not much different from mystery fiction or war stories or sea stories except to such fans as I was. Campbell had dazzling visions to share, and he kindled visions in a whole cluster of gifted new dreamers:

Asimov, Lester del Rey, Theodore Sturgeon, A. E. van Vogt, and
Heinlein himself. Discovering them and inspiring such adaptable survivors as de Camp, L. Ron Hubbard, and Cliff Simak, Campbell was
making science fiction something new.

Heinlein's early work was sometimes clumsy, but his ideas were
always exciting and he learned fast. By 1941, he had earned recognition as Guest of Honor at Denvention. He had a fine mind and
he knew a lot. Alertly critical of the world around him, he lived the
futures he wrote about and he made them live for us. His style was
utilitarian, deliberately unliterary but brightened with his own corn-
pone humor. I used to feel he was the most truly civilized person I
had ever known. Knowing him was one more good chapter in my
education.

He and Leslyn, his first wife, were living on Laurel Canyon, up
in the Hollywood hills, and I was vastly delighted when he invited
me to the little Saturday-night gatherings he called the Mañana Literary Society.

A remarkable group. Cleve Cartmill, crippled from polio, a sardonic but likable newspaperman who knew the seamy underside of
Los Angeles politics; later he made his name with "Deadfall," a story
that alarmed military security with all it said about how to build a
bomb. Cleve was no engineer, and most of the detail must have come
from Campbell.

Tony Boucher and Phyllis. Mick and Annette McComas. Sometimes I was allowed to bring Ray Bradbury, though he was still so
brash and noisy that Leslyn didn't always want him. Henry Kuttner
and C. L. Moore were there now and then. Leigh Brackett. Art
Barnes. Sometimes such visiting notables as Willy Ley and de Camp
and Hubbard. I remember a fetching redhead named Marda Brown.

We drank a little wine—mostly cheap white sherry—and told
shaggy dog stories and recited dirty limericks and talked about science fiction and life in the future and sex and nearly everything.

Legally, Tony was William Anthony Parker White—I think the
"Tony Boucher" name was coined to mean "fat check." He struck
me, as Heinlein did, as a citizen of a richer, wider culture where I
was still a naive stranger. He was a practising Catholic, a musicologist
specializing in Gregorian chant, and, as H. H. Holmes, a prolific
writer and reviewer of mystery novels. He put our society into his

1942 novel *Rocket to the Morgue*. Heinlein is there as Austin Carter, a chief suspect. Hubbard is D. Vance Wimple and Campbell is Don Stewart. Ed Hamilton and I are combined into Joe Henderson.

Tony had more sophisticated literary tastes than most of us. Both he and Mick McComas became discriminating editors. After the war, Mick and Ray Healy edited the first great science fiction anthology, *Adventures in Time and Space*, a landmark project which began convincing skeptics that science fiction books could sell.

A little later, Tony and Mick persuaded Lawrence Spivak to bankroll a trial issue of *The Magazine of Fantasy*. Soon renamed *Fantasy and Science Fiction*, it had a level of craftsmanship and quality new to the field. Mick resigned in 1954. Tony stayed on as sole editor until 1958. Such later editors as Ed Ferman have held *F&SF* to the same high curve.

In May of 1941, I came to the end of that second year with Dr. Tidd. Yet another, or even several more, might have done me good. I felt half anxious to go on, yet I had managed to fall behind again even with his nominal fees. That may have been the device of a still-rebellious unconscious in search of escape. However that may be, we agreed to suspend the analysis again.

THE FIREFLY TREE

They had come back to live on the old farm where his grandfather was born. His father loved it, but he felt lonely for his friends in the city. Cattle sometimes grazed through the barren sandhills beyond the barbed wire fences, but there were no neighbors. He found no friends except the firefly tree.

It grew in the old fruit orchard his grandfather had planted below the house. His mouth watered for the ripe apples and peaches and pears he expected, but when he saw the trees they were all dead or dying. They bore no fruit.

With no friends at all, he stayed with his father on the farm when his mother drove away every morning to work at the peanut mill. His father was always busy in the garden he made among the bare trees in the orchard. The old windmill had lost its wheel, but there was an electric pump for water. Cantaloupe and squash vines grew along the edge of the garden, with rows of tomatoes and beans, and then the corn that grew tall enough to hide the money trees.

He found the firefly tree one day while his father was chopping weeds and moving the pipes that sprayed water on his money trees. It was still tiny then, not as tall as his knee. The leaves were odd: thin arrowheads of glossy black velvet, striped with silver. A single lovely flower had three wide sky-colored petals and a bright yellow star at the center. He sat on the ground by it, breathing its strange sweetness, till his father came by with the hoe.

"Don't hurt it!" he begged. "Please!"

"That stinking weed?" his father grunted. "Get out of the way."
Something made him reach to catch the hoe.

"Okay." His father grinned and let it stay. "If you care that much."

He called it his tree, and watched it grow. When it wilted in a week with no rain, he found a bucket and carried water from the well. It grew taller than he was, with a dozen of the great blue flowers and then a hundred. The odor of them filled the garden.

Since there was no school, his mother tried to teach him at home. She found a red-backed reader for him, and a workbook with pages for him to fill out while she was away at work. He seldom got the lessons done.

"He's always mooning over that damn weed," his father muttered when she scolded him. "High as a kite on the stink of it."

The odor was strange and strong, but no stink at all. Not to him. He loved it and loved the tree. He carried more water and used the hoe to till the soil around it. Often he stood just looking at the huge blue blooms, wondering what the fruit would be.

One night he dreamed that the tree was swarming with fireflies. They were so real that he got out of bed and slipped out into the dark. The stars blazed brighter here than they had ever been in the city. They lit his way to the orchard, and he heard the fireflies before he came to the tree.

Their buzz rose and fell like the sound of the surf the time they went to visit his aunt who lived by the sea. Twinkling brighter than the stars, they filled the branches. One of them came to meet him. It hovered in front of his face and lit on the tip of his trembling finger, smiling at him with eyes as blue and bright as the flowers.

He had never seen a firefly close up. It was as big as a bumblebee. It had tiny hands that gripped his fingernail, and one blue eye squinted a little to study his face. The light came from a round topknot on its head. It flickered like something electric, from red to green, red to yellow to blue, maybe red again. The flashes were sometimes slower than his breath, sometimes so fast they blurred. He thought the flicker was meant to tell him something, but he had no way to understand.

Barefoot and finally shivering with cold, he stood there till it stopped. The firefly shook its crystal wings and flew away. The stars were fading into the dawn, and the tree was dark and silent when he looked. He was back in bed before he heard his mother rattling dishes in the kitchen, making breakfast.

The next night he dreamed that he was back under the tree, with the firefly perched again on his finger. Its tiny face seemed almost human in the dream, and he understood its winking voice. It told him how the tree had grown from a sharp-pointed acorn that came from the stars and planted itself when it struck the ground.

It told him about the firefly planet, far off in the sky. The fireflies belonged to a great republic spread across the stars. Thousands of different peoples lived in peace on thousands of different worlds. The acorn ship had come to invite the people of Earth to join their republic. They were ready to teach the Earth-people how to walk across space and travel to visit the stars. The dream seemed so wonderful that he tried to tell about it at breakfast.

"What did I tell you?" His father turned red and shouted at his mother. "His brain's been addled by the stink of that poison weed. I ought to cut it down and burn it."

"Don't!" He was frightened and screaming. "I love it. I'll die if you kill it."

"I'm afraid he would." His mother looked worried. "Leave the plant where it is, and I'll take him to Dr. Wong."

"Okay." His father nodded at him sternly. "If you'll promise to do your chores and stay out of the garden."

Trying to keep the promise, he washed the dishes after his mother was gone to work. He made the beds and swept the floors. He tried to do his lessons, though the stories in the reader seemed stupid to him now.

He did stay out of the garden, but the fireflies came again in his dreams. They carried him to see the shining forests on their own wonderful world. They took him to visit the planets of other peoples, people who lived under their seas, people who lived high in their skies, people as small as ants, people larger than the elephants he had seen in a circus parade. He saw ships that could fly faster than light from star to star, and huge machines he never understood, and cities more magical than fairyland.

He said no more about the dreams till the day his mother came home from work to take him to Dr. Wong. The nurse put a thermometer under his tongue and squeezed his arm with a rubber gadget and left him to wait with his mother for Dr. Wong. Dr. Wong was a friendly man who listened to his chest and looked at the nurse's chart and asked him about the fireflies.

"They're wonderful!" He thought the doctor would believe. "You must come at night to see them, sir. They love us. They came to show us the way to the stars."

"Listen to him!" His mother had never been out when the fireflies were shining. "That ugly weed has driven him out of his head!"

"An interesting case." The doctor smiled and patted his shoulder in a friendly way and turned to look at his mother. "One for the books. The boy should see a psychiatrist."

His mother had no money for that.

"I'll just take him home," she said, "and hope he gets better."

A police car was parked in front of the house when they got there. His father sat in the back, behind a metal grill. His head was bent. He wouldn't look up, not even when his mother called through a half-open window.

The police had more cars parked around the garden. They had chopped down all the money trees and thrown them into a pile. The firefly tree lay on top. It fragrance was lost in a reek of kerosene. The policemen made everybody move upwind and set the fire with a hissing blowtorch.

It spread slowly at first, then blazed so high they had to move farther away. Feeling sick at his stomach, he saw the branches of the tree twist and beat against the flames. He heard a long sharp scream. A cat caught in the fire, the policemen said, but he knew it wasn't a cat. Fireflies swarmed out of the thrashing branches and exploded like tiny bombs when the flames caught them.

His father was crying when the police took him away, along with a bundle of the money trees for evidence. His mother moved him back to the city. In school again, he tried to tell his new teachers about the fireflies and how they had come to invite the Earth into their great confederation of stars. The teachers sent him to the school psychologist, who called his mother to come for a conference.

They wanted him to forget the fireflies and find his old friends again, but he wanted no friends except the fireflies. He grieved for them and grieved for his father and grieved for all that might have been.

Recommended Reading by Jack Williamson

The Humanoids
Darker Than You Think
Brother to Demons, Brother to God
The Legion of Space
Lifeburst

CLIFFORD D. SIMAK

1904–1988

Clifford D. Simak was not only one of the best science fiction writers who ever lived. He was also one of the kindliest. In the late 1930s Simak took time out of his busy life (he was a full-time newspaperman, as well as a science fiction writer) to write long letters of encouragement and advice to such hopeful young sprigs as the teenaged Isaac Asimov.

He also found time for community affairs in the Minneapolis area. In fact, although Cliff and I had known each other pretty well by correspondence—I was his literary agent for a time—the first time I met Cliff in the flesh was when he came to New York in the early 1950s. There was nothing remarkable about a writer making the trek to New York City; that was the place where all the editors were, and writers do feel the need now and then to talk to their editors. That wasn't what brought Cliff to the Big Apple, though. A group of local Boy Scouts had won a visit to the city, and as one of the most obviously trustworthy adults around, Cliff had been drafted to come along as their chaperone. He was a good choice. Though Clifford Simak tolerated the eccentricities of others, his ideas of proper behavior were firmly rooted in the Midwest ethic of the 1920s, where he was growing up, and those sensibilities show up in most of his best work.

Clifford D. Simak's first appearance as a science fiction writer was with a story called "The World of the Red Sun" in 1931. In those days the only markets for science fiction in America were pulp magazines; appropriately, the stories they contained were more concerned with high-flying adventures on bizarre remote worlds than with literary merit. So with Simak's early stories; but after he had published only five of them, all in the space of a year or two, he took time out to regroup and reconsider. When he returned to writing SF, half a dozen years later, his editor of choice was John Campbell. The stories he wrote then showed a wholly new depth of character, climaxing with "City," the first story in his most famous series and the one that gave its title to the book that made his reputation.

By his fifties Simak was concentrating his writing on novels, all of them good, some remarkable. My personal favorite is *Way Station,* a nostalgically touching story about a lonely farmer in a state not unlike Simak's own Minnesota, who is charged with receiving and relaying to their destinations aliens traveling across the universe. The only reason *Way Station* is not included here is that its length would keep everything else out of the volume.

Like Jack Williamson, Clifford D. Simak began writing early, kept getting better, and never stopped. He was the third person to receive the Grand Master award. Few have deserved it more.

DESERTION

Four men, two by two, had gone into the howling maelstrom that was Jupiter and had not returned. They had walked into the keening gale—or rather, they had loped, bellies low against the ground, wet sides gleaming in the rain.

For they did not go in the shape of men.

Now the fifth man stood before the desk of Kent Fowler, head of Dome No. 3, Jovian Survey Commission.

Under Fowler's desk, old Towser scratched a flea, then settled down to sleep again.

Harold Allen, Fowler saw with a sudden pang, was young—too young. He had the easy confidence of youth, the face of one who never had known fear. And that was strange. For men in the domes of Jupiter did know fear—fear and humility. It was hard for Man to reconcile his puny self with the mighty forces of the monstrous planet.

"You understand," said Fowler, "that you need not do this. You understand that you need not go."

It was formula, of course. The other four had been told the same thing, but they had gone. This fifth one, Fowler knew, would go as well. But suddenly he felt a dull hope stir within him that Allen wouldn't go.

"When do I start?" asked Allen.

There had been a time when Fowler might have taken quiet pride in that answer, but not now. He frowned briefly.

"Within the hour," he said.

Allen stood waiting, quietly.

"Four other men have gone out and have not returned," said Fowler. "You know that, of course. We want you to return. We don't want you going off on any heroic rescue expedition. The main thing, the only thing, is that you come back, that you prove man can live in a Jovian form. Go to the first survey stake, no farther, then come back. Don't take any chances. Don't investigate anything. Just come back."

Allen nodded. "I understand all that."

"Miss Stanley will operate the converter," Fowler went on. "You need have no fear on that particular score. The other men were converted without mishap. They left the converter in apparently perfect condition. You will be in thoroughly competent hands. Miss Stanley is the best qualified conversion operator in the Solar System. She has had experience on most of the other planets. That is why she's here."

Allen grinned at the woman and Fowler saw something flicker across Miss Stanley's face—something that might have been pity, or rage—or just plain fear. But it was gone again and she was smiling back at the youth who stood before the desk. Smiling in that prim, school-teacherish way she had of smiling, almost as if she hated herself for doing it.

"I shall be looking forward," said Allen, "to my conversion."

And the way he said it, he made it all a joke, a vast, ironic joke. But it was no joke.

It was serious business, deadly serious. Upon these tests, Fowler knew, depended the fate of men on Jupiter. If the tests succeeded, the resources of the giant planet would be thrown open. Man would take over Jupiter as he already had taken over the other smaller planets. And if they failed—

If they failed, Man would continue to be chained and hampered by the terrific pressure, the greater force of gravity, the weird chemistry of the planet. He would continue to be shut within the domes, unable to set actual foot upon the planet, unable to see it with direct, unaided vision, forced to rely upon the awkward tractors and the televisor, forced to work with clumsy tools and mechanisms or through the medium of robots that themselves were clumsy.

For Man, unprotected and in his natural form, would be blotted out by Jupiter's terrific pressure of fifteen thousand pounds per square inch, pressure that made terrestrial sea bottoms seem a vacuum by comparison.

Even the strongest metal Earthmen could devise couldn't exist under pressure such as that, under the pressure and the alkaline rains that forever swept the planet. It grew brittle and flaky, crumbling like clay, or it ran away in little streams and puddles of ammonia salts. Only by stepping up the toughness and strength of that metal, by increasing its electronic tension, could it be made to withstand the weight of thousands of miles of swirling, choking gases that made up the atmosphere. And even when that was done, everything had to be coated with tough quartz to keep away the rain—the liquid ammonia that fell as bitter rain.

Fowler sat listening to the engines in the sub-floor of the dome—engines that ran on endlessly, the dome never quiet of them. They had to run and keep on running, for if they stopped the power flowing into the metal walls of the dome would stop, the electronic tension would ease up and that would be the end of everything.

Towser roused himself under Fowler's desk and scratched another flea, his leg thumping hard against the floor.

"Is there anything else?" asked Allen.

Fowler shook his head. "Perhaps there's something you want to do," he said. "Perhaps you—"

He had meant to say write a letter and he was glad he caught himself quick enough so he didn't say it.

Allen looked at his watch. "I'll be there on time," he said. He swung around and headed for the door.

Fowler knew Miss Stanley was watching him and he didn't want to turn and meet her eyes. He fumbled with a sheaf of papers on the desk before him.

"How long are you going to keep this up?" asked Miss Stanley and she bit off each word with a vicious snap.

He swung around in his chair and faced her then. Her lips were drawn into a straight, thin line, her hair seemed skinned back from her forehead tighter than ever, giving her face that queer, almost startling death-mask quality.

He tried to make his voice cool and level. "As long as there's any need of it," he said. "As long as there's any hope."

"You're going to keep on sentencing them to death," she said. "You're going to keep marching them out face to face with Jupiter. You're going to sit in here safe and comfortable and send them out to die."

"There is no room for sentimentality, Miss Stanley," Fowler said, trying to keep the note of anger from his voice. "You know as well as I do why we're doing this. You realize that Man in his own form simply cannot cope with Jupiter. The only answer is to turn men into the sort of things that can cope with it. We've done it on the other planets.

"If a few men die, but we finally succeed, the price is small. Through the ages men have thrown away their lives on foolish things, for foolish reasons. Why should we hesitate, then, at a little death in a thing as great as this?"

Miss Stanley sat stiff and straight, hands folded in her lap, the lights shining on her graying hair and Fowler, watching her, tried to imagine what she might feel, what she might be thinking. He wasn't exactly afraid of her, but he didn't feel quite comfortable when she was around. Those sharp blue eyes saw too much, her hands looked far too competent. She should be somebody's Aunt sitting in a rocking chair with her knitting needles. But she wasn't. She was the top-notch conversion unit operator in the Solar System and she didn't like the way he was doing things.

"There is something wrong, Mr. Fowler," she declared.

"Precisely," agreed Fowler. "That's why I'm sending young Allen out alone. He may find out what it is."

"And if he doesn't?"

"I'll send someone else."

She rose slowly from her chair, started toward the door, then stopped before his desk.

"Some day," she said, "you will be a great man. You never let a chance go by. This is your chance. You knew it was when this dome was picked for the tests. If you put it through, you'll go up a notch or two. No matter how many men may die, you'll go up a notch or two."

"Miss Stanley," he said and his voice was curt, "young Allen is going out soon. Please be sure that your machine—"

"My machine," she told him, icily, "is not to blame. It operates along the co-ordinates the biologists set up."

He sat hunched at his desk, listening to her footsteps go down the corridor.

What she said was true, of course. The biologists had set up the co-ordinates. But the biologists could be wrong. Just a hairbreath of difference, one iota of digression and the converter would be sending out something that wasn't the thing they meant to send. A mutant that might crack up, go haywire, come unstuck under some condition or stress of circumstance wholly unsuspected.

For Man didn't know much about what was going on outside. Only what his instruments told him was going on. And the samplings of those happenings furnished by those instruments and mechanisms had been no more than samplings, for Jupiter was unbelievably large and the domes were very few.

Even the work of the biologists in getting the data on the Lopers, apparently the highest form of Jovian life, had involved more than three years of intensive study and after that two years of checking to make sure. Work that could have been done on Earth in a week or two. But work that, in this case, couldn't be done on Earth at all, for one couldn't take a Jovian life form to Earth. The pressure here on Jupiter couldn't be duplicated outside of Jupiter and at Earth pressure and temperature the Lopers would simply have disappeared in a puff of gas.

Yet it was work that had to be done if Man ever hoped to go about Jupiter in the life form of the Lopers. For before the converter could change a man to another life form, every detailed physical characteristic of that life form must be known—surely and positively, with no chance of mistake.

Allen did not come back.

The tractors, combing the nearby terrain, found no trace of him, unless the skulking thing reported by one of the drivers had been the missing Earthman in Loper form.

The biologists sneered their most accomplished academic sneers when Fowler suggested the co-ordinates might be wrong. Carefully they pointed out, the co-ordinates worked. When a man was put into the converter and the switch was thrown, the man became a Loper. He left the machine and moved away, out of sight, into the soupy atmosphere.

Some quirk, Fowler had suggested; some tiny deviation from the thing a Loper should be, some minor defect. If there were, the biologists said, it would take years to find it.

And Fowler knew that they were right.

So there were five men now instead of four and Harold Allen had walked out into Jupiter for nothing at all. It was as if he'd never gone so far as knowledge was concerned.

Fowler reached across his desk and picked up the personnel file, a thin sheaf of paper neatly clipped together. It was a thing he dreaded but a thing he had to do. Somehow the reason for these strange disappearances must be found. And there was no other way than to send out more men.

He sat for a moment listening to the howling of the wind above the dome, the everlasting thundering gale that swept across the planet in boiling, twisting wrath.

Was there some threat out there, he asked himself? Some danger they did not know about? Something that lay in wait and gobbled up the Lopers, making no distinction between Lopers that were *bona fide* and Lopers that were men? To the gobblers, of course, it would make no difference.

Or had there been a basic fault in selecting the Lopers as the type of life best fitted for existence on the surface of the planet? The evident intelligence of the Lopers, he knew, had been one factor in that determination. For if the thing Man became did not have capacity for intelligence, Man could not for long retain his own intelligence in such a guise.

Had the biologists let that one factor weigh too heavily, using it to offset some other factor that might be unsatisfactory, even disastrous? It didn't seem likely. Stiffnecked as they might be, the biologists knew their business.

Or was the whole thing impossible, doomed from the very start? Conversion to other life forms had worked on other planets, but that did not necessarily mean it would work on Jupiter. Perhaps Man's intelligence could not function correctly through the sensory apparatus provided Jovian life. Perhaps the Lopers were so alien there was no common ground for human knowledge and the Jovian conception of existence to meet and work together.

Or the fault might lie with Man, be inherent with the race. Some mental aberration which, coupled with what they found outside, wouldn't let them come back. Although it might not be an aberration, not in the human sense. Perhaps just one ordinary human mental trait, accepted as commonplace on Earth, would be so violently at odds with Jovian existence that it would blast human sanity.

Claws rattled and clicked down the corridor. Listening to them, Fowler smiled wanly. It was Towser coming back from the kitchen, where he had gone to see his friend, the cook.

Towser came into the room, carrying a bone. He wagged his tail at Fowler and flopped down beside the desk, bone between his paws. For a long moment his rheumy old eyes regarded his master and Fowler reached down a hand to ruffle a ragged ear.

"You still like me, Towser?" Fowler asked and Towser thumped his tail.

"You're the only one," said Fowler.

He straightened and swung back to the desk. His hand reached out and picked up the file.

Bennett? Bennett had a girl waiting for him back on Earth.

Andrews? Andrews was planning on going back to Mars Tech just as soon as he earned enough to see him through a year.

Olson? Olson was nearing pension age. All the time telling the boys how he was going to settle down and grow roses.

Carefully, Fowler laid the file back on the desk.

Sentencing men to death. Miss Stanley had said that, her pale lips scarcely moving in her parchment face. Marching men out to die while he, Fowler, sat here safe and comfortable.

They were saying it all through the dome, no doubt, especially since Allen had failed to return. They wouldn't say it to his face, of course. Even the man or men he called before this desk and told they were the next to go, wouldn't say it to him.

But he would see it in their eyes.

He picked up the file again. Bennett, Andrews, Olson. There were others, but there was no use in going on.

Kent Fowler knew that he couldn't do it, couldn't face them, couldn't send more men out to die.

He leaned forward and flipped up the toggle on the intercommunicator.

"Yes, Mr. Fowler."

"Miss Stanley, please."

He waited for Miss Stanley, listening to Towser chewing halfheartedly on the bone. Towser's teeth were getting bad.

"Miss Stanley," said Miss Stanley's voice.

"Just wanted to tell you, Miss Stanley, to get ready for two more."

"Aren't you afraid," asked Miss Stanley, "that you'll run out of them? Sending out one at a time, they'd last longer, give you twice the satisfaction."

"One of them," said Fowler, "will be a dog."

"A dog!"

"Yes, Towser."

He heard the quick, cold rage that iced her voice. "Your own dog! He's been with you all these years—"

"That's the point," said Fowler. "Towser would be unhappy if I left him behind."

It was not the Jupiter he had known through the televisor. He had expected it to be different, but not like this. He had expected a hell of ammonia rain and stinking fumes and the deafening, thundering tumult of the storm. He had expected swirling clouds and fog and the snarling flicker of monstrous thunderbolts.

He had not expected the lashing downpour would be reduced to drifting purple mist that moved like fleeing shadows over a red and purple sward. He had not even guessed the snaking bolts of lightning would be flares of pure ecstasy across a painted sky.

Waiting for Towser, Fowler flexed the muscles of his body, amazed at the smooth, sleek strength he found. Not a bad body, he decided, and grimaced at remembering how he had pitied the Lopers when he glimpsed them through the television screen.

For it had been hard to imagine a living organism based upon ammonia and hydrogen rather than upon water and oxygen, hard to believe that such a form of life could know the same quick thrill of life that humankind could know. Hard to conceive of life out in the soupy maelstrom that was Jupiter, not knowing, of course, that through Jovian eyes it was no soupy maelstrom at all.

The wind brushed against him with what seemed gentle fingers and he remembered with a start that by Earth standards the wind was a roaring gale, a two-hundred-mile an hour howler laden with deadly gases.

Pleasant scents seeped into his body. And yet scarcely scents, for it was not the sense of smell as he remembered it. It was as if his whole being was soaking up the sensation of lavender—and yet not lavender. It was something, he knew, for which he had no word, undoubtedly the first of many enigmas in terminology. For the words he knew, the thought symbols that served him as an Earthman would not serve him as a Jovian.

The lock in the side of the dome opened and Towser came tumbling out—at least he thought it must be Towser.

He started to call to the dog, his mind shaping the words he meant to say. But he couldn't say them. There was no way to say them. He had nothing to say them with.

For a moment his mind swirled in muddy terror, a blind fear that eddied in little puffs of panic through his brain.

How did Jovians talk? How—

Suddenly he was aware of Towser, intensely aware of the bumbling, eager friendliness of the shaggy animal that had followed him from Earth to many planets. As if the thing that was Towser had reached out and for a moment sat within his brain.

And out of the bubbling welcome that he sensed, came words.

"Hiya, pal."

Not words really, better than words. Thought symbols in his brain, communicated thought symbols that had shades of meaning words could never have.

"Hiya, Towser," he said.

"I feel good," said Towser. "Like I was a pup. Lately I've been feeling pretty punk. Legs stiffening up on me and teeth wearing down to almost nothing. Hard to mumble a bone with teeth like that.

Besides, the fleas give me hell. Used to be I never paid much attention to them. A couple of fleas more or less never meant much in my early days."

"But . . . but—" Fowler's thoughts tumbled awkwardly. "You're talking to me!"

"Sure thing," said Towser. "I always talked to you, but you couldn't hear me. I tried to say things to you, but I couldn't make the grade."

"I understood you sometimes," Fowler said.

"Not very well," said Towser. "You knew when I wanted food and when I wanted a drink and when I wanted out, but that's about all you ever managed."

"I'm sorry," Fowler said.

"Forget it," Towser told him. "I'll race you to the cliff."

For the first time, Fowler saw the cliff, apparently many miles away, but with a strange crystalline beauty that sparkled in the shadow of the many-colored clouds.

Fowler hesitated. "It's a long way—"

"Ah, come on," said Towser and even as he said it he started for the cliff.

Fowler followed, testing his legs, testing the strength in that new body of his, a bit doubtful at first, amazed a moment later, then running with a sheer joyousness that was one with the red and purple sward, with the drifting smoke of the rain across the land.

As he ran the consciousness of music came to him, a music that beat into his body, that surged throughout his being, that lifted him on wings of silver speed. Music like bells might make from some steeple on a sunny, springtime hill.

As the cliff drew nearer the music deepened and filled the universe with a spray of magic sound. And he knew the music came from the tumbling waterfall that feathered down the face of the shining cliff.

Only, he knew, it was no waterfall, but an ammonia-fall and the cliff was white because it was oxygen, solidified.

He skidded to a stop beside Towser where the waterfall broke into a glittering rainbow of many hundred colors. Literally many hundred, for here, he saw, was no shading of one primary to another as human beings saw, but a clearcut selectivity that broke the prism down to its last ultimate classification.

"The music," said Towser.

"Yes, what about it?"

"The music," said Towser, "is vibrations. Vibrations of water falling."

"But Towser, you don't know about vibrations."

"Yes, I do," contended Towser. "It just popped into my head."

Fowler gulped mentally. "Just popped!"

And suddenly, within his own head, he held a formula—the formula for a process that would make metal to withstand the pressure of Jupiter.

He stared, astounded, at the waterfall and swiftly his mind took the many colors and placed them in their exact sequence in the spectrum. Just like that. Just out of the blue sky. Out of nothing, for he knew nothing either of metals or of colors.

"Towser," he cried. "Towser, something's happening to us!"

"Yeah, I know," said Towser.

"It's our brains," said Fowler. "We're using them, all of them, down to the last hidden corner. Using them to figure out things we should have known all the time. Maybe the brains of Earth things naturally are slow and foggy. Maybe we are the morons of the universe. Maybe we are fixed so we have to do things the hard way."

And, in the new sharp clarity of thought that seemed to grip him, he knew that it would not only be the matter of colors in a waterfall or metals that would resist the pressure of Jupiter. He sensed other things, things not yet quite clear. A vague whispering that hinted of greater things, of mysteries beyond the pale of human thought, beyond even the pale of human imagination. Mysteries, fact, logic built on reasoning. Things that any brain should know if it used all its reasoning power.

"We're still mostly Earth," he said. "We're just beginning to learn a few of the things we are to know—a few of the things that were kept from us as human beings, perhaps because we were human beings. Because our human bodies were poor bodies. Poorly equipped for thinking, poorly equipped in certain senses that one has to have to know. Perhaps even lacking in certain senses that are necessary to true knowledge."

He stared back at the dome, a tiny black thing dwarfed by the distance.

Back there were men who couldn't see the beauty that was Jupiter. Men who thought that swirling clouds and lashing rain obscured the planet's face. Unseeing human eyes. Poor eyes. Eyes that could not see the beauty in the clouds, that could not see through the storm. Bodies that could not feel the thrill of trilling music stemming from the rush of broken water.

Men who walked alone, in terrible loneliness, talking with their tongue like Boy Scouts wigwagging out their messages, unable to reach out and touch one another's mind as he could reach out and touch Towser's mind. Shut off forever from that personal, intimate contact with other living things.

He, Fowler, had expected terror inspired by alien things out here on the surface, had expected to cower before the threat of unknown things, had steeled himself against digust of a situation that was not of Earth.

But instead he had found something greater than Man had ever known. A swifter, surer body. A sense of exhilaration, a deeper sense of life. A sharper mind. A world of beauty that even the dreamers of the Earth had not yet imagined.

"Let's get going," Towser urged.

"Where do you want to go?"

"Anywhere," said Towser. "Just start going and see where we end up. I have a feeling . . . well, a feeling—"

"Yes, I know," said Fowler.

For he had the feeling, too. The feeling of high destiny. A certain sense of greatness. A knowledge that somewhere off beyond the horizons lay adventure and things greater than adventure.

Those other five had felt it, too. Had felt the urge to go and see, the compelling sense that here lay a life of fullness and of knowledge.

That, he knew, was why they had not returned.

"I won't go back," said Towser.

"We can't let them down," said Fowler.

Fowler took a step or two, back toward the dome, then stopped. Back to the dome. Back to that aching, poison-laden body he had left. It hadn't seemed aching before, but now he knew it was.

Back to the fuzzy brain. Back to muddled thinking. Back to the flapping mouths that formed signals others understood. Back to eyes that now would be worse than no sight at all. Back to squalor, back to crawling, back to ignorance.

"Perhaps some day," he said, muttering to himself.

"We got a lot to do and a lot to see," said Towser. "We got a lot to learn. We'll find things—"

Yes, they could find things. Civilizations, perhaps. Civilizations that would make the civilization of Man seem puny by comparison. Beauty and, more important, an understanding of that beauty. And a comradeship no one had never known before—that no man, no dog had ever known before.

And life. The quickness of life after what seemed a drugged existence.

"I can't go back," said Towser.

"Nor I," said Fowler.

"They would turn me back into a dog," said Towser.

"And me," said Fowler, "back into a man."

FOUNDING FATHER

W inston-Kirby walked home across the moor just before the twilight hour and it was then, he felt, that the land was at its best. The sun was sinking into a crimson froth of clouds and the first gray-silver light began to run across the swales. There were moments when it seemed all eternity grew quiet and watched with held breath.

It had been a good day and it would be a good homecoming, for the others would be waiting for him with the dinner table set and the fireplace blazing and the drinks set close at hand. It was a pity, he thought, that they would not go walking with him, although, in this particular instance, he was rather glad they hadn't. Once in a while, it was a good thing for a man to be alone. For almost a hundred years, aboard the ship, there had been no chance to be alone.

But that was over now and they could settle down, just the six of them, to lead the kind of life they'd planned. After only a few short weeks, the planet was beginning to seem like home; in the years to come, it would become in truth a home such as Earth had never been.

Once again he felt the twinge of recurring wonder at how they'd ever got away with it. That Earth should allow six of its immortals to slip through its clutches seemed unbelievable. Earth had real and urgent need for all of its immortals, and that not one, but six, of them should be allowed to slip away, to live lives of their own, was beyond all logic. And yet that was exactly what had happened.

There was something queer about it, Winston-Kirby told himself. On the century-long flight from Earth, they'd often talked about it and wondered how it had come about. Cranford-Adams, he recalled, had been convinced that it was some subtle trap, but after a hundred years there was no evidence of any trap and it had begun to seem Cranford-Adams must be wrong.

Winston-Kirby topped the gentle rise that he had been climbing and, in the gathering dusk, he saw the manor house—exactly the kind of house he had dreamed about for years, precisely the kind of house to be built in such a setting—except that the robots had built it much too large. But that, he consoled himself, was what one had to expect of robots. Efficient, certainly, and very well intentioned and obedient and nice to have around, but sometimes pretty stupid.

He stood on the hilltop and gazed down upon the house. How many times had he and his companions, at the dinner table, planned the kind of house they would build? How often had they speculated upon the accuracy of the specifications given for this planet they had chosen from the Exploratory Files, fearful that it might not be in every actuality the way it was described?

But here, finally, it was—something out of Hardy, something from the Baskervilles—the long imagining come to comfortable reality.

There was the manor house, with the light shining from its windows, and the dark bulk of the outbuildings built to house the livestock, which had been brought in the ship as frozen embryos and soon would be emerging from the incubators. And there the level land that in a few more months would be fields and gardens, and to the north the spaceship stood after years of roving. As he watched, the first bright star sprang out just beyond the spaceship's nose, and the spaceship and the star looked for all the world like a symbolic Christmas candle.

He walked down the hill, with the first night wind blowing in his face and the ancient smell of heather in the air, and was happy and exultant.

It was sinful, he thought, to be so joyful, but there was reason for it. The voyage had been happy and the planet-strike successful and here he was, the undisputed proprietor of an entire planet upon which, in the fullness of time, he would found a family and a dynasty.

And he had all the time there was. There was no need to hurry. He had all of eternity if he needed it.

And, best of all, he had good companions.

They would be waiting for him when he stepped through the door. There would be laughter and a quick drink, then a leisurely dinner, and, later, brandy before the blazing fire. And there'd be talk—good talk, sober and intimate and friendly.

It had been the talk, he told himself, more than anything else, which had gotten them sanely through the century of space flight. That and their mutual love and appreciation of the finer points of the human culture—understanding of the arts, love of good literature, interest in philosophy. It was not often that six persons could live intimately for a hundred years without a single spat, without a touch of cabin fever.

Inside the manor house, they would be waiting for him in the fire and candlelight, with the drinks all mixed and the talk already started, and the room would be warm with good fellowship and perfect understanding.

Cranford-Adams would be sitting in the big chair before the fire, staring at the flames and thinking, for he was the thinker of the group. And Allyn-Burbage would be standing, with one elbow on the mantel, a glass clutched in his hand and in his eyes the twinkle of good humor. Cosette-Middleton would be talking with him and laughing, for she was the gay one, with her elfin spirit and her golden hair. Anna-Quinze more than likely would be reading, curled up in a chair, and Mary-Foyle would be simply waiting, glad to be alive, glad to be with friends.

These, he thought, were the long companions of the trip, so full of understanding, so tolerant and gracious that a century had not dulled the beauty of their friendship.

Winston-Kirby hurried, a thing he almost never did, at the thought of those five who were waiting for him, anxious to be with them, to tell them of his walk across the moor, to discuss with them still again some details of their plans.

He turned into the walk. The wind was becoming cold, as it always did with the fall of darkness, and he raised the collar of his jacket for the poor protection it afforded.

He reached the door and stood for an instant in the chill, to savor the never-failing satisfaction of the massive timbering and the stout, strong squareness of the house. A place built to stand through the centuries, he thought, a place of dynasty with a sense of forev-erness.

He pressed the latch and thrust his weight against the door and it came slowly open. A blast of warm air rushed out to greet him. He stepped into the entry hall and closed the door behind him. As he took off his cap and jacket and found a place to hang them, he stamped and scuffed his feet a little to let the others know that he had returned.

But there were no greetings for him, no sound of happy laughter. There was only silence from the inner room.

He turned about so swiftly that his hand trailed across his jacket and dislodged it from the hook. It fell to the floor with a smooth rustle of fabric and lay there, a little mound of cloth.

His legs suddenly were cold and heavy, and when he tried to hurry, the best he could do was shuffle, and he felt the chill edge of fear.

He reached the entrance to the room and stopped, shocked into immobility. His hands went out and grasped the door jamb on either side of him.

There was no one in the room. And not only that—the room itself was different. It was not simply the companions who were gone. Gone, as well, were the rich furnishings of the rooms, gone the com-fort and the pride.

There were no rugs upon the floor, no hangings at the windows, no paintings on the wall. The fireplace was a naked thing of rough and jagged stone. The furniture—the little there was—was primitive, barely knocked together. A small trestle table stood before the fire-place, with a three-legged stool pulled up to a place that was set for one.

Winston-Kirby tried to call. The first time, the words gurgled in his throat and he could not get them out. He tried again and made it: "Job! Job, where are you?"

Job came running from somewhere in the house. "What's the trouble, sir?"

"Where are the others? Where have they gone? They should be waiting for me."

Job shook his head, just slightly, a quick move right and left. "Mister Kirby, sir, they were never here."

"Never here! But they were here when I left this morning. They knew I'd be coming back."

"You fail to understand, sir. There were never any others. There were just you and I and the other robots. And the embryos, of course."

Winston-Kirby let go of the door and walked a few feet forward.

"Job," he said, "you're joking." But he knew something was wrong—robots never joke.

"We let you keep them as long as we could," said Job. "We hated to have to take them from you, sir. But we needed the equipment for the incubators."

"But this room! The rugs, the furniture, the—"

"That was all part of it, sir. Part of the dimensino."

Winston-Kirby walked slowly across the room, used one foot to hook the three-legged stool out from the table. He sat down heavily.

"The dimensino?" he asked.

"Surely you remember."

He frowned to indicate he didn't. But it was coming back to him, some of it, slowly and reluctantly, emerging vaguely after all the years of forgetfulness.

He fought against the remembering and the knowledge. He tried to push it back into that dark corner of his mind from which it came. It was sacrilege and treason—it was madness.

"The human embryos," Job told him, "came through very well. Of the thousand of them, all but three are viable."

Winston-Kirby shook his head, as if to clear away the mist that befogged his brain.

"We have the incubators all set up in the outbuildings, sir," said Job. "We waited as long as we could before we took the dimensino equipment. We let you have it until the very last. It might have been easier, sir, if we could have done it gradually, but there is no provision for that. You either have dimensino or you haven't got it."

"Of course," said Winston-Kirby, mumbling just a little. "It was considerate of you. I thank you very much."

He stood up unsteadily and rubbed his hand across his eyes.

"It's not possible," he said. "It simply can't *be* possible. I lived for a hundred years with them. They were as real as I am. They were flesh and blood, I tell you. They were . . ."

The room still was bare and empty, a mocking emptiness, an alien mockery.

"It is possible," said Job gently. "It is just the way it should be. Everything has gone according to the book. You are here, still sane, thanks to the dimensino. The embryos came through better than expected. The equipment is intact. In eight months or so, the children will be coming from the incubators. By that time, we will have gardens and a crop on the way. The livestock embryos will also have emerged and the colony will be largely self-sustaining."

Winston-Kirby strode to the table, picked up the plate that was laid at the single place. It was lightweight plastic.

"Tell me," he said. "Have we any china? Have we any glassware or silver?"

Job looked as near to startled as a robot ever could. "Of course not, sir. We had no room for more than just the bare essentials this trip. The china and the silver and all the rest of it will have to wait until much later."

"And I have been eating ship rations?"

"Naturally," said Job. "There was so little room and so much we had to take . . ."

Winston-Kirby stood with the plate in his hand, tapping it gently on the table, remembering those other dinners—aboard the ship and since the ship had landed—the steaming soup in its satiny tureen, the pink and juicy prime ribs, the huge potatoes baked to a mealy turn, the crisp green lettuce, the shine of polished silver, the soft sheen of good china, the—

"Job," he said.

"Sir?"

"It was all delusion, then?"

"I am afraid it was. I am sorry, sir."

"And you robots?"

"All of us are fine, sir. It was different with us. We can face reality."

"And humans can't."

"Sometimes it is better if they can be protected from it."

"But not now?"

"Not any more," said Job. "It must be faced now, sir."

Winston-Kirby laid the plate down on the table and turned back to the robot. "I think I'll go up to my room and change to other clothes. I presume dinner will be ready soon. Ship rations, doubtless?"

"A special treat tonight," Job told him. "Hezekiah found some lichens and I've made a pot of soup."

"Splendid!" Winston-Kirby said, trying not to gag.

He climbed the stairs to the door at the head of the stairs.

As he was about to go into the room, another robot came tramping down the hall.

"Good evening, sir," it said.

"And who are you?"

"I'm Solomon," said the robot. "I'm fixing up the nurseries."

"Soundproofing them, I hope."

"Oh, nothing like that. We haven't the material or time."

"Well, carry on," said Winston-Kirby, and went into the room.

It was not his room at all. It was small and plain. There was a bunk instead of the great four-poster he had been sleeping in and there were no rugs, no full-length mirror, no easy chairs.

Delusion, he had said, not really believing it.

But here there was no delusion.

The room was cold with a dread reality—a reality, he knew, that had been long delayed. In the loneliness of this tiny room, he came face to face with it and felt the sick sense of loss. It was a reckoning that had been extended into the future as far as it might be—and extended not alone as a matter of mercy, of mere consideration, but because of a cold, hard necessity, a practical concession to human vulnerability.

For no man, no matter how well adjusted, no matter if immortal, could survive intact, in mind and body, a trip such as he had made. To survive a century under space conditions, there must be delusion and companionship to provide security and purpose from day to day. And that companionship must be more than human. For mere human companionship, however ideal, would give rise to countless ir-ritations, would breed deadly cabin fever.

Dimensino companionship was the answer, then, providing an il-lusion of companionship flexible to every mood and need of the human subject. Providing, as well, a background to that companionship

—a wish-fulfillment way of life that nailed down security such as humans under normal circumstances never could have known.

He sat down on the bunk and began to unlace his heavy walking shoes.

The practical human race, he thought—practical to the point of fooling itself to reach destination, practical to the point of fabricating the dimensino equipment to specifications which could be utilized, upon arrival, in the incubators.

But willing to gamble when there was a need to gamble. Ready to bet that a man could survive a century in space if he were sufficiently insulated against reality—insulated by seeming flesh and blood which, in sober fact, existed only by the courtesy of the human mind assisted by intricate electronics.

For no ship before had ever gone so far on a colonizing mission. No man had ever existed for even half as long under the influence of dimensino.

But there were few planets where Man might plant a colony under natural conditions, without extensive and expensive installations and precautions. The nearer of these planets had been colonized and the survey had shown that this one which he finally had reached was especially attractive.

So Earth and Man had bet. Especially one man, Winston-Kirby told himself with pride, but the pride was bitter in his mouth. The odds, he recalled, had been five to three against him.

And yet, even in his bitterness, he recognized the significance of what he had done. It was another breakthrough, another triumph for the busy little brain that was hammering at the door of all eternity.

It meant that the Galaxy was open, that Earth could remain the center of an expanding empire, that dimensino and immortal could travel to the very edge of space, that the seed of Man would be scattered wide and far, traveling as frozen embryos through the cold, black distance which hurt the mind to think of.

He went to the small chest of drawers and found a change of clothing, laid it on the bunk and began to take off his hiking outfit.

Everything was going according to the book, Job had said.

The house was bigger than he had wanted it, but the robots had been right—a big building would be needed to house a thousand babies. The incubators were set up and the nurseries were being readied and another far Earth colony was getting under way.

And colonies were important, he remembered, reaching back into that day, a hundred years before, when he and many others had laid their plans—including the plan whereby he could delude himself and thus preserve his sanity. For with more and more of the immortal mutations occurring, the day was not too distant when the human race would require all the room that it could grab.

And it was the mutant immortals who were the key persons in the colonizing programs—going out as founding fathers to supervise the beginning of each colony, staying on as long as needed, to act as a sort of elder statesman until that day when the colony could stand on its own feet.

There would be busy years ahead, he knew, serving as father, proctor, judge, sage and administrator, a sort of glorified Old Man of a brand-new tribe.

He pulled on his trousers, scuffed his feet into his shoes, rose to tuck in his shirt tail. And he turned, by force of habit, to the full-length mirror.

And the glass was there!

He stood astounded, gaping foolishly at the image of himself. And behind him, in the glass, he saw the great four-poster and the easy chairs.

He swung around and the bed and chairs were gone. There were just the bunk and the chest of drawers in the small, mean room.

Slowly he sat down on the edge of the bunk, clasping his hands so they wouldn't shake.

It wasn't true! It couldn't be! The dimensino was gone.

And yet it was with him still, lurking in his brain, just around the corner if he would only try.

He tried and it was easy. The room changed as he remembered it—with the full-length mirror and the massive bed upon which he sat, the thick rugs, the gleaming liquor cabinet and the tasteful drapes.

He tried to make it go away, barely remembering back in some deep, black closet of his mind that he must make it go.

But it wouldn't go away.

He tried and tried again, and it still was there, and he felt the will to make it go slipping from his consciousness.

"No!" he cried in terror, and the terror did it.

He sat in the small, bare room.

He found that he was breathing hard, as if he'd climbed a high, steep hill. His hands were fists and his teeth were clenched and he felt the sweat trickling down his ribs.

It would be easy, he thought, so easy and so pleasant to slip back to the old security, to the warm, deep friendship, to the lack of pressing purpose.

But he must not do it, for here was a job to do. Distasteful as it seemed now, as cold, as barren, it still was something he must do. For it was more than just one more colony. It was the breakthrough, the sure and certain knowledge, the proved knowledge, that Man no longer was chained by time or distance.

And yet there was this danger to be recognized; it was not something on which one might shut one's mind. It must be reported in every clinical detail so that, back on Earth, it might be studied and the inherent menace somehow remedied or removed.

Side effect, he wondered, or simply a matter of learning? For the dimensino was no more than an aid to the human mind—an aid to a very curious end, the production of controlled hallucinations operating on the wish-fulfillment level.

After a hundred years, perhaps, the human mind had learned the technique well, so well that there was no longer need of the dimensino.

It was something he should have realized, he insisted to himself. He had gone on long walks and, during all those hours alone, the delusion had not faded. It had taken the sudden shock of silence and emptiness, where he had expected laughter and warm greeting, to penetrate the haze of delusion in which he'd walked for years. And even now it lurked, a conditioned state of mind, to ambush him at every hidden thicket.

How long would it be before the ability would start to wear away? What might be done to wipe it out entirely? How does one unlearn a thing he's spent a century in learning? Exactly how dangerous was it—was there necessity of a conscious thought, an absolute command or could a man slip into it simply as an involuntary retreat from drear reality?

He must warn the robots. He must talk it over with them. Some sort of emergency measure must be set up to protect him against the wish or urge, some manner of drastic action be devised to rescue him, should he slip back into the old delusion.

Although, he thought, it would be so fine to walk out of the room and down the stairs and find the others waiting for him, with the drinks all ready and the talk well started. . . .

"Cut it out!" he screamed.

Wipe it from his mind—that was what he must do. He must not even think of it. He must work so hard that he would have no time to think, become so tired from work that he'd fall into bed and go to sleep at once and have no chance to dream.

He ran through his mind all that must be done—the watching of the incubators, preparing the ground for gardens and for crops, servicing the atomic generators, getting in timbers against the need of building, exploring and mapping and surveying the adjacent territory, overhauling the ship for the one-robot return flight to Earth.

He filled his mind with it. He tagged items for further thought and action. He planned the days and months and years ahead. And at last he was satisfied.

He had it under control.

He tied his shoes and finished buttoning his shirt. Then, with a resolute tread, he opened the door and walked out on the landing.

A hum of talk floating up the stairway stopped him in his tracks.

Fear washed over him. Then the fear evaporated. Gladness burst within him and he took a quick step forward.

At the top of the stairs, he halted and reached out a hand to grasp the banister.

Alarm bells were ringing in his brain and the gladness fell away. There was nothing left but sorrow, a terrible, awful grieving.

He could see one corner of the room below and he could see that it was carpeted. He could see the drapes and paintings and one ornate golden chair.

With a moan, he turned and fled to his room. He slammed the door and stood with his back against it.

The room was the way it should be, bare and plain and cold.

Thank God, he thought. Thank God!

A shout came up the stairway.

"Winston, what's wrong with you? Winston, hurry up!"

And another voice: "Winston, we're celebrating. We have a suckling pig."

And still another voice: "With an apple in its mouth."

He didn't answer.

They'll go away, he thought. They have to go away.

And even as he thought it, half of him—more than half—longed in sudden agony to open up the door and go down the stairs and know once again the old security and the ancient friendship.

He found that he had both his hands behind his back and that they were clutching the doorknob as if they were frozen there.

He heard steps on the stairway, the sound of many happy, friendly voices, coming up to get him.

GROTTO OF THE DANCING DEER

Luis was playing his pipe when Boyd climbed the steep path that led up to the cave. There was no need to visit the cave again; all the work was done, mapping, measuring, photographing, extracting all possible information from the site. Not only the paintings, although the paintings were the important part of it. Also there had been the animal bones, charred, and the still remaining charcoal of the fire in which they had been charred; the small store of natural earths from which the pigments used by the painters had been compounded—a cache of valuable components, perhaps hidden by an artist who, for some reason that could not now be guessed, had been unable to use them; the atrophied human hand, severed at the wrist (why had it been severed and, once severed, left there to be found by men thirty millennia removed?); the lamp formed out of a chunk of sandstone, hollowed to accommodate a wad of moss, the hollow filled with fat, the moss serving as a wick to give light to those who painted. All these and many other things, Boyd thought with some satisfaction; Gavarnie had turned out to be, possibly because of the sophisticated scientific methods of investigation that had been brought to bear, the most significant cave painting site ever studied—perhaps not as spectacular, in some ways, as Lascaux, but far more productive in the data obtained.

No need to visit the cave again, and yet there was a reason—the nagging feeling that he had passed something up, that in the rush and his concentration on the other work, he had forgotten something. It had made a small impression on him at the time, but now, thinking back on it, he was becoming more and more inclined to believe it might have importance. The whole thing probably was a product of his imagination, he told himself. Once he saw it again (if, indeed, he could find it again, if it were not a product of retrospective worry), it might prove to be nothing at all, simply an impression that had popped up to nag him.

So here he was again, climbing the steep path, geologist's hammer swinging at his belt, large flashlight clutched in hand, listening to the piping of Luis who perched on a small terrace, just below the mouth of the cave, a post he had occupied through all the time the work was going on. Luis had camped there in his tent through all kinds of weather, cooking on a camper's stove, serving as self-appointed watchdog, on alert against intruders, although there had been few intruders other than the occasional curious tourist who had heard of the project and tramped miles out of the way to see it. The villagers in the valley below had been no trouble; they couldn't have cared less about what was happening on the slope above them.

Luis was no stranger to Boyd; ten years before, he had shown up at the rock shelter project some fifty miles distant and there had stayed through two seasons of digging. The rock shelter had not proved as productive as Boyd initially had hoped, although it had shed some new light on the Azilian culture, the tag-end of the great Western European prehistoric groups. Taken on as a common laborer, Luis had proved an apt pupil and as the work went on had been given greater responsibility. A week after the work had started at Gavarnie, he had shown up again.

"I heard you were here," he'd said. "What do you have for me?"

As he came around a sharp bend in the trail, Boyd saw him, sitting crosslegged in front of the weatherbeaten tent, holding the primitive pipe to his lips, piping away.

That was exactly what it was—piping. Whatever music came out of the pipe was primitive and elemental. Scarcely music, although Boyd would admit that he knew nothing of music. Four notes—would it be four notes? he wondered. A hollow bone with an elongated slot as a mouthpiece, two drilled holes for stops.

Once he had asked Luis about it. "I've never seen anything like it," he had said. Luis had told him, "You don't see many of them.

In remote villages here and there, hidden away in the mountains."

Boyd left the path and walked across the grassy terrace, sat down beside Luis, who took down the pipe and laid it in his lap.

"I thought you were gone," Luis said. "The others left a couple of days ago."

"Back for one last look," said Boyd.

"You are reluctant to leave it?"

"Yes, I suppose I am."

Below them the valley spread out in autumn browns and tans, the small river a silver ribbon in the sunlight, the red roofs of the village a splash of color beside the river.

"It's nice up here," said Boyd. "Time and time again, I catch myself trying to imagine what it might have been like at the time the paintings were done. Not much different than it is now, perhaps. The mountains would be unchanged. There'd have been no fields in the valley, but it probably would have been natural pasture. A few trees here and there, but not too many of them. Good hunting. There'd have been grass for the grazing animals. I have even tried to figure out where the people would've camped. My guess would be where the village is now."

He looked around at Luis. The man still sat upon the grass, the pipe resting in his lap. He was smiling quietly, as if he might be smiling to himself. The small black beret sat squarely on his head, his tanned face was round and smooth, the black hair close-clipped, the blue shirt open at the throat. A young man, strong, not a wrinkle on his face.

"You love your work," said Luis.

"I'm devoted to it. So are you, Luis," Boyd said.

"It's not my work."

"Your work or not," said Boyd, "you do it well. Would you like to go with me? One last look around."

"I need to run an errand in the village."

"I thought I'd find you gone," said Boyd. "I was surprised to hear your pipe."

"I'll go soon," said Luis. "Another day or two. No reason to stay but, like you, I like this place. I have no place to go, no one needing me. Nothing's lost by staying a few more days."

"As long as you like," said Boyd. "The place is yours. Before too long, the government will be setting up a caretaker arrangement, but the government moves with due deliberation."

"Then I may not see you again," said Luis.

"I took a couple of days to drive down to Roncesvalles," said Boyd. "That's the place where the Gascons slaughtered Charlemagne's rear guard in 778."

"I've heard of the place," said Luis.

"I'd always wanted to see it. Never had the time. The Charlemagne chapel is in ruins, but I am told masses are still said in the village chapel for the dead paladins. When I returned from the trip, I couldn't resist the urge to see the cave again."

"I am glad of that," said Luis. "May I be impertinent?"

"You're never impertinent," said Boyd.

"Before you go, could we break bread once more together? Tonight, perhaps. I'll prepare an omelet."

Boyd hesitated, gagging down a suggestion that Luis dine with him. Then he said, "I'd be delighted, Luis. I'll bring a bottle of good wine."

Holding the flashlight centered on the rock wall, Boyd bent to examine the rock more closely. He had not imagined it; he had been right. Here, in this particular spot, the rock was not solid. It was broken into several pieces, but with the several pieces flush with the rest of the wall. Only by chance could the break have been spotted. Had he not been looking directly at it, watching for it as he swept the light across the wall, he would have missed it. It was strange, he thought, that someone else, during the time they had been working in the cave, had not found it. There'd not been much that they'd missed.

He held his breath, feeling a little foolish at the holding of it, for, after all, it might mean nothing. Frost cracks, perhaps, although he knew that he was wrong. It would be unusual to find frost cracks here.

He took the hammer out of his belt, and holding the flashlight in one hand, trained on the spot, he forced the chisel end of the hammer into one of the cracks. The edge went in easily. He pried gently and the crack widened. Under more pressure, the piece of rock moved out. He laid down the hammer and flash, seized the slab of rock, and pulled it free. Beneath it were two other slabs and they both came free as easily as the first. There were others as well and he also took them out. Kneeling on the floor of the cave, he directed the light into the fissure that he had uncovered.

Big enough for a man to crawl into, but at the prospect he remained for the moment undecided. Alone, he'd be taking a chance to do it. If something happened, if he should get stuck, if a fragment of rock should shift and pin him or fall upon him, there'd be no rescue. Or probably no rescue in time to save him. Luis would come back to the camp and wait for him, but should he fail to make an appearance, Luis more than likely would take it as a rebuke for impertinence, or an American's callous disregard of him. It would never occur to him that Boyd might be trapped in the cave.

Still, it was his last chance. Tomorrow he'd have to drive to Paris to catch his plane. And this whole thing was intriguing; it was not something to be ignored. The fissure must have some significance; otherwise, why should it have been walled up so carefully? Who, he wondered, would have walled it up? No one, certainly, in recent times. Anyone, finding the hidden entrance to the cave, almost immediately would have seen the paintings and would have spread the word. So the entrance to the fissure must have been blocked by one who would have been unfamiliar with the significance of the paintings or by one to whom they would have been commonplace.

It was something, he decided, that could not be passed up; he would have to go in. He secured the hammer to his belt, picked up the flashlight, and began the crawl.

The fissure ran straight and easy for a hundred feet or more. It offered barely room enough for crawling but, other than that, no great difficulties. Then, without warning, it came to an end. Boyd lay in it, directing the flash beam ahead of him, staring in consternation at the smooth wall of rock that came down to cut the fissure off.

It made no sense. Why should someone go to the trouble of walling off an empty fissure? He could have missed something on the way, but thinking of it, he was fairly sure he hadn't. His progress had been slow and he had kept the flash directed ahead of him every inch of the way. Certainly if there had been anything out of the ordinary, he would have seen it.

Then a thought came to him and slowly, with some effort, he began to turn himself around, so that his back, rather than his front, lay on the fissure floor. Directing the beam upward, he had his answer. In the roof of the fissure gaped a hole.

Cautiously he raised himself into a sitting position. Reaching up, he found handholds on the projecting rock and pulled himself erect. Swinging the flash around, he saw that the hole opened not into another fissure, but into a bubblelike cavity—small, no more than six feet in any dimension. The walls and ceiling of the cavity were smooth, as if a bubble of plastic rock had existed here for a moment at some time in the distant geologic past when the mountains had been heaving upward, leaving behind it as it drained away a bubble forever frozen into smooth and solid stone.

As he swung the flash across the bubble, he gasped in astonishment. Colorful animals capered around the entire expanse of stone. Bison played leapfrog. Horses cantered in a chorus line. Mammoths turned somersaults. All around the bottom perimeter, just above the floor, dancing deer, standing on their hind legs, joined hands and jigged, antlers swaying gracefully.

"For the love of Christ!" said Boyd.

Here was Stone Age Disney.

If it was the Stone Age. Could some jokester have crawled into the area in fairly recent times to paint the animals in this grotto? Thinking it over, he rejected the idea. So far as he had been able to ascertain, no one in the valley, nor in the entire region, for that matter, had known of the cave until a shepherd had found it several years before when a lamb had blundered into it. The entrance was small and apparently for centuries had been masked by a heavy growth of brush and bracken.

Too, the execution of the paintings had a prehistoric touch to them. Perspective played but a small part. The paintings had that curious flat look that distinguished most prehistoric art. There was no background—no horizon line, no trees, no grass or flowers, no clouds, no sense of sky. Although, he reminded himself, anyone who had any knowledge of cave painting probably would have been aware of all these factors and worked to duplicate them.

Yet, despite the noncharacteristic antics of the painted animals, the pictures did have the feeling of cave art. What ancient man, Boyd asked himself, what kind of ancient man, would have painted gamboling bison and tumbling mammoths? While the situation did not hold in all cave art, all the paintings in this particular cave were deadly serious—conservative as to form and with a forthright, honest attempt to portray the animals as the artists had seen them. There was no frivolity, not even the imprint of paint-smeared human hands, as so often happened in other caves. The men who had worked in this cave had not as yet been corrupted by the symbolism that had crept in, apparently rather late in the prehistoric painting cycle.

So who had been this clown who had crept off by himself in this hidden cavern to paint his comic animals? That he had been an accomplished painter, there could be no doubt. This artist's techniques and executions were without flaw.

Boyd hauled himself up through the hole, slid out onto the two-foot ledge that ran all around the hole, crouching, for there was no room to stand. Much of the painting, he realized, must have been done with the artist lying flat upon his back, reaching up to work on the curving ceiling.

He swept the beam of the flashlight along the ledge. Halfway around, he halted the light and jiggled it back and forth to focus upon something that was placed upon the ledge, something that undoubtedly had been left by the artist when he had finished his work and gone away.

Leaning forward, Boyd squinted to make out what it was. It looked like the shoulder blade of a deer; beside the shoulder blade lay a lump of stone.

Cautiously he edged his way around the ledge. He had been right. It was the shoulder blade of a deer. Upon the flat surface of it lay a lumpy substance. Paint? he wondered, the mixture of animal fats and mineral earths the prehistoric artists used as paints? He focused the flash closer and there was no doubt. It was paint, spread over the surface of the bone, which had served as a palette, with some of the paint lying in thicker lumps ready for use, but never used, paint dried and mummified and bearing imprints of some sort. He leaned close, bringing his face down to within a few inches of the paint, shining the light upon the surface. The imprints, he saw, were fingerprints, some of them sunk deep—the signature of that ancient, long-dead man who had worked here, crouching even as Boyd now crouched, shoulders hunched against the curving stone. He put out his hand to touch the palette, then pulled it back. Symbolic, yes, this move to touch, this reaching out to touch the man who painted—but symbolic only, a gesture with too many centuries between.

He shifted the flashlight beam to the small block of stone that lay beside the shoulder blade. A lamp—hollowed-out sandstone, a hollow to hold the fat and the chunk of moss that served as a wick. The fat and wick were long since gone, but a thin film of soot still remained around the rim of the hollow that had held them.

Finishing his work, the artist had left his tools behind him, had even left the lamp, perhaps still guttering, with the fat almost finished—had left it here and let himself down into the fissure, crawling it in darkness. To him, perhaps, there was no need of light. He could crawl the tunnel by touch and familiarity. He must have crawled the route many times, for the work upon these walls had taken long, perhaps many days.

So he had left, crawling through the fissure, using the blocks of stone to close the opening to the fissure, then had walked away, scrambling down the slope to the valley where grazing herds had lifted their heads to watch him, then had gone back to grazing.

But when had this all happened? Probably, Boyd told himself, after the cave itself had been painted, perhaps even after the paintings in the cave had lost much of whatever significance they originally would have held—one lone man coming back to paint his secret animals in his secret place. Painting them as a mockery of the pompous, magical importance of the main cave paintings? Or as a protest against the stuffy conservatism of the original paintings? Or simply as a bubbling chuckle, an exuberance of life, perhaps even a joyous rebellion against the grimness and the simplemindedness of the hunting magic? A rebel, he thought, a prehistoric rebel—an intellectual rebel? Or perhaps simply a man with a viewpoint slightly skewed from the philosophy of his time?

But this was that other man, that ancient man. Now how about himself? Having found the grotto, what did he do next? What would be the best way to handle it? Certainly he could not turn his back upon it and walk away, as the artist, leaving his palette and his lamp behind him, had walked away. For this was an important discovery. There could be no question of that. Here was a new and unsuspected approach to the prehistoric mind, a facet of ancient thinking that never had been guessed.

Leave everything as it lay, close up the fissure and make a phone call to Washington and another one to Paris, unpack his bags, and settle down for a few more weeks of work. Get back the photographers and other members of the crew—do a job of it. Yes, he told himself, that was the way to do it.

Something lying behind the lamp, almost hidden by the sandstone lamp, glinted in the light. Something white and small.

Still crouched over, Boyd shuffled forward to get a better look.

It was a piece of bone, probably a leg bone from a small grazing animal. He reached out and picked it up and, having seen what it was, hunched unmoving over it, not quite sure what to make of it.

It was a pipe, a brother to the pipe that Luis carried in his jacket pocket, had carried in his pocket since that first day he'd met him, years ago. There was the mouthpiece slot, there the two round stops. In that long-gone day when the paintings had been done, the artist had hunched here, in the flickering of the lamp, and had played softly to himself those simple piping airs that Luis had played almost every evening, after work was done.

"Merciful Jesus," Boyd said, almost prayerfully, "it simply cannot be!"

He stayed there, frozen in his crouch, the thoughts hammering in his mind while he tried to push the thoughts away. They would not go away. He'd drive them away for just a little distance, then they'd come surging back to overwhelm him.

Finally, grimly, he broke the trance in which the thoughts had held him. He worked deliberately, forcing himself to do what he knew must be done.

He took off his windbreaker and carefully wrapped the shoulderblade palette and the pipe inside it, leaving the lamp. He let himself down into the fissure and crawled, carefully protecting the bundle that he carried. In the cave again, he meticulously fitted the blocks of stone together to block the fissure mouth, scraped together handfuls of soil from the cave floor, and smeared it on the face of the blocks, wiping it away, but leaving a small, clinging film to mask the opening to all but the most inquiring eye.

Luis was not at his camp on the terrace below the cave mouth; he was still on his errand into the village.

When he reached his hotel, Boyd made his telephone call to Washington. He skipped the call to Paris.

The last leaves of October were blowing in the autumn wind, and a weak sun, not entirely obscured by the floating clouds, shone down on Washington.

John Roberts was waiting for him on the park bench. They nodded at one another, without speaking, and Boyd sat down beside his friend.

"You took a big chance," said Roberts. "What would have happened if the customs people . . ."

"I wasn't too worried," Boyd said. "I knew this man in Paris. For years he's been smuggling stuff into America. He's good at it and he owed me one. What have you got?"

"Maybe more than you want to hear."

"Try me."

"The fingerprints match," said Roberts.

"You were able to get a reading on the paint impressions?"

"Loud and clear."

"The FBI?"

"Yes, the FBI. It wasn't easy, but I have a friend or two."

"And the dating?"

"No problem. The bad part of the job was convincing my man this was top secret. He's still not sure it is."

"Will he keep his mouth shut?"

"I think so. Without evidence, no one would believe him. It would sound like a fairy story."

"Tell me."

"Twenty-two thousand. Plus or minus three hundred years."

"And the prints do match. The bottle prints and . . ."

"I told you they match. Now will you tell me how in hell a man who lived twenty-two thousand years ago could leave his prints on a wine bottle that was manufactured last year."

"It's a long story," said Boyd. "I don't know if I should. First, where do you have the shoulder blade?"

"Hidden," said Roberts. "Well hidden. You can have it back, and the bottle, any time you wish."

Boyd shrugged. "Not yet. Not for a while. Perhaps never."

"Never?"

"Look, John, I have to think it out."

"What a hell of a mess," said Roberts. "No one wants the stuff. No one would dare to have it. Smithsonian wouldn't touch it with a ten-foot pole. I haven't asked. They don't even know about it. But I know they wouldn't want it. There's something, isn't there, about sneaking artifacts out of a country . . ."

"Yes, there is," said Boyd.

"And now you don't want it."

"I didn't say that. I just said let it stay where it is for a time. It's safe, isn't it?"

"It's safe. And now . . ."

"I told you it is a long story. I'll try to make it short. There's this man—a Basque. He came to me ten years ago when I was doing the rock shelter . . ."

Roberts nodded. "I remember that one."

"He wanted work and I gave him work. He broke in fast, caught on to the techniques immediately. Became a valuable man. That often happens with native laborers. They seem to have the feel for their own antiquity. And then when we started work on the cave he showed up again. I was glad to see him. The two of us, as a matter of fact, are fairly good friends. On my last night at the cave he cooked a marvelous omelet—eggs, tomato, green pimientoes, onions, sausages, and home-cured ham. I brought a bottle of wine."

"*The* bottle?"

"Yes, *the* bottle."

"So go ahead."

"He played a pipe. A bone pipe. A squeaky sort of thing. Not too much music in it . . ."

"There was a pipe . . ."

"Not that pipe. Another pipe. The same kind of pipe, but not the one our man has. Two pipes the same. One in a living man's pocket, the other beside the shoulder blade. There were things about this man I'm telling you of. Nothing that hit you between the eyes. Just little things. You would notice something and then, some time later, maybe quite a bit later, there'd be something else, but by the time that happened, you'd have forgotten the first incident and not tie the two together. Mostly it was that he knew too much. Little things a man like him would not be expected to know. Even things that no one knew. Bits and pieces of knowledge that slipped out of him, maybe without his realizing it. And his eyes. I didn't realize that until later, not until I'd found the second pipe and began to think about the other things. But I was talking about his eyes. In appearance he is a young man, a never-aging man, but his eyes are old . . ."

"Tom, you said he is a Basque."

"That's right."

"Isn't there some belief that the Basques may have descended from the Cro-Magnons?"

"There is such a theory. I have thought of it."

"Could this man of yours be a Cro-Magnon?"

"I'm beginning to think he is."

"But think of it—twenty thousand years!"

"Yes, I know," said Boyd.

Boyd heard the piping when he reached the bottom of the trail that led up to the cave. The notes were ragged, torn by the wind. The Pyrenees stood up against the high blue sky.

Tucking the bottle of wine more securely underneath his arm, Boyd began the climb. Below him lay the redness of the village rooftops and the sere brown of autumn that spread across the valley. The piping continued, lifting and falling as the wind tugged at it playfully.

Luis sat crosslegged in front of the tattered tent. When he saw Boyd, he put the pipe in his lap and sat waiting.

Boyd sat down beside him, handing him the bottle. Luis took it and began working on the cork.

"I heard you were back," he said. "How went the trip?"

"It went well," said Boyd.

"So now you know," said Luis.

Boyd nodded. "I think you wanted me to know. Why should you have wanted that?"

"The years grow long," said Luis. "The burden heavy. It is lonely, all alone."

"You are not alone."

"It's lonely when no one knows you. You now are the first who has really known me."

"But the knowing will be short. A few years more and again no one will know you."

"This lifts the burden for a time," said Luis. "Once you are gone, I will be able to take it up again. And there is something . . ."

"Yes, what is it, Luis?"

"You say when you are gone there'll be no one again. Does that mean . . ."

"If what you're getting at is whether I will spread the word, no, I won't. Not unless you wish it. I have thought on what would happen to you if the world were told."

"I have certain defenses. You can't live as long as I have if you fail in your defenses."

"What kind of defenses?"

"Defenses. That is all."

"I'm sorry if I pried. There's one other thing. If you wanted me to know, you took a long chance. Why, if something had gone wrong, if I had failed to find the grotto . . ."

"I had hoped, at first, that the grotto would not be necessary. I had thought you might have guessed, on your own."

"I knew there was something wrong. But this is so outrageous I couldn't have trusted myself even had I guessed. You know it's outrageous, Luis. And if I'd not found the grotto . . . Its finding was pure chance, you know."

"If you hadn't, I would have waited. Some other time, some other year, there would have been someone else. Some other way to betray myself."

"You could have told me."

"Cold, you mean?"

"That's what I mean. I would not have believed you, of course. Not at first."

"Don't you understand? I could not have told you. The concealment now is second nature. One of the defenses I talked about. I simply could not have brought myself to tell you, or anyone."

"Why me? Why wait all these years until I came along?"

"I did not wait, Boyd. There were others, at different times. None of them worked out. I had to find, you must understand, someone who had the strength to face it. Not one who would run screaming madly. I knew you would not run screaming."

"I've had time to think it through," Boyd said. "I've come to terms with it. I can accept the fact, but not too well, only barely. Luis, do you have some explanation? How come you are so different from the rest of us?"

"No idea at all. No inkling. At one time I thought there must be others like me and I sought for them. I found none. I no longer seek."

The cork came free and he handed the bottle of wine to Boyd. "You go first," he said steadily.

Boyd lifted the bottle and drank. He handed it to Luis. He watched him as he drank. Wondering, as he watched, how he could be sitting here, talking calmly with a man who had lived, who had stayed young through twenty thousand years. His gorge rose once again against acceptance of the fact—but it had to be a fact. The shoulder blade, the small amount of organic matter still remaining in the pigment, had measured out to 22,000 years. There was no question that the prints in the paint had matched the prints upon the bottle. He had raised one question back in Washington, hoping there might be evidence of hoax. Would it have been possible, he had asked, that the ancient pigment, the paint used by the prehistoric artist, could have been reconstituted, the fingerprints impressed upon it, and then replaced in the grotto? *Impossible* was the answer. Any reconstitution of the pigment, had it been possible, would have shown up in the analysis. There had been nothing of the sort—the pigment dated to 20,000 years ago. There was no question of that.

"All right, Cro-Magnon," said Boyd, "tell me how you did it. How does a man survive as long as you have? You do not age, of course. Your body will not accept disease. But I take it you are not immune to violence or to accident. You've lived in a violent world.

How does a man sidestep accident and violence for two hundred centuries?"

"There were times early," Luis said, "when I came close to not surviving. For a long time I did not realize the kind of thing I was. Sure, I lived longer, stayed younger than all the others—I would guess, however, that I didn't begin to notice this until I began to realize that all the people I had known in my early life were dead— dead for a long, long time. I knew then that I was different from the rest. About the same time, others began to notice I was different. They became suspicious of me. Some of them resented me. Others thought I was some sort of evil spirit. Finally I had to flee the tribe. I became a skulking outcast. That was when I began to learn the principles of survival."

"And those principles?"

"You keep a low profile. You don't stand out. You attract no attention to yourself. You cultivate a cowardly attitude. You are never brave. You take no risks. You let others do the dirty work. You never volunteer. You skulk and run and hide. You grow a skin that's thick; you don't give a damn what others think of you. You shed all your noble attributes, your social consciousness. You shuck your loy-alty to tribe or folk or country. You're not a patriot. You live for yourself alone. You're an observer, never a participant. You scuttle around the edges of things. And you become so self-centered that you come to believe that no blame should attach to you, that you are living in the only logical way a man can live. You went to Ron-cesvalles the other day, remember?"

"Yes. I mentioned I'd been there. You said you'd heard of it."

"Heard of it? Hell, I was there the day it happened—August 15, 778. An observer, not a participant. A cowardly little bastard who tagged along behind that noble band of Gascons who did in Roland. Gascons, hell. That's the fancy name for them. They were Basques, pure and simple. The meanest crew of men who ever drew the breath of life. Some Basques may be noble, but not this band. They weren't the kind of warriors who'd stand up face to face with the Franks. They hid up in the pass and rolled rocks down on all those puissant knights. But it wasn't the knights who held their interest. It was the wagon train. They weren't out to fight a war or to avenge a wrong. They were out for loot. Although little good it did them."

"Why do you say that?"

"It was this way," said Luis. "They knew the rest of the Frankish army would return when the rear guard didn't come up, and they had not the stomach for that. They stripped the dead knights of their golden spurs, their armor and fancy clothes, the money bags they carried, and loaded all of it on the wagons and got out of there. A few miles farther on, deep in the mountains, they holed up and hid. In a deep canyon where they thought they would be safe. But if they should be found, they had what amounted to a fort. A half-mile or so below the place they camped, the canyon narrowed and twisted sharply. A lot of boulders had fallen down at that point, forming a barricade that could have been held by a handful of men against any assault that could be launched against it. By this time I was a long way off. I smelled something wrong, I knew something most unpleasant was about to happen. That's another thing about this survival business. You develop special senses. You get so you can smell out trouble, well ahead of time. I heard what happened later."

He lifted the bottle and had another drink. He handed it to Boyd.

"Don't leave me hanging," said Boyd. "Tell me what did happen."

"In the night," said Luis, "a storm came up. One of those sudden, brutal summer thunderstorms. This time it was a cloudburst. My brave fellow Gascons died to the man. That's the price of bravery."

Boyd took a drink, lowered the bottle, held it to his chest, cuddling it.

"You know about this," he said. "No one else does. Perhaps no one had ever wondered what happened to those Gascons who gave Charlemagne the bloody nose. You must know of other things. Christ, man, you've lived history. You didn't stick to this area."

"No. At times I wandered. I had an itching foot. There were things to see. I had to keep moving along. I couldn't stay in one place any length of time or it would be noticed that I wasn't aging."

"You lived through the Black Death," said Boyd. "You watched the Roman legions. You heard firsthand of Attila. You skulked along on Crusades. You walked the streets of ancient Athens."

"Not Athens," said Luis. "Somehow Athens was never to my

taste. I spent some time in Sparta. Sparta, I tell you—that was really something."

"You're an educated man," said Boyd. "Where did you go to school?"

"Paris, for a time, in the fourteenth century. Later on at Oxford. After that at other places. Under different names. Don't try tracing me through the schools that I attended."

"You could write a book," said Boyd. "It would set new sales records. You'd be a millionaire. One book and you'd be a millionaire."

"I can't afford to be a millionaire. I can't be noticed, and millionaires are noticed. I'm not in want. I've never been in want. There's always treasure for a skulker to pick up. I have caches here and there. I get along all right."

Luis was right, Boyd told himself. He couldn't be a millionaire. He couldn't write a book. In no way could he be famous, stand out in any way. In all things he must remain unremarkable, always anonymous.

The principles of survival, he had said. And this was part of it, although not all of it. He had mentioned the art of smelling trouble, the hunch ability. There would be, as well, the wisdom, the street savvy, the cynicism that a man would pick up along the way, the expertise, the ability to judge character, an insight into human reaction, some knowledge concerning the use of power, power of every sort, economic power, political power, religious power.

Was the man still human, he wondered, or had he, in 20,000 years, become something more than human? Had he advanced that one vital step that would place him beyond humankind, the kind of being that would come after man?

"One thing more," said Boyd. "Why the Disney paintings?"

"They were painted some time later than the others," Luis told him. "I painted some of the earlier stuff in the cave. The fishing bear is mine. I knew about the grotto. I found it and said nothing. No reason I should have kept it secret. Just one of those little items one hugs to himself to make himself important. I know something you don't know—silly stuff like that. Later I came back to paint the grotto. The cave art was so deadly serious. Such terribly silly magic. I told myself painting should be fun. So I came back after the tribe had moved, and painted simply for the fun of it. How did it strike you, Boyd?"

"Damn good art," said Boyd.

"I was afraid you wouldn't find the grotto and I couldn't help you. I knew you had seen the cracks in the wall; I watched you one day looking at them. I counted on your remembering them. And I counted on your seeing the fingerprints and finding the pipe. All pure serendipity, of course. I had nothing in mind when I left the paint with the fingerprints and the pipe. The pipe, of course, was the tipoff, and I was confident you'd at least be curious. But I couldn't be sure. When we ate that night, here by the campfire, you didn't mention the grotto and I was afraid you'd blown it. But when you made off with the bottle, sneaking it away, I knew I had it made. And now the big question. Will you let the world in on the grotto paintings?"

"I don't know. I'll have to think about it. What are your thoughts on the matter?"

"I'd just as soon you didn't."

"Okay," said Boyd. "Not for the time at least. Is there anything else I can do for you? Anything you want?"

"You've done the best possible," said Luis. "You know who I am, what I am. I don't know why that's so important to me, but it is. A matter of identity, I suppose. When you die, which I hope will be a long time from now, then, once again, there'll be no one who knows. But the knowledge that one man did know, and what is more important, understood, will sustain me through the centuries. A minute—I have something for you."

He rose and went into the tent, came back with a sheet of paper, handing it to Boyd. It was a topographical survey of some sort.

"I've put a cross on it," said Luis. "To mark the spot."

"What spot?"

"Where you'll find the Charlemagne treasure of Roncesvalles. The wagons and the treasure would have been carried down the canyon in the flood. The turn in the canyon and the boulder barricade I spoke of would have blocked them. You'll find them there, probably under a deep layer of gravel and debris."

Boyd looked up questioningly from the map.

"It's worth going after," said Luis. "Also it provides another check against the validity of my story."

"I believe you," said Boyd. "I need no further evidence."

"Ah, well!" said Luis. "It wouldn't hurt. And now it's time to go."

"Time to go! We have a lot to talk about."

"Later, perhaps," said Luis. "We'll bump into one another from time to time. I'll make it a point we do. But now it's time to go."

He started down the path, and Boyd sat watching him.

After a few steps, Luis halted and half turned back to Boyd.

"It seems to me," he said in explanation, "it's always time to go."

Boyd stood and watched him move down the trail toward the village. There was about the moving figure a deep sense of loneliness— the most lonely man in all the world.

Recommended Reading by Clifford D. Simak

Way Station
The Goblin Reservation
City
A Heritage of Stars
They Walked Like Men

L . SPRAGUE DE CAMP

b. 1907

Although L. Sprague de Camp was one of the brighter stars in
the contellation of John W. Campbell's "Golden Age" of *Astounding
Science Fiction*, he actually anticipated Campbell's tenure there by a
few months; de Camp's first story in *Astounding*, "The Isolinguals,"
was accepted and published, in 1937, by Campbell's predecessor, F.
Orlin Tremaine. All the same, de Camp was Campbell's kind of guy:
he had been trained as an engineer at Caltech, MIT, and Stevens
Institute, shared Campbell's ideas of what science fiction could be
and—not unimportantly—had the right kind of name for a byline
in *Astounding*. (That is, a name that was a lot like "Campbell." It
was John Campbell's fixed opinion that the customers really preferred
to have their stories written by people with Scotch-Irish names as
much as possible; for which reason he insisted H. L. Gold use "Clyde
Crane Campbell" as a pen name on his early stories, and urged other
writers to adopt WASPish pseudonyms. This just goes to show that
even a great editor has peccadilloes.) John Campbell took note of
this new de Camp fellow, encouraged him, became close friends with
him, and made him a regular in *Astounding* and—as soon as it
appeared—in Campbell's companion fantasy magazine, *Unknown*.

For those years of *Astounding* de Camp produced an unending
series of bright, inventive stories such as his "Johnny Black" series,
concerning an intelligent bear, and such more traditional works as
"Divide and Rule." A particularly endearing trait of de Camp's was
his portrayal of the protagonist characters of his stories. They seldom
were scientists, almost never swashbuckling adventurers. More than

anything else, they resembled idealized versions of the boy next door, or the pump jockey at the neighborhood filling station: smart, decent, resourceful, and very, very easy for the average young male reader of *Astounding* to identify with.

The story that converted de Camp into an instant superstar, however, appeared in Campbell's *Unknown*. That was "Lest Darkness Fall," a time-travel story about a twentieth-century American, Martin Padway, who is somehow (it is never made clear exactly how) transported to sixth-century Rome.

There is no doubt that "Lest Darkness Fall" owes some of its inspiration to Mark Twain's *A Connecticut Yankee in King Arthur's Court*. That doesn't matter. William Shakespeare's *The Merchant of Venice* has a similar debt to Christopher Marlowe's *The Jew of Malta*, but a masterpiece is a masterpiece whatever its provenance. "Lest Darkness Fall" is all of that. Martin Padway is stuck in the sixth century, but he isn't defeated by it. He sets about doing something about it, and no small thing, at that. He doesn't propose to settle for simply increasing his own physical comforts by introducing such future fads as brandy, printing presses, and soap. He knows where the history of the world is headed. He can see that the Dark Ages are looming ahead and, very simply, he decides to prevent that from happening. And, unlike Twain's Sir Boss, he succeeds.

My personal acquaintance with Sprague de Camp goes back to 1939. I was then nineteen and, through little virtue of my own except for happening to be in the right place at the right time, I found myself the full-fledged editor of two professional science fiction magazines, *Astonishing Stories* and *Super Science Stories*. They were definitely low-budget also-rans in the expanding science fiction magazine field, to be sure, but they were *real*! And I was in heaven.

Editors are supposed to outrank writers in the T/O of the publishing biz, but I was not only a very *young* editor but a very recent pure fan. I was in great awe of the established pros of the field. It was severe and disorienting culture shock for me to meet, and to be able to buy stories from, these Titans. They included great names that are now almost forgotten—including Manly Wade Wellman, Ray Cummings, Malcolm Jameson, Raymond Z. Gallun—and a few who definitely have not been forgotten, including the remarkable one we're talking about now, L. Sprague de Camp.

Shortly after getting the job I invited Sprague to join me for an editorial lunch. That was a real stretch for me, considering that I had not much of a paycheck and no entertainment budget at all, and I remain in Sprague's debt for the fact that, at the end, he insisted on splitting the check. The whole luncheon was pure humane generosity on Sprague's part, because, although we talked about the kind of stories I hoped he might write for me, I knew as well as he did that all I was ever going to see from him were the ones John Campbell and other more solvent editors didn't want. (But even the best of editors may have more than one kind of blind spot. Among the Campbell rejects were some splendid work. One of the ones I was lucky enough to get from Sprague was a longish collaboration with P. Schuyler Miller, "Genus Homo," a far-future story about a human from the present finding himself in a time when the human race has finally done itself in and the world has come to be ruled by intelligently evolved other primates. If you've seen or read *Planet of the Apes*, forget it. Go out and search for a copy of the earlier, and far better, "Genus Homo.")

World War II interrupted de Camp's writing, as it did for so many others; he served in that Philadelphia Navy Yard research team that included Heinlein and Asimov. But when the Axis was defeated de Camp came back stronger than ever, notably with his "Viagens Interplanetarias" stories, such as "Rogue Queen," set in a world in which Brazil has become the world's dominant interplanetary power. He wasn't confining himself to writing science fiction, though. Among other areas, Sprague's clear voice for sanity was raised in articles, essays, and talks devoted to exposing the nonsense quotient in such fads as phony religions, superstitions, flying saucers, and other human aberrations.

While de Camp's solo work is outstanding, he also did well in collaboration with other writers—with P. Schuyler Miller, as mentioned above; with Fletcher Pratt in their wonderful series of fantasies in *The Incomplete Enchanter* and the tall stories in the *Tales from Gavagan's Bar*. With Willy Ley, prince of science populizers, he wrote the nonfiction *Lands Beyond,* and, of course, he was one of the leading members of the team of writers who brought Robert E. Howard's unfinished manuscripts to completion, and Conan the Barbarian to his present status as a household name.

Sadly, none of those erstwhile literary partners are still with us, but de Camp found another first-class writer to work with who was nearer to home. This was his wife, Catherine Crook de Camp, a writer in her own right, and for the last dozen years his principal collaborator on nearly all of his later works.

A GUN FOR DINOSAUR

No, I'm sorry, Mr. Seligman, but I can't take you hunting Late Mesozoic dinosaur.

Yes, I know what the advertisement says.

Why not? How much d'you weigh? A hundred and thirty? Let's see; that's under ten stone, which is my lower limit.

I could take you to other periods, you know. I'll take you to any period in the Cenozoic. I'll get you a shot at an entelodont or a uintathere. They've got fine heads.

I'll even stretch a point and take you to the Pleistocene, where you can try for one of the mammoths or the mastodon.

I'll take you back to the Triassic where you can shoot one of the smaller ancestral dinosaurs. But I will jolly well not take you to the Jurassic or Cretaceous. You're just too small.

What's your size got to do with it? Look here, old boy, what did you think you were going to shoot your dinosaur with?

Oh, you hadn't thought, eh?

Well, sit there a minute. . . . Here you are: my own private gun for that work, a Continental .600. Does look like a shotgun, doesn't it? But it's rifled, as you can see by looking through the barrels. Shoots a pair of .600 Nitro Express cartridges the size of bananas; weighs fourteen and a half pounds and has a muzzle energy of over seven thousand foot-pounds. Costs fourteen hundred and fifty dollars. Lot of money for a gun, what?

I have some spares I rent to the sahibs. Designed for knocking down elephant. Not just wounding them, knocking them base-over-apex. That's why they don't make guns like this in America, though I suppose they will if hunting parties keep going back in time.

Now, I've been guiding hunting parties for twenty years. Guided 'em in Africa until the game gave out there except on the preserves. And all that time I've never known a man your size who could handle the six-nought-nought. It knocks 'em over, and even when they stay on their feet they get so scared of the bloody cannon after a few shots that they flinch. And they find the gun too heavy to drag around rough Mesozoic country. Wears 'em out.

It's true that lots of people have killed elephant with lighter guns: the .500, .475, and .465 doubles, for instance, or even .375 magnum repeaters. The difference is, with a .375 you have to hit something vital, preferably the heart, and can't depend on simple shock power.

An elephant weighs—let's see—four to six tons. You're proposing to shoot reptiles weighing two or three times as much as an elephant and with much greater tenacity of life. That's why the syndicate decided to take no more people dinosaur hunting unless they could handle the .600. We learned the hard way, as you Americans say. There were some unfortunate incidents. . . .

I'll tell you, Mr. Seligman. It's after seventeen-hundred. Time I closed the office. Why don't we stop at the bar on our way out while I tell you the story?

. . . It was about the Raja's and my fifth safari into time. The Raja? Oh, he's the Aiyar half of Rivers and Aiyar. I call him the Raja because he's the hereditary monarch of Janpur. Means nothing nowadays, of course. Knew him in India and ran into him in New York running the Indian tourist agency. That dark chap in the photograph on my office wall, the one with his foot on the dead saber-tooth.

Well, the Raja was fed up with handing out brochures about the Taj Mahal and wanted to do a bit of hunting again. I was at loose ends when we heard of Professor Prochaska's time machine at Washington University.

Where's the Raja now? Out on safari in the Early Oligocene after titanothere while I run the office. We take turn about, but the first few times we went out together.

Anyway, we caught the next plane to St. Louis. To our morti-fication, we found we weren't the first. Lord, no! There were other hunting guides and no end of scientists, each with his own idea of the right way to use the machine.

We scraped off the historians and archeologists right at the start. Seems the ruddy machine won't work for periods more recent than 100,000 years ago. It works from there up to about a billion years.

Why? Oh, I'm no four-dimensional thinker; but, as I understand it, if people could go back to a more recent time, their actions would affect our own history, which would be a paradox or contradiction of facts. Can't have that in a well-run universe, you know.

But, before 100,000 B.C., more or less, the actions of the expe-ditions are lost in the stream of time before human history begins. At that, once a stretch of past time has been used, say the month of January, one million B.C., you can't use that stretch over again by sending another party into it. Paradoxes again.

The professor isn't worried, though. With a billion years to ex-ploit, he won't soon run out of eras.

Another limitation of the machine is the matter of size. For technical reasons, Prochaska had to build the transition chamber just big enough to hold four men with their personal gear, and the cham-ber wallah. Larger parties have to be sent through in relays. That means, you see, it's not practical to take jeeps, launches, aircraft, and other powered vehicles.

On the other hand, since you're going to periods without human beings, there's no whistling up a hundred native bearers to trot along with your gear on their heads. So we usually take a train of asses—burros, they call them here. Most periods have enough natural forage so you can get where you want to go.

As I say, everybody had his own idea for using the machine. The scientists looked down their noses at us hunters and said it would be a crime to waste the machine's time pandering to our sadistic amuse-ments.

We brought up another angle. The machine cost a cool thirty million. I understand this came from the Rockefeller Board and such people, but that accounted for the original cost only, not the cost of operation. And the thing uses fantastic amounts of power. Most of the scientists' projects, while worthy enough, were run on a shoe-string, financially speaking.

Now, we guides catered to people with money, a species with which America seems well stocked. No offense, old boy. Most of these could afford a substantial fee for passing through the machine into the past. Thus we could help finance the operation of the machine for scientific purposes, provided we got a fair share of its time. In the end, the guides formed a syndicate of eight members, one member being the partnership of Rivers and Aiyar, to apportion the machine's time.

We had rush business from the start. Our wives—the Raja's and mine—raised hell with us for a while. They'd hoped that, when the big game gave out in our own era, they'd never have to share us with lions and things again, but you know how women are. Hunting's not really dangerous if you keep your head and take precautions.

On the fifth expedition, we had two sahibs to wet-nurse; both Americans in their thirties, both physically sound, and both solvent. Otherwise they were as different as different can be.

Courtney James was what you chaps call a playboy: a rich young man from New York who'd always had his own way and didn't see why that agreeable condition shouldn't continue. A big bloke, almost as big as I am; handsome in a florid way, but beginning to run to fat. He was on his fourth wife and, when he showed up at the office with a blond twist with "model" written all over her, I assumed that this was the fourth Mrs. James.

"Miss Bartram," she corrected me, with an embarrassed giggle.

"She's not my wife," James explained. "My wife is in Mexico, I think, getting a divorce. But Bunny here would like to go along—"

"Sorry," I said, "we don't take ladies. At least, not to the Late Mesozoic."

This wasn't strictly true, but I felt we were running enough risks, going after a little-known fauna, without dragging in people's do-mestic entanglements. Nothing against sex, you understand. Mar-velous institution and all that, but not where it interferes with my living.

"Oh, nonsense!" said James. "If she wants to go, she'll go. She skis and flies my airplane, so why shouldn't she—"

"Against the firm's policy," I said.

"She can keep out of the way when we run up against the dangerous ones," he said.

"No, sorry."

"Damn it!" said he, getting red. "After all, I'm paying you a goodly sum, and I'm entitled to take whoever I please."

"You can't hire me to do anything against my best judgment," I said. "If that's how you feel, get another guide."

"All right, I will," he said. "And I'll tell all my friends you're a God-damned—" Well, he said a lot of things I won't repeat, until I told him to get out of the office or I'd throw him out.

I was sitting in the office and thinking sadly of all that lovely money James would have paid me if I hadn't been so stiff-necked, when in came my other lamb, one August Holtzinger. This was a little slim pale chap with glasses, polite and formal. Holtzinger sat on the edge of his chair and said:

"Uh—Mr. Rivers, I don't want you to think I'm here under false pretenses. I'm really not much of an outdoorsman, and I'll probably be scared to death when I see a real dinosaur. But I'm determined to hang a dinosaur head over my fireplace or die in the attempt."

"Most of us are frightened at first," I soothed him, "though it doesn't do to show it." And little by little I got the story out of him.

While James had always been wallowing in the stuff, Holtzinger was a local product who'd only lately come into the real thing. He'd had a little business here in St. Louis and just about made ends meet when an uncle cashed in his chips somewhere and left little Augie the pile.

Now Holtzinger had acquired a fiancée and was building a big house. When it was finished, they'd be married and move into it. And one furnishing he demanded was a ceratopsian head over the fireplace. Those are the ones with the big horned heads with a parrot-beak and a frill over the neck, you know. You have to think twice about collecting them, because if you put a seven-foot *Triceratops* head into a small living room, there's apt to be no room left for anything else.

We were talking about this when in came a girl: a small girl in her twenties, quite ordinary looking, and crying.

"Augie!" she cried. "You can't! You mustn't! You'll be killed!" She grabbed him round the knees and said to me:

"Mr. Rivers, you mustn't take him! He's all I've got! He'll never stand the hardships!"

"My dear young lady," I said, "I should hate to cause you distress, but it's up to Mr. Holtzinger to decide whether he wishes to retain my services."

"It's no use, Claire," said Holtzinger. "I'm going, though I'll probably hate every minute of it."

"What's that, old boy?" I said. "If you hate it, why go? Did you lose a bet, or something?"

"No," said Holtzinger. "It's this way. Uh—I'm a completely undistinguished kind of guy. I'm not brilliant or big or strong or handsome. I'm just an ordinary Midwestern small businessman. You never even notice me at Rotary luncheons, I fit in so perfectly.

"But that doesn't say I'm satisfied. I've always hankered to go to far places and do big things. I'd like to be a glamorous, adventurous sort of guy. Like you, Mr. Rivers."

"Oh, come," I said. "Professional hunting may seem glamorous to you, but to me it's just a living."

He shook his head. "Nope. You know what I mean. Well, now I've got this legacy, I could settle down to play bridge and golf the rest of my life, and try to act like I wasn't bored. But I'm determined to do something with some color in it, once at least. Since there's no more real big-game hunting in the present, I'm gonna shoot a dinosaur and hang his head over my mantel if it's the last thing I do. I'll never be happy otherwise."

Well, Holtzinger and his girl argued, but he wouldn't give in. She made me swear to take the best care of her Augie and departed, sniffling.

When Holtzinger had left, who should come in but my vile-tempered friend Courtney James? He apologized for insulting me, though you could hardly say he groveled.

"I don't really have a bad temper," he said, "except when people won't cooperate with me. Then I sometimes get mad. But so long as they're cooperative I'm not hard to get along with."

I knew that by "cooperate" he meant to do whatever Courtney James wanted, but I didn't press the point. "How about Miss Bartram?" I asked.

"We had a row," he said. "I'm through with women. So, if there's no hard feelings, let's go on from where we left off."

"Very well," I said, business being business.

The Raja and I decided to make it a joint safari to eighty-five million years ago: the Early Upper Cretaceous, or the Middle Cretaceous as some American geologists call it. It's about the best period for dinosaur in Missouri. You'll find some individual species a little larger in the Late Upper Cretaceous, but the period we were going to gives a wider variety.

Now, as to our equipment: The Raja and I each had a Continental .600, like the one I showed you, and a few smaller guns. At this time we hadn't worked up much capital and had no spare .600s to rent.

August Holtzinger said he would rent a gun, as he expected this to be his only safari, and there's no point in spending over a thousand dollars for a gun you'll shoot only a few times. But, since we had no spare .600s, his choice lay between buying one of those and renting one of our smaller pieces.

We drove into the country and set up a target to let him try the .600. Holtzinger heaved up the gun and let fly. He missed completely, and the kick knocked him flat on his back.

He got up, looking paler than ever, and handed me back the gun, saying: "Uh—I think I'd better try something smaller."

When his shoulder stopped hurting, I tried him out on the smaller rifles. He took a fancy to my Winchester 70, chambered for the .375 magnum cartridge. This is an excellent all-round gun— perfect for the big cats and bears, but a little light for elephant and definitely light for dinosaur. I should never have given in, but I was in a hurry, and it might have taken months to have a new .600 made to order for him. James already had a gun, a Holland & Holland .500 double express, which is almost in a class with the .600.

Both sahibs had done a bit of shooting, so I didn't worry about their accuracy. Shooting dinosaur is not a matter of extreme accuracy, but of sound judgment and smooth coordination so you shan't catch twigs in the mechanism of your gun, or fall into holes, or climb a small tree that the dinosaur can pluck you out of, or blow your guide's head off.

People used to hunting mammals sometimes try to shoot a dinosaur in the brain. That's the silliest thing you can do, because dinosaur haven't got any. To be exact, they have a little lump of tissue the size of a tennis ball on the front end of their spines, and how are you going to hit that when it's imbedded in a six-foot skull?

The only safe rule with dinosaur is: always try for a heart shot. They have big hearts, over a hundred pounds in the largest species, and a couple of .600 slugs through the heart will slow them up, at least. The problem is to get the slugs through that mountain of meat around it.

Well, we appeared at Prochaska's laboratory one rainy morning: James and Holtzinger, the Raja and I, our herder Beauregard Black, three helpers, a cook, and twelve jacks.

The transition chamber is a little cubbyhole the size of a small lift. My routine is for the men with the guns to go first in case a hungry theropod is standing near the machine when it arrives. So the two sahibs, the Raja, and I crowded into the chamber with our guns and packs. The operator squeezed in after us, closed the door, and fiddled with his dials. He set the thing for April twenty-fourth, eighty-five million B.C., and pressed the red button. The lights went out, leaving the chamber lit by a little battery-operated lamp. James and Holtzinger looked pretty green, but that may have been the lighting. The Raja and I had been through all this before, so the vibration and vertigo didn't bother us.

The little spinning black hands of the dials slowed down and stopped. The operator looked at his ground-level gauge and turned the handwheel that raised the chamber so it shouldn't materialize underground. Then he pressed another button, and the door slid open.

No matter how often I do it, I get a frightful thrill out of stepping into a bygone era. The operator had raised the chamber a foot above ground level, so I jumped down, my gun ready. The others came after.

"Right-ho," I said to the chamber wallah, and he closed the door. The chamber disappeared, and we looked around. There weren't any dinosaur in sight, nothing but lizards.

In this period, the chamber materializes on top of a rocky rise, from which you can see in all directions as far as the haze will let you. To the west, you see the arm of the Kansas Sea that reaches across Missouri and the big swamp around the bayhead where the sauropods live.

To the north is a low range that the Raja named the Janpur Hills, after the Indian kingdom his forebears once ruled. To the east, the land slopes up to a plateau, good for ceratopsians, while to the south is flat country with more sauropod swamps and lots of ornithopod: duckbill and iguanodont.

The finest thing about the Cretaceous is the climate: balmy like the South Sea Islands, but not so muggy as most Jurassic climates. It was spring, with dwarf magnolias in bloom all over.

A thing about this landscape is that it combines a fairly high rainfall with an open type of vegetation cover. That is, the grasses hadn't yet evolved to the point of forming solid carpets over all the open ground. So the ground is thick with laurel, sassafras, and other shrubs, with bare earth between. There are big thickets of palmettos and ferns. The trees round the hill are mostly cycads, standing singly and in copses. You'd call 'em palms. Down towards the Kansas Sea are more cycads and willows, while the uplands are covered with screw pine and ginkgoes.

Now, I'm no bloody poet—the Raja writes the stuff, not me—but I can appreciate a beautiful scene. One of the helpers had come through the machine with two of the jacks and was pegging them out, and I was looking through the haze and sniffing the air, when a gun went off behind me—*bang! bang!*

I whirled round, and there was Courtney James with his .500, and an ornithomime legging it for cover fifty yards away. The ornithomimes are medium-sized running dinosaurs, slender things with long necks and legs, like a cross between a lizard and an ostrich. This kind is about seven feet tall and weighs as much as a man. The beggar had wandered out of the nearest copse, and James gave him both barrels. Missed.

I was upset, as trigger-happy sahibs are as much a menace to their party as theropods. I yelled: "Damn it, you idiot! I thought you weren't to shoot without a word from me?"

"And who the hell are you to tell me when I'll shoot my own gun?" he said.

We had a rare old row until Holtzinger and the Raja got us calmed down. I explained:

"Look here, Mr. James, I've got reasons. If you shoot off all your ammunition before the trip's over, your gun won't be available in a pinch, as it's the only one of its caliber. If you empty both barrels at an unimportant target, what would happen if a big theropod charged before you could reload? Finally, it's not sporting to shoot everything in sight, just to hear the gun go off. Do you understand?"

"Yeah, I guess so," he said.

The rest of the party came through the machine, and we pitched our camp a safe distance from the materializing place. Our first task was to get fresh meat. For a twenty-one-day safari like this, we calculate our food requirements closely, so we can make out on tinned stuff and concentrates if we must, but we count on killing at least one piece of meat. When that's butchered, we go off on a short tour, stopping at four or five camping places to hunt and arriving back at base a few days before the chamber is due to appear.

Holtzinger, as I said, wanted a ceratopsian head, any kind. James insisted on just one head: a tyrannosaur. Then everybody'd think he'd shot the most dangerous game of all time.

Fact is, the tyrannosaur's overrated. He's more a carrion eater than an active predator, though he'll snap you up if he gets the chance. He's less dangerous than some of the other theropods— the flesh eaters, you know—such as the smaller *Gorgosaurus* from the period we were in. But everybody's read about the tyrant lizard, and he does have the biggest head of the theropods.

The one in our period isn't the *rex*, which is later and a bit bigger and more specialized. It's the *trionyches*, with the forelimbs not quite so reduced, though they're still too small for anything but picking the brute's teeth after a meal.

When camp was pitched, we still had the afternoon. So the Raja and I took our sahibs on their first hunt. We had a map of the local terrain from previous trips.

The Raja and I have worked out a system for dinosaur hunting. We split into two groups of two men each and walk parallel from twenty to forty yards apart. Each group has a sahib in front and a guide following, telling him where to go. We tell the sahibs we put them in front so they shall have the first shot. Well, that's true, but another reason is they're always tripping and falling with their guns cocked, and if the guide were in front he'd get shot.

The reason for two groups is that if a dinosaur starts for one, the other gets a good heart shot from the side.

As we walked, there was the usual rustle of lizards scuttling out of the way: little fellows, quick as a flash and colored like all the jewels in Tiffany's, and big gray ones that hiss at you as they plod off. There were tortoises and a few little snakes. Birds with beaks full of teeth flapped off squawking. And always there was that marvelous mild Cretaceous air. Makes a chap want to take his clothes off and dance with vine leaves in his hair, if you know what I mean.

Our sahibs soon found that Mesozoic country is cut up into millions of nullahs—gullies, you'd say. Walking is one long scramble, up and down, up and down.

We'd been scrambling for an hour, and the sahibs were soaked with sweat and had their tongues hanging out, when the Raja whistled. He'd spotted a group of bonehead feeding on cycad shoots.

These are the troödonts, small ornithopods about the size of men with a bulge on top of their heads that makes them look almost intelligent. Means nothing, because the bulge is solid bone. The males butt each other with these heads in fighting over the females.

These chaps would drop down on all fours, munch up a shoot, then stand up and look around. They're warier than most dinosaur, because they're the favorite food of the big theropods.

People sometimes assume that because dinosaur are so stupid, their senses must be dim, too. But it's not so. Some, like the sauropods, are pretty dim-sensed, but most have good smell and eyesight and fair hearing. Their weakness is that having no minds, they have no memories. Hence, out of sight, out of mind. When a big theropod comes slavering after you, your best defense is to hide in a nullah or behind a bush, and if he can neither see you nor smell you he'll just wander off.

We skulked up behind a patch of palmetto downwind from the bonehead. I whispered to James:

"You've had a shot already today. Hold your fire until Holtzinger shoots, and then shoot only if he misses or if the beast is getting away wounded."

"Uh-huh," said James.

We separated, he with the Raja and Holtzinger with me. This got to be our regular arrangement. James and I got on each other's nerves, but the Raja's a friendly, sentimental sort of bloke nobody can help liking.

We crawled round the palmetto patch on opposite sides, and Holtzinger got up to shoot. You daren't shoot a heavy-caliber rifle prone. There's not enough give, and the kick can break your shoulder.

Holtzinger sighted round the last few fronds of palmetto. I saw his barrel wobbling and waving. Then he lowered his gun and tucked it under his arm to wipe his glasses.

Off went James's gun, both barrels again.

The biggest bonehead went down, rolling and thrashing. The others ran away on their hindlegs in great leaps, their heads jerking and their tails sticking up behind.

"Put your gun on safety," I said to Holtzinger, who'd started forward. By the time we got to the bonehead, James was standing over it, breaking open his gun and blowing out the barrels. He looked as smug as if he'd come into another million and was asking the Raja to take his picture with his foot on the game.

I said: "I thought you were to give Holtzinger the first shot?"

"Hell, I waited," he said, "and he took so long I thought he must have gotten buck fever. If we stood around long enough, they'd see us or smell us."

There was something in what he said, but his way of saying it put my monkey up. I said: "If that sort of thing happens once more, we'll leave you in camp the next time we go out."

"Now, gentlemen," said the Raja. "After all, Reggie, these aren't experienced hunters."

"What now?" said Holtzinger. "Haul him back ourselves or send out the men?"

"We'll sling him under the pole," I said. "He weighs under two hundred."

The pole was a telescoping aluminum carrying pole I had in my pack, with padded yokes on the ends. I brought it because, in such eras, you can't count on finding saplings strong enough for proper poles on the spot.

The Raja and I cleaned our bonehead to lighten him and tied

him to the pole. The flies began to light on the offal by thousands. Scientists say they're not true flies in the modern sense, but they look and act like flies. There's one huge four-winged carrion fly that flies with a distinctive deep thrumming note.

The rest of the afternoon we sweated under that pole, taking turn about. The lizards scuttled out of the way, and the flies buzzed round the carcass.

We got to camp just before sunset, feeling as if we could eat the whole bonehead at one meal. The boys had the camp running smoothly, so we sat down for our tot of whiskey, feeling like lords of creation, while the cook broiled bonehead steaks.

Holtzinger said: "Uh—if I kill a ceratopsian, how do we get his head back?"

I explained: "If the ground permits, we lash it to the patent aluminium roller frame and sled it in."

"How much does a head like that weigh?" he asked.

"Depends on the age and the species," I told him. "The biggest weigh over a ton, but most run between five hundred and a thousand pounds."

"And all the ground's rough like it was today?"

"Most of it," I said. "You see, it's the combination of the open vegetation cover and the moderately high rainfall. Erosion is frightfully rapid."

"And who hauls the head on its little sled?"

"Everybody with a hand," I said. "A big head would need every ounce of muscle in this party. On such a job there's no place for side."

"Oh," said Holtzinger. I could see he was wondering whether a ceratopsian head would be worth the effort.

The next couple of days we trekked round the neighborhood. Nothing worth shooting; only a herd of ornithomimes, which went bounding off like a lot of ballet dancers. Otherwise there were only the usual lizards and pterosaurs and birds and insects. There's a big lace-winged fly that bites dinosaurs, so, as you can imagine, its beak makes nothing of a human skin. One made Holtzinger leap and dance like a Red Indian when it bit him through his shirt. James joshed him about it, saying:

"What's all the fuss over one little bug?"

The second night, during the Raja's watch, James gave a yell that brought us all out of our tents with rifles. All that had happened was that a dinosaur tick had crawled in with him and started drilling under his armpit. Since it's as big as your thumb even when it hasn't fed, he was understandably startled. Luckily he got it before it had taken its pint of blood. He'd pulled Holtzinger's leg pretty hard about the fly bite, so now Holtzinger repeated the words:

"What's all the fuss over one little bug, buddy?"

James squashed the tick underfoot with a grunt, not much liking to be hoist by his own what-d'you-call-it.

We packed up and started on our circuit. We meant to take the sahibs first to the sauropod swamp, more to see the wildlife than to collect anything.

From where the transition chamber materializes, the sauropod swamp looks like a couple of hours' walk, but it's really an all-day scramble. The first part is easy, as it's downhill and the brush isn't heavy. Then, as you get near the swamp, the cycads and willows grow so thickly that you have to worm your way among them.

I led the party to a sandy ridge on the border of the swamp, as it was pretty bare of vegetation and afforded a fine view. When we got to the ridge, the sun was about to go down. A couple of crocs slipped off into the water. The sahibs were so tired that they flopped down in the sand as if dead.

The haze is thick round the swamp, so the sun was deep red and weirdly distorted by the atmospheric layers. There was a high layer of clouds reflecting the red and gold of the sun, too, so altogether it was something for the Raja to write one of his poems about. A few little pterosaur were wheeling overhead like bats.

Beauregard Black got a fire going. We'd started on our steaks, and that pagoda-shaped sun was just slipping below the horizon, and something back in the trees was making a noise like a rusty hinge, when a sauropod breathed out in the water. They're the really big ones, you know. If Mother Earth were to sigh over the misdeeds of her children, it would sound like that.

The sahibs jumped up, shouting: "Where is he? Where is he?"

I said: "That black spot in the water, just to the left of that point."

They yammered while the sauropod filled its lungs and disappeared. "Is that all?" said James. "Won't we see any more of him?"

Holtzinger said: "I read that they never come out of the water because they're too heavy to walk."

"No," I explained. "They can walk perfectly well and often do, for egg-laying and moving from one swamp to another. But most of the time they spend in the water, like hippopotamus. They eat eight hundred pounds of soft swamp plants a day, all through those little heads. So they wander about the bottoms of lakes and swamps, chomping away, and stick their heads up to breathe every quarter-hour or so. It's getting dark, so this fellow will soon come out and lie down in the shallows to sleep."

"Can we shoot one?" demanded James.

"I wouldn't," said I.

"Why not?"

I said: "There's no point in it, and it's not sporting. First, they're almost invulnerable. They're even harder to hit in the brain than other dinosaurs because of the way they sway their heads about on those long necks. Their hearts are too deeply buried to reach unless you're awfully lucky. Then, if you kill one in the water, he sinks and can't be recovered. If you kill one on land, the only trophy is that little head. You can't bring the whole beast back because he weighs thirty tons or more, and we've got no use for thirty tons of meat."

Holtzinger said: "That museum in New York got one."

"Yes," said I. "The American Museum of Natural History sent a party of forty-eight to the Early Cretaceous with a fifty-caliber machine gun. They killed a sauropod and spent two solid months skinning it and hacking the carcass apart and dragging it to the time machine. I know the chap in charge of that project, and he still has nightmares in which he smells decomposing dinosaur. They had to kill a dozen big theropods attracted by the stench, so they had them lying around and rotting, too. And the theropods ate three men of the party despite the big gun."

Next morning, we were finishing breakfast when one of the helpers said: "Look, Mr. Rivers, up there!"

He pointed along the shoreline. There were six big crested duckbill, feeding in the shallows. They were the kind called *Parasauro-lophus*, with a long spike sticking out the back of their heads and a web of skin connecting this with the back of their necks.

"Keep your voices down!" I said. The duckbill, like the other ornithopods, are wary beasts because they have neither armor nor weapons. They feed on the margins of lakes and swamps, and when a gorgosaur rushes out of the trees they plunge into deep water and swim off. Then when *Phobosuchus*, the supercrocodile, goes for them in the water, they flee to the land. A hectic sort of life, what?

Holtzinger said: "Uh—Reggie! I've been thinking over what you said about ceratopsian heads. If I could get one of those yonder, I'd be satisfied. It would look big enough in my house, wouldn't it?"

"I'm sure of it, old boy," I said. "Now look here. We could detour to come out on the shore near here, but we should have to plow through half a mile of muck and brush, and they'd hear us coming. Or we can creep up to the north end of this sandspit, from which it's three or four hundred yards—a long shot but not impossible. Think you could do it?"

"Hm," said Holtzinger. "With my scope sight and a sitting po-sition—okay, I'll try it."

"You stay here, Court," I said to James. "This is Augie's head, and I don't want any argument over your having fired first."

James grunted while Holtzinger clamped his scope to his rifle. We crouched our way up the spit, keeping the sand ridge between us and the duckbill. When we got to the end where there was no more cover, we crept along on hands and knees, moving slowly. If you move slowly enough, directly toward or away from a dinosaur, it probably won't notice you.

The duckbill continued to grub about on all fours, every few seconds rising to look round. Holtzinger eased himself into the sitting position, cocked his piece, and aimed through his scope. And then—

Bang! bang! went a big rifle back at the camp.

Holtzinger jumped. The duckbills jerked their heads up and leaped for the deep water, splashing like mad. Holtzinger fired once and missed. I took one shot at the last duckbill before it vanished too, but missed. The .600 isn't built for long ranges.

Holtzinger and I started back toward the camp, for it had struck us that our party might be in theropod trouble.

What had happened was that a big sauropod had wandered down past the camp underwater, feeding as it went. Now, the water shoaled about a hundred yards offshore from our spit, halfway over to the swamp on the other side. The sauropod had ambled up the slope until its body was almost all out of water, weaving its head from side to side and looking for anything green to gobble. This is a species of *Alamosaurus,* which looks much like the well-known *Brontosaurus* except that it's bigger.

When I came in sight of the camp, the sauropod was turning round to go back the way it had come, making horrid groans. By the time we reached the camp, it had disappeared into deep water, all but its head and twenty feet of neck, which wove about for some time before they vanished into the haze.

When we came up to the camp, James was arguing with the Raja. Holtzinger burst out:

"You crummy bastard! That's the second time you've spoiled my shots."

"Don't be a fool," said James. "I couldn't let him wander into the camp and stamp everything flat."

"There was no danger of that," said the Raja. "You can see the water is deep offshore. It's just that our trigger-happee Mr. James cannot see any animal without shooting."

I added: "If it did get close, all you needed to do was throw a stick of firewood at it. They're perfectly harmless."

This wasn't strictly true. When the Comte de Lautrec ran after one for a close shot, the sauropod looked back at him, gave a flick of its tail, and took off the Comte's head as neatly as if he'd been axed in the tower. But, as a rule, they're inoffensive enough.

"How was I to know?" yelled James, turning purple. "You're all against me. What the hell are we on this miserable trip for, except to shoot things? Call yourselves hunters, but I'm the only one who hits anything!"

I got pretty wrothy and said he was just an excitable young skite with more money than brains, whom I should never have brought along.

"If that's how you feel," he said, "give me a burro and some food, and I'll go back to the base by myself. I won't pollute your pure air with my presence!"

"Don't be a bigger ass than you can help," I said. "What you propose is quite impossible."

"Then I'll go alone!" He grabbed his knapsack, thrust a couple of tins of beans and an opener into it, and started off with his rifle.

Beauregard Black spoke up: "Mr. Rivers, we cain't let him go off like that. He'll git lost and starve, or be et by a theropod."

"I'll fetch him back," said the Raja, and started after the runaway.

He caught up with James as the latter was disappearing into the cycads. We could see them arguing and waving their hands in the distance. After a while, they started back with arms around each other's necks like old school pals.

This shows the trouble we get into if we make mistakes in planning such a do. Having once got back in time, we had to make the best of our bargain.

I don't want to give the impression, however, that Courtney James was nothing but a pain in the rump. He had good points. He got over these rows quickly and next day would be as cheerful as ever. He was helpful with the general work of the camp, at least when he felt like it. He sang well and had an endless fund of dirty stories to keep us amused.

We stayed two more days at that camp. We saw crocodile, the small kind, and plenty of sauropod—as many as five at once—but no more duckbill. Nor any of those fifty-foot supercrocodiles.

So, on the first of May, we broke camp and headed north toward the Janpur Hills. My sahibs were beginning to harden up and were getting impatient. We'd been in the Cretaceous a week, and no trophies.

We saw nothing to speak of on the next leg, save a glimpse of a gorgosaur out of range and some tracks indicating a whopping big iguanodont, twenty-five or thirty feet high. We pitched camp at the base of the hills.

We'd finished off the bonehead, so the first thing was to shoot fresh meat. With an eye to trophies, too, of course. We got ready the morning of the third, and I told James:

"See here, old boy, no more of your tricks. The Raja will tell you when to shoot."

"Uh-huh, I get you," he said, meek as Moses.

We marched off, the four of us, into the foothills. There was a good chance of getting Holtzinger his ceratopsian. We'd seen a couple on the way up, but mere calves without decent horns.

As it was hot and sticky, we were soon panting and sweating. We'd hiked and scrambled all morning without seeing a thing except lizards, when I picked up the smell of carrion. I stopped the party and sniffed. We were in an open glade cut up by those little dry nullahs. The nullahs ran together into a couple of deeper gorges that cut through a slight depression choked with denser growth, cycad, and screw pine. When I listened, I heard the thrum of carrion flies.

"This way," I said. "Something ought to be dead—ah, here it is!"

And there it was: the remains of a huge ceratopsian lying in a little hollow on the edge of the copse. Must have weighed six or eight ton alive; a three-horned variety, perhaps the penultimate species of *Triceratops*. It was hard to tell, because most of the hide on the upper surface had been ripped off, and many bones had been pulled loose and lay scattered about.

Holtzinger said: "Oh, shucks! Why couldn't I have gotten to him before he died? That would have been a darned fine head."

I said: "On your toes, chaps. A theropod's been at this carcass and is probably nearby."

"How d'you know?" said James, with sweat running off his round red face. He spoke in what was for him a low voice, because a nearby theropod is a sobering thought to the flightiest.

I sniffed again and thought I could detect the distinctive rank odor of theropod. I couldn't be sure, though, because the carcass stank so strongly. My sahibs were turning green at the sight and smell of the cadaver. I told James:

"It's seldom that even the biggest theropod will attack a full-grown ceratopsian. Those horns are too much for them. But they love a dead or dying one. They'll hang round a dead ceratopsian for weeks, gorging and then sleeping off their meals for days at a time. They usually take cover in the heat of the day anyhow, because they can't stand much direct hot sunlight. You'll find them lying in copses like this or in hollows, wherever there's shade."

"What'll we do?" asked Holtzinger.

"We'll make our first cast through this copse, in two pairs as usual. Whatever you do, don't get impulsive or panicky."

I looked at Courtney James, but he looked right back and merely checked his gun.

"Should I still carry this broken?" he asked.

"No, close it, but keep the safety on till you're ready to shoot," I said. "We'll keep closer than usual, so we shall be in sight of each other. Start off at that angle, Raja; go slowly, and stop to listen between steps."

We pushed through the edge of the copse, leaving the carcass but not its stench behind us. For a few feet, you couldn't see a thing.

It opened out as we got in under the trees, which shaded out some of the brush. The sun slanted down through the trees. I could hear nothing but the hum of insects and the scuttle of lizards and the squawks of toothed birds in the treetops. I thought I could be sure of the theropod smell, but told myself that might be imagination. The theropod might be any of several species, large or small, and the beast itself might be anywhere within a half-mile's radius.

"Go on," I whispered to Holtzinger. I could hear James and the Raja pushing ahead on my right and see the palm fronds and ferns lashing about as they disturbed them. I suppose they were trying to move quietly, but to me they sounded like an earthquake in a crockery shop.

"A little closer!" I called.

Presently, they appeared slanting in toward me. We dropped into a gully filled with ferns and scrambled up the other side. Then we found our way blocked by a big clump of palmetto.

"You go round that side; we'll go round this," I said. We started off, stopping to listen and smell. Our positions were the same as on that first day, when James killed the bonehead.

We'd gone two-thirds of the way round our half of the palmetto when I heard a noise ahead on our left. Holtzinger heard it too, and pushed off his safety. I put my thumb on mine and stepped to one side to have a clear field of fire.

The clatter grew louder. I raised my gun to aim at about the height of a big theropod's heart. There was a movement in the foliage—and a six-foot-high bonehead stepped into view, walking solemnly across our front and jerking its head with each step like a giant pigeon.

I heard Holtzinger let out a breath and had to keep myself from laughing. Holtzinger said: "Uh—"

Then that damned gun of James's went off, *bang! bang!* I had a glimpse of the bonehead knocked arsy-varsy with its tail and hindlegs flying.

"Got him!" yelled James. "I drilled him clean!" I heard him run forward.

"Good God, if he hasn't done it again!" I said.

Then there was a great swishing of foliage and a wild yell from James. Something heaved up out of the shrubbery, and I saw the head of the biggest of the local flesh eaters, *Tyrannosaurus trionyches* himself.

The scientists can insist that *rex* is the bigger species, but I'll swear this blighter was bigger than any *rex* ever hatched. It must have stood twenty feet high and been fifty feet long. I could see its big bright eye and six-inch teeth and the big dewlap that hangs down from its chin to its chest.

The second of the nullahs that cut through the copse ran athwart our path on the far side of the palmetto clump. Perhaps it was six feet deep. The tyrannosaur had been lying in this, sleeping off its last meal. Where its back stuck up above the ground level, the ferns on the edge of the nullah masked it. James had fired both barrels over the theropod's head and woke it up. Then the silly ass ran forward without reloading. Another twenty feet and he'd have stepped on the tyrannosaur.

James, naturally, stopped when this thing popped up in front of him. He remembered that he'd fired both barrels and that he'd left the Raja too far behind for a clear shot.

At first, James kept his nerve. He broke open his gun, took two rounds from his belt, and plugged them into the barrels. But, in his haste to snap the gun shut, he caught his hand between the barrels and the action. The painful pinch so startled James that he dropped his gun. Then he went to pieces and bolted.

The Raja was running up with his gun at high port, ready to snap it to his shoulder the instant he got a clear view. When he saw James running headlong toward him, he hesitated, not wishing to shoot James by accident. The latter plunged ahead, blundered into the Raja, and sent them both sprawling among the ferns. The tyrannosaur collected what little wits it had and stepped forward to snap them up.

And how about Holtzinger and me on the other side of the palmettos? Well, the instant James yelled and the tyrannosaur's head appeared, Holtzinger darted forward like a rabbit. I'd brought my gun up for a shot at the tyrannosaur's head, in hope of getting at least an eye; but, before I could find it in my sights, the head was out of sight behind the palmettos. Perhaps I should have fired at hazard, but all my experience is against wild shots.

When I looked back in front of me, Holtzinger had already disappeared round the curve of the palmetto clump. I'd started after him when I heard his rifle and the click of the bolt between shots: bang—click-click—bang—click-click, like that.

He'd come up on the tyrannosaur's quarter as the brute started to stoop for James and the Raja. With his muzzle twenty feet from the tyrannosaur's hide, Holtzinger began pumping .375s into the beast's body. He got off three shots when the tyrannosaur gave a tremendous booming grunt and wheeled round to see what was stinging it. The jaws came open, and the head swung round and down again.

Holtzinger got off one more shot and tried to leap to one side. As he was standing on a narrow place between the palmetto clump and the nullah, he fell into the nullah. The tyrannosaur continued its lunge and caught him. The jaws went chomp, and up came the head with poor Holtzinger in them, screaming like a damned soul.

I came up just then and aimed at the brute's face, but then realized that its jaws were full of my sahib and I should be shooting him, too. As the head went on up like the business end of a big power shovel, I fired a shot at the heart. The tyrannosaur was already turning away, and I suspect the ball just glanced along the ribs. The beast took a couple of steps when I gave it the other barrel in the jack. It staggered on its next step but kept on. Another step, and it was nearly out of sight among the trees, when the Raja fired twice. The stout fellow had untangled himself from James, got up, picked up his gun, and let the tyrannosaur have it.

The double wallop knocked the brute over with a tremendous crash. It fell into a dwarf magnolia, and I saw one of its huge birdlike hindlegs waving in the midst of a shower of pink-and-white petals.

But the tyrannosaur got up again and blundered off without even dropping its victim. The last I saw of it was Holtzinger's legs dangling out one side of its jaws (he'd stopped screaming) and its big tail banging against the tree trunks as it swung from side to side.

The Raja and I reloaded and ran after the brute for all we were worth. I tripped and fell once, but jumped up again and didn't notice my skinned elbow till later. When we burst out of the copse, the tyrannosaur was already at the far end of the glade. We each took a quick shot but probably missed, and it was out of sight before we could fire again.

We ran on, following the tracks and spatters of blood, until we had to stop from exhaustion. Never again did we see that tyrannosaur. Their movements look slow and ponderous, but with those tremendous legs they don't have to step very fast to work up considerable speed.

When we'd got our breath, we got up and tried to track the tyrannosaur, on the theory that it might be dying and we should come up to it. But, though we found more spoor, it faded out and left us at a loss. We circled round, hoping to pick up, but no luck.

Hours later, we gave up and went back to the glade.

Courtney James was sitting with his back against a tree, holding his rifle and Holtzinger's. His right hand was swollen and blue where he'd pinched it, but still usable. His first words were:

"Where the hell have you two been?"

I said: "We've been occupied. The late Mr. Holtzinger. Remember?"

"You shouldn't have gone off and left me; another of those things might have come along. Isn't it bad enough to lose one hunter through your stupidity without risking another one?"

I'd been preparing a warm wigging for James, but his attack so astonished me that I could only bleat: "What? We lost . . . ?"

"Sure," he said. "You put us in front of you, so if anybody gets eaten it's us. You send a guy up against these animals undergunned. You—"

"You Goddamn' stinking little swine!" I said. "If you hadn't been a blithering idiot and blown those two barrels, and then run like the yellow coward you are, this never would have happened. Holtzinger died trying to save your worthless life. By God, I wish he'd failed!

He was worth six of a stupid, spoiled, muttonheaded bastard like you—"

I went on from there. The Raja tried to keep up with me, but ran out of English and was reduced to cursing James in Hindustani.

I could see by the purple color on James's face that I was getting home. He said: "Why, you—" and stepped forward and sloshed me one in the face with his left fist.

It rocked me a bit, but I said: "Now then, my lad, I'm glad you did that! It gives me a chance I've been waiting for. . . ."

So I waded into him. He was a good-sized boy, but between my sixteen stone and his sore right hand he had no chance. I got a few good ones home, and down he went.

"Now get up!" I said. "And I'll be glad to finish off!"

James raised himself to his elbows. I got set for more fisticuffs, though my knuckles were skinned and bleeding already. James rolled over, snatched his gun, and scrambled up, swinging the muzzle from one to the other of us.

"You won't finish anybody off!" he panted through swollen lips. "All right, put your hands up! Both of you!"

"Do not be an idiot," said the Raja. "Put that gun away!"

"Nobody treats me like that and gets away with it!"

"There's no use murdering us," I said. "You'd never get away with it."

"Why not? There won't be much left of you after one of these hits you. I'll just say the tyrannosaur ate you, too. Nobody could prove anything. They can't hold you for a murder eighty-five million years old. The statute of limitations, you know."

"You fool, you'd never make it back to the camp alive!" I shouted.

"I'll take a chance—" began James, setting the butt of his .500 against his shoulder, with the barrels pointed at my face. Looked like a pair of bleeding vehicular tunnels.

He was watching me so closely that he lost track of the Raja for a second. My partner had been resting on one knee, and now his right arm came up in a quick bowling motion with a three-pound rock. The rock bounced off James's head. The .500 went off. The ball must have parted my hair, and the explosion jolly well near broke my eardrums. Down went James again.

"Good work, old chap!" I said, gathering up James's gun.

"Yes," said the Raja thoughtfully, as he picked up the rock he'd thrown and tossed it. "Doesn't quite have the balance of a cricket ball, but it is just as hard."

"What shall we do now?" I said. "I'm inclined to leave the beggar here unarmed and let him fend for himself."

The Raja gave a little sigh. "It's a tempting thought, Reggie, but we really cannot, you know. Not done."

"I suppose you're right," I said. "Well, let's tie him up and take him back to camp."

We agreed there was no safety for us unless we kept James under guard every minute until we got home. Once a man has tried to kill you, you're a fool if you give him another chance.

We marched James back to camp and told the crew what we were up against. James cursed everybody.

We spent three dismal days combing the country for that tyrannosaur, but no luck. We felt it wouldn't have been cricket not to make a good try at recovering Holtzinger's remains. Back at our main camp, when it wasn't raining, we collected small reptiles and things for our scientific friends. The Raja and I discussed the question of legal proceedings against Courtney James, but decided there was nothing we could do in that direction.

When the transition chamber materialized, we fell over one another getting into it. We dumped James, still tied, in a corner, and told the chamber operator to throw the switches.

While we were in transition, James said: "You two should have killed me back there."

"Why?" I said. "You don't have a particularly good head."

The Raja added: "Wouldn't look at all well over a mantel."

"You can laugh," said James, "but I'll get you some day. I'll find a way and get off scot-free."

"My dear chap!" I said. "If there were some way to do it, I'd have you charged with Holtzinger's death. Look, you'd best leave well enough alone."

When we came out in the present, we handed him his empty gun and his other gear, and off he went without a word. As he left, Holtzinger's girl, that Claire, rushed up crying:

"Where is he? Where's August?"

There was a bloody heartrending scene, despite the Raja's skill at handling such situations.

We took our men and beasts down to the old laboratory building that the university has fitted up as a serai for such expeditions. We paid everybody off and found we were broke. The advance payments from Holtzinger and James didn't cover our expenses, and we should have precious little chance of collecting the rest of our fees either from James or from Holtzinger's estate.

And speaking of James, d'you know what that blighter was doing? He went home, got more ammunition, and came back to the university. He hunted up Professor Prochaska and asked him:

"Professor, I'd like you to send me back to the Cretaceous for a quick trip. If you can work me into your schedule right now, you can just about name your own price. I'll offer five thousand to begin with. I want to go to April twenty-third, eighty-five million B.C."

Prochaska answered: "Why do you wish to go back again so soon?"

"I lost my wallet in the Cretaceous," said James. "I figure if I go back to the day before I arrived in that era on my last trip, I'll watch myself when I arrived on that trip and follow myself around till I see myself lose the wallet."

"Five thousand is a lot for a wallet," said the professor.

"It's got some things in it I can't replace," said James.

"Well," said Prochaska, thinking. "The party that was supposed to go out this morning has telephoned that they would be late, so perhaps I can work you in. I have always wondered what would happen when the same man occupied the same stretch of time twice."

So James wrote out a check, and Prochaska took him to the chamber and saw him off. James's idea, it seems, was to sit behind a bush a few yards from where the transition chamber would appear and pot the Raja and me as we emerged.

Hours later, we'd changed into our street clothes and phoned our wives to come and get us. We were standing on Forsythe Boulevard waiting for them when there was a loud crack, like an explosion, and a flash of light not fifty feet from us. The shock wave staggered us and broke windows.

We ran toward the place and got there just as a bobby and

several citizens came up. On the boulevard, just off the kerb, lay a human body. At least, it had been that, but it looked as if every bone in it had been pulverized and every blood vessel burst, so it was hardly more than a slimy mass of pink protoplasm. The clothes it had been wearing were shredded, but I recognized an H. & H. .500 double-barreled express rifle. The wood was scorched and the metal pitted, but it was Courtney James's gun. No doubt whatever.

Skipping the investigations and the milling about that ensued, what had happened was this: nobody had shot at us as we emerged on the twenty-fourth, and that couldn't be changed. For that matter, the instant James started to do anything that would make a visible change in the world of eighty-five million B.C., such as making a footprint in the earth, the space-time forces snapped him forward to the present to prevent a paradox. And the violence of the passage practically tore him to bits.

Now that this is better understood, the professor won't send anybody to a period less than five thousand years prior to the time that some time traveler has already explored, because it would be too easy to do some act, like chopping down a tree or losing some durable artifact, that would affect the later world. Over longer periods, he tells me, such changes average out and are lost in the stream of time.

We had a rough time after that, with the bad publicity and all, though we did collect a fee from James's estate. Luckily for us, a steel manufacturer turned up who wanted a mastodon's head for his den.

I understand these things better now, too. The disaster hadn't been wholly James's fault. I shouldn't have taken him when I knew what a spoiled, unstable sort of bloke he was. And if Holtzinger could have used a really heavy gun, he'd probably have knocked the tyrannosaur down, even if he didn't kill it, and so have given the rest of us a chance to finish it.

So, Mr. Seligman, that's why I won't take you to that period to hunt. There are plenty of other eras, and if you look them over I'm sure you'll find something to suit you. But not the Jurassic or the Cretaceous. You're just not big enough to handle a gun for dinosaur.

LITTLE GREEN MEN FROM AFAR

In 1950, when the flying-saucer craze was enjoying its first boom, Francis F. Broman, an instructor in general science at the University of Denver, staged an experiment to test his students' judgment of evidence. He presented to his class a self-styled flying-saucer expert. Broman told his students to judge this man's tale by five criteria: that the report be first-hand; that the teller show no obvious bias or prejudice; that he be a trained observer; that the data be available for checking; and that the teller be clearly identified.

The class met on March 8. Students invited friends, so the classroom was crowded with strange and eager faces. The speaker was one Silas Newton.

He had, Newton said, learned from government officials that three unidentified flying objects, containing a total of thirty-four extraterrestrials, had crashed, killing all their occupants. These were little blond, beardless men, around three and a half feet tall. They became green only in later versions of the story.

A fourth saucer landed unharmed, and the little men got out. But they fled when officials approached them, and their vehicle vanished.

Broman's class unanimously flunked Newton's story on all five criteria. He had, for instance, shown a bias against the U.S. Air Force. The tale, however, appeared in the Denver newspapers. Reporters flocked to interview Newton, who, it appeared, was promoting an alleged magnetic method of prospecting for oil. Newton repeated his story with embellishments. The vehicles, he said, were powered by magnetic lines of force, and those that crashed had run into something he called a "magnetic fault." This is pseudoscientific gobbledygook, signifying nothing. Also, he said, the government was trying to suppress all news of this visitation.

Even if Broman's students did not believe the story, many others did. Newton sold several articles about his saucerians. His friend Frank Scully, a theatrical journalist living in Hollywood, California, published a book, *Behind the Flying Saucers*. This puffed up Newton's claims and denounced the government for suppressing the truth about the saucerians.

Such circular logic is commonly used by pseudoscientists. You start by assuming what you wish to prove. If you assume that saucers have landed, why haven't they been exposed to view? Obviously, because the government has censored the news, and the fact that the government has squelched this information proves that the saucers exist. QED.

The tale of the shy saucerians has grown with retelling, so that the pygmy visitors are now firmly established in American folklore. Newton's tale has generated the usual imitations and elaborations. Recently, a pair of enterprising Texans, Marshall Applewhite and Bonnie Lu Nettles, were traveling about calling themselves Bo and Peep, or simply the "Two." They have collected a gaggle of followers by promising to carry them all off in UFOs to a happier life on some other world. All the Two wanted was for their disciples to abandon all family ties and give the Two all their money.

In the history of cultism, one is always experiencing a feeling of *déjà vu*. Cultist beliefs have been confuted countless times but bob up again as lively as ever. The idea that the earth was once devastated by a comet began in the seventeenth century with a Cambridge professor, William Whiston. It was revived in the eighteenth by Count Gian Rinaldo Carli. It was revived again in the nineteenth by Ignatius Donnelly, who also made popular cults out of earlier scholarly speculations about the lost Atlantis and the idea that Bacon wrote Shakespeare. In our own times, the cometary-collision hypothesis has been revived with stunning success by Immanuel Velikovsky.

The story of the Two seems like a replay, with modern embellishments, of the Millerite agitation of 1843. William Miller, an up-state New York farmer, because convinced by his biblical studies that the world was about to end. When a shower of meteors and a passing comet aroused excitement, Miller gathered a following, who sold or gave away all their property in anticipation of the End. Their logic is hard to follow, since after the End nobody would have any use for property anyway.

On the appointed night, Millerites in white robes gathered on hilltops, the more easily to be caught up to Heaven with the rest of the righteous. Needless to say, nothing happened, and the dupes were obliged to go back to scratching a living as best they could.

The Newton episode and its sequels form but one thread in the long and tangled web of pseudoscientific belief. Beginning a decade ago, a Swiss bank employee named Erich von Däniken widely popularized the notion that no mere human beings could have built the pyramids of Egypt, the statues on Easter Island, and similar feats of pre-industrial engineering. These must, therefore, have been constructed by extraterrestrial visitors. The fact that von Däniken's books are solid masses of misstatements, errors, and wild guesses presented as fact, unsupported by anything resembling scientific data, has not stopped them from earning their author a much better living than he ever made back in Switzerland.

The idea of enlighteners from afar was not new when von Däniken took it up. It formed part of the teachings of Helena Petrovna Blavatsky, the founder of the Theosophy, and her successors. Madame Blavatsky was a big, fat Russian adventuress who, when she launched her cult in the 1870s, had already led a colorful career. She had lived in Europe, Egypt, and the United States. She had been a circus bareback rider, a professional pianist, a businesswoman, and a spiritualist medium. She had also been the mistress of, among others, a Slovenian singer, a Russian baron, and an English businessman.

In 1878 she moved to India, where her organization took final form. In 1885, she left India for good, after exposure of some of her magical tricks by a pair of disgruntled accomplices. Three years later, she published her *chef-d'oeuvre*, *The Secret Doctrine*, in which her credo took permanent if wildly confused shape. This work, in six volumes, is a mass of plagiarism and fakery, based upon contemporary scientific, pseudoscientific, mythological, and occult works, cribbed without credit and used in a blundering way that shows only skin-deep acquaintance with the topics discussed.

In addition to the gaudy Theosophical cosmos of multiple planes of existence and chains of planets, following each other in cycles from plane to plane, we are told that life on earth has evolved through seven cycles or Rounds. Man develops through seven Root Races, each comprising seven sub-races.

The First Root Race, we learn, was a kind of invisible astral jellyfish, dwelling in the polar Imperishable Sacred Land. The Second Root Race, a little more substantial, lived in the arctic continent of Hyperborea (derived, like Atlantis, from Greek myths and speculations). The Third Root Race were the gigantic, green, apelike, hermaphroditic, egg-laying Lemurians, with four arms, and eyes in the backs of their heads. Edgar Rice Burroughs probably used Madame Blavatsky's Lemurians as models for his Martian green men.

The downfall of the Lemurians came with their discovery of sex. Madame Blavatsky took a dim view of sex, at least after she got too old to be interested in it herself. Lemuria, like Hyperborea before it, broke up by the subsidence of its parts, while Atlantis took shape. The Fourth Root Race were the wholly human Atlantians; we are the Fifth; the Sixth and Seventh are yet to come.

After Madame Blavatsky died in 1891, her successors clothed her skeletal account of lost continents and prehistoric races with a substantial body of detail. Her associate A. P. Sinnett, in *The Growth of the Soul* (1896), wrote:

> From Venus, as all students of esoteric teaching will be aware, the guardians of our infant humanity in the later third and early fourth race of this world period descended to stimulate in our family the growth of the mânistic principle [P. 277]

Madame's successor as head of the Theosophical Society, Annie Besant, said in *The Pedigree of Man* (1908):

> The third class of Mânasaputras consists of Beings who come to our earth from another planetary chain. They . . . come from

outside, from the Chain wherein the planet Venus, [or] Shûkra,
is Globe D. [P. 96]

Not even Madame Blavatsky originated the idea of the enlighteners from afar. The concept belongs to a class of myths and legends
of culture heroes, who taught mankind what it needed to know in
order to thrive. In Greece, the culture hero was Prometheus, who
stole fire from Heaven and gave it to mankind against the orders of
Zeus. In Egypt, he was Osiris. Among the North American Indians,
he was often called the Coyote.

In the naïve old days when the earth was flat, the culture hero
used to come down from Heaven. Astronomy, by showing that
Heaven was mostly empty space, scotched this idea. Then the discovery that the planets were worlds provided a substitute. The idea
that such worlds might be inhabited was broached in the second
century by the Syrian satirist Loukianos, or Lucian of Samosata. In
his *True History*, Lucian told how a boatload of adventurers, snatched
up into the heavens by a whirlwind, got involved in a war between
the king of the sun and the king of the moon over the colonization
of Venus.

Voltaire, in his *Micromegas* (1752), brought to earth an eight-
mile-high visitor from Sirius and a slightly smaller native of Saturn.
Because of their size, these beings have a hard time deciding whether
there is intelligent life on earth. Some of us have trouble deciding
that, too.

The reason for this persistent desire to credit the early advances of
mankind to superior beings—angels, demigods, or extraterrestrials—is
simple. The vast majority never have a new idea that is at once original, practicable, and a significant contribution to human progress. For
this majority, to admit that some human beings do have such ideas is
to admit that such people are more intelligent than they. Nobody likes
to confess that he is stupider than someone else.

This is especially true now, when the world is high on an equality kick. It is fashionable in some circles to believe that all men are
created literally equal. If they are not, it is unfair and undemocratic,
and we should pretend that they are. To think otherwise is called
elitism, and you know what a wicked thing that is said to be.

So the enlighteners from afar, whether green or some other color, will be with us for some time to come. No explanation of how the little brown men of the Nile Valley actually built the pyramids will banish these exotic pedagogues, because belief in them panders to human vanity. Most people want reassurance, consolation, and flattery more than they want scientific facts.

The story of pseudoscientific cultism, of which the enlighteners in UFOs form but one small part, is depressing to believers in human rationality. Some cultist ideas, such as Cyrus Teed's notion of the 1890s that the earth is a hollow sphere with us inside, or the more recent one that fluoridation of drinking water is a Communist conspiracy by those notorious red-plotters Dwight Eisenhower, John Foster Dulles, and Earl Warren, are so absurd that they beguile few followers and soon fade away. Others attract huge followings and persist for generations.

During the past century, hundreds of thousands of such credophiles (as I like to call them) have believed, despite clear evidence to the contrary—

that Plato's Atlantis not only existed but also gave rise to all other civilizations;

that the descendants of the Lost Ten Tribes of Israel are the British, the Irish, the Japanese, the American Indians, or some other modern folk;

that the Great Pyramid of King Khufu at Giza embodies in its measurements a revelation of the wisdom of the ages and a prophecy of the future of man;

that in early historic times, a comet hit the earth, reversing its rotation and changing the length of its day;

that creatures from some other planet are keeping us under surveillance from spacecraft;

that visitors from another fictitious continent—Lemuria, in the Pacific—still dwell on Mount Shasta, in California, where they perform mystic rites with magical fireworks;

that William Shakespeare's plays were written by Sir Francis Bacon, or the Earl of Oxford, or some other Elizabethan worthy;

that the ancient Babylonian superstition of astrology is an effective means of analyzing a personality and predicting the vicissitudes of the one possessing it;

and that in various parts of the world lurk large, picturesque animals left over from some prehistoric era, such as dinosaurs, ape-men, or the plesiosaur of Loch Ness.

As all good monster-fanciers know, the story of Nessie started with a tale of Saint Columba, a sixth-century Irish priest who went to Scotland and converted some of the Picts to Christianity. According to his biographer, another Irish cleric named Adomnan, about the year A.D. 565:

> . . . when the blessed man was for a number of days in the province of the Picts, he had to cross the river Nes. When he reached its bank, he saw a poor fellow being buried by other inhabitants; and the buriers said that, while swimming not long before, he had been seized and most savagely bitten by a water beast. Some men, going to his rescue in a wooden boat, though too late, had put out hooks and caught hold of his wretched corpse. When the blessed man heard this, he ordered notwithstanding that one of his companions should swim out and bring back to him, by sailing, a boat that stood on the opposite bank. Hearing this order of the holy and memorable man, Lugne mocu-Min obeyed without delay, and putting off his clothes, excepting his tunic, plunged into the water. But the monster, whose appetite had earlier been not so much sated as whetted for prey, lurked in the depth of the river. Feeling the water above disturbed by Lugne's swimming, it suddenly swam up to the surface, and with gaping mouth and with great roaring rushed towards the man swimming in the middle of the stream. While all that were there, barbarians and even the brothers, were struck down with extreme terror, the blessed man, who was watching, raised his holy hand and drew the saving sign of the cross in the empty air; and then, invoking the name of God, he commanded the savage beast, and said: "You will go no further. Do not touch the man; turn backward speedily." Then, hearing this command of the saint, the beast, as if pulled back with ropes, fled terrified in swift retreat; although it had before approached so close to Lugne as he swam

that there was no more than the length of one short pole between man and beast.

Then, seeing that the beast had withdrawn and that their fellow-soldier Lugne had returned to them unharmed and safe, in the boat, the brothers with great amazement glorified God in the blessed man. And also the pagan barbarians who were there at the time, impelled by the magnitude of this miracle that they themselves had seen, magnified the God of the Christians.

According to Adomnan, Columba also, with God's help, saw events taking place far away or in the future, cast out demons, healed the sick, raised the dead, controlled the winds, calmed storms at sea, summoned water from a rock, turned water into wine, and destroyed evil-doers by his curses. If you believe these marvels, there is no reason why you should not believe in Nessie, too.

It is true that new species of animals are discovered from time to time. Only last year, a supposedly extinct species of peccary turned up alive in the Gran Chaco of Paraguay. It seems increasingly unlikely, however, that any more large air-breathers remain to be found. So to discover new species, the most promising fields are either the deep-sea or very small organisms. The likeliest of all is the largest single order, in number of species, of all animals: the Coleoptera, or beetles. Of the million-odd known species of animals, about one fifth are beetles. So, if you itch to discover a new species, a new kind of beetle is your best bet.

Nowadays, however, instead of hunting for new species, it is more to the point to try to keep the species we already know from being exterminated, as many are in danger of being.

Why do such cults and their dogmas survive endless exposures, discreditings, and confutations? What gives them the regenerative powers of the Lernaean Hydra, which grew two new heads for every one that Herakles knocked off?

Well, men have always had a voracious appetite for tall tales of colorful, exciting wonders. They accept them and pass them along, often with embellishments, because it is *fun*. Nearly all histories, before modern times, were full of marvels. Thus the skeptical Roman historian Titus Livius collected hundreds of stories of portents. During Hannibal's invasion of Italy, he wrote:

> . . . *many portents occurred in Rome or in the neighborhood, or at all events, many were reported and easily gained credence, for when men's minds have been excited by superstitious fears they easily believe these things. A six-month-old child, of freeborn parents, is said to have shouted "Io Triumphe" in the vegetable market, whilst in the Forum Boarum, an ox is reported to have climbed up of its own accord to the third story of a house, and then, frightened by the noisy crowd which gathered, it threw itself down. A phantom navy was seen shining in the sky; the temple of Hope in the vegetable market was struck by lightning; at Lanuvium Juno's spear moved of itself, and a crow had flown down to the temple and settled on her couch; in the territory of Amiternum beings in human shape and clothed in white were seen at a distance.* [The Annals of the Roman People XXI xlii, 1]

Some of these events may have been natural, if unusual. But to show how these things grow, Livy gave a later list, in which the child spoke in its mother's womb, the ox talked in a human voice, and the beings in white stood around an altar in the sky.

For a later example, the thirteenth-century Icelandic *Njal's Saga* tells how, before the battle of Clontarf in 1014, which enabled the Irish to throw the Vikings out of Ireland, on three successive nights, one of the Norse contingents suffered first a rain of blood from the sky, then the men's own weapons leaped into the air and attacked them, and finally they were assailed by flocks of fierce ravens. One could go on like this all day.

Another factor in the ebullient recent growth of pseudoscience is the weakening of traditional religions as sources of facts about man and the universe. As science advances, it finds the true explanations for many questions that have long puzzled men. These explanations often contradict those given in the sacred books.

Thus the authors of the Bible obviously believed the world to be flat, but it's round. We are not descended from Adam and Eve but from a hairy ground-ape living in Africa twenty million years ago. Plagues are not sent by God to punish disobedient peoples but are caused by bacterial infections. Hence the traditional religions are less and less relied upon for material facts. Increasingly, they have been relegated to being teachers of morals and social-service organizations.

This decline has left a blank in the human psyche. Efforts to substitute some secular philogophy, such as Stoicism, Confucianism, or Marxism, for religion, as a guide and comforter to sinful man, have not been spectacularly successful. Science does not offer a very comforting substitute. It is the best way of finding out what is what, but it makes men neither better nor worse; and the impersonal universe it reveals is bleakly indifferent to human hopes and desires.

Further, by its very nature, science becomes more complex, specialized, and difficult as time goes on. It thus becomes progressively harder for an ordinary mind to keep abreast of scientific discovery. Pseudoscientific cults, on the other hand, give the believer the feeling of being in the "modern" scientific swim, or of knowing things hidden from the unenlightened mass, without compelling him to master anything really hard.

Furthermore, the ease of transportation and communication has fostered the multiplication of cults. When people were more closely tied to their birthplaces, their kin, and the social milieux into which they were born, they were compelled to associate with a variety of people, many of them uncongenial, with whom they were connected by accidents of birth or geography. But at least they had to face other viewpoints, and obvious foolishness was hooted down.

Of course, new ideas that turned out to be right were also hooted down. With the dizzy speed of change in the presentday world, however, many people have developed minds that are not merely open but gaping. They swallow any new idea, no matter how fantastic, if it is forcefully presented by a charismatic leader.

Also, more and more find it possible, by easy travel and communication, to confine their social lives to those who share their own outlooks and prejudices. Wherever they go, they seek out others of their own peculiar views, since most folk prefer having their existing beliefs confirmed to having them refuted. In such a limited milieu, the most bizarre ideas can be solemnly embraced, because the cultists, seeing only one another outside of working hours, are never forced to consider other points of view. Hence a leader, if he can isolate his followers long enough, can convince them that the moon is made of green cheese. Since they never hear him contradicted, they believe it indefinitely.

Thus contemporary society tends to become more and more subdivided into small, exclusive, mentally self-isolated groups. Each has its own version of the True Faith and never listens to any other.

What can be done about this? Something, but not a great deal. If one is in academe, one can drill one's students in the criteria for judging a statement, as Instructor Broman did at the University of Denver. He seems to have made it work; at least, his students were not fooled by Newton's tale. One can warn one's students against the stigmata of the charlatan: arrogance, garrulity, appeals to emotion, authoritarianism, incomprehensible language, conviction of his own grandeur and persecution, and certainty that those who reject his ideas are scoundrels or madmen.

Few, however, seem able to examine new ideas with the calm, evenhanded intelligence, and the unemotional balance of receptivity and skepticism, needed correctly to evaluate such ideas every time. Pseudoscientific cultism, therefore, seems destined for a long and prosperous career.

Its endurance would be assured, if by nothing else, by the fact that there is money in it. Donald Menzel wrote a book effectively debunking flying saucers, and more recently Lawrence Kusche has published one debunking the Bermuda Triangle. You may be sure that the sales of these books have been only a tiny fraction of the sales of books promoting the original vagaries. If I undertook a thorough analysis of one of von Däniken's books, the result would be a book several times the size of the original. It would take years of my time; and if I were mad enough to write it, who would then read it?

Nor should we expect help from the government. When the government gets into such a dispute, its weight is thrown to the beliefs of its leaders, and they can be as wrong as anyone else. Governmental intervention resulted in the compulsory Aryanism of Hitler's Germany and the rule of Lysenko's pseudogenetics in Stalin's Russia. In the United States, the Fundamentalist crusade of the 1920s, led by the eminent William Jennings Bryan, sought a constitutional amendment against the teaching of evolution. Luckily, that effort petered out. In recent years, however, it has been revived, especially in California. There it had the blessing of the then governor Ronald Reagan. Goodness knows what might happen if a real, red-hot Fundamentalist were to become President of the United States.

Still, this is no reason for not knocking a head off this particular hydra whenever we can. The scientific debunker's job may be compared to that of the trash collector. The fact that the garbage truck comes by today does not mean that there won't be another load tomorrow. But if the garbage were not collected at all, the results would be worse, as some cities have found when the sanitation workers struck.

So let us do our best to get rid of this ideological garbage, lest it inundate the earth. Our work will never be decisive, since old cults are almost unkillable and new ones keep springing up; but that is no reason for not doing what we can. If we can save even a few from the lure of the higher nonsense, our efforts will have been worthwhile.

To close on a lighter note, I dabble in light verse and have composed a jingle called "The Little Green Men." It runs like this:

Ah, little green fellows from Venus
Or some other planet afar:
From Mars or Calypso or, maybe,
A world of an alien star!

According to best-selling authors—
Blavatsky to von Däniken—
They taught us the skills that were needed
To make super-apes into men.

They guided our faltering footsteps
From savagery into the dawns

Of burgeoning civilization
With cities and writing and bronze.

By them were the Pyramids builded;
They reared the first temples in Hind;
Drew lines at Peruvian Nazca
To uplift the poor Amerind.

With all of these wonders they gave us
It's sad these divine astronauts
Revealed not the answers to questions
That foil our most rational thoughts.

Such puzzles as riches and paupers,
The problems of peace and of war,
Relations between the two sexes,
Or crime and chastisement therefore.

So when we feel dim and defeated
By problems immune to attack,
Let's send out a prayer electronic:
"O little green fellows, come back!"

LIVING FOSSIL

W here the rivers flowed together, the country was flat and, in places, swampy. The combined waters spread out and crawled around reedy islands. Back from the banks, the ground rose into low tree-crowned humps.

The May flies were swarming that day, and as thousands of them danced, the low afternoon sun, whose setting would bring death to them all, glinted on their wings. There was little sound, other than the hum of a belated cicada and the splashing of an elephantlike beast in the southern tributary.

The beast suddenly raised its head, its great mulish ears swiveling forward and its upraised trunk turning this way and that like a periscope. It evidently disapproved of what it smelled, for it heaved its bulk out of its bath and ambled off up a creek bed, the feet on its columnar legs making loud sucking noises as they pulled out of the mud.

Two riders appeared from downstream, each leading an animal similar to the one he rode. The animals' feet swished through the laurel beds and went *squilch-squilch* as they struck patches of muck. As they crossed the creek bed, the leading rider pulled up his mount and pointed to the tracks made by the elephantine beast.

"Giant tapir!" he said in his own harsh, chattering language. "A big one. What a specimen he'd make!"

"*Ngoy?*" drawled his companion, meaning approximately "Oh, yeah?" He continued: "And how would we get it back to South

America? Carry it slung from a pole?"

The first rider made the grating noise in his throat that was his race's equivalent of laughter. "I didn't suggest shooting it. I just said it would make a good specimen. We'll have to get one some day. The museum hasn't a decent mounted example of the species."

The riders were anthropoid, but not human. Their large prehensile tails, rolled up behind them on the saddle, and the thick coats of brown and black hair that covered them, precluded that. Their thumblike halluces or big toes jutted out from the mid-portion of their feet and were hooked into the stirrups, which were about the size and shape of napkin rings. Below the large liquid eyes in their prognathous faces there were no external noses, just a pair of narrow nostrils set wide apart. The riders weighed about one hundred and fifty pounds each. A zoölogist of today would have placed them in the family *Cebidæ*, the capuchin monkeys, and been right. They would have had more difficulty in classifying the zoölogist, because in their time the science of paleontology was young, and the family tree of the primates had not been worked out fully.

Their mounts were the size of mules; tailless, round-eared, and with catlike whiskers sprouting from their deep muzzles. They absurdly resembled colossal guinea pigs, which they were; or rather, they were colossal agoutis, the ordinary agouti being a rabbit-sized member of the cavy family.

The leading rider whistled. His mount and the lead pack agouti bucked up the creek bank and headed at their tireless trot toward one of the mounds. The rider dismounted and began poking around between the curiously regular granite blocks scattered among the green-and-brown-spotted trunks of the sycamores. Grasshoppers exploded from under his feet as he walked.

He called, "Chujee!"

The other rider trotted up and got off. The four agoutis went to work with their great chisel teeth on the low-drooping branches.

"Look," the first rider said, turning over one of the blocks. "Those faces are too nearly parallel to have been made that way by accident. And here's one with two plane surfaces at a perfect right angle. I think we've found it."

"*Ngoy?*" drawled the other. "You mean the site of a large city of Men? Maybe." Skepticism was patent in his tone as he strolled about, poking at the stones with his foot. Then his voice rose. "Naw-putta! You think *you've* found something; look at this!" He uprighted a large stone. Its flat face was nearly smooth, but when it was turned so that the sun's rays were almost parallel with the face, a set of curiously regular shadows sprang out on the surface.

Nawputta—he had a given name as well, but it was both un-pronounceable and unnecessary to reproduce here—scowled at it, trying in his mind to straighten the faint indentations into a series of inscribed characters. He fished a camera out of his harness and snapped several pictures, while Chujee braced the stone. The mark-ings were as follows:

NATIO

ANK OF

TTSBURGH

"It's an inscription, all right," Nawputta remarked, as he put his camera away. "Most of it's weathered away, which isn't surprising, considering that the stone's been here for five or ten million years, or however long Man has been extinct. The redness of this sand bears out the theory. It's probably full of iron oxide. Men must have used an incredible amount of steel in their buildings."

Chujee asked: "Have you any idea what the inscription says?" In his voice there was the trace of awe which the capuchins felt toward these predecessors who had risen so high and vanished so utterly.

"No. Some of our specialists will have to try to decipher it from my photographs. That'll be possible only if it's in one of the lan-guages of Man that have been worked out. He had dozens of different languages that we know of, and probably hundreds that we don't. The commonest was En-gel-iss-ha, which we can translate fairly well. It's too bad there aren't some live Men running around. They could answer a lot of questions that puzzle us."

"Maybe," said Chujee. "And maybe it's just as well there aren't. They might have killed *us* off if they'd thought we were going to become civilized enough to compete with them."

"Perhaps you're right. I never thought of that. I wish we could take the stone back with us."

Chujee grunted. "When you hired me to guide you, you told me the museum just wanted you to make a short reconnaissance. And every day you see something weighing a ton or so that you want to collect. Yesterday it was that bear we saw on the cliff; it weighed a ton and a half at least."

"But," expostulated Nawputta, "that was a new subspecies!"

"Sure," growled the guide. "That makes it different. New subspecies aren't really heavy; they only look that way. You scientific guys! We should have brought along a derrick, a steam tractor, and a gang of laborers from the Colony." His grin took the sting out of his words. "Well, old-timer, I see you'll be puttering around after relics all day; I might as well set up camp." He collected the agoutis and went off to find a dry spot near the river.

Presently he was back. "I found a place," he said. "But we aren't the first ones. There's the remains of a recent fire."

Nawputta, the zoölogist, looked disappointed. "Then we aren't the first to penetrate this far into the Eastern Forest. Who do you suppose it was?"

"Dunno. Maybe a timber scout from the Colony. They're trying to build up a lumber export business, you know. They don't like being too dependent on their salt and sulphur—Yeow!" Chujee jumped three feet straight up. "Snake!"

Nawputta jumped, too; then laughed at their timidity. He bent over and snatched up the little reptile as it slithered among the stones. "It's perfectly harmless," he said. "Most of them are, this far north."

"I don't care if it is," barked Chujee, backing up rapidly. "You keep that damn thing away from me!"

Next day they pushed up the south tributary. The character of the vegetation slowly changed as they climbed. A few miles up, they came to another fork. They had to swim the main stream in order to follow the smaller one, as Nawputta wished to cast toward the line of hills becoming visible in the east, before turning back. As they swam their agoutis across the main street, a black-bellied cloud that had crept up behind them suddenly opened with a crash of thunder, and pelting rain whipped the surface to froth.

As they climbed out on the far bank, Nawputta began absent-mindedly unrolling his cape. He almost had it on when a whoop from Chujee reminded him that he was thoroughly soaked already. The rain had slackened to a drizzle and presently ceased.

The scientist sniffed. "Wood smoke," he said.

Chujee grunted. "Either that's our mysterious friend, or we're just in time to stop a forest fire, if the rain hasn't done that for us." He kicked his mount forward. In the patch of pine they were traversing, the agoutis' feet made no sound on the carpet of needles. Thus they came upon the fire and the capuchin who was roasting a slab of venison over it before the latter saw them.

At the snap of a twig, the stranger whirled and snatched up a heavy rifle.

"Well?" he said in a flat voice. "Who be you?" In his cape, which he was still wearing after the rain, he looked like a caricature of Little Red Ridinghood.

The explorers automatically reached for the rifles in their saddle boots, but thought better of it in the face of that unwavering muzzle. Nawputta identified himself and the guide.

The stranger relaxed. "Oh! Just another one of those damn bug hunters. Sorry I scared you. Make yourselves at home. I'm Nguchoy tsu Chaw, timber scout for the Colony. We—I—came up in that canoe yonder. Made it ourselves out of birch bark. Great stuff, birch bark."

"We?" echoed Nawputta.

The scout's shoulders drooped sadly. "Just finished burying my partner. Rattlesnake got him. Name was Jawga; Jawga tsu Shrr. Best partner a scout ever had. Say, could you let me have some flea powder? I'm all out."

As he rubbed the powder into his fur, he continued: "We'd just found the biggest stand of pine you ever saw. This river cuts through a notch in the ridge about thirty miles up. Beyond that it's gorges and rapids for miles, and beyond that it cuts through another ridge and breaks up into little creeks. We had to tie the boat up and hike. Great country; deer, bear, giant rabbit, duck, and all kinds of game. Not so thick as they say it is on the western plains, but you can shoot your meat easy." He went on to say that he was making a cast up the main stream before returning to the Colony with his news.

After Nguchoy had departed early the following morning, Chujee, the guide, scratched his head. "Guess I must have picked up some fleas from our friend. Wonder why he held a gun on us until he found who we were? That's no way to treat a stranger."

Nawputta wiggled his thumbs, the capuchin equivalent of a shrug. "He was afraid at being alone, I imagine."

Chujee still frowned. "I can understand his grabbing it before he knew what was behind him; we might have been a lion. But he kept pointing it after he saw we were *Jmu*"—the capuchin word for "human"—"like himself. There aren't any criminals around here for him to be scared of. Oh, well, I guess I'm just naturally mistrustful of these damned Colonials. Do you want to look at this 'great country'?"

"Yes," said Nawputta. "If we go on another week, we can still get out before the cold weather begins." (Despite their fur, the capuchins were sensitive to cold, for which reason exploration had lagged behind the other elements of their civilization.) "Nguchoy's description agrees with what Chmrrgoy saw from his balloon, though, as you recall, he never got up this far on foot. He landed by the river forty miles down and floated down the Big Muddy to the Colony on a raft."

"Say," said Chujee. "Do you suppose they'll ever get a flying machine that'll go where you want it to, instead of being blown around like these balloons? You know all about these scientific things."

"Not unless they can get a much lighter engine. By the time you've loaded your boiler, your engine proper, and your fuel and feed water aboard, your flying machine has as much chance of taking off as a granite boulder. There's a theory that Men had flying machines, but the evidence isn't conclusive. They may have had engines powered by mineral oils, which they pumped out of beds of oil-bearing sand. Our geologists have traced some of their borings. They used up nearly all the oils, so *we* have to be satisfied with coal."

It was a great country, the explorers agreed when they reached it. The way there had not been easy. Miles before they reached the notch, they had had to cut their way through a forest of alders that stretched along the sides of the river. Chujee had gone ahead on foot, swinging an ax in time to his strides with the effortless skill of an old woodsman. With each swing the steel bit clear through the soft white wood of a slim trunk. Behind him, Nawputta had stumbled, the leading agouti's reins gripped in his tail.

When they had passed through the notch, they climbed up the south side of the gorge in which they found themselves and in the distance saw another vast blue rampart, like the one they had just cut through stretching away to the northeast. (This had once been called the Allegheny Mountains.) Age-old white pines raised their somber blue-green spires above them. A huge buffalo-shaped cervid, who was rubbing the velvet from his antlers against a tree trunk, smelled them, snorted, and lumbered off.

"What's that noise?" asked Nawputta.

They listened, and heard a faint rhythmical thumping that seemed to come out of the ground.

"Dunno," said Chujee. "Tree trunks knocking together, maybe? But there isn't enough wind."

"Perhaps it's stones in a pothole in the river," said Nawputta without conviction.

They kept on to where the gorge widened out. Nawputta suddenly pulled his agouti off the game trail and jumped down. Chujee rode over and found the scientist examining a pile of bones.

Ten minutes later he was still turning the bones over.

"Well," said Chujee impatiently, "aren't you going to let me in on the secret?"

"Sorry. I didn't believe my own senses at first. These are the bones of Men! Not fossils; *fresh* bones! From the looks of them they're the remains of a meal. There were three of them. From the holes in the skulls I'd say that our friend Nguchoy or his partner shot them. I'm going to get a whole specimen, if it's the last thing I do."

Chujee sighed. "For a fellow who claims he hates to kill things, you're the bloodthirstiest cuss I ever saw when you hear about a new species."

"You don't understand, Chujee," objected Nawputta. "I'm what's called a fanatical conservationist. Hunting for fun not only doesn't amuse me; it makes me angry when I hear about it. But securing a scientific specimen is different."

"Oh," said Chujee.

They peered out of the spruce thicket at the Man. He was a strange object to them, almost hairless, so that the scars on his yellow-brown skin showed. He carried a wooden club, and padded noiselessly over the pine needles, pausing to sniff the air. The sun glinted on the wiry bronze hair that sprouted from his chin.

Nawputta squeezed his trigger; the rifle went off with a deafening *ka-pow!* A fainter *ka-pow!* bounced back from the far wall of the gorge as the Man's body struck the ground.

"Beautiful!" cried Chujee. "Right through the heart! Couldn't have done better myself. But I'd feel funny about shooting one; they look so *Jmu.*"

Nawputta, getting out his camera, tape measure, notebook, and skinning knife, said: "In the cause of science I don't mind. Besides, I couldn't trust you not to try for a brain shot and ruin the skull."

Hours later he was still dissecting his prize and making sketches. Chujee had long since finished the job of salting the hide, and was lolling about trying to pick up a single pine needle with his tail.

"Yeah," he said, "I know it's a crime that we haven't got a tank of formaldehyde so we could pack the whole carcass back, instead of just the skin and skeleton. But we haven't got it, and never did have it, so why bellyache?"

Much as he respected Nawputta, the zoölogist got on his nerves at times. Not that he didn't appreciate the scientific point of view; he was well-read and had some standing as an amateur naturalist. But, having managed expeditions for years, he had long been resigned to the fact that you can carry only so much equipment at a time.

He sat up suddenly with a warning "S-s-st!" Fifty feet away a human face peered out of a patch of brake ferns. He reached stealthily for his rifle; the face vanished. The hair on Chujee's neck and scalp rose. He had never seen such a concentration of malevolent hatred in one countenance. The ferns moved, and there was a brief flash of yellow-brown skin among the trees.

"Better hurry," he said. "The things may be dangerous when one of 'em's been killed."

Nawputta murmured vaguely that he'd have the skeleton cleaned in a few minutes. He was normally no more insensitive to danger than the guide, but in the presence of this scientific wonder, a complete Man, the rest of the world had withdrawn itself into a small section of his mind.

Chujee, still peering into the forest, growled: "It's funny that Nguchoy didn't say anything to us about the Men. That is, unless he *wanted* us to be eaten by the things. And why should he want that? Say, isn't that pounding louder? I'll bet it's a Man pounding a hollow log for a signal. If Nguchoy wanted to get rid of us, he picked an ingenious method. He and his partner kill some of the Men, and we come along just when they've got nicely stirred up and are out for *Jmu* blood. Let's get out of here!"

Nawputta was finished at last. They packed the skin and skeleton of the Man, mounted, and rode back the way they had come, glancing nervously into the shadows around them. The pounding was louder.

They had gone a couple of miles and were beginning to relax, when something soared over their heads and buried itself quivering in the ground. It was a crude wooden spear. Chujee fired his rifle into the underbrush in the direction from which the spear had come. A faint rustle mocked him. The pounding continued.

The notch loomed high before them, though still several miles away. The timber was smaller here, and there was more brush. They had originally come along the river, and followed game trails up the side of the gorge at this point. They hesitated whether or not to go back the same way.

"I don't like to let them get above me," complained Nawputta.

"We'll have to," argued Chujee. "The sides of the notch are too craggy; we'd never get the agoutis over it."

They started down the slope, on which the trees thinned out. A chorus of yells brought them up sharply. The hairless things were pouring out of the deep woods and racing toward them.

"The agoutis won't make it with those loads," snapped Chujee, and he flung himself off his mount.

Nawputta did likewise, and his rifle crashed almost as soon as the guide's. The echoes of their rapid fire made a deafening uproar in the gorge. Nawputta, as he fired and worked the lever of his gun, wondered what he'd do when the magazine was empty.

Then the Men were bounding back into the shelter of the woods, shrieking with fear. They vanished. Two of their number lay still, and a third thrashed about in a raspberry bush and screeched.

"I can't see him suffer," said Nawputta. He drew a bead on the Man's head and fired. The Man quieted, but from the depths of the forest came screams of rage.

Chujee said dryly, "They didn't interpret that as an act of mercy," as he remounted.

The agoutis were trembling. Nawputta noticed that he was shaking a bit himself. He had counted his shots, and knew before he started to reload that he had had just one shot left.

The yelping cries of the Men followed them as they headed into the notch, but the things didn't show themselves long enough for a shot.

"That was too close for comfort," said Nawputta in a low voice, not taking his eyes from the woods. "Say, hasn't somebody invented a rifle whose recoil automatically reloads it, so that one can shoot it as fast as one pulls the trigger?"

Chujee grunted. "Yeah, he was up in the Colony demonstrating it last year. I tried it out. It jammed regularly every other shot. Maybe they'll be practical some day, but for the present I'll stick to the good old lever action. I suppose you were thinking of what would have happened to us if the Men had kept on coming. I—Say, look!" He halted his animal. "Look up yonder!"

Nawputta looked, and said: "Those boulders weren't piled up on top of the cliff when we came this way, were they?"

"That's right. When we get into the narrowest part of the notch, they'll roll them down on us. They'll be protected from our guns by the bulge of the cliff. There's no pathway on the other side of the river. We can't swim the animals because of the rapids, and even if we could, the river's so narrow that the rocks would bounce and hit us anyway."

Nawputta pondered. "We'll have to get through that bottle neck somehow; it'll be dark in a couple of hours."

Both were silent for a while.

Chujee said: "There's something wrong about this whole business; Nguchoy and his partner, I mean. If we ever get out of this—"

Nawputta interrupted him: "Look! I could swim one agouti over here, and climb a tree on the other side. I could get a good view of the top of the cliffs. There's quite an open space there, and I could try to keep the Men away from the boulders with my gun, while you took the agoutis down through the notch. Then, if you can find a corresponding tree below the bottle neck, you could repeat the process while I followed you down."

"Right! I'll fire three shots when I'm ready for you."

Nawputta tethered his animal and hoisted himself up the big pine, his rifle held firmly in his tail. He found a place where he could rest the gun on a branch to sight, and waved to the guide, who set off at a trot down the narrow shelf along the churning waters.

Sure enough, the Men presently appeared on top of the cliff. They looked smaller over the sights of Nawputta's rifle than he had expected; too small to make practical targets as individuals even. He aimed into the thick of these dancing pink midges and fired twice. The crash of the rifle was flung back sharply from the south wall of the gorge. He couldn't see whether he had hit anything, but the spidery things disappeared.

Then he waited. The sun had long since disappeared behind the ridge, but a few slanting rays poked through the notch; insects were briefly visible as motes of light as they flew through these rays. Overhead a string of geese flapped southward.

When Nawputta heard three shots, he descended, swam his agouti back across the river, and headed downstream. The dark walls of the gorge towered almost vertically over him. Above the roar of the rapids he heard a shot, then another. The agouti flinched at the reports, but kept on. The shots continued. The Men were evidently determined not to be balked of their prey this time. Nawputta counted—seven—eight. The firing ceased, and the zoölogist knew that his companion was reloading.

There was a rattle of loose rock. A boulder appeared over his head, swelled like a balloon, swished past him, and went *plunk* in the river beside him, throwing spray over him and his mount. He kicked the animal frantically and it bounded forward, nearly pitching its rider into the river at a turn.

Nawputta wondered desperately why Chujee hadn't begun shooting again. He looked up, and saw that the air over his head seemed to be full of boulders hanging suspended. They grew as he watched, and every one seemed headed straight for him. He bent low and urged the animal; he saw black water under him as the agouti cleared a recess in the trail with a bucking jump. He thought: "Why doesn't he shoot? But it's too late now."

The avalanche of rock struck the trail and the river behind him with a roar; one rock passed him so closely that he felt its wind. The agouti in its terror almost skidded off the trail. Then they were out in the sunlight again, and the animal's zigzag leaps settled into a smooth gallop.

Nawputta pulled up opposite Chujee's tree.

The guide was already climbing down with his rifle in his tail. He called: "Did you get hit? I thought you were a goner sure when the rock fall commenced. Got a twig caught in my breech while I was reloading."

Nawputta tried to call back reassurance, but found he couldn't make a sound.

When Chujee pulled his dripping mount up the bank, he got out his binoculars and looked at the south shoulder of the notch. He said: "Come on! They've already climbed down toward us; they haven't given up yet. But I think we can lose them if we can find that trail we cut through the alders. They don't know about it yet, and they'll probably scatter trying to find which way we've gone."

Nawputta yawned, stretched, and sat up. Chujee was sitting by the fire at Nguchoy's camp, his rifle, in his lap. Both still looked a trifle haggard after their sleepless flight down the river. They had strung the four agoutis in a column, and taken turns riding backward on the last one of the string to keep watch against another attack. But though the pounding had continued, the Men had not shown themselves again. When they arrived at Nguchoy's camp, the timber scout was not to be seen, evidently not having returned.

Chujee said: "I've been thinking, while you were catching up on sleep, about this Nguchoy and his yarns. I don't reckon he intended us to return, though we couldn't prove anything against him.

"And I wonder how it happened that his partner died at such a convenient time . . . for him. He needed this Jawga person to help him paddle up the rivers. But once they got to the head of navigation, Nguchoy could get back downstream easy enough without help. And when they'd found that great pine forest, it would be mighty convenient if an accident happened to Jawga. When Nguchoy went back to the Colony, he wouldn't have to share the credit for the find, and the bonus, with anybody."

Nawputta raised his eyebrows, and without a word began hunting in their duffel for a spade.

In half an hour they had dug up all that was mortal of Jawga tsu Shrr. Nawputta examined the remains, which were in a most unpleasant state of decay.

"See!" he said. "Two holes in the skull, which weren't made by any rattlesnake. The one on the left side is just about right for a No. 14 rifle bullet going in."

They were silent. Over the swish of the wind in the trees came a faint rhythmical pounding.

"Do we want to pinch him?" asked Chujee. "It's a long way back to the Colony."

Nawputta thought. "I have a better idea. We'll rebury the corpse for the present."

"Nothing illegal," said Chujee firmly.

"N-no, not exactly. It's this way. Have you ever seen a Colony lumberjack gang in action?"

Nawputta shoved the corpse into the grave. The pounding was louder. Both capuchins looked to see that their rifles were within easy reach.

A tuneless whistling came through the trees.

"Quick!" whispered Nawputta. "Sprinkle some leaves on the grave. When he arrives, you get his attention. Talk about anything."

The whistling stopped, and presently the timber scout appeared. If he was surprised to see the explorers, he did not show it.

"Hello," he said. "Have a good trip?"

He paused and sniffed the air. The explorers realized that there had been one thing they couldn't put back in the grave. Nguchoy looked at the grave, but made no remark.

"Sure, we did," said Chujee in his best good-fellow manner, and went on to talk about the splendor of the gorge and the magnificence of the pines.

The pounding was becoming louder, but nobody seemed to notice.

"Nguchoy," said Nawputta suddenly, "did you and Jawga see any traces of live Men in the forest?"

The timber scout snorted. "Don't be a sap. Men have been— what's that word?—extinct for millions of years. How could we see them?"

"Well," the scientist went on, "we did." He paused. The only sound was the pounding. Or were there faint yelping cries? "Moreover, we've just had a look at the remains of your late-lamented partner."

There was silence again, except for the ominous sounds of the approach of Men.

"Are you going to talk to us?" asked Nawputta.

Nguchoy grinned. "Sure, I'll talk to you." He sprang back to the tree against which he had left his rifle standing. "With this!" He snatched up the weapon and pulled the trigger.

The rifle gave out a metallic click.

Nawputta opened his fist, showing a handful of cartridges. Then he calmly picked up his own rifle and covered the timber scout.

"Chujee," he said, "you take his knife and hatchet and the rest of his ammunition."

The guide, dumbfounded by the decisive way of his usually impractical companion, obeyed.

"Now," said Nawputta, "tie the four agoutis together, and hitch the leading one to the end of Nguchoy's canoe. We're pulling out."

"But what?" asked Chujee uncertainly.

Nawputta snapped: "I'll explain later. Hurry."

As the explorers piled into the boat, the timber scout woke to life.

"Hey!" he shouted. "Aren't you taking me along? The Men'll be here any minute, and they'll eat me! They even eat their own kind when one's been killed!"

"No," said Nawputta, "we aren't taking you."

The canoe pulled out into the river, the agoutis following unwillingly till only their heads and loads showed above water.

"Hey!" screamed Nguchoy. "Come back! I'll confess!"

The canoe kept on, the agoutis swimming in its wake.

As the site of the camp receded, there was a sudden commotion among the trees. The now-familiar yells of the Men were mingled with despairing shrieks from the timber scout. The shrieks ceased, and the voices of the Men were raised in a rhythmical but tuneless chant, which the explorers could hear long after the camp was hidden from view.

Chujee, paddling low, stared straight before him for a while in silence. Finally he turned around in his seat and said deliberately: "That's the lowest damned trick I ever saw in my life. To leave him there defenseless like that to be eaten by those hairless things. I don't care if he *was* a liar and a murderer."

Nawputta's expression of smugness vanished, and he looked slightly crestfallen. "You don't approve, do you? I was afraid you wouldn't. But I had to do it that way."

"Well, why?"

Nawputta took a long breath and rested his paddle. "I started to explain before, but I didn't have time. Nguchoy had killed his partner, and was going to return to the Colony with the news of the forest. He tried to have us killed by the Men, and when that didn't work, he'd have killed us himself if I hadn't emptied his gun behind his back.

"When he got back to the Colony, a timber gang would have been sent out. They'd have wiped out that forest in a few years, and you'll admit that it's probably the finest in the whole Eastern Mountain area. Moreover, they'd have killed off the wild life, including the Men, partly for food, partly for self-protection, and partly because they like to shoot.

"We thought Man had been extinct for millions of years, after having spread all over the world and reached a state of civilization as high as or higher than ours. The Men that we saw may well be the last of their species. You're a practical fellow, and I don't know whether I can make you understand a biologist's feeling toward a living fossil like that. To us it's simply priceless, and there's nothing we won't do to preserve it.

"If we can get back to South America before the news of the pine stand reaches the Colony, I can pull the necessary wires to have the area set aside as a park or preserve. The Colony can just as well go elsewhere for its lumber. But if the Colony hears about it first, I shan't have a chance.

"If we'd taken Nguchoy back with us, even if we'd brought him to justice, he'd still have been able to give the news away, especially since he could probably have purchased leniency by it. And that would be the end of my park idea.

"If we'd taken the law into our own hands, even if I'd been able to overcome your objections to doing so, we'd have been in a fix when, as will inevitably happen, the Colony sends an officer up to investigate the disappearance of their scout. If we said he died of a snake bite, for instance, and the officer found a body with a bullet hole through the head, or alternatively if he'd found no body at all, he'd have been suspicious. As it is, we can truthfully say, when they ask us, that Nguchoy was alive and sound of wind and limb the last time we saw him. The officer will then find the remains, having obviously been eaten by the Men. Of course, we needn't volunteer any information until the park proposal is in the bag.

"The reason I took his canoe is that I remembered that Men probably can't swim. At least, the chimpanzee, which is the nearest living relative of Man, can't, whereas we can swim instinctively as soon as we're able to walk.

"But there's a bigger issue than Nguchoy and the Men. You probably think I'm a bit cracked, with my concern for conservation.

"We know that Man, during the period of his civilization, was prodigally wasteful of his resources. The exhaustion of the mineral oils is an example. And the world-wide extinction of the larger mammals at the close of the last ice age was probably his doing, at least in part. We're sure that he was responsible for wiping out all the larger species of whales, and we suspect that he also killed off all but two of the twenty or more species of elephant that abounded at that time. Most of the large mammals of today have evolved in the last few million years from forms that were small enough to sit in your hand in Man's time.

"We don't know just why he became extinct, or almost extinct. Perhaps a combination of war and disease did it. Perhaps the exhaustion of his resources had a share. You know what a hardboiled materialist I am in most things; but it always has seemed to me that it was a case of outraged nature taking its revenge. That's not rational, but it's the way I feel. And I've dedicated my life to seeing that we don't make the same mistake.

"Now do you see why I had to do what I did?"

Chujee was silent for a moment, then said: "Perhaps I do. I won't say I approve . . . yet. But I'll think it over for a few days. Say, we'll have to land soon; the agoutis are getting all tired out from swimming."

The canoe slid on down the river in the Indian-summer sunshine. The white men who had applied the name "Indian summer" to that part of the year were gone, as were the Indians after whom it had been named. Of mighty Man, the only remnant was a little savage tribe in the Alleghenies. A representative of a much more ancient order, a dragonfly, hovered over the bow, its four glassy wings glittering in the sunlight. Then with a faint whir it wheeled and fled.

Recommended Reading by L. Sprague de Camp

Lest Darkness Fall
The Incomplete Enchanter (with Fletcher Pratt)
Divide and Rule
Rogue Queen
The Stone of Nomuru (with Catherine Crook de Camp)

FRITZ LEIBER

1910–1992

Fritz Leiber's early stories were all signed "Fritz Leiber, Jr." in order to avoid confusion with his father, who was not only still around but actually pretty famous. The elder Fritz Leiber was an actor, Shakespearean by preference, but perhaps best known for the movies in which he played an endless series of roles as the evil cardinal or the sinister plotter. Fritz inherited his father's acting talent (though he gave up his own stage career early on, later putting in some time as a coach for other actors). He also inherited his father's commanding physical presence—tall, dark, formidably good-looking—and his father's mellifluous organ voice. One of my most cherished memories of Fritz was a weekend at the late Fletcher Pratt's huge old summer house in Highlands, New Jersey, with Fritz lying on the floor of the cardroom, a beautiful blonde snuggled up one each side and a drink in his hand, holding a roomful of pretty unimpressable writers and artists spellbound with his majestic recitation of "Dover Beach."

Early in his life Fritz considered becoming a minister; I remember his pointing out the seminary he had attended, in New York's Chelsea neighborhood, one day as we drove by. For a time, later on, he was the editor of *Science Digest*, one of the better science-oriented periodicals for laymen. But what he was best at was writing, both science fiction and fantasy. His first sale was a short story, "Two Sought Adventure," to John Campbell's short-lived but unforgettable fantasy magazine, *Unknown*; this turned out to be Fritz's first cut at his long-lasting and award-winning series of the adventures of Fafhrd and the Gray Mouser. *Unknown* also published Leiber's first novel, *Conjure Wife*, a scarily plausible novel about witchcraft among the faculty wives at a school not unlike the University of Chicago (which Fritz had attended briefly). Although *Conjure Wife* was Leiber's first book, it may also have been his most successful one. Print writers count themselves lucky when Hollywood picks up a story to make into a film. *Conjure Wife* was made into two of the things—*Weird Woman* (1944) and *Burn, Witch, Burn* (1961)—and was also adapted for television.

Leiber's best-known early work was fantasy, but when he turned to science fiction for his principal interest he showed equal mastery. Two of his SF novels, *The Big Time* and *The Wanderer*, won well-deserved best-of-the-year Hugo awards, and in the 1950s, mostly for the new magazine edited by Horace Gold, *Galaxy*, he produced a series of fine, perceptive, pointed short stories including "Coming Attraction," "The Nice Girl with Five Husbands," and "A Bad Day for Sales."

Among Leiber's finest traits as a writer was a willingness to take risks. He didn't find himself a single comfortable writing niche and stay tucked inside it for life. He pushed at the envelope, always breaking new ground. When his novel *The Big Time* was offered to editor Horace Gold for serialization in his magazine, *Galaxy*, Gold rejected it outright; he was afraid that the tricks Leiber played in the story, in characterization and in switched time frames, were too confusing for *Galaxy*'s readers to follow. (But then Gold could not get the novel out of his mind. Complex or not, it was just too good to pass up. He called the manuscript back and published it, and the readers responded by giving it the Hugo award.)

Leiber trusted his readers. He was confident that they could follow him wherever his always inquiring mind took him, whether in investigating the solipsist fallacy in stories such as *The Big Time* or in sharing his fondness for the ordinaries of life. (He loved cats, which produced the short story "Space-Time for Springers," and chess, leading to the novella *The Sixty-four Square Madhouse*.)

Perhaps it was this trait of constant exploration that made his work so rewarding. He began well, and kept on getting better, as long as he lived.

•   •   •

Fritz Leiber had a fine and productive career, for which he was re-
warded with more than two dozen of the science fiction and fantasy
fields' top literary awards. His success was not all easily attained,
though.

For most of his adult life Fritz waged an exhausting and destructive war against alcoholism, which sometimes put him in the hospital
for months at a time or longer, and seriously damaged his health.
One can only wonder what other great stories he would have found
to tell us if it had not been for those time-outs, and for those other
times when he was doing his best to stay sober, but all too often
failed.

SANITY

"Come in, Phy, and make yourself comfortable."

The mellow voice—and the suddenly dilating doorway—caught the general secretary of the World playing with a blob of greenish gasoid, squeezing it in his fist and watching it ooze between his fingers in spatulate tendrils that did not dissipate. Slowly, crookedly, he turned his head. World Manager Carrsbury became aware of a gaze that was at once oafish, sly, vacuous. Abruptly the expression was replaced by a nervous smile. The thin man straightened himself, as much as his habitually drooping shoulders would permit, hastily entered, and sat down on the extreme edge of a pneumatically form-fitting chair.

He embarrassedly fumbled the blob of gasoid, looking around for a convenient disposal vent or a crevice in the upholstery. Finding none, he stuffed it hurriedly into his pocket. Then he repressed his fidgetings by clasping his hands resolutely together, and sat with downcast eyes.

"How are you feeling, old man?" Carrsbury asked in a voice that was warm with a benign friendliness.

The general secretary did not look up.

"Anything bothering you, Phy?" Carrsbury continued solicitously. "Do you feel a bit unhappy, or dissatisfied, about your . . . er . . . transfer, now that the moment has arrived?"

Still the general secretary did not respond. Carrsbury leaned forward across the dully silver, semicircular desk and, in his most winning tones, urged, "Come on, old fellow, tell me all about it."

The general secretary did not lift his head, but he rolled up his strange, distant eyes until they were fixed directly on Carrsbury. He shivered a little, his body seemed to contract, and his bloodless hands tightened their interlocking grip.

"I know," he said in a low, effortful voice. "You think I'm insane."

Carrsbury sat back, forcing his brows to assume a baffled frown under the mane of silvery hair.

"Oh, you needn't pretend to be puzzled," Phy continued, swiftly now that he had broken the ice. "You know what that word means as well as I do. Better—even though we both had to do historical research to find out."

"Insane," he repeated dreamily, his gaze wavering. "Significant departure from the norm. Inability to conform to basic conventions underlying all human conduct."

"Nonsense!" said Carrsbury, rallying and putting on his warmest and most compelling smile. "I haven't the slightest idea of what you're talking about. That you're a little tired, a little strained, a little distraught—that's quite understandable, considering the burden you've been carrying, and a little rest will be just the thing to fix you up, a nice long vacation away from all this. But as for your being . . . why, ridiculous!"

"No," said Phy, his gaze pinning Carrsbury. "You think I'm insane. You think I'm insane. You think all my colleagues in the World Management Service are insane. That's why you're having us replaced with those men you've been training for ten years in your Institute of Political Leadership—ever since, with my help and connivance, you became World manager."

Carrsbury retreated before the finality of the statement. For the first time his smile became a bit uncertain. He started to say something, then hesitated and looked at Phy, as if half hoping he would go on.

But that individual was once again staring rigidly at the floor.

Carrsbury leaned back, thinking. When he spoke it was in a more natural voice, much less consciously soothing and fatherly.

"Well, all right, Phy. But look here, tell me something, honestly. Won't you—and the others—be a lot happier when you've been relieved of all your responsibilities?"

Phy nodded somberly. "Yes," he said, "we will . . . but"—his face became strained—"you see—"

"But—?" Carrsbury prompted.

Phy swallowed hard. He seemed unable to go on. He had gradually slumped toward one side of the chair, and the pressure had caused the green gasoid to ooze from his pocket. His long fingers crept over and kneaded it fretfully.

Carrsbury stood up and came around the desk. His sympathetic frown, from which perplexity had ebbed, was not quite genuine.

"I don't see why I shouldn't tell you all about it now, Phy," he said simply. "In a queer sort of way I owe it all to you. And there isn't any point now in keeping it a secret . . . there isn't any danger—"

"Yes," Phy agreed with a quick bitter smile, "you haven't been in any danger of a *coup d'état* for some years now. If ever we should have revolted, there'd have been"—his gaze shifted to a point in the opposite wall where a faint vertical crease indicated the presence of a doorway—"your secret police."

Carrsbury started. He hadn't thought Phy had known. Disturbingly, there loomed in his mind a phrase *The cunning of the insane.* But only for a moment. Friendly complacency flooded back. He went behind Phy's chair and rested his hands on the sloping shoulders.

"You know, I've always had a special feeling toward you, Phy," he said, "and not only because your whims made it a lot easier for me to become World manager. I've always felt that you were different from the others, that there were times when—" He hesitated.

Phy squirmed a little under the friendly hands. "When I had my moments of sanity?" he finished flatly.

"Like now," said Carrsbury softly, after a nod the other could not see. "I've always felt that sometimes, in a kind of twisted, unrealistic way, you *understood*. And that has meant a lot to me. I've been alone, Phy, dreadfully alone, for ten whole years. No companionship anywhere, not even among the men I've been training in the Institute of Political Leadership—for I've had to play a part with them too, keep them in ignorance of certain facts, for fear they would

try to seize power over my head before they were sufficiently prepared. No companionship anywhere, except for my hopes—and for
occasional moments with you. Now that it's over and a new regime
is beginning for us both, I can tell you that. And I'm glad."

There was a silence. Then—Phy did not look around, but one
lean hand crept up and touched Carrsbury's. Carrsbury cleared his
throat. Strange, he thought, that there could be even a momentary
rapport like this between the sane and the insane. But it was so.

He disengaged his hands, strode rapidly back to his desk, turned.

"I'm a throwback, Phy," he began in a new, unused, eager
voice. "A throwback to a time when human mentality was far
sounder. Whether my case was due chiefly to heredity, or to certain
unusual accidents of environment, or to both, is unimportant. The
point is that a person had been born who was in a position to criticize
the present state of mankind in the light of the past, to diagnose its
condition, and to begin its cure. For a long time I refused to face
the facts, but finally my researches—especially those in the literature
of the twentieth century—left me no alternative. The mentality of
mankind had become—aberrant. Only certain technological advances, which had resulted in making the business of living infinitely
easier and simpler, and the fact that war had been ended with the
creation of the present world state, were staving off the inevitable
breakdown of civilization. But only staving it off—delaying it. The
great masses of mankind had become what would once have been
called hopelessly neurotic. Their leaders had become . . . you said it
first, Phy . . . insane. Incidentally, this latter phenomenon—the drift
of psychological aberrants toward leadership—has been noted in all
ages."

He paused. Was he mistaken, or was Phy following his words
with indications of a greater mental clarity than he had ever noted
before, even in the relatively non-violent World secretary? Perhaps—
he had often dreamed wistfully of the possibility—there was still a
chance of saving Phy. Perhaps, if he just explained to him clearly
and calmly—

"In my historical studies," he continued, "I soon came to the
conclusion that the crucial period was that of the Final Amnesty,
concurrent with the founding of the present world state. We are
taught that at that time there were released from confinement mil-

lions of political prisoners—and millions of others. Just who were those others? To this question, our present histories gave only vague and platitudinous answers. The semantic difficulties I encountered were exceedingly obstinate. But I kept hammering away. Why, I asked myself, have such words as insanity, lunacy, madness, psychosis, disappeared from our vocabulary—and the concepts behind them from our thought? Why has the subject 'abnormal psychology' disappeared from the curricula of our schools? Of greater significance, why is our modern psychology strikingly similar to the field of abnormal psychology as taught in the twentieth century, and to that field alone? Why are there no longer, as there were in the twentieth century, any institutions for the confinement and care of the psychologically aberrant?"

Phy's head jerked up. He smiled twistedly. "Because," he whispered slyly, "everyone's insane now."

The cunning of the insane. Again that phrase loomed warningly in Carrsbury's mind. But only for a moment. He nodded.

"At first I refused to make that deduction. But gradually I reasoned out the why and wherefore of what had happened. It wasn't only that a highly technological civilization had subjected mankind to a wider and more swiftly-tempoed range of stimulations, conflicting suggestions, mental strains, emotional wrenchings. In the literature of the twentieth century psychiatry there are observations on a kind of psychosis that results from success. An unbalanced individual keeps going so long as he is fighting something, struggling toward a goal. He reaches his goal—and goes to pieces. His repressed confusions come to the surface, he realizes that he doesn't know what he wants at all, his energies hitherto engaged in combatting something outside himself are turned against himself, he is destroyed. Well, when war was finally outlawed, when the whole world became one unified state, when social inequality was abolished . . . you see what I'm driving at?"

Phy nodded slowly. "That," he said in a curious, distant voice, "is a very interesting deduction."

"Having reluctantly accepted my main premise," Carrsbury went on, "everything became clear. The cyclic six-months' fluctuations in world credit—I realized at once that Morganstern of Finance must be a manic-depressive with a six-months' phase, or else a duel personality with one aspect a spendthrift, the other a miser. It turned out to be the former. Why was the Department of Cultural Advancement stagnating? Because Manager Hobart was markedly catatonic. Why the boom in Extraterrestrial Research? Because McElvy was a euphoric."

Phy looked at him wonderingly. "But naturally," he said, spreading his lean hands, from one of which the gasoid dropped like a curl of green smoke.

Carrsbury glanced at him sharply. He replied. "Yes, I know that you and several of the others have a certain warped awareness of the differences between your . . . personalities, though none whatsoever of the basic aberration involved in them all. But to get on. As soon as I realized the situation, my course was marked out. As a sane man, capable of entertaining fixed realistic purposes, and surrounded by individuals of whose inconsistencies and delusions it was easy to make use, I was in a position to attain, with time and tact, any goal at which I might aim. I was already in the Managerial Service. In three years I became World manager. Once there, my range of influence was vastly enhanced. Like the man in Archimedes' epigram, I had a place to stand from which I could move the world. I was able, in various guises and on various pretexts, to promulgate regulations the actual purpose of which was to soothe the great neurotic masses by curtailing upsetting stimulations and introducing a more regimented and orderly program of living. I was able, by humoring my fellow executives and making the fullest use of my greater capacity for work, to keep world affairs staggering along fairly safely—at least stave off the worst. At the same time I was able to begin my Ten Years' Plan—the training, in comparative isolation, first in small numbers, then in larger, as those instructed could in turn become instructors, of a group of prospective leaders carefully selected on the basis of their relative freedom from neurotic tendencies."

"But that—" Phy began rather excitedly, starting up.

"But what?" Carrsbury inquired quickly.

"Nothing," muttered Phy dejectedly, sinking back.

"That about covers it," Carrsbury concluded, his voice suddenly grown a little duller. "Except for one secondary matter. I couldn't afford to let myself go ahead without any protection. Too much depended on me. There was always the risk of being wiped out by some ill-co-ordinated but none the less effective spasm of violence, momentarily uncontrollable by tack, on the part of my fellow executives. So, only because I could see no alternative, I took a dangerous step. I created"—his glance strayed toward the faint crease in the side wall—"my secret police. There is a type of insanity known as paranoia, an exaggerated suspiciousness involving delusions of persecution. By means of the late twentieth century Rand technique of hypnotism, I inculated a number of these unfortunate individuals with the fixed idea that their lives depended on me and that I was threatened from all sides and must be protected at all costs. A distasteful expedient, even though it served its purpose. I shall be glad, very glad to see it discontinued. You can understand, can't you, why I had to take that step?"

He looked questioningly at Phy—and became aware with a shock that that individual was grinning at him vacuously and holding up the gasoid between two fingers.

"I cut a hole in my couch and lot of this stuff came out," Phy explained in a thick naive voice. "Ropes of it got all over my office. I kept tripping." His fingers patted at it deftly, sculpturing it into the form of a hideous transparent green head, which he proceeded to squeeze out of existence. "Queer stuff," he rambled on. "Rarefied liquid. Gas of fixed volume. And all over my office floor, tangled up with the furniture."

Carrsbury leaned back and shut his eyes. His shoulders slumped. He felt suddenly a little weary, a little eager for his day of triumph to be done. He knew he shouldn't be despondent because he had failed with Phy. After all, the main victory was won. Phy was the merest of side issues. He had always known that, except for flashes, Phy was hopeless as the rest. Still—

"You don't need to worry about your office floor, Phy," he said with a listless kindliness. "Never any more. Your successor will have to see about cleaning it up. Already, you know, to all intents and purposes, you have been replaced."

"That's just it!" Carrsbury started at Phy's explosive loudness.

The World secretary jumped up and strode toward him, pointing an excited hand. "That's what I came to see you about! That's what I've been trying to tell you! I can't be replaced like that! None of the others can, either! It won't work! You can't do it!"

With a swiftness born of long practice, Carrsbury slipped behind his desk. He forced his features into that expression of calm, smiling benevolence of which he had grown unutterably weary.

"Now, now, Phy," he said brightly, soothingly, "if I can't do it, of course I can't do it. But don't you think you ought to tell me why? Don't you think it would be very nice to sit down and talk it all over and you tell me why?"

Phy halted and hung his head, abashed.

"Yes, I guess it would," he said slowly, abruptly falling back into the low, effortful tones. "I guess I'll have to. I guess there just isn't any other way. I had hoped, though, not to have to tell you everything." The last sentence was half question. He looked up wheedlingly at Carrsbury. The latter shook his head, continuing to smile. Phy went back and sat down.

"Well," he finally began, gloomily kneading the gasoid, "it all began when you first wanted to be World manager. You weren't the usual type, but I thought it would be kind of fun—yes, and kind of helpful." He looked up at Carrsbury. "You've really done the world a lot of good in quite a lot of ways, always remember that," he assured him. "Of course," he added, again focusing the tortured gasoid, "they weren't exactly the ways you thought."

"No?" Carrsbury prompted automatically. *Humor him. Humor him.* The wornout refrain droned in his mind.

Phy sadly shook his head. "Take those regulations you promulgated to soothe people—"

"Yes?"

"—they kind of got changed on the way. For instance, your prohibition, regarding reading tapes, of all exciting literature . . . oh, we tried a little of the soothing stuff you suggested at first. Everyone got a great kick out of it. They laughed and laughed. But afterwards, well, as I said, it kind of got changed—in this case to a prohibition of all *unexciting* literature."

Carrsbury's smile broadened. For a moment the edge of his mind had toyed with a fear, but Phy's last remark had banished it.

"Every day I coast past several reading stands," Carrsbury said gently. "The fiction tapes offered for sale are always in the most chastely and simply colored containers. None of those wild and lurid pictures that one used to see everywhere."

"But did you ever buy one and listen to it? Or project the visual text?" Phy questioned apologetically.

"For ten years I've been a very busy man," Carrsbury answered. "Of course I've read the official reports regarding such matters, and at times glanced through sample resumes of taped fiction."

"Oh, sure, that sort of official stuff," agreed Phy, glancing up at the wall of tape files beyond the desk. "What we did, you see, was to keep the monochrome containers but go back to the old kind of contents. The contrast kind of tickled people. Remember, as I said before, a lot of your regulations have done good. Cut out a lot of unnecessary noise and inefficient foolishness, for one thing."

That sort of official stuff. The phrase lingered unpleasantly in Carrsbury's ears. There was a trace of irrepressible suspicion in his quick over-the-shoulder glance at the tiered tape files.

"Oh, yes," Phy went on, "and that prohibition against yielding to unusual or indecent impulses, with a long listing of specific categories. It went into effect all right, but with a little rider attached: 'unless you really want to.' That seemed absolutely necessary, you know." His fingers worked furiously with the gasoid. "As for the prohibition of various stimulating beverages—well, in this locality they're still served under other names, and an interesting custom has grown up of behaving very soberly while imbibing them. Now when we come to that matter of the eight-hour working day—"

Almost involuntarily, Carrsbury had got up and walked over to the outer wall. With a flip of his hand through an invisible U-shaped beam, he switched on the window. It was as if the outer wall had disappeared. Through its near-perfect transparency, he peered down with fierce curiosity past the sleekly gleaming facades to the terraces and parkways below.

The modest throngs seemed quiet and orderly enough. But then there was a scurry of confusion—a band of people, at this angle all tiny heads with arms and legs, came out from a shop far below and began to pelt another group with what looked like foodstuffs. While, on a side parkway, two small ovoid vehicles, seamless drops of silver because their vision panels were invisible from the outside, butted each other playfully. Someone started to run.

Carrsbury hurriedly switched off the window and turned around. Those were just off-chance occurrences, he told himself angrily. Of no real statistical significance whatever. For ten years mankind had steadily been trending toward sanity despite occasional relapses. He'd seen it with his own eyes, seen the day-to-day progress—at least enough to know. He'd been a fool to let Phy's ramblings effect him— only tired nerves had made that possible.

He glanced at his timepiece.

"Excuse me," he said curtly, striding past Phy's chair, "I'd like to continue this conversation, but I have to get along to the first meeting of the new Central Managerial Staff."

"Oh but you can't!" Instantly Phy was up and dragging at his arm. "You just can't do it, you know! It's impossible!"

The pleading voice rose toward a scream. Impatiently Carrsbury tried to shake loose. The seam in the side wall widened, became a doorway. Instantly both of them stopped struggling.

In the doorway stood a cadaverous giant of a man with a stubby dark weapon in his hand. Straggly black beard shaded into gaunt cheeks. His face was a cruel blend of suspicion and fanatical devotion, the first directed along with the weapon at Phy, the second— and the somnambulistic eyes—at Carrsbury.

"He was threatening you?" the bearded man asked in a harsh voice, moving the weapon suggestively.

For a moment an angry, vindictive light glinted in Carrsbury's eyes. Then it flicked out. What could he have been thinking, he asked himself. This poor lunatic World secretary was no one to hate.

"Not at all, Hartman," he remarked calmly. "We were discussing something and we became excited and allowed our voices to rise. Everything is quite all right."

"Very well," said the bearded man doubtfully, after a pause. Reluctantly he returned his weapon to its holster, but he kept his hand on it and remained standing in the doorway.

"And now," said Carrsbury, disengaging himself, "I must go."

He had stepped on to the corridor slidewalk and had coasted

halfway to the elevator before he realized that Phy had followed him and was plucking timidly at his sleeve.

"You can't go off like this," Phy pleaded urgently, with an apprehensive backward glance. Carrsbury noted that Hartman had also followed—an ominous pylon two paces to the rear. "You must give me a chance to explain, to tell you why, just like you asked me."

Humor him. Carrsbury's mind was deadly tired of the drone, but mere weariness prompted him to dance to it a little longer. "You can talk to me in the elevator," he conceded, stepping off the slidewalk. His finger flipped through a U-beam and a serpentine movement of light across the wall traced the elevator's obedient rise.

"You see, it wasn't just that matter of prohibitory regulations," Phy launched out hurriedly. "There were lots of other things that never did work out like your official reports indicated. Departmental budgets for instance. The reports showed, I know, that appropriations for Extraterrestrial Research were being regularly slashed. Actually, in your ten years of office, they increased tenfold. Of course, there was no way for you to know that. You couldn't be all over the world at once and see each separate launching of supra-stratospheric rockets."

The moving light became stationary. A seam dilated. Carrsbury stepped into the elevator. He debated sending Hartman back. Poor babbling Phy was no menace. Still—*the cunning of the insane.* He decided against it, reached out and flipped the control beam at the sector which would bring them to the hundredth and top floor. The door snipped softly shut. The cage became a surging darkness in which floor numerals winked softly. Twenty-one. Twenty-two. Twenty-three.

"And then there was the Military Service. You had it sharply curtailed."

"Of course I did." Sheer weariness stung Carrsbury into talk. "There's only one country in the world. Obviously, the only military requirement is an adequate police force. To say nothing of the risks involved in putting weapons into the hands of the present world population."

"I know," Phy's answer came guiltily from the darkness. "Still, what's happened is that, unknown to you, the Military Service has been increased in size, and recently four rocket squadrons have been added."

Fifty-seven. Fifty-eight. *Humor him.* "Why?"

"Well, you see we've found out that Earth is being reconnoitered. Maybe from Mars. Maybe hostile. Have to be prepared. We didn't tell you . . . well, because we were afraid it might excite you."

The voice trailed off. Carrsbury shut his eyes. How long, he asked himself, how long? He realized with dull surprise that in the last hour people like Phy, endured for ten years, had become unutterably weary to him. For the moment even the thought of the conference over which he would soon be presiding, the conference that was to usher in a sane world, failed to stir him. Reaction to success? To the end of a ten years' tension?

"Do you know how many floors there are in this building?"

Carrsbury was not immediately conscious of the new note in Phy's voice, but he reacted to it.

"One hundred," he replied promptly.

"Then," asked Phy, "just where are we?"

Carrsbury opened his eyes to the darkness. One hundred twenty-seven, blinked the floor numeral. One hundred twenty-eight. One hundred twenty-nine.

Something cold dragged at Carrsbury's stomach, pulled at his brain. He felt as if his mind were being slowly and irresistibly twisted. He thought of hidden dimensions, of unsuspected holes in space. Something remembered from elementary physics danced through his thoughts: If it were possible for an elevator to keep moving upward with uniform acceleration, no one inside an elevator could determine whether the effects they were experiencing were due to acceleration or to gravity—whether the elevator were standing motionless on some planet or shooting up at everincreasing velocity through free space.

One hundred forty-one. One hundred forty-two.

"Or as if you were rising through consciousness into an unsuspected realm of mentality lying above," suggested Phy in his new voice, with its hint of gentle laughter.

One hundred forty-six. One hundred forty-seven. It was slowing now. One hundred forty-nine. One hundred fifty. It had stopped.

This was some trick. The thought was like cold water in Carrsbury's face. Some cunning childish trick of Phy's. An easy thing to hocus the numerals. Carrsbury groped irascibly about in the darkness, encountered the slick surface of a holster, Hartman's gaunt frame.

"Get ready for a surprise," Phy warned from close at his elbow.

As Carrsbury turned and grabbed, bright sunlight drenched him, followed by a gripping, heartstopping spasm of vertigo.

He, Hartman, and Phy, along with a few insubstantial bits of furnishings and controls, were standing in the air fifty stories above the hundred-story summit of World Managerial Center.

For a moment he grabbed frantically at nothing. Then he realized they were not falling and his eyes began to trace the hint of walls and ceiling and floor and, immediately below them, the ghost of a shaft.

Phy nodded. "That's all there is to it," he assured Carrsbury casually. "Just another of those charmingly odd modern notions against which you have legislated so persistently—like our incomplete staircases and roads to nowhere. The Buildings and Grounds Committee decided to extend the range of the elevator for sightseeing purposes. The shaft was made air-transparent to avoid spoiling the form of the original building and to improve the view. This was achieved so satisfactorily that an electronic warning system had to be installed for the safety of passing airjets and other craft. Treating the surfaces of the cage like windows was an obvious detail."

He paused and looked quizzically at Carrsbury. "All very simple," he observed, "but don't you find a kind of symbolism in it? For ten years now you've been spending most of your life in that building below. Every day you've used this elevator. But not once have you dreamed of these fifty extra stories. Don't you think that something of the same sort may be true of your observations of other aspects of contemporary social life?"

Carrsbury gaped at him stupidly.

Phy turned to watch the growing speck of an approaching aircraft. "You might look at it too," he remarked to Carrsbury, "for it's going to transport you to a far happier, more restful life."

Carrsbury parted his lips, wet them. "But—" he said, unsteadily. "But—"

Phy smiled. "That's right, I didn't finish my explanation. Well, you might have gone on being World manager all your life, in the isolation of your office and your miles of taped official reports and your occasional confabs with me and the others. Except for your Institute of Political Leadership and your Ten-Year-Plan. That upset things. Of course, we were as much interested in it as we were in you. It had definite possibilities. We hoped it would work out. We would have been glad to retire from office if it had. But, most fortunately, it didn't. And that sort of ended the whole experiment."

He caught the downward direction of Carrsbury's gaze.

"No," he said, "I'm afraid your pupils aren't waiting for you in the conference chamber on the hundredth story. I'm afraid they're still in the Institute." His voice became gently sympathetic. "And I'm afraid that it's become . . . well . . . a somewhat different sort of institute."

Carrsbury stood very still, swaying a little. Gradually his thoughts and his will power were emerging from the waking nightmare that had paralyzed them. *The cunning of the insane*—he had neglected that trenchant warning. In the very moment of victory—

No! He had forgotten Hartman! This was the very emergency for which that counterstroke had been prepared.

He glanced sideways at the chief member of his secret police. The black giant, unconcerned by their strange position, was glaring fixedly at Phy as if at some evil magician from whom any malign impossibility could be expected.

Now Hartman became aware of Carrsbury's gaze. He divined his thought.

He drew his dark weapon from its holster, pointed it unwaveringly at Phy.

His black-bearded lips curled. From them came a hissing sound. Then, in a loud voice, he cried, "You're dead, Phy! I disintegrated you."

Phy reached over and took the weapon from his hand.

"That's another respect in which you completely miscalculated the modern temperament," he remarked to Carrsbury, a shade argumentatively. "All of us have certain subjects on which we're a trifle unrealistic. That's only human nature. Hartman's was his suspiciousness—a weakness for ideas involving plots and persecutions. You gave him the worst sort of job—one that catered to and encouraged his weaknesses. In a very short time he became hopelessly unrealistic. Why for years he's never realized that he's been carrying a dummy pistol."

He passed it to Carrsbury for inspection.

"But," he added, "give him the proper job and he'd function well enough—say something in creation or exploration. Fitting the man to the job is an art with infinite possibilities. That's why we had Morgenstern in Finance—to keep credit fluctuating in a safe, predictable rhythm. That's why a euphoric is made manager of Extraterrestial Research—to keep it booming. Why a catatonic is given Cultural Advancement—to keep it from tripping on its face in its haste to get ahead."

He turned away. Dully, Carrsbury observed that the aircraft was hovering close to the cage and sidling slowly in.

"But in that case why—" he began stupidly.

"Why were you made World manager?" Phy finished easily. "Isn't that fairly obvious? Haven't I told you several times that you did a lot of good, indirectly? You interested us, don't you see? In fact, you were practically unique. As you know, it's our cardinal principle to let every individual express himself as he wants to. In your case, that involved letting you become World manager. Taken all in all it worked out very well. Everyone had a good time, a number of constructive regulations were promulgated, we learned a lot—oh, we didn't get everything we hoped for, but one never does. Unfortunately, in the end, we were forced to discontinue the experiment."

The aircraft had made contact.

"You understand, of course, why that was necessary?" Phy continued hurriedly, as he urged Carrsbury toward the opening port. "I'm sure you must. It all comes down to a question of sanity. What is sanity—now, in the twentieth century, any time? Adherence to a norm. Conformity to certain basic conventions underlying all human conduct. In our age, departure from the norm has become the norm. Inability to conform has become the standard of conformity. That's quite clear, isn't it? And it enables you to understand, doesn't it, your own case and that of your proteges? Over a long period of years you persisted in adhering to a norm, in conforming to certain basic conventions. You were completely unable to adapt yourself to the society around you. You could only pretend—and your proteges wouldn't have been able to do even that. Despite your many engaging personal characteristics, there was obviously only one course of action open to us."

In the port Carrsbury turned. He had found his voice at last. It was hoarse, ragged. "You mean that all these years you've just been *humoring* me?"

The port was closing. Phy did not answer the question.

As the aircraft edged out, he waved farewell with the blob of green gasoid.

"It'll be very pleasant where you're going," he shouted encouragingly. "Comfortable quarters, adequate facilities for exercise, and a complete library of twentieth century literature to while away your time."

He watched Carrsbury's rigid face, staring whitely from the vision port, until the aircraft had diminished to a speck.

Then he turned away, looked at his hands, noticed the gasoid, tossed it out the open door of the cage, studied its flight for a few moments, then flicked the downbeam.

"I'm glad to see the last of that fellow," he muttered, more to himself than to Hartman, as they plummeted toward the roof. "He was beginning to have a very disturbing influence on me. In fact, I was beginning to fear for my"—his expression became suddenly vacuous—"sanity."

THE MER SHE

1

The ripening newrisen moon of the world of Nehwon shone yellowly down on the marching swells of the Outer Sea, flecking with gold their low lacy crests and softly gilding the taut triangular sail of the slim galley hurrying northwest. Ahead, the last sunset reds were fading while black night engulfed the craggy coast behind, shrouding its severe outlines.

At *Seahawk's* stern, beside old Ourph, who had the tiller, stood the Gray Mouser with arms folded across his chest and a satisfied smile linking his cheeks, his short stalwart body swaying as the ship slowly rocked, moving from shallow trough to low crest and to trough again with the steady southwest wind on her loadside beam, her best point of sailing. Occasionally he stole a glance back at the fading lonely lights of No-Ombrulsk, but mainly he looked straight ahead where lay, five nights and days away, Rime Isle and sweet Cif, and poor one-hand Fafhrd and the most of their men and Fafhrd's Afreyt, whom the Mouser found rather austere.

Ah, by Mog and by Loki, he thought, what satisfaction equals that of captain who at last heads home with ship well ballasted with the get of monstrously clever trading? None! he'd warrant. Youth's erotic capturings and young manhood's slayings—yea, even the masterworks and life-scrolls of scholar and artist—were the merest baubles by compare, callow fevers all.

In his self-enthusiasm the Mouser couldn't resist going over in his mind each last item of merchant plunder—and also to assure himself that each was stowed to best advantage and stoutly secured, in case of storm or other ill-hap.

First, lashed to the sides, in captain's cabin beneath his feet, were the casks of wine, mostly fortified, and the small kegs of bitter brandy, Fafhrd's favorite tipple—those assuredly could not be stored elsewhere or entrusted to another's overwatching (except perhaps yellow old Ourph's here), he reminded himself as he lifted a small leather flask from his belt to his lips and took a measured sup of elixir of Ool Hruspan grape; he had strained his throat bellowing orders for *Seahawk*'s stowing and swift departure, and its raw membranes wanted healing before winter air came to try them further.

And amongst the wine in his cabin was also stored, in as many equally stout, tight barrels, their seams tarred, the wheaten flour— plebeian stuff to the thoughtless, but all-important for an isle that could grow no grain except a little summer barley.

Forward of captain's cabin—and now with his self-enthusiasm at glow point, the Mouser's mused listing-over turned to actual tour of inspection, he first speaking word to Ourph and then moving prow-wards catlike along the moonlit ship—forward of captain's cabin was chiefest prize, the planks and beams and mast-worthy rounds of seasoned timber such as Fafhrd had dreamed of getting at Ool Plerns, south where trees grew, when his stump was healed and could carry hook, such same timber won by cunningest bargaining maneuvers at No-Ombrulsk, where no more trees were than at Rime Isle (which got most of its gray wood from wrecks and nothing much bigger than bushes grew) and where they (the 'Brulskers) would sooner sell their wives than lumber! Yes, rounds and squares and planks of the precious stuff, all lashed down lengthwise to the rowers' benches from poop to forecastle beneath the boom of the great single sail, each layer lashed down separately and canvased and tarred over against the salt spray and wet, with a precious long vellum-thin sheet of beaten copper between layers for further protection and firming, the layers going all the way from one side of *Seahawk* to the other, and all the way up, tied-down timber and thin copper alternating, until the topmost layer was a tightly lashed, canvased deck, its seams tarred, level with the bulwarks—a miracle of stowage. (Of course, this would make rowing difficult if such became needful, but oars were rarely required on voyages such as the remainder of this one promised to be, and there were always some risks that had to be run by even the most prudent sea commander.)

Yes, it was a great timber-bounty that *Seahawk* was bearing to wood-starved Rime Isle, the Mouser congratulated himself as he moved slowly forward alongside the humming, moonlit sail, his softly shod feet avoiding the tarred seams of the taut canvas deck, while his nostrils twitched at an odd, faint, goaty-musky scent he caught, but it (the timber) never would have been won except for his knowledge of the great lust of Lord Logben of No-Ombrulsk for rare strange ivories to complete his White Throne. The 'Brulskers would sooner part with their girl-concubines than their timber, true enough, but the lust of Lord Logben for strange ivories was a greater desire than either of those, so that when with low drummings the Kleshite trading scow had put into 'Brulsk's black harbor and the Mouser had been among the first to board her and had spotted the behemoth tusk amongst the Kleshite trading treasures, he had bought it at once in exchange for a double-fist lump of musk-odorous ambergris, common stuff in Rime Isle but more precious than rubies in Klesh, so that they were unable to resist it.

Thereafter the Kleshites had proffered their lesser ivories in vain to Lord Logben's major-domo, wailing for the mast-long giant snow serpent's white furred skin, that was *their* dearest desire, procured by Lord Logben's hunters in the frigid mountains known as the Bones of the Old Ones, and in vain had Lord Logben offered the Mouser its weight in electrum for the tusk. Only when the Kleshites had added their pleas to the Mouser's demands that the 'Brulskers sell him timber, offering for the unique snow serpent skin not only their lesser ivories but half their spices, and the Mouser had threatened to sink the tusk in the bottomless bay rather than sell it for less than wood, had the 'Brulskers been forced by their Lord to yield up a quarter shipload of seasoned straight timber, as grudgingly as the Mouser had seemed to part with the tusk—whereafter all the trading (even in timber) had gone more easily.

Ah, that had been most cunningly done, a masterstroke! the Mouser assured himself soberly.

As these most pleasant recollections were sorting themselves to best advantage within the Mouser's wide, many-shelved skull, his noiseless feet had carried him to the thick foot of the mast, where the false deck made by the timber cargo ended. Three yards farther on began the decking of the forecastle, beneath which the rest of the cargo was stowed and secured: ingots of bronze and little chests of dyes and spices and a larger chest of silken fabrics and linens for Cif and Afreyt—that was to show his crew he trusted them with all things except mind-fuddling, duty-betraying wine—but mostly the forward cargo was tawny grain and white and purple beans and sun-dried fruit, all bagged in wool against the sea-damp: food for the hungry Isle. There was your real thinking man's treasure, he told himself, beside which gold and twinkling jewels were merest trinkets, or the pointy breasts of young love or words of poets or the pointed stars themselves that astrologers cherished and that made men drunk with distance and expanse.

In the three yards between false deck and true, their upper bodies in the shadow of the latter and their feet in a great patch of moonlight, on which his own body cast its supervisory shadow, his crew slept soundly while the sea cradle-rocked 'em: four wiry Mingols, three of his short, nimble sailor-thieves with their lieutenant Mikkidu, and Fafhrd's tall lieutenant Skor, borrowed for this voyage. Aye, they slept soundly enough! he told himself with relish (he could clearly distinguish the bird-twittering snores of ever-apprehensive Mikkidu and the lion-growling ones of Skor), for he had kept tight rein on them all the time in No-Ombrulsk and then deliberately worked them mercilessly loading and lashing the timber at the end, so that they'd fallen asleep in their tracks after the ship had sailed and they had supped (just as he'd cruelly disciplined himself and permitted himself no freedom all time in port, no slightest recreation, even such as was desirable for hygienic reasons), for he knew well the appetites of sailors and the dubious, debilitating attractions of 'Brulsk's dark alleys—why, the whores had paraded daily before Seahawk to distract his crew. He remembered in particular one hardly-more-than-child among them, an insolent skinny girl in tattered tunic faded silver-gray, same shade as her precociously silver hair, who had moved a little apart from the other whores and had seemed to be forever flaunting herself and peering up at Seahawk wistfully yet somehow tauntingly, with great dark waifish eyes of deepest green.

Yes, by fiery Loki and by eight-limbed Mog, he told himself, in the discharge of his captain's duties he'd disciplined himself most rigorously of all, expending every last ounce of strength, wisdom, cunning (and voice!) and asking no reward at all except for the knowledge of responsibilities manfully shouldered—that, and gifts for his friends. Suddenly the Mouser felt nigh to bursting with his virtues and somehow a shade sorry about it, especially the "no reward at all" bit, which now seemed manifestly unfair.

Keeping careful watch upon his wearied-out men, and with his ears attuned to catch any cessation of, or the slightest variation in their snorings, he lifted his leathern pottle to his lips and let a generous, slow, healthful swallow soothe his raw throat.

As he thrust the lightened pottle back into his belt, securely hooking it there, his gaze fastened on one item of cargo stored forward that seemed to have strayed from its appointed place—either his concentrated watching or else some faint unidentified sound had called it to his attention. (At the same instant he got another whiff of the musky, goaty, strangely attractive sea odor. Ambergris?) It was the chest of silks and thick ribbons and linens and other costly fabrics intended chiefly for his gift to Cif. It was standing out a little way from the ship's side, almost entirely in the moonlight, as if its lashings had loosened, and now as he studied it more closely he saw that it wasn't lashed at all and that its top was wedged open a finger's breadth by a twist of pale orange fabric protruding near a hinge.

What monstrous indiscipline did this signify?

He dropped noiselessly down and approached the chest, his nostrils wrinkling. Was unsold ambergris cached inside it? Then, carefully keeping his shadow off it, he gripped the top and silently threw it wide open on its hinges.

The topmost silk was a thick lustrous copper-colored one chosen to match the glints in Cif's dark hair.

Upon this rich bedding, like a kitten stolen in to nap on fresh-laundered linens, reposed, with arms and legs somewhat drawn in but mostly on her back, and with one long-fingered hand twisting down through her tousled silvery hair so as to shadow further her lidded eyes—reposed that self-same wharf-waif he'd but now been recalling. The picture of innocence, but the odor (he knew it now) all sex. Her slender chest rose and fell gently and slowly with her sleeping inhalations, her small breasts and rather larger nipples out-denting the flimsy fabric of her ragged tunic, while her narrow lips smiled faintly. Her hair was somewhat the same shade as that of silver-blond, thirteen-year-old Gale back on Rime Isle, who'd been one of Odin's maidens. And she was, apparently, not a great deal older.

Why, this was worse than monstrous, the Mouser told himself as he wordlessly stared. That one or two or more of all of his crew should conspire to smuggle this girl aboard for his or their hot plea-sure, tempting her with silver or feeing her pimp or owner (or else kidnapping her, though that was most unlikely in view of her un-bound state) was bad enough, but that they should presume to do this not only without their captain's knowledge but also in complete disregard of the fact that *he* enjoyed no such erotic solacing, but rather worked himself to the bone on their behalf and *Seahawk*'s, solicitous only of their health and welfare and the success of the voyage—why, this was not only wantonest indiscipline but also ran-kest ingratitude!

At this dark point of disillusionment with his fellow man, the Mouser's one satisfaction was his knowledge that his crew slept deeply from exhaustion he'd inflicted on them. The chorus of their unaltering snores was music to his ears, for it told him that although they'd managed to smuggle the girl aboard successfully, not one of them had yet enjoyed her (at least since the loading and business of getting under way was done). No, they'd been smote senseless by fatigue, and would not now wake for a hurricane. And that thought in turn pointed out to him the way to their most appropriate and condign punishment.

Smiling widely, he reached his left hand toward the sleeping girl, and, where it made a small peak in her worn silver-faded tunic, delicately yet somewhat sharply tweaked her right nipple. As she came shuddering awake with a suck of indrawn breath, her eyes opening and her parted lips forming an exclamation, he swooped his face toward hers, frowning most sternly and laying his finger across his now disapprovingly set lips, enjoining silence.

She shrank away, staring at him in wonder and dread and keeping obediently still. He drew back a little in turn, noting the twin reflections of the misshapen moon in her wide dark eyes and how strangely the lustrous coppery silk on which she cowered contrasted with her hair tangled upon it, fine and silver pale as a ghost's.

From around them the chorus of snores continued unchanged as the crew slept on.

From beside her slender naked feet the Mouser plucked up a black roll of thick silken ribbon and unsheathing his dirk Cat's Claw, proceeded to cut three hanks from it, staring broodingly at the shrinking girl all the while. Then he motioned to her and crossed his wrists to indicate what was wanted of her.

Her chest lifting in a silent sigh, and shrugging her shoulders a little, she crossed her slender wrists in front of her. He shook his head and pointed behind her.

Again divining his command, she crossed them there, turning upon her side a little to do so.

He bound her wrists together crosswise and tightly, then bound her elbows together also, noting that they met without undue strain upon her slender shoulders. He used the third hank to tie her legs together firmly just above the knees. Ah, discipline! he thought— good for one and all, but in particular the young!

In the end she lay supine upon her bound arms, gazing up at him. He noted that there seemed to be more curiosity and speculation in that gaze than dread and that the twin reflections of the gibbous moon did not waver with any eye-blinking or -watering.

How very pleasant this all was, he mused: his crew asleep, his ship driving home full-laden, the slim girl docile to his binding of her, he meting out justice as silently and secretly as does a god. The taste of undiluted power was so satisfying to him that it did not trouble him that the girl's silken-smooth flesh glowed a little more silvery pale than even moonlight would easily account for.

Without any warning or change in his own brooding expression, he flicked inside the protruding twist of fabric and closed the lid of the chest upon her.

Let the confident minx worry a bit, he thought, as to whether I intend to suffocate her or perchance cast the chest overboard, she being in it. Such incidents were common enough, he told himself, at least in myth and story.

Tiny wavelets gently slapped *Seahawk*'s side, the moonlit sail hummed as softly, and the crew snored on.

The Mouser wakened the two brawniest Mingols by twisting a big toe of each and silently indicated that they should take up the chest without disturbing their comrades and bear it back to his cabin. He did not want to risk waking the crew with sound of words. Also, using gestures spared his strained throat.

If the Mingols were privy to the secret of the girl, their blank expressions did not show it, although he watched them narrowly. Nor did old Ourph betray any surprise. As they came nigh him, the ancient Mingol's gaze slipped over them and roved serenely ahead and his gnarled hands rested lightly on the tiller, as though the shifting about of the chest were a matter of no consequence whatever.

The Mouser directed the younger Mingols in their setting of the chest between the lashed cases that narrowed the cabin and beneath the brass lamp that swung on a short chain from the low ceiling. Laying finger to compressed lips, he signed them to keep strict silence about the chest's midnight remove. Then he dismissed them with a curt wave. He rummaged about, found a small brass cup, filled it from a tiny keg of Fafhrd's bitter brandy, drank off half, and opened the chest.

The smuggled girl gazed up at him with a composure he told himself was creditable. She had courage, yes. He noted that she took three deep breaths, though, as if the chest had indeed been a bit stuffy. The silver glow of her pale skin and hair pleased him. He motioned her to sit up, and when she did so, set the cup against her lips, tilting it as she drank the other half. He unsheathed his dirk, inserted it carefully between her knees, and drawing it upward, cut the ribbon confining them. He turned, moved away aft, and settled himself on a low stool that stood before Fafhrd's wide bunk. Then with crooked forefinger he summoned her to him.

When she stood close before him, chin high, slender shoulders thrown back by virtue of the ribbons binding her arms, he eyed her significantly and formed the words, "What is your name?"

"Ississi," she responded in a lisping whisper that was like the ghosts of wavelets kissing the hull. She smiled.

2

On deck, Ourph had directed one of the younger Mingols to take the tiller, the other to heat him gahveh. He sheltered from the wind behind the false deck of the timber cargo, looking toward the cabin and shaking his head wonderingly. The rest of the crew snored in the forecastle's shadow. While on Rime Isle in her low-ceilinged yellow bedroom Cif woke with the thought that the Gray Mouser was in peril. As she tried to recollect her nightmare, moonlight creeping along the wall reminded her of the mer-ghost which had murdered Zwaaken and lured off Fafhrd from sister Afreyt for a space, and she wondered how Mouser would react to such a dangerous challenge.

3

Bright and early the next morning the Mouser threw on a short gray robe, belted it, and rapped sharply on the cabin's ceiling. Speaking in a somewhat hoarse whisper, he told the impassive Mingol thus summoned that he desired the instant presence of Master Mikkidu. He had cast a disguising drape across the transported chest that stood between the crowding casks that narrowed farther the none-too-wide cabin, and now sat behind it on the stool, as though it were a captain's flat desk. Behind him on the crosswise bunk that occupied the cabin's end Ississi reposed and either slept or shut-eyed waked, he knew not which, blanket-covered except for her streaming silver hair and unconfined save for the thick black ribbon tying one ankle securely to the bunk's foot beneath the blanket.

(*I'm no egregious fool,* he told himself, *to think that one night's love brings loyalty.*)

He nursed his throat with a cuplet of bitter brandy, gargled and slowly swallowed.

(*And yet she'd make a good maid for Cif, I do believe, when I have*

done with disciplining her. Or perchance I'll pass her on to poor maimed
and isle-locked Fafhrd.)

He impatiently finger-drummed the shrouded chest, wondering
what could be keeping Mikkidu. A guilty conscience? Very likely!

Save for a glimmer of pale dawn filtering through the curtained
hatchway and the two narrow side ports glazed with mica, which the
lashed casks further obscured, the oil-replenished swaying lamp still
provided the only light.

4

There was a flurry of running footsteps coming closer, and then Mikkidu simultaneously rapped at the hatchway and thrust tousle-pated
head and distracted eyes between the curtains. The Mouser beckoned
him in, saying in a soft, brandy-smoothed voice, "Ah, Master Mikkidu, I'm glad your duties, which no doubt must be pressing, at last
permit you to visit me, because I do believe I ordered that you come
at once."

"Oh, Captain, sir," the latter replied rapidly, "there's a chest
missing from the stowage forward. I saw that it was gone as soon as
Trenchi wakened me and gave me your command. I only paused to
rouse my mates and question them before I hurried here."

(*Ah-ha,* the Mouser thought, *he knows about Ississi, I'm sure of*
it, he's much too agitated, he had a hand in smuggling her aboard. But
he doesn't know what's happened to her now—suspects everything and
everyone, no doubt—and seeks to clear himself with me of all suspicion
by reporting to me the missing chest, the wretch!)

"A chest? Which chest?" the Mouser meanwhile asked blandly.
"What did it contain? Spices? Spicy things?"

"Fabrics for Lady Cif, I do believe," Mikkidu answered.

"Just fabrics for the Lady Cif and nothing else?" the Mouser
inquired, eyeing him keenly. "Weren't there some other things?
Something of *yours,* perhaps?"

"No, sir, nothing of mine," Mikkidu denied quickly.

"Are you sure of that?" the Mouser pressed. "Sometimes one will
tuck something of one's own inside another's chest—for safekeeping,
as it were, or perchance to smuggle it across a border."

"Nothing of mine at all," Mikkidu maintained. "Perhaps there were some fabrics also for the other lady . . . and, well, just fabrics, sir and—oh, yes—some rolls of ribbon."

"Nothing but fabrics and ribbon?" the Mouser went on, prodding him. "No fabrics made into garments, eh?—such as a short silvery tunic of some lacy stuff, for instance?"

Mikkidu shook his head, his eyebrows rising.

"Well, well," the Mouser said smoothly, "what's happened to this chest, do you suppose? It must be still on the ship—unless someone has dropped it overboard. Or was it perhaps stolen back in 'Brulsk?"

"I'm sure it was safe aboard when we sailed," Mikkidu asserted. Then he frowned. "I *think* it was, that is." His brow cleared. "Its lashings lay beside it, loose on the deck!"

"Well, I'm glad you found something of it," the Mouser said. "Where on the ship do you suppose it can be? Think, man, where can it be?" For emphasis, he pounded the muffled chest he sat at.

Mikkidu shook his head helplessly. His gaze wandered about, past the Mouser.

(*Oh-ho*, the latter thought, *does he begin to get a glimmering at last of what has happened to his smuggled girl? Whose plaything she is now? This might become rather amusing.*)

He recalled his lieutenant's attention by asking, "What were your men able to tell you about the runaway chest?"

"Nothing, sir. They were as puzzled as I am. I'm sure they know nothing. I *think*."

"Hmn. What did the Mingols have to say about it?"

"They're on watch, sir. Besides, they answer only to Ourph—or yourself, of course, sir."

(*You can trust a Mingol*, the Mouser thought, *at least where it's a matter of keeping silent.*)

"What about Skor, then?" he asked. "Did Captain Fafhrd's man know anything about the chest's vanishment?"

Mikkidu's expression became a shade sulky. "Lieutenant Skor is not under my command," he said. "Besides that, he sleeps very soundly."

There was a thuddingly loud double knock at the hatchway.

"Come in," the Mouser called testily, "and next time don't try to pound the ship to pieces."

Fafhrd's chief lieutenant thrust bent head with receding reddish hair through the curtains and followed after. He had to bend both back and knees to keep from bumping his naked pate on the beams. (*So Fafhrd too would have had to go about stooping when occupying his own cabin,* the Mouser thought. *Ah, the discomforts of size.*)

Skor eyed the Mouser coolly and took note of Mikkidu's presence. He had trimmed his russet beard, which gave it a patchy appearance. Save for his broken nose, he rather resembled a Fafhrd five years younger.

"Well?" the Mouser said peremptorily.

"Your pardon, Captain Mouser," the other replied, "but you asked me to keep particular watch on the stowage of cargo, since I was the only one who had done any long voyaging on *Seahawk* before this faring, and knew her behavior in different weathers. So I believe that I should report to you that there is a chest of fabrics— you know the one, I think—missing from the fore steer-side storage. Its lashings lie all about, both those which roped it shut and those which tied it securely in place."

(*Ah-ha,* the Mouser thought, *he's guilty too and seeks to cover it by making swift report, however late. Never trust a bland expression. The lascivious villain!*)

With his lips he said, "Ah yes, the missing chest—we were just speaking of it. When do you suppose it became so?—I mean missing. In 'Brulsk?"

Skor shook his head. "I saw to its lashing myself—and noted it still tied fast to the side as my eyes closed in sleep a league outside that port. I'm sure it's still on *Seahawk*."

(*He admits it, the effrontrous rogue!* the Mouser thought. *I wonder he doesn't accuse Mikkidu of stealing it. Perhaps there's a little honor left 'mongst thieves and berserks.*)

Meanwhile the Mouser said, "Unless it has been dropped overboard—that is a distinct possibility, do you not think? Or mayhap we were boarded last night by soundless and invisible pirates while you both snored, who raped the chest away and nothing else. Or perchance a crafty and shipwise octopus, desirous of going richly clad and with arms skillful at tying and untying knots—"

He broke off when he noted that both tall Skor and short Mikkidu were peering wide-eyed beyond him. He turned on his stool. A little more of Ississi showed above the blanket—to wit, a small patch of pale forehead and one large green silver-lashed eye peering unwinking through her long silvery hair.

He turned back very deliberately and, after a sharp "Well?" to get their attention, asked in his blandest voice, "Whatever are you looking at so engrossedly?"

"Uh—nothing at all," Mikkidu stammered, while Skor only shifted gaze to look at the Mouser steadily.

"Nothing at all?" the Mouser questioned. "You don't perhaps see the chest somewhere in this cabin? Or perceive some clue to its present disposition?"

Mikkidu shook his head, while after a moment Skor shrugged, eyeing the Mouser strangely.

"Well, gentlemen," the Mouser said cheerily, "that sums it up. The chest must be aboard this ship, as you both say. So hunt for it! Scour *Seahawk* high and low—a chest that large can't be hid in a seaman's bag. And use your eyes, both of you!" He thumped the shrouded box once more for good measure. "And now—dismiss!"

(They both know all about it, I'll be bound. The deceiving dogs! the Mouser thought. *And yet . . . I am not altogether satisfied of that.)*

5

When they were gone (after several hesitant, uncertain backward glances), the Mouser stepped back to the bunk and, planting his hands to either side of the girl, stared down at her green eye, supporting himself on stiff arms. She rocked her head up and down a little and to either side, and so worked her entire face free of the blanket and her eyes of the silken hair veiling them and stared up at him expectantly.

He put on an inquiring look and flirted his head toward the hatchway through which the men had departed, then directed the same look more particularly at her. It was strange, he mused, how he avoided speaking to her whenever he could except with pointings and gestured commands. Perhaps it was that the essence of power lay in getting your wishes gratified without ever having to speak them out, to put another through all his paces in utter silence, so that no god might overhear and know. Yes, that was part of it at least.

He formed with his lips and barely breathed the question, "How did you *really* come aboard *Seahawk?*"

Her eyes widened and after a while her peach-down lips began to move, but he had to turn his head and lower it until they moistly and silkily brushed his best ear as they enunciated, before he could clearly hear what she was saying—in the same Low Lankhmarese as he and Mikkidu and Skor had spoken, but with a delicious lisping accent that was all little hisses and gasps and warblings. He recalled how her scent had seemed all sex in the chest, but now infinitely flowery, dainty, and innocent.

"I was a princess and lived with the prince Mordroog, my brother, in a far country where it was always spring," she began. "There a watery influence filtered all harshness from the sun's beams, so that he shone no more bright than the silvery moon, and winter's rages and summer's droughts were tamed, and the roaring winds moderated to eternal balmy breezes, and even fire was cool—in that far country."

Every whore tells the same tale, the Mouser thought. *They were all princesses before they took to the trade.* Yet he listened on.

"We had golden treasure beyond all dreaming," she continued, "unicorns that flew and kittens that flowed were my pets, and we were served by nimble companies of silent servitors and guarded by soft-voiced monsters—great Slasher and vasty All-Gripper, and Deep Rusher, who was greatest of all.

"But then came ill times. One night while our guardians slept, our treasure was stolen away and our realm became lonely, farther off and more secret still. My brother and I went searching for our treasure and for allies, and in that search I was raped away by bold scoundrels and taken to vile, vile 'Brulsk, where I came to know all the evil there is under the hateful sun."

This too is a familiar part of each harlot's story, the Mouser told himself, *the raping away, the loss of innocence, instruction in every vice.* Yet he went on listening to her ticklesome whispering.

"But I knew that one day *that one* would come who would be king over me and carry me back to my realm and dwell with me in power and silvery glory, our treasures being restored. And then *you* came."

Ah, now the personal appeal, the Mouser thought. *Very familiar indeed. Still, let's hear her out. I like her tongue in my ear. It's like being a flower and having a bee suck your nectar.*

"I went to your ship each day and stared at you. I could do naught else at all, however I tried. And you would never look at me for long, and yet I knew that our paths lay together. I knew you were a masterful man and that you'd visit upon me rigors and inflictions besides which those I'd suffered in dreadful 'Brulsk would be nothing, and yet I could not turn aside for an instant, or take my eyes away from you and your dark ship. And when it was clear you would not notice me, or act upon your true feelings, or any of your men provide a means for me to follow you, I stole aboard unseen while they were all stowing and lashing and you were commanding them."

(*Lies, lies, all lies,* the Mouser thought—and continued to listen.)

"I managed to conceal myself by moving about amongst the cargo. But when at last you'd sailed from harbor and your men slept, I grew cold, the deck was hard, I suffered keenly. And yet I dared not seek your cabin yet, or otherwise disclose myself, for fear you would put back to 'Brulsk to put me off. So I gradually freed of its lashings a chest of fabrics I'd marked, working and working like a mouse or shrew—the knots were hard, but my fingers are clever and nimble, and strong whenever the need is—until I could creep inside and slumber warm and soft. And then you came for me, and here I am."

The Mouser turned his head and looked down into her large green eyes, across which golden gleams moved rhythmically with the lamp's measured swinging. Then he briefly pressed a finger across her soft lips and drew down the blanket until her ribbon-fettered ankle was revealed and he admired her beautiful small body. It was well, he told himself, for a man to have always a beautiful young woman close by him—like a beautiful cat, yes, a young cat, independent but with kitten ways still. It was well when such a one talked, speaking lies much as any cat would (*'Twas crystal clear she must have had help getting aboard—Skor and Mikkidu both, likely enough*), but best not to talk to her too much, and wisest to keep her well bound. You could trust folk when they were secured—indeed, trussed!—and not otherwise, no, not at all. And that was the essence of power—binding all others, binding all else! Keeping his eyes hypnotically upon hers, he reached across her for the loose hanks of black ribbon. It would be well to fetter her three other limbs to foot and head of bunk, not tightly, yet not so loosely that she could reach either wrist with other hand or with her pearly teeth—so he could take a turn on deck, confident that she'd be here when he returned.

6

On Rime Isle Cif, strolling alone across the heath beyond Salthaven, plucked from the slender pouch at her girdle a small male figure of sewn cloth stuffed with lint. He was tall as her hand was long and his waist was constricted by a plain gold ring which would have fitted one of her fingers—and that was a measure of the figure's other dimensions. He was dressed in a gray tunic and gray, gray-hooded cloak. She regarded his featureless linen face and for a space she meditated the mystery of woven cloth—one set of threads or lines tying or at least restraining another such set, with a uniquely pro-tective pervious surface the result. Then some odd hint of expression in the faintly brown, blank linen face suggested to her that the Gray Mouser might be in need of more golden protection than the ring afforded, and thrusting the doll feet-first back into her pouch, she strode back toward Salthaven, the council hall, and the recently ghost-raped treasury. The north wind coming unevenly rippled the heather.

7

His throat burning from the last swallow of bitter brandy he'd taken, the Mouser slipped through the hatchway curtains and stole silently on deck. His purpose was to check on his crew (surprise 'em if need be!) and see if they were all properly occupied with sailorly duties (tied to their tasks, as it were!), including the fool's search for the missing chest he'd sent them on in partial punishment for smuggling Ississi aboard. (She was secure below, the minx, he'd seen to that!)

The wind had freshened a little and *Seahawk* leaned to steerside
a bit farther as she dashed ahead, lead-weighted keel balancing the
straining sail. The Mingol steersman leaned on the tiller while his
mate and old Ourph scanned with sailorly prudence the southwest
for signs of approaching squalls. At this rate they might reach Rime
Isle in three more days instead of four. The Mouser felt uneasy at
that, rather than pleased. He looked over the steerside apprehen-
sively, but the rushing white water was still safely below the oarholes,
each of which had a belaying pin laid across it, around which the
ropes lashing down the middle tier of the midship cargo had been
passed. This reminder of the security of the ship unaccountably did
not please him either.

Where was the rest of the crew? he asked himself. A-search
forward below for the missing chest? Or otherwise busy? Or merely
skulking? He'd see for himself! But as he strode forward across the
taut canvas sheathing the timber treasure, the reason for his sudden
depression struck him, and his steps slowed.

He did not like the thought of soon arrival or of the great gifts
he was bringing (in fact, *Seahawk*'s cargo had now become hateful
to him) because all that represented ties binding him and his future
to Cif and crippled Fafhrd and haughty Afreyt too and all his men
and every last inhabitant of Rime Isle. Endless responsibility—that
was what he was sailing back to. Responsibility as husband (or some
equivalent) of Cif, old friend to Fafhrd (who was already tied to
Afreyt, no longer comrade), captain (and guardian!) of his men,
father to all. Provider and protector!—and first thing you knew they,
or at least one of them, would be protecting *him*, confining and
constraining him for his own good in tyranny of love or fellowship.

Oh, he'd be a hero for an hour or two, praised for his sumptuous
get. But next day? Go out and do it again! Or (worse yet) stay at
home and do it. And so on, *ad infinitum*. Such a future ill sorted
with the sense of power he'd had since last night's sailing and which
the girl-whore Ississi had strangely fed. Himself bound instead of
binding others, and adventuring on to bind the universe mayhap and
put it through its paces, enslave the very gods. Not free to adventure,
discover, and to play with life, tame it by all-piercing knowledge and
by shrewd commands and put it through its paces, search out each

dizzy height and darksome depth. The Mouser *bound*? No, no, no, no!

As his feelings marched with that great repeated negation, his inching footsteps had carried him forward almost to the mast, and through the sail's augmented hum and the wind's and the water's racket against the hull, he became aware of two voices contending vehemently in strident whispers.

He instantly and silently dropped on his belly and crawled on very cautiously until the top half of his face overlooked the gap between timber cargo and forecastle.

His three sailor-thieves and the two other Mingols sprawled higgledy piggledy, lazily napping, while immediately below him Skor and Mikkidu argued in what might be called loud undertones. He could have reached down and patted their heads—or rapped them with fisted knuckles.

"There you go bringing in the chest again," Mikkidu was whispering hotly, utterly absorbed in the point he was making. "There *is* no longer any chest on *Seahawk*! We've searched every place on the ship and not found it, so it has to have been cast overboard—that's the only explanation!—but only after (most like) the rich fabrics it contained were taken out and hid deviously in any number of ways and places. And there I must, with all respect, suspect old Ourph. He was awake while we slept, you can't trust Mingols (or get a word out of them, for that matter), he's got merchant's blood and can't resist snatching any rich thing, he's also got the cunning of age, and—"

Mikkidu perforce paused to draw breath and Skor, who seemed to have been patiently waiting for just that, cut in with, "Searched every place *except* the Captain's cabin. And we searched that pretty well with our eyes. So the chest has to be the draped oblong thing he sat behind and even thumped on. It was exactly the right size and shape—"

"That was the Captain's desk," Mikkidu asserted in outraged tones.

"There *was* no desk," Skor rejoined, "when Captain Fafhrd occupied the cabin, or on our voyage down. Stick to the facts, little man. Next you'll be denying again he had a girl with him."

"There was no girl!" Mikkidu exploded, using up at once all the

breath he'd managed to draw, for Skor was able to continue without raising his voice, "There was indeed a girl, as any fool could see who was not oversunk in doggish loyalty—a dainty delicate piece just the right size for him with long, long silvery hair and a great green eye casting out lustful gleams—"

"That wasn't a girl's long hair you saw, you great lewd oaf," Mikkidu cut in, his lungs replenished at last. "That was a large dried frond of fine silvery seaweed with a shining, sea-rounded green pebble caught up in it—such a curio as many a captain's cabin accumulates—and your woman-starved fancy transformed it to a wench, you lickerish idiot—

"Or else," he recommenced rapidly, cutting in on himself, as it were, "it was a lacy silver dress with a silver-set green gem at its neck—the Captain questioned me closely about just such a dress when he was quizzing me about the chest before you came."

My, my, the Mouser thought, *I never dreamed Mikkidu had such a quick fancy or would spring to my defense so loyally. But it does now appear, I must admit, that I have falsely suspected these two men and that Ississi somehow did board Seahawk solo. Unless one of the others— no, that's unlikely. Truth from a whore—there's a puzzler for you.*

Skor said triumphantly, "But if it was the dress you saw on's bunk and the dress had been in the chest, doesn't that prove the chest too was in the cabin? Yes, it may well have been a filmy silver dress we saw, now that I think of it, which the girl slipped teasingly and lasciviously out of before leaping between the sheets, or else your Captain Mouser ripped it off her (it looked torn), for he's as hot and lusty as a mink and ever boasting of his dirksmanship—I've heard Captain Fafhrd say so again and again, or at least imply it."

What infamy was this now? the Mouser asked himself, suddenly indignant, glaring down at Skor's balding head from his vantage point. *It was his own place to chide Fafhrd for his womanizing, not hear himself so chidden for the same fault (and boastfulness to boot) by this bogus Fafhrd, this insolent, lofty, jumped-up underling.* He involuntarily whipped up his fist to smite.

"Yes, boastful, devious, a martinet, and mean," Skor continued while Mikkidu spluttered. "What think you of a captain who drives his crew hard in port, holds back their pay, puritanically forbids shore leave, denies 'em all discharge of their natural urges—and then brings a girl aboard for his own use and flaunts her in their faces? and *then* plays games with them about her, sends them on idiot's hunt. *Petty*—that's what I've heard Captain Fafhrd call it—or at least show he thought so by his looks."

The Mouser, furious, could barely restrain himself from striking out. *Defend me, Mikkidu,* he inwardly implored. *Oh the monstrousness of it—to invoke Fafhrd. Had Fafhrd really—*

"Do you really think so?" he heard Mikkidu say, only a little doubtfully. "You really think he's got a girl in there? Well, if that's the case I must admit he is a very devil!"

The cry of pure rage that traitorous utterance drew from the sprung-up Mouser made the two lieutenants throw back their heads and stare, and brought the nappers fully awake and almost to their feet.

He opened his mouth to utter rebuke that would skin them alive—and then paused, wondering just what form that rebuke could take. After all, there *was* a naked girl in his cabin with her legs tied wide—in fact, spread-eagled. His glance lit on the lashings of the chest of fabrics still lying loose on the deck.

"Clear up that strewage!" he roared, pointing it out. "Use it to tie down doubly those grain sacks there." He pointed again. "And while you're at it—" (he took a deep breath) "double lash the entire cargo! I am not satisfied that it won't shift if hurricane strikes." He directed that last remark chiefly at the two lieutenants, who peered puzzledly at the blue sky as they moved to organize the work.

"Yes, double lash it all down tight as eelskin," he averred, beginning to pace back and forth as he warmed to his task. "Pass the timber's extra ropings around belaying pins set *inside* the oarholes and then draw them tight across the deck. See that those wool sacks of grain and fruit are lashed really tight—imagine you're corsetting a fat woman, put your foot in her back and really pull those laces. For I'm not convinced those bags would stay in place if we had green water aboard and dragging at them. And when all that is done, bring a gang aft to further firm the casks and barrels in my cabin, marry them indissolubly to *Seahawk*'s deck and sides. Remember, all of you," he finished as he danced off aft, "if you tie things up carefully enough—your purse, your produce, or your enemies, and eke your lights of love—nothing can ever surprise you, or escape from you, or harm you!"

8

Cif untied the massive silver key from the neck of her soft leather tunic, where it had hung warm inside, unlocked the heavy oaken door of the treasury, opened it cautiously and suspiciously, inspected the room from the threshold—she'd been uneasy about the place ever since the sea-ghost's depredations. Then she went in and re-locked the door behind her. A small window with thumb-thick bars of bronze illumined not too well the wooden room. On a shelf re-posed two ingots of pale silver, three short stacks of silver coins, and a single golden stack, still shorter. The walls of the room crowded in on a low circular table, in the gray surface of which a pentacle had been darkly burnt. She named over to herself the five golden objects standing at the points: the Arrow of Truth, kinked from Fafhrd's tugging of it from the demoness; the Rule of Prudence, a short rod circled by ridges; the Cup of Measured Hospitality, hardly larger than a thimble; the Circles of Unity, so linked that if any one were taken away, the other two fell apart; and the strange skeletal globe that Fafhrd had recovered with the rest and suggested might be the Cube of Square-Dealing smoothly deformed (something she rather doubted). She took the Mouser doll from her pouch and laid it in their midst, at pentalpha's center. She sighed with relief, sat down on one of the three stools there were, and gazed pensively at the doll's blank face.

9

As the Mouser approved the last cask's double lashings and then dismissed as curtly his still-baffled lieutenants and their weary work gang—fairly drove 'em from his cabin!—he felt a surge of power inside, as if he'd just stepped or been otherwise carried over an invisible boundary into a realm where each last object was plainly labeled "Mine Alone!"

Ah, that had been sport of the best, he told himself—closely supervising the gang's toil while standing all the while in their midst atop the draped chest he'd had them hunting all day long, and while the girl Ississi lay naked and securely spread-eagled beneath the blanket spread across his bunk—and they all somehow conscious of her delectable presence yet never quite daring to refer to it. Power sport indeed!

In a transport of self-satisfaction he whipped the drape from the chest, threw back its top, and admired the expanse of coppery silk so revealed and the bolts of black ribbon. Now *there* was a bed fit for a princess's nuptials, he told himself as he filled and downed a brass cup of brandy, a couch somewhat small, but sufficient and soft all the way down to the bottom.

His mind and his feet both dancing with all manner of imaginings and impulses, he moved to the bunk and whirled off its coverings and—

The bunk's coarse gray single sheeting was covered by a veritable black snow-sprinkle of ribbon scraps and shreds. Of Ississi there was no sign.

After a long moment's searching of it with his astounded eyes, he fairly dove across the bunk and fumbled frantically all the way around the thin mattress's edges and under them, searching for the razor-keen knife or scissors that had done this or (who knew?) some sharp-toothed, ribbon-shredding small animal secretly attendant on the girl whore and obedient to her command.

A trilling sigh of blissful contentment made him switch convulsively around. In the midst of the new-opened, chest, got there by sleights he could scarce dream of, Ississi sat cross-legged facing him. Her arms were lifted while her nimble hands were swiftly braiding her long straight silvery hair, an action which showed off her slender waist and dainty small breasts to best advantage, while her green eyes flashed and her lips smiled at him, "Am I not exceedingly clever? Surpassingly clever and wholly delightful?"

The Mouser frowned at her terribly, then sent the same expression roving to either side, as if spying for a route by which she could have got unseen from bunk to chest past the double-lashed and closely abutting casks—and mayhap for her confederates, animal, human, or demonic. Next he got off the bunk and, approaching her, edged his way around the chest and back, eyeing her up and down as though searching for concealed weapons, even so little as a sharpened fingernail, and turning his own body so that his frown was always fixed on her and he never lost sight of her for an instant, until he faced her once more.

His nostrils flared with his deep breathing, while the lamp's yellow beams and shadows swayed measuredly across his dark angry presence and her moon-pale skin.

She continued to braid her hair and to smile and to warble and trill, and after a short while her trillings and warblings became a sort of rough song of recitation, one shot with seeming improvisations, as though she were translating it into Low Lankhmarese from another language:

"Oh, the golden gifts of my land are six, And round you now they're straitly fixed. The Golden Shaft of Death and Desire, The Rod of Command whose smart's like fire, The Cup of Close Confinement and Minding, The Circles of Fate whose ways are winding. The Cubical Prison of god and of elf, The Many-Barred Globe of Simorgya and Self. Deep, oh deep is my far country, Where gold will carry us, me and thee."

The Mouser shook his finger before her face in dark challenge and dire warning. Then he slashed lengths of ribbed black silk ribbon from a roll, twisting and tugging it to test its strength, continuing to eye her all the while, and he bound her legs together as they were, slender ankle to calf, just below the knee, and slender calf to ankle. Then he held out his hand for hers imperiously. She rapidly finished plaiting her hair, whipped the braid round her head and tucked it in, so that it became a sort of silvery coronet. Then with a sigh and a turning away of her somewhat narrow face, she held out her wrists to him close together, the palms of her hands upward.

He seized them contemptuously and drew them behind her and bound them there, as he had on the previous night, and her elbows too, drawing her shoulders backward. And then he tipped her over forward so that her face was buried in the coppery silk intended for Cif (how long ago?) and led a double ribbon from her bound wrists down her spine to her crosswise-bound lower legs, and drew it tight as he could, so that her back was perforce arched and her face lifted free of the silk.

But despite his mounting excitement, the thought nagged him that there had been something in her warbled ditty which he had not liked. Ah yes, the mention of Simorgya. What place had that sunken kingdom in a whore's never-never lands? And all her earlier babble of moist and watery influences in the imagined land where she queened, or rather princessed it—There, she was at it again!

"Come, Brother Mordroog, to royally escort us," she warbled over the orangy silk, seemingly unmindful of her acute discomforts. "Come with our guardians, Deep Rusher your horse—your behemoth, rather, and you in his castle. Come also with Slasher and vasty All-Gripper, to shatter our prison and ferry us home. And send all your spirits coursing before you, so our minds are engulfed—"

The shadows steadied unnaturally as the lamp's swing shortened quiveringly, then stopped.

On the deck immediately above their heads there was consternation. The wind had unaccountably faded and the sea grown oily calm. The tiller in Skor's grip was lifeless, the sheet that Mikkidu fingered slack. The sky did not appear to be overcast, yet there was a shadowed, spectral quality to the sunlight, as though an unpredicted eclipse or other ominous event impended. Then without warning the dark sea mounded up boiling scarce a spear's cast off steerside—and subsided again without any diminishment in the feeling of foreboding. The spreading wave jogged *Seahawk*. The two lieutenants and Ourph stared about wonderingly and then at each other. None of them marked the trail of bubbles leading from the place of the mounding toward the becalmed sailing galley.

10

In the treasury Cif had the sudden feeling that the Mouser stood in need of more protection. The doll looked lonely there at pentagram's center. Perhaps he was too far from the ikons. She gathered the ikons together and after a moment's hesitation thrust the doll, doubled up, into the barred globe. Then she poked the ruler and the crooked arrow in along with him, transfixing the globe (more gold close to him!), almost as an afterthought clapped the tiny cup like a helmet on the protruding doll's head, and set all down on the linked rings.

Then she seated herself again, staring doubtfully at what she had done.

11

In the cabin the Gray Mouser rolled the bound Ississi over on her back and regarded the silvery girl opened up for his enjoyment. The blood pounded in his head and he felt an increasing pressure there, as if his brain had grown too large for his skull. The motionless cabin grew spectral, there was a sense of thronging presences, and then it was as if part of him only remained there while another part whirled away into a realm where he was a giant coursing through rushing darkness, uncertain of his humanity, while the pressure inside his skull grew and grew.

But the part of him in the cabin still was capable of sensation, though hardly of action, and this one watched helpless and aghast, through air that seemed to thicken and become more like water, the silvery, smiling trussed-up Ississi writhe and writhe yet again while her skin grew more silvery still—scaly silvery—and her elfin face narrowed and her green eyes swam apart, while from her head and back and shoulders, and along the backs of her legs and her hands and arms, razor-sharp spines erected themselves in crests and, as she writhed once more again mightily, cut through all the black ribbons at once so they floated in shreds about her. Then through the curtained hatchway there swam a face like her own new one, and she came up from the coppery silk in a great forward undulation and reached the palms of her back-crested hands out toward the Mouser's cheeks lovingly on arms that seemed to grow longer and longer, saying in a strange deep voice that seemed to bubble from her, "In moments this prison will be broken, Deep Rusher will smash it, and we will be free."

At those words the other part of the Mouser realized that the darkness through which he was now coursing upward was the deep sea, that he was engulfed in the whale-body and great-foreheaded brain of Deep Rusher, her monster, that it was the tiny hull of *Seahawk* far above him that his massive forehead was aimed at, and that he could no more evade that collision than his other self in the cabin could avoid the arms of Ississi.

12

In the treasury Cif could not bear the woeful expression with which the blank linen face of the doll appeared to gaze out at her from under the jammed-down golden helmet, nor the sudden thought that the sea demoness had recently fondled all that gold hemming in the doll. She grabbed it up with its prison, withdrew it from the barred globe and snatched off its helmet, and while the ikons chinked down on the table she clutched the stuffed cloth to her bosom and bent her lips to it and cherished and kissed it, breathing it words of endearment.

13

In the cabin the Mouser was able to dodge aside from those questing silvery spined hands, which went past him, while in the dark realm his giant self was able to veer aside from *Seahawk's* hull at the last moment and burst out of the darkness, so that his two selves were one again and both back in the cabin—which now lurched as though *Seahawk* were capsizing.

On deck all gaped, flinching, as a black shape thicker than *Seahawk* burst resoundingly from the dark water beside them, so close the ship's hull shook and they might have reached out and touched the monster. The shape erected itself like a windowless tower built all of streaming black boot leather, down which sheets of water cascaded. It shot up higher and higher, dragging their gazes skyward, then it narrowed and with a sweep of its great flukes left the water altogether, and for a long moment they watched the dark dripping underbelly of black leviathan pass over *Seahawk*, vast as a storm cloud, lacking lightning perhaps but not thunder, as he breached entire from the ocean. But then they were all snatching for handholds as *Seahawk* lurched down violently sideways, as though trying to shake them from her back. At least there was no shortage of lashings to grab onto as she slid with the collapsing waters into the great chasm left by leviathan. There came the numbing shock of that same beast smiting the sea beyond them as he returned to his element. Then salt ocean closed over them as they sank down, down, and down.

Afterward the Mouser could never determine how much of what next happened in the cabin transpired underwater and how much in a great bubble of air constrained by that other element so that it became more akin to it. (No question, he was wholly underwater toward the end.) There was a somewhat slow or, rather, measured dreamlike quality to all subsequent movements there—his, the transformed Ississi's, and the creature he took to be her brother—as if they were made against great pressures. It had elements both of a savage struggle—a fierce, life-and-death fight—and of a ceremonial dance with beasts. Certainly his position during it was always in the center, beside or a little above the open chest of fabrics, and certainly the transformed Ississi and her brother circled him like sharks and darted in alternately to attack, their narrow jaws gaping to show razorlike teeth and closing like great scissors snipping. And always there was that sense of steadily increasing pressure, though not now within his skull particularly, but over his entire body and centering, if anywhere, upon his lungs.

It began, of course, with his evading of Ississi's initial loving and murderous lunge at him, and his moving past her to the chest she had just quitted. Then, as she turned back to assault him a second time (all jaws now, arms merged into her silver-scaled sides and her crested legs merged, but eyes still great and green), and as he, in turn, turned to oppose her, he was inspired to grab up with both hands from the chest the topmost fabric and, letting it unfold sequentially and spread as he did so, whirl it between him and her in a great lustrous, baffling coppery sheet, or pale rosy-orange cloud. And she was indeed distracted from her main purpose by this timely interposition, although her silvery jaws came through it more than once, shredding and shearing and altogether making sorry work of Cif's intended cloak or dress of state or treasurer's robes, or whatever.

Then, as the Mouser completed his whirling turn, he found himself confronting the in-rushing silver-crested Mordroog, and to hold *him* off snatched up and whirlingly interposed the next rich silken fabric in the chest, which happened to be a violet one, his reluctant gift for Afreyt, so now it became a great pale purple cloud-wall soon slashed to lavender streaks and streamers, through which Mordroog's silver and jaw-snapping visage showed like a monstrous moon.

This maneuver brought the Mouser back in turn to face Ississi, who was closing in again through coppery shreds, and this attack was in turn thwarted by the extensive billowing-out of a sheet of bold scarlet silk, which he had meant to present to the capable whore-turned-fisherwoman Hilsa, but now was as effectively reduced to scraps and tatters as any incarnadined sunset is by conquering night.

And so it went, each charming or at least clever fabric gift in turn sacrificed—brassy yellow satin for Hilsa's comrade Rill, a rich brown worked with gold for Fafhrd, lovely sea-green and salmon pink sheets (also for Cif), a sky blue one (still another for Afreyt—to appease Fafhrd), a royal purple one for Pshawri (in honor of his first lieutenancy), and even one for Groniger (soberest black)—but each sheet successively defeating a dire attack by silvery sea demon or demoness, until the cabin had been filled with a most expensive sort of confetti and the bottom of the chest had been reached.

But by then, mercifully, the demonic attacks had begun to lessen in speed and fury, grow weaker and weaker, until they were but surly and almost aimless switchings-about (even floppings-about, like those of fish dying), while (*most* mercifully—almost miraculously) the dreadful suffocating pressure, instead of increasing or even holding steady, had started to fall off, to lessen, and now was continuing to do so, more and more swiftly.

What had happened was that when *Seahawk* had slid into the hole left by leviathan, the lead in her keel (which made her seaworthy) had tended to drag her down still farther, abetted by the mass of her great cargo, especially the bronze ingots and copper sheetings in it. But on the other hand, the greater part of her cargo by far consisted of items that were *lighter than water*—the long stack of dry, well seasoned timber, the tight barrels of flour, and the woollen sacks of grain, all of these additionally having considerable amounts of air trapped in them (the timber by virtue of the tarred canvas sheathing it, the grain because of the greasy raw wool of the sacks, so they acted as so many floats). So long as these items were above the water they tended to press the ship more deeply into it, but once they were underwater, their effect was to drag *Seahawk* upward, toward the surface.

Now under ordinary conditions of stowage—safe, adequate stowage, even—all these items might well have broken loose and floated up to the surface individually, the timber stack emerging like a great disintegrating raft, the sacks bobbing up like so many balloons, while *Seahawk* continued on down to a watery grave carrying along with it those trapped below decks and any desperately clinging seamen too shocked and terror-frozen to loosen their panic-grips.

But the imaginative planning and finicky overseeing the Mouser had given the stowage of the cargo at 'Brulsk, so that Fafhrd or Cif or (Mog forbid!) Skor should never have cause to criticize him, and also in line with his determination, now he had taken up merchanting, to be the cleverest and most foresighted merchant of them all, taken in conjunction with the mildly sadistic fury with which he had driven the men at their stowage work, insured that the wedgings and lashings-down of this cargo were something exceptional. And then when, earlier today and seemingly on an insane whim, he had insisted that all those more-than-adequate lashings be doubled, and then driven the men to that work with even greater fury, he had unknowingly guaranteed *Seahawk*'s survival.

To be sure, the lashings were strained, they creaked and boomed underwater (they were lifting a whole sailing galley), but not a single one of them parted, not a single air-swollen sack escaped before *Seahawk* reached the surface.

14

And so it was that the Mouser was able to swim through the hatchway and see untained blue sky again and blessedly fill his lungs with their proper element and weakly congratulate Mikkidu and a Mingol paddling and gasping beside him on their most fortunate escape. True, *Seahawk* was water-filled and awash, but she floated upright, her tall mast and bedraggled sail were intact, the sea was calm and windless still, and (as was soon determined) her entire crew had survived, so the Mouser knew there was no insurmountable obstacle in the way of their clearing her of water first by bailing, then by pumping (the oarholes could be plugged, if need be), and continuing their voyage. And if in the course of that clearing, a few fish, even a couple of big ones, should flop overside after a desultory snap or two (best be wary of all fish!) and then dive deep into *their* proper element and return to their own rightful kingdom—why, that was all in the Nehwonian nature of things.

15

A fortnight later, being a week after *Seahawk*'s safe arrival in Salthaven, Fafhrd and Afreyt rented the Sea Wrack and gave Captain Mouser and his crew a party, which Cif and the Mouser had to help pay for from the profits of the latter's trading voyage. To it were invited numerous Isler friends. It coincided with the year's first blizzard, for the winter gales had held off and been providentially late coming. No matter, the salty tavern was snug and the food and drink all that could be asked for—with perhaps one exception.

"There was a faint taste of wool fat in the fruit soup," Hilsa observed. "Nothing particularly unpleasant, but noticeable."

"That'll have been from the grease in the sacking," Mikkidu enlightened her, "which kept the salt sea out of 'em, so they buoyed us up powerfully when we sank. Captain Mouser thinks of everything."

"Just the same," Skor reminded him sotto voce, "it turned out he did have a girl in the cabin all the while—and that damned chest of fabrics too! You can't deny he's a great liar whenever he chooses."

"Ah, but the girl turned out to be a sea demon, and he needed the fabrics to defend himself from her, and that makes all the difference," Mikkidu rejoined loyally.

"I never saw her as aught but a ghostly and silver-crested sea demon," old Ourph put in. "The first night out from No-Ombrulsk I saw her rise from the cabin through the deck and stand at the taffrail, invoking and communing with sea monsters."

"Why didn't you report that to the Mouser?" Fafhrd asked, gesturing toward the venerable Mingol with his new bronze hook.

"One never speaks of a ghost in its presence," the latter explained, "or while there is chance of its reappearance. It only gives it strength. As always, silence is silver."

"Yes, and speech is golden," Fafhrd maintained.

Rill boldly asked the Mouser across the table, "But just how did you deal with the sea demoness while she was in her girl-guise? I gather you kept her tied up a lot, or tried to?"

"Yes," Cif put in from beside him. "You were even planning at one point to train her to be a maid for me, weren't you?" She smiled curiously. "Just think, I lost that as well as those lovely materials."

"I attempted a number of things that were rather beyond my powers," the Gray One admitted manfully, the edges of his ears turning red. "Actually, I was lucky to escape with my life." He turned toward Cif. "Which I couldn't have done if you hadn't snatched me from the tainted gold in the nick of time."

"Never mind, it was I put you amongst the tainted gold in the first place," she told him, laying her hand on his on the table, "but now it's been hopefully purified." (She had directed that ceremony of exorcism of the ikons herself, with the assistance of Mother Grum, to free them of all baleful Simorgyan influence got from their handling by the demoness. The old witch was somewhat dubious of the complete efficacy of the ceremony.)

Later Skor described leviathan arching over *Seahawk*. Afreyt nodded appreciatively, saying, "I was once in a dory when a whale breached close alongside. It is not a sight to be forgotten."

"Nor is it when viewed from the other side of the gunnel," the Mouser observed reflectively. Then he winced. "Mog, what a head thump that would have been!"

A BAD DAY FOR SALES

The big bright doors parted with a *whoosh* and Robie glided suavely onto Times Square. The crowd that had been watching the fifty-foot tall clothing-ad girl get dressed, or reading the latest news about the Hot Truce scrawl itself in yard-high script, hurried to look.

Robie was still a novelty. Robie was fun. For a little while yet he could steal the show.

But the attention did not make Robie proud. He had no more vanity than the pink plastic giantess, and she did not even flicker her blue mechanical eyes.

Robie radared the crowd, found that it surrounded him solidly, and stopped. With a calculated mysteriousness, he said nothing.

"Say, ma, he doesn't look like a robot at all. He looks sort of like a turtle."

Which was not completely inaccurate. The lower part of Robie's body was a metal hemisphere hemmed with sponge rubber and not quite touching the sidewalk. The upper was a metal box with black holes in it. The box could swivel and duck.

A chromium-bright hoopskirt with a turret on top.

"Reminds me too much of the Little Joe Baratanks," a veteran of the Persian War muttered, and rapidly rolled himself away on wheels rather like Robie's.

His departure made it easier for some of those who knew about Robie to open a path in the crowd. Robie headed straight for the gap. The crowd whooped.

Robie glided very slowly down the path, deftly jogging aside whenever he got too close to ankles in skylon or sockassins. The rubber buffer on his hoopskirt was merely an added safeguard.

The boy who had called Robie a turtle jumped in the middle of the path and stood his ground, grinning foxily.

Robie stopped two feet short of him. The turret ducked. The crowd got quiet.

"Hello, youngster," Robie said in a voice that was smooth as that of a TV star, and was in fact a recording of one.

The boy stopped smiling. "Hello," he whispered.

"How old are you?" Robie asked.

"Nine. No, eight."

"That's nice," Robie observed. A metal arm shot down from his neck, stopped just short of the boy. The boy jerked back.

"For you," Robie said gently.

The boy gingerly took the red polly-lop from the neatly-fashioned blunt metal claws. A gray-haired woman whose son was a paraplegic hurried on.

After a suitable pause Robie continued, "And how about a nice refreshing drink of Poppy Pop to go with your polly-lop?" The boy lifted his eyes but didn't stop licking the candy. Robie wiggled his claws ever so slightly. "Just give me a quarter and within five seconds—"

A little girl wriggled out of the forest of legs. "Give me a polly-lop too, Robie," she demanded.

"Rita, come back here," a woman in the third rank of the crowd called angrily.

Robie scanned the newcomer gravely. His reference silhouettes were not good enough to let him distinguish the sex of children, so he merely repeated, "Hello, youngster."

"Rita!"

"Give me a polly-lop!"

Disregarding both remarks, for a good salesman is single-minded and does not waste bait, Robie said winningly, "I'll bet you read *Junior Space Killers*. Now I have here—"

"Uh-hhh, I'm a girl. *He* got a polly-lop."

At the word "girl" Robie broke off. Rather ponderously he said, "Then—" After another pause he continued, "I'll bet you read *Gee-*

Gee Jones, Space Stripper. Now I have here the latest issue of that thrilling comic, not yet in the stationary vending machines. Just give me fifty cents and within five—"

"Please let me through. I'm her mother."

A young woman in the front rank drawled over her powder-sprayed shoulder. "I'll get her for you," and slithered out on six-inch platforms. "Run away, children," she said nonchalantly and lifting her arms behind her head, pirouetted slowly before Robie to show how much she did for her bolero half-jacket and her form-fitting slacks that melted into skylon just above the knees. The little girl glared at her. She ended the pirouette in profile.

At this age-level Robie's reference silhouettes permitted him to distinguish sex, though with occasional amusing and embarrassing miscalls. He whistled admiringly. The crowd cheered.

Someone remarked critically to his friend. "It would go better if he was built more like a real robot. You know, like a man."

The friend shook his head. "This way it's subtler."

No one in the crowd was watching the newscript overhead as it scribbled, "Ice Pack for Hot Truce? Vanadin hints Russ may yield on Pakistan."

Robie was saying, ". . . in the savage new glamor-tint we have christened Mars Blood, complete with spray applicator and fit-all fingerstalls that mask each finger completely except for the nail. Just give me five dollars—uncrumpled bills may be fed into the revolving rollers you see beside my arm—and within five seconds—"

"No thanks, Robie," the young woman yawned.

"Remember," Robie persisted, "for three more weeks seductiv-ising Mars Blood will be unobtainable from any other robot or human vendor."

"No thanks."

Robie scanned the crowd resourcefully. "Is there any gentleman here . . ." he began just as a woman elbowed her way through the front rank.

"I told you come back!" she snarled at the little girl.

"But I didn't get my polly-lop!"

". . . who would care to . . ."

"Rita!"

"Robie cheated. Ow!"

Meanwhile the young woman in the half-bolero had scanned the nearby gentlemen on her own. Deciding that there was less than a fifty per cent chance of any of them accepting the proposition Robie seemed about to make, she took advantage of the scuffle to slither gracefully back into the ranks. Once again the path was clear before Robie.

He paused, however, for a brief recapitulation of the more magical properties of Mars Blood, including a telling phrase about "the passionate claws of a Martian sunrise."

But no one bought. It wasn't quite time yet. Soon enough silver coins would be clinking, bills going through the rollers faster than laundry, and five hundred people struggling for the privilege of having their money taken away from them by America's only genuine mobile salesrobot.

But how was too soon. There were still some tricks that Robie did free, and one certainly should enjoy those before starting the more expensive fun.

So Robie moved on until he reached the curb. The variation in level was instantly sensed by his under-scanners. He stopped. His head began to swivel. The crowd watched in eager silence. This was Robie's best trick.

Robie's head stopped swiveling. His scanners had found the traffic light. It was green. Robie edged forward. But then it turned red. Robie stopped again, still on the curb. The crowd softly *ahhed* its delight.

Oh, it was wonderful to be alive and watching Robie on such a wonderful day. Alive and amused in the fresh, weather-controlled air between the lines of bright skyscrapers with their winking windows and under a sky so blue you could almost call it dark.

(But way, way up, where the crowd could not see, the sky was darker still. Purple-dark, with stars showing. And in that purple-dark, a silver-green something, the color of a bud, plunged downward at better than three miles a second. The silver-green was a paint that foiled radar.)

Robie was saying, "While we wait for the light there's time for you youngsters to enjoy a nice refreshing Poppy Pop. Or for you adults—only those over five feet are eligible to buy—to enjoy an exciting Poppy Pop fizz. Just give me a quarter or—I'm licensed to dispense intoxicating liquors—in the case of adults one dollar and a quarter and within five seconds . . ."

But that was not cutting it quite fine enough. Just three seconds later the silver-green bud bloomed above Manhattan into a globular orange flower. The skyscrapers grew brighter and brighter still, the brightness of the inside of the sun. The windows winked white fire.

The crowd around Robie bloomed too. Their clothes puffed into petals of flame. Their heads of hair were torches.

The orange flower grew, stem and blossom. The blast came. The winking windows shattered tier by tier, became black holes. The walls bent, rocked, cracked. A stony dandruff dribbled from their cornices. The flaming flowers on the sidewalk were all leveled at once. Robie was shoved ten feet. His metal hoopskirt dimpled, regained its shape.

The blast ended. The orange flower, grown vast, vanished overhead on its huge, magic beanstalk. It grew dark and very still. The cornice-dandruff pattered down. A few small fragments rebounded from the metal hoopskirt.

Robie made some small, uncertain movements, as if feeling for broken bones. He was hunting for the traffic light, but it no longer shone, red or green.

He slowly scanned a full circle. There was nothing anywhere to interest his reference silhouettes. Yet whenever he tried to move, his under-scanners warned him of low obstructions. It was very puzzling.

The silence was disturbed by moans and a crackling sound, faint at first as the scampering of rats.

A seared man, his charred clothes fuming where the blast had blown out the fire, rose from the curb. Robie scanned him.

"Good day, sir," Robie said. "Would you care for a smoke? A truly cool smoke? Now I have here a yet-unmarketed brand . . ."

But the customer had run away, screaming, and Robie never ran after customers, though he could follow them at a medium brisk roll. He worked his way along the curb where the man had sprawled, carefully keeping his distance from the low obstructions, some of which writhed now and then, forcing him to jog. Shortly he reached a fire hydrant. He scanned it. His electronic vision, though it still worked, had been somewhat blurred by the blast.

"Hello, youngster," Robie said. Then, after a long pause, "Cat got your tongue? Well, I've got a little present for you. A nice, lovely polly-lop." His metal arm snaked down.

"Take it, youngster," he said after another pause. "It's for you. Don't be afraid."

His attention was distracted by other customers, who began to rise up oddly here and there, twisting forms that confused his reference silhouettes and would not stay to be scanned properly. One cried, "Water," but no quarter clinked in Robie's claws when he caught the word and suggested, "How about a nice refreshing drink of Poppy Pop?"

The rat-crackling of the flames had become a jungle muttering. The blind windows began to wink fire again.

A little girl marched up, stepping neatly over arms and legs she did not look at. A white dress and the once taller bodies around her had shielded her from the brilliance and the blast. Her eyes were fixed on Robie. In them was the same imperious confidence, though none of the delight, with which she had watched him earlier.

"Help me, Robie," she said. "I want my mother."

"Hello, youngster," Robie said. "What would you like? Comics? Candy?"

"Where is she, Robie? Take me to her."

"Balloons? Would you like to watch me blow up a balloon?"

The little girl began to cry. The sound triggered off another of Robie's novelty circuits.

"Is something wrong?" he asked. "Are you in trouble? Are you lost?"

"Yes, Robie. Take me to my mother."

"Stay right here," Robie said reassuringly, "and don't be frightened. I will call a policeman." He whistled shrilly, twice.

Time passed. Robie whistled again. The windows flared and roared. The little girl begged, "Take me away, Robie," and jumped onto a little step in his hoopskirt.

"Give me a dime," Robie said. The little girl found one in her pocket and put it in his claws.

"Your weight," Robie said, "is fifty-four and one-half pounds, exactly."

"Have you seen my daughter, have you seen her?" a woman was

crying somewhere. "I left her watching that thing while I stepped inside—Rita!"

"Robie helped me," the little girl was telling her moments later. "He knew I was lost. He even called a policeman, but he didn't come. He weighed me too. Didn't you, Robie?"

But Robie had gone off to peddle Poppy Pop to the members of a rescue squad which had just come around the corner, more robot-like than he in their fireproof clothing.

Recommended Reading by Fritz Leiber

Conjure Wife
The Big Time
The Wanderer
A Specter Is Haunting Texas
Gather, Darkness